The Low Countries Journal of Social and Economic History 18:1 (2021)

www.tseg.nl

W0280838

# Table of Contents

**BOOK REVIEWS** 161

Rudolf A.A. Bosch, *Stedelijke macht tussen overvloed en stagnatie. Stadsfinanciën, sociaal-politieke structuren en economie in het hertogdom Gelre, ca. 1350-1550* (Jaco Zuijderduijn) – Jessica Dijkman and Bas van Leeuwen (eds.), *An Economic History of Famine Resilience* (Michiel de Haas) – Jan Luiten van Zanden, Tine de Moor and Sarah Carmichael, *Capital Women. The European Marriage Pattern, Female Empowerment and Economic Development in Western Europe 1300-1800* (Anna Bellavitis) – Marianne Eekhout, *Memorabilia van de Tachtigjarige Oorlog* (Michel van Duijnen) – Hittjo Kruyswijk, *Gek, niet ziek? Lucas Lindeboom, Abraham Kuyper en de stichting van gereformeerde ziekenhuizen in Nederland (1880-1940)* (Meindert Fennema) – Maarten Hell, *De Amsterdamse herberg 1450-1800. Geestrijk centrum van het openbare leven* (Anne Wegener Sleeswijk) – Sharika D. Crawford, *The Last Turtlemen of the Caribbean. Waterscapes of Labor, Conservation, and Boundary Making* (Stephanie van Dam) – Lodewijk Petram en Samuël Kruizinga, *De oorlog tegemoet. Nederlanders en de strijd om Spanje, 1936-1939* (Bart van der Steen) – David Onnekink and Gijs Rommelse, *The Dutch in the Early Modern World. A History of a Global Power* (Elisabeth Heijmans) – Ewout Frankema and Anne Booth (eds.), *Fiscal Capacity and the Colonial State in Asia and Africa, c. 1850-1960* (Ellen Hillbom) – Thomas Max Safley, *Family Firms and Merchant Capitalism in Early Modern Europe. The Business, Bankruptcy and Resilience of the Höchstetters of Augsburg* (Jeroen Puttevils)

# Not so Consensual after All

*A New Perspective on the Dutch 1980s*

Rosa Kösters, Bram Mellink, Merijn Oudenampsen & Matthias van Rossum

TSEG 18 (1): 5–18
DOI: 10.18352/tseg.1196

In January 1980, the American broadcaster PBS aired the first episode of the documentary series *Free to Choose* by Rose and Milton Friedman. At that time, politicians and policymakers were, in fact, *forced* to choose. Western economies were mired in the most serious economic crisis since the 1930s. Keynesians desperately searched for a way to combat the crisis within the constraints of the existing economic order. Neoliberal economists, such as the Friedmans, challenged the Keynesian understanding of economics and offered pro-market policy alternatives, which came into full swing as the new decade commenced. Less than one year before *Free to Choose* aired, Margaret Thatcher had taken office as prime minister of Great Britain. The election of Ronald Reagan as president of the United States was only months away. Forty years later, it is common knowledge that the 'war of ideas' between neoliberals and Keynesians ended with the downfall of the old Keynesian order. As the metaphor indicates, the British and American confrontation between Keynesians and neoliberals was both polarized and contentious and has been documented as such.[1]

1 R. Cockett, *Thinking the unthinkable. Think-tanks and the economic counter-revolution 1931-1983* (London 1995); M. Blyth, *Great transformations. Economic ideas and institutional change in the twentieth century* (Cambridge 2002); P.A. Hall, 'Policy paradigms, social learning, and the state. The case of economic policymaking in Britain', *Comparative Politics* 25:3 (1993) 275-296; M. Prasad, *The politics of free markets. The rise of neoliberal economic policies in Britain, France, Germany, and the United States* (Chicago 2006).

The Netherlands has long been cast as a contrast to Anglo-American developments: an island of tranquility in a tempestuous global scene. Various leading studies have claimed that the Dutch avoided open conflict and charted a consensual path to market-oriented reform.[2] Peter Katzenstein was the first to make this argument. In his 1986 classic *Small States in World Markets*, a comparative study of small Western European countries, he argued that small states with open economies could not enact protectionist measures, nor could they push through policies in a polarized and authoritarian manner.[3] Instead, economic policymakers in these countries relied on a corporatist strategy, enlisting the co-operation of trade unions and business associations to secure broad support for market-oriented reforms. Corporatist coordination thus smoothened the process of economic adjustment. Published in the middle of Ronald Reagan's presidency, *Small States* was as much an exercise in comparative political economy as a criticism of the polarized nature of American politics.

Roughly ten years later, Jelle Visser and Anton Hemerijck drove home Katzenstein's point in their influential book *A Dutch Miracle*. They heralded the Dutch corporatist approach as a superior alternative to the polarizing 'state-led institutional and paradigmatic overhaul' of Reagan and Thatcher.[4] At the center of their account was the bipartite 'Wassenaar Accord' from 1982, in which Dutch trade unions and employers' organizations agreed to exchange wage moderation for reduced working hours to combat the economic crisis. Visser and Hemerijck depicted this agreement as the return of corporatist consensus in the Netherlands, which allowed the passage of a series of austerity measures and supply-side reforms. When the Dutch economy made a strong recovery in the mid-1990s, this was hailed as 'the Dutch miracle'. The Dutch approach soon acquired international fame as the 'polder model'. Visser and Hemerijck's emphasis on consensus as driver of policy change became the staple of the literature on Dutch welfare state reform.[5] While, internationally speaking, the neoliberal turn became the

2 J. Visser and A. Hemerijck, *'A Dutch miracle'. Job growth, welfare reform and corporatism in the Netherlands, changing welfare states* (Amsterdam 1997); I. Bruff, *Culture and consensus in European varieties of capitalism* (Basingstoke 2008); E. Jones, *Economic adjustment and political transformation in small states* (Oxford 2008); F. Hendriks, *Polder politics. The re-invention of consensus democracy in the Netherlands* (London 2017); C. Hendriks, *The story behind the Dutch model. The consensual politics of wage restraint* (Oisterwijk 2011).

3 P.J. Katzenstein, *Small states in world markets. Industrial policy in Europe* (Ithaca 1985).

4 Visser and Hemerijck, *A Dutch miracle*, 79.

5 A. Hemerijck and M. Schludi, 'Sequences of policy failures and effective policy responses', in: W.

dominant scholarly narrative of the 1980s, in the Netherlands it was the rise of the polder model. Dutch corporatist consensus was presented by Dutch scholars as an alternative to neoliberalism.[6]

Miracles however, tend to sow skepticism. Over the years, a range of authors have challenged the 'polder model' narrative.[7] They have argued that the degree of consensus has generally been overstated and that corporatist institutions were less important than commonly assumed. Rather than consensus, they asserted, the 1980s were a period of deep and lasting controversies over economic policy. The political scientist Steven Wolinetz was among the first of these critics. In response to Katzenstein, he argued that the Dutch case did not really fit his thesis of smooth corporatist adjustment. The market-oriented shift in Dutch economic policy, Wolinetz noted, did not originate in corporatist institutions.[8] Instead, he pointed to 'the relatively autonomous role of the government in determining policy'. Wolinetz saw the reforms of the 1980s not as a consensual strategy of adjustment but rather as a state-led overhaul. The Dutch trade unions, he noted, were allowed 'scant influence on government policy', while the Dutch state decided to consciously 'circumvent corporatist structures in order to orchestrate a response to economic change'.[9] Wolinetz's argument was later taken up by authors such as Uwe Becker, Wiener Salverda, Jacques Woldendorp and Hans Keman.[10]

Scharpf and V.A. Schmidt (eds.), *Welfare and work in the open economy,* vol. 1 (Oxford 2000) 125-228; H. Keman, 'Explaining miracles. Third ways and work and welfare', *West European Politics* 26:2 (2003) 115-135; V.A. Schmidt, 'How, where and when does discourse matter in small states' welfare state adjustment?', *New Political Economy* 8:1 (2003) 127-146.

6 A. Hemerijck, 'Het leervermogen van de overlegeconomie', in: F. Hendriks and T. Toonen (eds.), *Schikken en plooien. De stroperige staat bij nader inzien* (Assen 1998) 117-134; A. Hemerijck and J. Visser, 'The Dutch model. An obvious candidate for the "Third way"?', *Archives Européennes de Sociologie/ European Journal of Sociology/Europäisches Archiv Für Soziologie* (1999) 103-121.

7 U. Becker, "Miracle' by consensus? Consensualism and dominance in Dutch employment development', *Economic and Industrial Democracy* 22:4 (2001) 453-483; Idem, 'An example of competitive corporatism? The Dutch political economy 1983-2004 in critical examination', *Journal of European Public Policy* 12:6 (2005) 1078-1102; J. Woldendorp, *The polder model – from disease to miracle? Dutch neo-corporatism 1965-2000* (Amsterdam 2005); J. Woldendorp and H. Keman, 'The polder model reviewed. Dutch corporatism 1965-2000', *Economic and Industrial Democracy* 28:3 (2007) 317-347; R.A. Andeweg, 'From Dutch disease to Dutch model? Consensus government in practice', *Parliamentary Affairs* 53:4 (2000) 697-709.

8 S.B. Wolinetz, 'Socio-economic bargaining in the Netherlands. Redefining the post-war policy coalition', *West European Politics* 12:1 (1989) 90.

9 Wolinetz, 'Socio-economic bargaining', 90, 95.

10 Becker, 'Miracle by consensus?' 453-483; Idem, 'A "Dutch" model. Employment growth by corporatist consensus and wage restraint? A critical account of an idyllic view', *New Political Economy* 6:1 (2001)

This less flattering analysis of the 1980s policy shift possesses a number of analytical advantages over the established 'polder model' narrative. First, it identifies the state as the crucial driver of institutional reform. In comparison, advocates of the consensus view offer a surprisingly elusive account of the dynamics of the Dutch policy shift, remarking that compromise was 'in the air' and that the 'sudden agreement' in Wassenaar ended 'a twenty year period of polarisation'.[11] Second, Wolinetz acknowledged that the outcomes of the negotiations suited employers far better than advocates of the trade unions. In contrast, proponents of the consensus view take as their point of departure the far less satisfactory assumption that all stakeholders involved somehow detached themselves from the 'short-term interests of some of their constituency' during the negotiations at Wassenaar, so as to focus exclusively on the long-term 'general' interest.[12] Third, and finally, state-driven reform is easier to reconcile with the speed and depth of Dutch reforms than accounts based on corporatist consensus and concomitant incrementalism.[13] In the Netherlands, reforms have been relatively fast and thorough. Of comparable OECD countries, the Netherlands has cut back its welfare state the most.[14] As political scientist Vivien Schmidt observed, the Netherlands transformed from 'one of the most conservative of continental welfare states to the most liberal' throughout the 1980s and 1990s.[15] The Netherlands was quick to turn to privatization and the liberalization of financial markets, while its flexibilization of the labor market was relatively extensive. Flexible job contracts had doubled from an estimated 12 percent of the working population (500,000 – 600,000

19-43; Idem, 'An example of competitive corporatism?' 1078-1102; W. Salverda, 'The Dutch model. Magic in a flat landscape?', in: U. Becker and H. Schwartz (eds.), *Employment 'miracles'. A critical comparison of the Dutch, Scandinavian, Swiss, Australian and Irish cases versus Germany and the US* (Amsterdam 2005) 39-64; Woldendorp, *The polder model*; Woldendorp and Keman, 'The polder model reviewed'.

11 D. Hellema, *Nederland en de jaren zeventig* (Amsterdam 2012) 221, 263-265; H. de Liagre Böhl, 'Consensus en polarisatie. Spanning in de verzorgingsstaat, 1945-1990', in: R. Aerts et al., *Land van kleine gebaren. Een politieke geschiedenis van Nederland, 1780-1990* (Nijmegen 2001) 321-322; J. Kennedy, *Een beknopte geschiedenis van Nederland* (Amsterdam 2017) 367.

12 Visser and Hemerijck, *'A Dutch miracle'*, 62.

13 Katzenstein, *Small states in world markets*, 198.

14 C. Green-Pedersen, *The politics of justification. Party competition and welfare-state retrenchment in Denmark and the Netherlands from 1982 to 1998* (Amsterdam 2002).

15 Schmidt, 'How, where and when does discourse matter', 132. See also L.J. Touwen, 'How does a coordinated market economy evolve? Effects of policy learning in the Netherlands in the 1980s', *Labor History* 49:4 (2008) 439-464.

employees) in 1987, to 22 percent (1,092,000 employees) in 2003, rising to 34 percent in 2019.[16]

In light of these analytical shortcomings of the 'polder model' narrative, a revision appears to be in order. This special issue builds on the existing critiques of the polder model discourse and aims to broaden the analysis of the Dutch 1980s. We argue that the Dutch case conforms more closely to the international literature on the neoliberal turn than accounted for thus far. The work of critics such as Steven Wolinetz and Uwe Becker serves as a point of departure, though it requires further elaboration. The critique and revision of the polder model proposed by the contributors to this special issue, centers on four major themes. Before we turn to the different contributions of this special issue, it is useful to briefly expand on these themes.

## Themes: conflict, the state, ideas and research methods

What do we actually mean when we refer to conflict or consensus in politics? This is a crucial preliminary question that warrants some expansion, so as to clarify the overarching argument of this special issue. The literature on corporatist consensus builds on the work of Arend Lijphart and his understanding of 'consensus democracy'. Lijphart used this term to refer to an institutional process of decision-making that 'aims at broad participation in government and broad agreement on the policies the government should pursue'.[17] Lijphart contrasted 'consensus democracy' to the Anglo-American model of majoritarian democracy, where minority opinions can potentially be ignored by vote-winning majorities. Consensus in this specific sense of the word does not mean there are no lasting differences of opinion. It is, rather, a commonly agreed upon process of dealing with these differences through a process of give and take, involving the structural participation of a broad range of societal actors. Katzenstein builds on this definition and defines democratic corporatism in terms of 'the continuous political bargaining between interest groups, state bureaucracies and political par-

16 M. van Dijk et al., *Precaire polder. Rapport in het kader van het onderzoeksproject Historische Verkenning Vakbeweging* (Amsterdam 2018) 30; Centraal Bureau voor de Statistiek, 'Werkzame beroepsbevolking; positie in de werkkring', 15 augustus 2020, https://www.cbs.nl/nl-nl/cijfers/detail/82646NED?dl=31E77.

17 A. Lijphart, *Patterns of democracy. Government forms and performance in thirty-six countries* (New Haven 1999) 2.

ties', where 'important social actors are systematically included in the policy network'.[18] Visser and Hemerijck similarly use corporatist consensus to refer to 'ongoing negotiations' between capital, labour and the state. They state that corporatist consensus involves a 'reconciliation of purposes', in which the participants 'learn to interpret reality in broadly the same way and to value generally the same thing'.[19]

We argue that the policy shift of the 1980s does not conform to this notion of corporatist consensus: participants did not all participate in government or policymaking, they did not interpret reality in a similar way, nor did they value the same things. Participants were miles apart. To begin with, trade union participation in government policymaking was relatively minimal. When the first Lubbers cabinet enacted a fundamental shift in economic policy at the beginning of the 1980s, its unilateral approach was closer to that of a vote-winning majority ignoring minority opinion, rather than Lijphart's 'broad participation' and 'broad agreement'. The Social Democrats and trade unions were largely excluded from the decision-making process. There was little room for give and take, since the 'government's commitment to deficit reduction and market-led recovery offered few opportunities for the trade unions or the left to influence government policy', as Wolinetz rightly remarked.[20] Unsurprisingly, frustrations regarding the lack of influence on government policies prevailed among trade unionists. In 1983, one year after the Wassenaar Accord, trade union chairman Wim Kok deemed the dominant 'neoliberal approach' in government circles 'catastrophic' in its consequences, as it 'led to an accelerated breakdown of employment in the market sector and the (semi)public sector.'[21]

In addition, actors interpreted the economic developments of the 1980s in fundamentally different ways. Evidently, there was a circumscribed agreement that something needed to be done to bring down wages and tackle the deficit. Yet expert opinion was fundamentally divided: on one side, there was a Keynesian coalition that emphasized stabilization of effective demand and on the other, a neoliberal supply-side coalition that prioritized deficit reduction and the restoration of corporate profitability. These differences of opinion were so fundamental, and the crisis so severe, that they could not be bridged in a

18 Katzenstein, *Small states in world markets*, 32.

19 Visser and Hemerijck, *'A Dutch miracle'*, 67-68.

20 Wolinetz, 'Socio-economic bargaining in the Netherlands', 93.

21 W. Kok, 'Volledige werkgelegenheid. Uitdagingen voor de jaren tachtig', *Socialisme & Democratie* 7/8 (1983) 5.

consensual process of give and take. Corporatist institutions such as the Social and Economic Council were largely ineffective in the 1980s, paralyzed by internal disagreement.[22] Of course, this does not mean that the Dutch 1980s saw open conflict as bad as Thatcher's confrontation with the miners or Reagan's conflict with the air traffic controllers, but neither was consensual decision-making attainable, let alone dominant. This revision of the polder model thesis is theoretically important, since it brings power back into the equation. The 1980s policy shift is more readily understood as a dominant party imposing its viewpoint on a subaltern party, rather than a wholly voluntary 'reconciliation of purposes'. The Wassenaar Accord thus emerges as the formalization of a power shift between the state, employers and trade unions, in which especially the trade unions lost much of their former influence on public policy.

Our second theme concerns the state. This special issue argues that the role of the Dutch state in the 1980s policy shift has been underappreciated in existing 'polder model' accounts. A key argument in the literature on corporatism is the qualification of the role of the state. The state is assumed to have limited capacity for independent policymaking, due to its continuous interaction with interest groups. Instead, corporatist actors are assumed to be in the driver's seat. Visser and Hemerijck for example, have contrasted their work with the 'very state-centered' analysis of the rise of British monetarism under Thatcher, by the political scientist Peter Hall. They themselves seem to have made the opposite mistake, though, by largely ignoring and downplaying the role of the state. This has led them to claim that the Netherlands did not experience a 'state-led institutional and paradigmatic overhaul' in the 1980s.[23] We believe the opposite to be the case. We contend that the Dutch policy shift in the 1980s was first and foremost an initiative taken by the Dutch state. The first and second Lubbers cabinets acted relatively unilaterally in the 1980s and hardly consulted the trade unions or the Social Democrat opposition in parliament.[24] Insofar as corporatist institutions were involved in policymaking, the state was effec-

22 Wolinetz, 'Socio-economic bargaining in the Netherlands', 90. See also T. Jaspers and F. Pennings, 'Sociale zekerheid en zorg. De SER als moderator', in: T. Jaspers, B. van Bavel and J. Peet (eds.), *SER 1950-2010. Zestig jaar denkwerk voor draagvlak* (Amsterdam 2010) 133-161; For internal controversy see the 1984 report from the Committee of Economic Experts (CED) within the SER, which noted that the economic policymaking field was principally divided between a Keynesian and Monetarist camp: CED, *Rapport over het conjunctuurbeleid in de jaren tachtig* (The Hague 1984) 55.

23 Visser and Hemerijck, *'A Dutch miracle'*, 79.

24 Wolinetz, 'Socio-economic bargaining in the Netherlands', 93.

tively 'bullying the social partners into bipartite agreements', as Rudy Andeweg has pointed out.[25] While a shift in emphasis to the Dutch state as a driver of reform is necessary, this does not fully resolve the matter. We need to acknowledge that the state is not a single or monolithic actor. Researchers should therefore attempt to break down the state and expose the 'fragmentation' and internal power dynamics within, between different political currents, departments and interest groups.[26] These internal controversies raise the question why certain policy ideas became dominant at the cost of others. Instead of portraying economic reforms as self-evident, as mere pragmatism or as an economic 'reality check' for profligate politicians, the contributors to this special issue identify the rise of neoliberal economic ideas within the state as a crucial inspiration for the economic reforms of the 1980s.[27]

Here we come to our third major theme: the role of ideas. The Dutch reforms of the 1980s have generally been described as a pragmatic response to changes in the world economy, and that is certainly part of the story. Yet it was also the result of a changing perspective on the working of the economy itself. In other words, the way politicians, policymakers and the wider public *viewed* the economy changed fundamentally in the 1970s and 1980s, and this shift had consequences. Internationally, this development has generally been described as a move from a Keynesian to a neoliberal (or monetarist) paradigm.[28] As institutionalist scholars have argued, such paradigm shifts generally take the form of a 'battle of ideas'. Surprisingly, however, the major Dutch economic debates of the 1970s have hardly been studied by scholars. Relatively little is known of the Keynesian and neoliberal paradigms: who were their major advocates, and how did they achieve dominance?

An intriguing study by historian Duco Hellema demonstrates that the consensus among politicians, journalists and economists shifted towards market reforms at a late stage: in the middle of the 1970s, the left still gained successes in its attempts to combat the stagflation crisis

25 Andeweg, 'From Dutch disease to Dutch model?'

26 Cf. J.F.M. Koppenjan and A.B. Ringeling, 'Bewegend beleid', in: A.J.G.M. Bekke, J.L.M. Hakvoort and J.M. de Heer (eds.), *Departementen in beweging* (The Hague 1994) 203-221, 211-212.

27 R. Kuiper, *De terugkeer van het algemeen belang. Privatiseringsverdriet en de toekomst van Nederland* (Amsterdam 2014). S. Heijne and H. Noten, *Fantoomgroei* (Amsterdam 2020); D. Hellema and M. van Lith, *Dat hadden we nooit moeten doen. De PvdA en de neoliberale revolutie van de jaren negentig* (Amsterdam 2020).

28 P. Hall, 'Policy paradigms, social learning, and the state. The case of economic policymaking in Britain', *Comparative Politics* 25:3 (1993) 275-296; Blyth, *Great transformations*; V.A. Schmidt, *The futures of European capitalism* (Oxford 2002).

with Keynesian policy instruments, while public support for left-wing regimes in Western Europe remained considerable.[29] In the Netherlands, a group of leading Keynesian economists in prominent positions – including Tinbergen, De Galan, Halberstadt, Van der Zwan, Driehuis, Heertje and Pen – issued a public appeal in 1977 to vote for the left. They pleaded for the continuation of the expansionary policies of Labour Party leader Den Uyl and warned not to 'one-sidedly blame the tax burden or wages for unemployment'.[30] Merely five years later, this Keynesian perspective had been relegated to the margins. Like Reagan and Thatcher, the first Lubbers cabinet heralded a fundamental shift in economic thinking. As Anton Knoester wrote, it was 'the first government in the post-war period to make a wholesale break with the Keynesian ideas that have long been such an important influence on economic policy'.[31] This intellectual – or ideological – shift among politicians and policymakers has received little attention from scholars. This is partly a result of the dominant focus on 'corporatist consensus', 'policy learning' and 'shared understandings' and partly due to the fact that the qualitative analysis of political and economic ideas is traditionally not a very prominent approach in Dutch academia.

This brings us to our final theme: research methods. The road from ideas to policy can only be charted by means of a wider array of research methods. An important flaw of the existing literature on corporatism is its predominant focus on policy outcomes. This has resulted in a relatively narrow technocratic perspective and drove the debate mainly towards the interactions between government, employers' and employees' organizations. Their ideas and behavior have mostly been interpreted within the confines of corporatist institutions and a shared consensus. The impact of institutional actors on reformulating the dynamics of this political-economic arena (and thus on redefining the 'rules of the game'), but also the internal dynamics of such actors (from ministries, planning offices, to employer organizations and labour unions), all too often remain unstudied. This special issue explores other ways to study the development of the (Dutch) political economy. It connects methods from the history of ideas to institutional, policy and social history analysis in order to reinterpret the economic transformation of the 1980s.

29 D. Hellema, *The global 1970s. Radicalism, reform and crisis* (London 2018) 191.

30 'Oproep hoogleraren economie', *Trouw* 21 May (1977).

31 A. Knoester, *Economische politiek in Nederland* (Leiden 1989) 126.

## Overview of the contributions

Covering different aspects of the Dutch political and economic transformations of the 1980s, the articles of this special issue expand on existing critiques of the polder model and, taken together, offer an alternative explanation for the policy shift of the 1980s. Based on their study of senior civil servants, Bram Mellink and Merijn Oudenampsen bring the state back into the analysis. They argue that bureaucratic or administrative elites were crucial drivers of the paradigm shift in Dutch economic policy. Mellink and Oudenampsen see little evidence for social learning and corporatist consensus. They point to the innovative and powerful role of senior policymakers in the ministries of Finance and Economic Affairs. Inspired by a historical policy repertoire from the supply-side industrialization policies in the 1950s, these leading policymakers laid the groundwork for the neoliberal reforms of the 1980s.

One of the crucial debates of the 1970s revolved around the rise of public spending and how it could be controlled. In his contribution, Tom Kayzel focuses on the public choice tradition in the Netherlands, as well as the discussions it engendered within the Dutch Labour Party (PvdA). Public choice is an international current of economic thought commonly considered to be closely aligned with the broader neoliberal movement. Kayzel explains the rise of these ideas with the Dutch Labour Party against the background of a larger backlash against the agenda of democratization and social planning. Public choice theorists such as Theo Stevers and Hans Daudt argued that the power of pressure groups had led to an incontrollable rise of public spending, ultimately threatening the very continuity of the capitalist order. Kayzel shows how these ideas challenged established Keynesian policy and contributed to a new ideal of economic planning, which Kayzel calls 'the politics of restraint'. With his study, Kayzel underlines the importance of a (partly concealed) contest of ideas from the mid-1970s onwards.

The case of the Amsterdam shipyards, studied by Sjoerd Keulen and Ronald Kroeze from a multi-level governance-perspective, puts us in the center of the storm of the economic crisis. Their study highlights the conflicts and controversies arising around the state support and the closure of the shipyards. They contend that the transformation of state policy, with the state effectively withdrawing economic support for the shipyards, was promoted and counteracted on different government levels. The introduction of a new political actor (and level), the European Commission, created a sudden change in the landscape of policymaking and provided an important and transformative push towards neoliberal policies. Keulen and Kroeze not only emphasize the role of Dutch policy officials but also point to civil servants of the European Commission and management consultants such as McKinsey in the dissemination and implementation of neoliberal economic ideas. They underline need for a multi-level approach, including various levels of interaction between policymakers, ranging from local deliberations to negotiations at the level of the European Union.

Studying the position and strategy of the largest federation in the Dutch labor union movement on the rising flexibilization of labor relations in the 1980s, Rosa Kösters, Loran van Diepen, Moira van Dijk and Matthias van Rossum argue that the Federation of Dutch Trade Unions, or FNV, grudgingly held on to the institutional agreements set forth in the Wassenaar Accord with employer organizations, despite the clear negative effects from an employee's viewpoint. The agreements in the accord intended to boost employment through work time reduction measures in exchange for wage moderation by the labor unions, but this left the field wide open for employer strategies to flexibilize labor relations. The authors study the attitude and strategy of the trade union movement towards flexibilization, focusing on questions of power and the underlying strategies of employers and labor unions at multiple levels, rather than on the formation of political-economic consensus or ideas at the top. They argue that the responses and strategies of different levels of the labour union movement, or in many respects the lack of it, are an important factor in understanding the increasing labor flexibilization.

## Implications

Reviving the critique on the 'polder model' perspective in the Dutch societal and academic understanding of recent economic and political history, this special issue demonstrates that the developments in the Netherlands from the late 1970s onwards marked not the birth of a unique corporatist consensus model but instead a particular Dutch manifestation of a wider global neoliberal turn. Research in this area is still in its infancy, and far from attempting to cover the Dutch neoliberal turn in its entirety, we aim to (re)open the debate regarding a fundamental shift in economic policymaking that seems to have left no continent untouched.[32]

This last observation may therefore also serve as an opening for future research. Since the Dutch transformation was part of a wider, global development that witnessed a rise of neoliberal policies in different countries, the implications of this remarkably wide-ranging shift need to be fleshed out further. As various contributions to this special issue suggest, such research may benefit from an eye toward the different aims and motives of actors within institutions, on the one hand, and a sensitivity for the level of analysis, on the other, all the while moving between local, regional, national and international domains.

Secondly, even a superficial overview of the available literature demonstrates that although the neoliberal reforms of the 1970s and 1980s swept over various continents, they gained traction under very different circumstances with widely divergent effects. In Europe and the United States, for instance, the neoliberal turn was accompanied by de-industrialization and the rise of service industries, while countries of the Global South witnessed rapid expansion of their industrial sectors as a result of market-oriented reforms. The expansion of industrialization in the Global South was accompanied by a pronounced informalization of labour relations, while Europe and the United States witnessed a continued flexibilization of labour in the new service industries.[33] Despite their different manifestations, processes of fragmentation have marginalized the previously often institutionalized roles of labour unions and have led to new forms of organization and collectivity by workers in many regions across the globe.[34]A recent worldwide overview already pointed to the commonality of postindustrial neoliberal ideology and ruling practices.[35] At the same time, such observations merely reveal how the worldwide structural changes that made the simultaneous global political turn of the 1980s possible still awaits a full-scale analysis. How should we understand the globally diverging and

32 Hellema, *The global 1970s*.

33 E.g. J. Breman, *At work in the informal economy of India. A perspective from the Bottom Up* (Oxford 2013); M. van der Linden and J. Breman, 'Informalizing the economy. The return of the social question at a global level', *Development and Change* 45:5 (2014) 920-940.

34 E.g. S. Bhattacharya and R.P. Behal (eds.), *The vernacularization of labour politics* (Delhi 2016); D. Azzellini and M.G. Kraft (eds.), *The class strikes back. Self-organised workers' struggles in the twenty-first century* (Leiden 2018); M. van der Linden, 'San Precario, a new inspiration for labor historians', *Labor: Studies in Working-Class History of the Americas* 10:1 (2014) 9-21.

35 G. Therborn, 'Preface. The terrifying converges of the three worlds of the "social question", in: J. Breman et al. (eds.) *The social question in the twenty-first century. A global view* (Oakland 2019) ix-xii.

converging effects? How do these patterns help us to improve our analyses of national cases, such as the Netherlands, or to carve out the connections created in the process, for example, by large and globally operating multinationals, or by the exchange of ideas through international organizations, political movements and economic actors?

Finally, we hope to have demonstrated the urgent need for deeper analyses of the complex relations between interests, institutions and ideas. Social scientists and historians have long acted as if interests and ideas could be left out of the equation, or only played a minor role. However, institutions can only govern society if they somehow align to certain interests, and these interests depend on the ideas we employ to interpret the (inherently political) world around us.[36] It is therefore up to scholars who seek to understand economic reforms to trace the ascension of political ideas and convictions, pinpoint them to specific actors and interest groups and demonstrate how such parties manage to turn their ideas into institutions, as well as establish a new political reality. Apart from offering a reinterpretation of the economic shift of the 1980s, we hope that the contributions to this special issue may also help pave the road for a broader array of methods that will enable historians and social scientists to trace the complex processes underpinning policy change.

36 Blyth, *Great transformations*, 20, 35-37.

# Bureaucrats First

*The Leading Role of Policymakers in the Dutch Neoliberal Turn of the 1980s**

Merijn Oudenampsen and Bram Mellink

TSEG 18 (1): 19–52
DOI: 10.18352/tseg.1197

**Abstract**

In the 1980s, a fundamental shift took place in Dutch economic policy: Keynesian demand-management was exchanged for a neoliberal supply-side approach. The single most influential account of this transformation has focused on consensus among corporatist policymakers as key to the reforms. It is the origin story of the Dutch 'polder model'. The problem however, is that there is surprisingly little evidence for corporatist consensus in the 1980s. Instead of consensus, we argue that there has been a conflict of ideas between Keynesians and supply-siders. And instead of corporatism, we point to bureaucratic elites as a crucial factor in the Dutch policy shift. From the mid-1970s onwards, an influential group of senior public officials emerged that successfully advocated for a supply-side policy, inspired by the industrialization policies developed in the 1950s. In so doing, we believe the Dutch case exemplifies the pathbreaking role of administrative elites as highlighted by Skocpol, Weir and Heclo, rather than corporatist consensus.

## Introduction: false learning

When the former Prime Minister Wim Kok passed away in October 2018, he was commemorated in Dutch newspapers as the personification of the Dutch 'polder model'.[1] As leader of the largest Dutch trade

* We would like to thank the editors, referees and contributors to this special issue for their critical comments.

1 J. Lindner and R. Meijer, 'Wim Kok (1938-2018). Jongen uit de armoedige polder werd na alle tegenwind een sterke en sobere minister-president', *De Volkskrant* 20 October (2018); Redactie, 'Wim Kok was de polder in persoon', *NRC Handelsblad* 20 October (2018).

union, FNV, in the 1970s and early 1980s. Wim Kok negotiated the renowned 1982 'Wassenaar Accord' with the Dutch employers federation. The agreement became the symbol of the Dutch wage moderation strategy and was part of a wider shift from Keynesian demand-management to a market-oriented supply-side framework.

While the Wassenaar Accord was not originally seen as very significant, the economic recovery in the mid-1990s gave rise to the idea of the 'polder model'. The term referred to a specifically Dutch corporatist and consensual way of boosting competitiveness and reforming the welfare state that began in 1982 with Wassenaar. The historical roots of this model, it was argued, could be traced back to the age-old Dutch history of dikes and polders, and the need to collaborate in order to keep the water out; hence the name 'polder model'.[2] In an *in memoriam* of Kok, the leading Dutch historian Piet de Rooy praised the former Prime Minister for his contribution to the Wassenaar Accord that laid the groundwork for 'The Dutch Miracle' in the 1990s: 'the awe-inspiring job growth and the resulting economic prosperity.'[3] Dutch Prime Minister Mark Rutte lauded his predecessor as 'architect and constructor of the Dutch polder model'. And from the other side of the Atlantic, former US president Bill Clinton praised Kok as a visionary who 'developed innovative policies to seize the opportunities and meet the challenges' of globalization, and 'built the consensus to implement them'.[4] In this way, the death of a former Prime Minister became a eulogy for a model.

This particular interpretation of Dutch socio-economic history – which has since become part of the national imaginary – gained most of its academic credibility from the analysis put forward by social scientists Jelle Visser and Anton Hemerijck. In their influential book *A Dutch Miracle*, they praised the success of the wage moderation and welfare reforms of the 1980s and presented this paradigm shift in economic policy as a result of 'social learning' by the trade unions. In the 1970s, Dutch politicians, trade unions, and employers were at loggerheads and policymaking at the corporatist institutions came to a standstill. The explosive rise of unemployment, Visser and Hemerijck argued, 'creat-

2 See M. Prak and J.L. van Zanden, *Nederland en het poldermodel. Sociaal-economische geschiedenis van Nederland, 1000-2000* (Amsterdam 2013).

3 P. de Rooy, 'Met Kok verdween het vertrouwen', *NRC Handelsblad* 26 October (2018).

4 Redactie, 'Wim Kok herdacht als zowel "architect als aannemer" van het poldermodel', *De Volkskrant* 20 October (2018); 'Statement from President Clinton on the passing of former prime minister of the Netherlands, Wim Kok', *Clinton Foundation* 22 October (2018) www.clintonfoundation.org/press-releases/statement-president-clinton-passing-former-prime-minister-Netherlands-wim-kok. Accessed January 21, 2020.

ed a sense of urgency to "make things better"' and made the trade unions 'support reforms against the short-term interests of some of their constituency'.[5] Naturally, the centre-right coalition governments under Ruud Lubbers were important too in the 1980s, since these initiated the shift to a market-oriented approach. But for Visser and Hemerijck the 1982 Wassenaar Accord formed the crucial turning point, heralding a 'broad consensus over central policy goals' among the social partners.[6] The Dutch unions consented to wage moderation and social security retrenchment as a precondition for economic recovery and employment growth. This corporatist path to supply-side reform, Visser and Hemerijck contended, was a superior alternative to the polarizing state-led overhaul under Reagan and Thatcher.[7] The Dutch economic recovery of the 1990s showed that competitiveness and employment growth could be combined with still relatively generous social benefits. In their eyes, the Dutch case exemplified Peter Katzenstein's contention in *Small States in World Markets* that democratic corporatism facilitated and eased adjustment to changing global economic conditions.[8] The focus on consensus as a driver of fundamental transformation has become central to the literature on Dutch welfare state reform.[9]

At the time of publication, the analysis of Visser and Hemerijck was received with much enthusiasm. The Dutch economic recovery of the 1990s had made the Dutch 'polder model' the object of international admiration. In 1997, the Dutch bipartite Labour Foundation, where employers and trade unions deliberate over socio-economic policy, received the prestigious Carl Bertelsmann prize for social innovations.[10]

5 J. Visser and A. Hemerijck, *'A Dutch miracle'. Job growth, welfare reform and corporatism in the Netherlands* (Amsterdam 1997) 62; See for similar accounts: I. Bruff, *Culture and consensus in European varieties of capitalism* (Basingstoke 2008); F. Hendriks, *Polder politics. The re-invention of consensus democracy in the Netherlands* (London 2017); J.L. van Zanden, *The economic history of the Netherlands 1914-1995. A small open economy in the 'long' twentieth century* (London, 2005). See for more recent discussion: J. Jonker, 'The Netherlands and the polder model – Nederland en het poldermodel', *BMGN – Low Countries Historical Review* 129:1 (2014) 88-89; M. Keune (ed.), *Nog steeds een mirakel? De legitimiteit van het poldermodel in de eenentwintigste eeuw* (Amsterdam 2016).

6 Visser and Hemerijck, *'A Dutch miracle'*, 74.

7 Ibid., 79.

8 P.J. Katzenstein, *Small states in world markets. Industrial policy in Europe* (Ithaca 1985).

9 See A. Hemerijck and M. Schludi, 'Sequences of policy failures and effective policy responses', in: F.W. Scharpf and V.A. Schmidt, *Welfare and work in the open economy. From vulnerability to competitiveness in comparative perspective*, vol. 1 (Oxford 2000) 125-228; H. Keman, 'Explaining miracles. Third ways and work and welfare', *West European Politics* 26:2 (2003) 115-135; V.A. Schmidt, 'How, where and when does discourse matter in small states' welfare state adjustment?', *New Political Economy* 8:1 (2003) 127-146.

10 F. van Empel, *The Dutch model. The power of consultation* (The Hague 1997).

The Dutch reforms served as an important inspiration for the Third Way, the social democrat turn to the market under Tony Blair and Bill Clinton.[11] As a result, the polder model developed into an important political symbol, both domestically and internationally.

Yet Visser and Hemerijck's argument contained significant flaws. As FNV-leader Johan Stekelenburg pointed out after receiving the Bertelsmann prize, the prevailing international image of the 'polder model' and the 'Dutch miracle' was somewhat of a myth. Dutch employment growth was less impressive and labour relations more polarised than generally assumed.[12] In the following years, a series of scholars challenged the 'Dutch Miracle' account on these grounds. They argued that Dutch economic performance was not so miraculous after all, that the amount of consensus among policymakers had been overstated and that the policymaking role of corporatist institutions in the 1980s was far less consequential than assumed.[13] The 1980s, these scholars contended, were not a time of consensus in economic policymaking, but rather of deep and sustained divisions, which lasted well into the first half of the 1990s. Corporatist policymakers may have agreed on wage moderation, yet they strongly disagreed on the broader market-oriented policy shift enacted by the first Lubbers cabinet (1982-1986). In the summer of 1983 FNV trade union leader Wim Kok wrote in the journal of the social democrat party that its readers 'barely need to be told that the current government policy is in almost every way at odds with the approach advocated by the FNV':

> Achievements of the welfare state, such as the welfare-linked benefits, the statutory minimum wages and the dismissal law, must suffer in this

11 W. Bos, 'De Derde Weg voorbij. 21e Den Uyl-lezing', (Amsterdam, 25 January 2010); M. Oudenampsen, "Opkomst en voortbestaan van de Derde Weg. Het raadsel van de missende veren', *B en M. Tijdschrift voor Beleid, Politiek en Maatschappij* 43:3 (2016) 23-45.

12 Van Empel, *The Dutch model*, 14.

13 See U. Becker, 'Miracle by consensus? Consensualism and dominance in Dutch employment development', *Economic and Industrial Democracy* 22:4 (2001) 453-483; U. Becker, 'A "Dutch" model. Employment growth by corporatist consensus and wage restraint? A critical account of an idyllic view', *New Political Economy* 6:1 (2001) 19-43; U. Becker, 'An example of competitive corporatism? The Dutch political economy 1983-2004 in critical examination', *Journal of European Public Policy* 12:6 (2005) 1078-1102; W. Salverda, 'The Dutch model. Magic in a flat landscape?', in: U. Becker and H. Schwartz (eds.), *Employment 'miracles'. A critical comparison of the Dutch, Scandinavian, Swiss, Australian and Irish cases versus Germany and the US* (Amsterdam 2005) 39-64; J. Woldendorp, *The polder model. From disease to miracle? Dutch neo-corporatism 1965-2000* (Amsterdam 2005); J. Woldendorp and H. Keman, 'The polder model reviewed. Dutch corporatism 1965-2000', *Economic and Industrial Democracy* 28:3 (2007) 317-347; S. Wolinetz, 'Socio-economic bargaining in the Netherlands. Redefining the post-war policy coalition', *West European Politics* 12:1 (1989) 79-98.

> neo-liberal approach. [...] The reduction of the financing deficit has been declared the highest policy priority. The consequences are catastrophic, socially and economically. In 1983, the government knowingly unleashed a deflationary process with gigantic austerity measures and tax increases, which has so far only led to an accelerated breakdown of employment the market sector and the (semi-) public sector.[14]

The statement was far from exceptional. In a lecture in 1985, Kok opposed 'the ideology of government retrenchment' and proposed a fiscal stimulus to fight unemployment, instead of 'an "overkill" of austerity measures'.[15] In 1987, as newfound leader of the Dutch social democrat party, Kok argued that the reforms of the 1980s reflected a development in which 'the free play of (market – BM & MO) forces triumphs over the striving towards social consensus'.[16] As these statements make clear, Wim Kok was a forceful critic of the economic reforms that later became associated with the 'Dutch miracle' and with his own trade union leadership. Political narratives of Wim Kok as the 'visionary' or 'architect' who 'built the consensus' to implement the reform agenda of the 1980s therefore warrant a degree of skepticism.

As the debate on the Dutch polder model is still ongoing, we will not attempt to settle it here.[17] Suffice it to say that there is serious controversy regarding the thesis of social learning and corporatist consensus as a driver of the reforms in the 1980s. We will limit ourselves to summarizing the key criticisms of the polder model thesis, as the main thrust of this paper lies elsewhere. What we believe is lacking in the debate thus far, is an alternative explanation of the 1980s policy shift. This paper sets out to develop such an alternative, consisting of three interconnected elements. One, rather than corporatism, we point to bureaucratic elites as a crucial factor in the Dutch policy shift. Two, rather than consensus, we argue that the policy shift was the product of a conflict of ideas between Keynesians and supply-siders. And three, the relatively early ascent of supply-side ideas in the ministries we argue, is due to

14 W. Kok, 'Volledige werkgelegenheid. Uitdagingen voor de jaren tachtig', *Socialisme & Democratie* 7/8 (1983) 5.

15 Idem, 'Een maakbare samenleving. Enkele overwegingen', *Tijdschrift voor Politieke Economie* 9:2 (1985) 24-34.

16 Idem, 'Het bestuurlijke in de economie. Een kritiek op de nieuwe zakelijkheid', in: A. Knoester (ed.), *Lessen uit het verleden. 125 jaar Vereniging voor de Staathuishoudkunde* (Leiden 1987) 367-374, 373.

17 See for a more recent discussion: Jonker, '"The Netherlands and the Polder Model", 88-89; M. Keune (ed.), *Nog steeds een mirakel? De legitimiteit van het poldermodel in de eenentwintigste eeuw* (Amsterdam 2016).

the existing experience with a successful supply-side paradigm in the 1950s: the Dutch post-war industrialisation policy.

In a theoretical sense, we argue that the Dutch case exemplifies, not so much corporatism but rather the innovative role of bureaucratic elites, as put forward by Skocpol, Weir and Heclo.[18] The contention in the sociological classic *Bringing the State Back In* is that government is not just a neutral and passive arena where interest groups negotiate policy. Government is an actor in and of itself, and policymakers can take the lead in diagnosing political problems and offering policy solutions. The state bureaucracy has a powerful institutional infrastructure for the production of ideas, and the administrative biases therein can help explain political change. The ideas underpinning the policy shift of the 1980s did not originate in corporatist institutions, but rather in the ministries. We think that 'bringing the state back in' can lead to a more convincing account of political transformation in the Netherlands in the 1980s. To be clear, this is not an argument about the brute power of administrative elites per se, but rather about the power of ideas, which brings us to our next point.

Rather than consensus, we argue that the contest of ideas has played a crucial role in the 1970s. Our argument builds on institutional analysis, a tradition of research that stresses the crucial role of ideas in times of paradigmatic crisis.[19] When an existing policy paradigm enters into crisis, the dominant understanding of how the economy functions and how it should be run, loses its explanatory power. This is followed by a contest of ideas, in which the advocates of a new policy paradigm seek to make their understanding of the economy accepted as the new norm. The classical example is the stagflation crisis in the 1970s, when the reigning Keynesian policy paradigm came under fire. A new set of economic ideas – monetarism, rational expectations, public choice, supply-side economics – came to the fore that was critical of Keynesianism and would form the basis of neoliberal policy paradigm. That

18 M. Weir and T. Skocpol, 'State structures and the possibilities for "Keynesian" responses to the Great Depression in Sweden, Britain and the United States', in: P.B. Evans, D. Rueschemeyer and T. Skocpol (eds.), *Bringing the state back in* (Cambridge 1985) 107-163; H. Heclo, *Modern social politics in Britain and Sweden.* (New Haven 1974).

19 For a more extensive discussion of the Dutch case in relation to institutional theory, see: M. Blyth, *Great transformations. Economic ideas and institutional change in the twentieth century* (Cambridge 2002); P.A. Hall, 'Policy paradigms, social learning, and the state. The case of economic policymaking in Britain', *Comparative Politics* 25:3 (1993) 275-296; C. Hay, 'Ideas, interests and institutions in the comparative political economy of great transformations', *Review of International Political Economy* 11:1 (2004) 204-226; V.A. Schmidt, *The futures of European capitalism* (Oxford 2002).

paradigm became dominant with the election of Thatcher and Reagan in the Anglophone world, while similar, sometimes more moderate shifts occurred in other countries.[20] We argue that the Netherlands was no exception to this trend and we show the rise of these new ideas among policymakers in the ministries.

As our analysis demonstrates, Dutch economic policymakers were highly critical of the Keynesian policy paradigm at a surprisingly early stage. They advocated for wage moderation, welfare state retrenchment and marketization, long before that conviction became dominant among political parties and trade unions. Why did senior civil servants take the lead in proposing market-led reform? Skocpol, Weir and Heclo point to existing political legacies and policy models as crucial influences on policymakers. We argue that this was also the case in the Netherlands, and that existing legacies can help explain the relatively early ascent of anti-Keynesian sentiment among policymakers. Building on the seminal work of Peter Hall and Monica Prasad, our hypothesis is that Keynesian ideas have never been as dominant in the Netherlands as they were in countries like the U.S. and the U.K.[21] This is because the Netherlands has a prominent supply-side tradition of wage restraint and market-oriented supply-side thinking that underpinned the economic recovery and industrialisation policies of the 1950s.[22] Although Keynesianism was politically hegemonic in the decade after the Dutch post-war wage moderation paradigm collapsed (from 1965 till 1975), Keynesian ideas never came to fully dominate policy-making institutions. In the stagflation crisis of the 1970s, policymakers were able to quickly fall back on the earlier tradition of wage moderation and supply side thinking. The economic policies of the 1950s, as we will see, became a prominent inspiration for the reforms of the 1980s.

Our argument is based on an extensive analysis of the writings of economic policy makers that partook in the economic debates in the 1970s, in which Keynesianism came under attack. An analysis of a selected corpus of inaugural addresses and PhD-theses allowed us to identify the different positions in the Dutch debate. We have looked specifically at the senior policymakers at the Ministry of Economic Af-

20 See M. Fourcade-Gourinchas and S.L. Babb, 'The rebirth of the liberal creed. Paths to neoliberalism in four countries', *American Journal of Sociology* 108:3 (2002) 533-579, https://doi.org/10.1086/367922; M. Prasad, *The politics of free markets. The rise of neoliberal economic policies in Britain, France, Germany, and the United States* (Chicago 2006).

21 P. Hall, *The political power of economic ideas. Keynesianism across nations* (Princeton 1989); Prasad, *The politics of free markets*.

22 Becker, 'Miracle by consensus?', 473.

fair and the Ministry of Finance, and analysed their publications and academic background. We have had fifteen in-depth interviews with ministers, economists, and senior public officials to examine how supply-side ideas were translated into policy. Finally, we analyse the post-war policies with the help of minutes from the Main Committee for Industrialization, extensive parliamentary sources and the memoirs of Minister of Economic Affairs Jan van den Brink (1948-1952).

The structure of the paper is as follows: the first section expands on the existing criticisms of the idea that corporatist consensus has been a driver of reform in the 1980s. Then we move on to the role of bureaucratic elites, showing their early ascendance and crucial role in advocating for the market-oriented reforms of the 1980s. This then raises the question why leading policymakers in senior positions were early advocates of a shift to a supply-side framework. In the third section, we suggest that Keynesian ideas never became fully dominant in the Netherlands, due to the presence of an older market-oriented supply side tradition, with its roots in the 1950s. We conclude with a reflection on the theoretical implications.

## Critiques of the consensus view

Before we turn to the role of ideas, bureaucratic elites and the 1950s, it is necessary to expand on the critiques of the argument that consensus and social learning among corporatist policymakers has been the driver behind the 1980s policy shift. Scholarly criticism of the 'Dutch Miracle' argument has developed along several lines.

First, scholars found talk of a 'Dutch miracle' in economic performance and employment growth to be exaggerated. The Dutch economy performed relatively well, but not miraculously in the 1990s. The total number of people employed may have risen sharply, but many of them were part-time workers.[23] Considered in terms of hours worked, Dutch job growth was far less impressive or exceptional. And whether wage moderation was key to Dutch economic recovery is difficult to establish with certainty, since other factors such as an international recovery and a boom in mortgage-backed consumption were important too.[24]

23 Visser and Hemerijck acknowledge this point in the introduction of *A Dutch miracle*, but this does not lead them to modify their central thesis. Visser and Hemerijck, *A Dutch miracle*, 11-12.

24 Becker, 'A "Dutch" model'; Becker, 'An example of competitive corporatism?'; Salverda, 'The Dutch model'.

A second point of critique is that the amount of consensus in the 1980s had been overstated: the 'broad consensus over central policy goals' assumed by Visser and Hemerijck did not exist in practice.[25] Of course, there was some degree of consensus on the need for wage moderation in the market sector, as shown by the Wassenaar Accord.[26] But opinions diverged widely on the broader 1980s agenda of market-oriented reform, state retrenchment and social security cutbacks. As Steven Wolinetz, Uwe Becker, Jaap Woldendorp and Hans Keman have shown, the Dutch trade unions remained critical of the economic policies of the Lubbers cabinets throughout the 1980s. They favoured deficit financing, stimulus spending and work-sharing solutions rather than fiscal consolidation and social security retrenchment.[27] In fact, the text of the Wassenaar Accord contained a clause referring to this controversy. It stipulated that the agreement had been made 'with each party maintaining their own opinions and feelings with regard to the policy proposals of the new government'.[28] This controversy over economic policy manifested itself clearly in the years after Wassenaar. In 1983, the public sector unions organised one of the longest and largest strikes in Dutch post-war history against the lowering of public sector wages. As Wolinetz has shown, trade union leaders were largely in opposition in the 1980s and 'assumed a tribune-like role' against the government.[29] Due to this controversy, the principal corporatist policymaking body, the Social and Economic Council (SER), was internally divided and had scant influence on government policy.[30]

Becker, Keman and Woldendorp argue that it is more realistic to describe Dutch labour relations in a more competitive sense: in terms of

25 Visser and Hemerijck, *A Dutch miracle*, 74.

26 Uwe Becker posits that there was actually no consensus on the need for wage moderation. Trade unions did not sign the agreement because they were convinced of the need for wage moderation, but rather because they saw it as the only way to implement work-sharing solutions. See: Becker, 'Miracle by consensus?'.

27 See Wolinetz, 'Socio-economic bargaining in the Netherlands'; Becker, 'Miracle by consensus?'; Woldendorp and Keman, 'The polder model reviewed'.

28 Stichting van de Arbeid, *Centrale aanbevelingen inzake aspecten van het werkgelegenheidsbeleid* (The Hague 1982) 2-3.

29 Wolinetz, 'Socio-economic bargaining in the Netherlands', 93.

30 Ibid., 90. See also T. Jaspers and F. Pennings, 'Sociale zekerheid en zorg. De SER als moderator', in: T. Jaspers, B. van Bavel and J. Peet (eds.), *SER 1950-2010. Zestig jaar denkwerk voor draagvlak* (Amsterdam 2010) 133-161; For internal controversy see the 1984 report from the Committee of Economic Experts (CED) within the SER, which noted that the economic policymaking field was principally divided between a Keynesian and Monetarist camp, CED, *Rapport over het conjunctuurbeleid in de jaren tachtig* (The Hague 1984) 55.

dominance and acquiescence, rather than consensus.[31] The trade unions eventually acquiesced to a new policy mix that was largely imposed by the Dutch state and by employers. This period of conflict and fundamental disagreement concerning the corporatist institutional framework lasted at least till the mid-1990s. Senior politicians and policymakers, such as the director of the Netherlands Bureau for Economic Policy Analysis (*Centraal Planbureau*, CPB) and the Minister of Economic Affairs, took aim against the extension of industrial agreements, a cornerstone of Dutch corporatism, in 1992 and 1994.[32] Only from 1995 onwards, when economic recovery set in, did a more consensual period commence, wherein the trade unions gradually came to embrace the new policy mix and corporatist institutions revived. It seems that this belated consensus has subsequently been projected backwards in time, to Wassenaar, obscuring the more conflictual origins of the Dutch economic policy shift.

Thirdly, the emphasis on corporatist consensus in existing accounts has led to an underappreciation of the role of politicians and civil servants in pushing for wage moderation, fiscal consolidation and social security retrenchment. Various Dutch governments had pursued wage moderation since the middle of the seventies through wage controls. The Wassenaar Accord was made under threat of a similar wage measure by the first Lubbers cabinet. In other words, the social partners of the 1980s did not initiate wage moderation, but took up a policy that was already in place.[33] Politicians who had been active in the 1980s, also remembered the key significance of political action and political conflict during that decade in later life. Bert de Vries, parliamentary leader of the Christian Democrat party (1982-1989) and minister of Social Affairs (1989-1994), criticizes the consensual 'mythology' constructed around the Wassenaar Accord.[34] The impression created after the Wassenaar Accord that economic reform was arrived at in the harmony of the polder, was decidedly incorrect. 'Also after Wassenaar, it was war between the trade unions and the government', De Vries con-

31 Becker, 'Miracle by consensus?'; Woldendorp and Keman, 'The polder model reviewed'.

32 G. Zalm, 'Betekenis en toekomst van de algemeen-verbindendverklaring', *ESB* 3842 15 January (1992); G. van Loenen, 'Twaalf jaar loonmatiging en toch slaat Andriessen alarm', *Trouw* 24 March (1994).

33 Becker, 'Miracle by consensus?'; B. de Vries, *Een halve eeuw werk. Werk en de werking van de arbeidsmarkt* (Rotterdam 1995).

34 B. de Vries, interview by Merijn Oudenampsen (Bennekom, 27 November 2019); see also De Vries, *Een halve eeuw werk*; Idem, *Ontspoord kapitalisme* (Amsterdam 2020).

tended.[35] Frits Bolkestein, the leader of the right-wing liberal party VVD in the 1990s, likewise concluded that 'the golden formula of austerity and wage moderation was not thanks to the so-called polder model, it was the result of a tough political battle'.[36]

## The contest of ideas

A vast body of international literature has recently highlighted the crucial role of policymakers and economists in the shift from a Keynesian demand-management policy paradigm, to a neoliberal supply-side framework. The rise of neoliberal ideas in policy circles is generally associated with the emergence of new schools of economic thinking in the 1970s, most notably from the United States.[37] The single most important challenge to Keynesianism was formed by the rise of monetarism, a school of thought developed by authors such as Milton Friedman, Allan Meltzer and Karl Brunner. It argued that Keynesian fiscal and monetary policy was both dangerous and redundant and that the economy could best be managed by controlling the money supply.[38]

An equally significant development was new classical economics (or rational expectations) developed by Chicago School laureates Robert Lucas and Thomas Sargent. It held that expansionary Keynesian macro-economic policy was ineffective because rational actors could anticipate the future effects of that policy (a higher rate of inflation) and act accordingly. The so-called 'rational expectations revolution' effectively reinstated many of the neoclassical assumptions that had been discredited by the Keynesian revolution of the 1930s.[39] Then there was public choice, an economy theory of political action developed by Chicago School laureates such as James Buchanan, Gordon Tullock and George Stigler. Its core premise was that politicians and civil servants

35 J. van Tijn and M. van Weezel, *Inzake het kabinet Lubbers* (Amsterdam 1986) 186.

36 F. Bolkestein, *Overmoed en onverstand. Beschouwingen over politiek* (Amsterdam 2008) 20.

37 See: Blyth, *Great transformations*; Hall, 'Policy paradigms'; C. Hay, 'The "crisis" of Keynesianism and the rise of neoliberalism in Britain. An ideational institutionalist approach', in: J. Campbell and O. Pedersen (eds.), *The rise of neoliberalism and institutional analysis* (Princeton 2001) 193-218; Prasad, *The politics of free markets*.

38 See: T. Congdon, *Monetarism. An essay in definition* (London 1978); M. Friedman, *Inflation and employment. Nobel memorial prize lecture* (London 1977); K. Brunner and A.H. Meltzer (eds), *The Phillips curve and labor markets. Carnegie-Rochester conference series on public policy*, vol. 1 (Amsterdam 1976).

39 P. Miller (ed.) *The rational expectations revolution. Readings from the front line* (Cambridge Mass. 1994); S. Fischer, *Rational expectations and economic policy* (Chicago 1980).

acted in a self-interested fashion, and that under such conditions, market exchange was in many ways superior to public provision.[40] A fourth important strand of ideas was supply-side economics, a controversial theory popularized in the late 1970s by Jude Wanniski and Arthur Laffer within the ambit of the US Republican Party. It suggested that extensive tax cuts could be enacted in a budgetary neutral way, since they generated extra economic activity and therefore extra tax income.[41]

Despite their differences, these currents of economic thought complemented each other in the discrediting of the established Keynesian framework. All four schools of thought shared an explicit political character and an activist stance in limiting government. Their rise formed part of a politicization of the field of economics in this period.[42] In the Anglophone world, influential free market think tanks such as the Institute of Economic Affairs (IEA), the Centre for Policy Studies, the Cato Institute, The Heritage Foundation and the American Enterprise Institute (AEI) famously facilitated the spread of these new economic ideas. The administrations of Ronald Reagan and Margaret Thatcher were instrumental in their intellectual breakthrough to the mainstream of economic policymaking, amid a polarizing war of ideas with the advocates of Keynesianism.[43]

The Netherlands was certainly not immune to the changing ideological tides. In the 1970s, monetarist, new classical, public choice and supply side ideas received a warm welcome in the Dutch economic policymaking field. Senior economic policymakers took the lead in making the case for wage moderation, welfare state retrenchment and marketization, inspired by the aforementioned international developments in economic thinking. An important difference was that the challenge to Keynesian orthodoxy in the US and the UK came from outside the established institutions, while in the Netherlands, that opposition emerged from within the ministries.[44]

40 J. Buchanan and G. Tullock, *The calculus of consent. Logical foundations of constitutional democracy* (Ann Arbor 1965); S. Brittan, 'The economic contradictions of democracy', *British Journal of Political Science* 5:2 (1975) 129-159.

41 A. Laffer (ed.), *The economics of the tax revolt. A reader* (New York 1979); J. Wanniski, *The way the world works* (New York 1978).

42 R. Heilbroner and W. Milberg, *The crisis of vision in modern economic thought* (Cambridge 1995) 126-127.

43 See D.S. King, *The new right. Politics, markets and citizenship* (Basingstoke 1987); A. Gamble, *The free economy and the strong state. The politics of Thatcherism* (Basingstoke 1988). A. Burgin, *The great persuasion. Reinventing free markets since the Depression* (Cambridge Mass. 2012); Prasad, *The politics of free markets*. R. Cockett, *Thinking the unthinkable. Think-tanks and the economic counter-revolution 1931-1983* (London 1995).

44 Hall, 'Policy paradigms', 286.

Already at the end of the 1960s, criticism of Keynesian economics resonated loudly among Dutch economic policy makers. Especially the Ministry of Finance and the Ministry of Economic Affairs were notable for their anti-Keynesian views. The senior officials in these ministries pushed for welfare state retrenchment and wage moderation as a solution to Dutch economic ills. They became known in the course of the 1970s as *aanbodeconomen* ('supply-side' economists). While that term denoted a specific theory with a rather controversial and party-political connotation in the US, in the Netherlands it served as a container-term, that referred in a broader sense to economists that advocated market-oriented reform.[45]

From 1963 onwards, the post-war policy paradigm of state-led wage moderation and sober social services started to collapse. Wages rose rapidly, public spending increased in great leaps, and Keynesian ideas became more dominant.[46] These were the years in which the Dutch welfare state was built up and rapidly expanded by subsequent centre-right Christian Democrat-led coalitions. In response to this development, an economic debate emerged on the desirability of increased public spending.[47]

Especially the Ministry of Finance became increasingly outspoken in its opposition to this trend. One of the leading critics of the increase in public spending was Willem Drees jr., a senior civil servant at the Ministry of Finance and a passionate advocate of small government.[48] When he was appointed to the highest position (Accountant General) in the ministry in 1969, Drees publicly declared that the Ministry of Finance was involved in 'a fight against groups that want (too) much money from the treasury', as part of its mission to 'protect taxpayers'.[49] That same year, together with economists Cees Goedhart and Theo Ste-

45 On the use of the term 'aanbodeconomie', see: J. van Duyn, interview by Merijn Oudenampsen (Maassluis, 6 November 2019). J. van Sinderen, interview by Merijn Oudenampsen (The Hague, 1 November 2019); Van Duyn, *De economie van het aanbod*; Van Sinderen, *Belastingheffing, economische groei en belastingopbrengst*.

46 Van Zanden, *The economic history of the Netherlands 1914-1995*, 64.

47 While this was framed as a largely technical debate on how to curb spending, at its core was an unmistakably political question: what level of government spending was deemed desirable. For fiscal hawks such as Drees jr., Goedhart and Stevers, the small and sober government from the 1950s was the ideal. See *Het Parool*, 'Thesaurie werkt op drie fronten', *Het Parool* 21 October (1969); 'Prof. dr. W. Drees Jr: "Overheidsuitgaven door pressiegroepen bepaald,"' *NRC Handelsblad* 21 October (1970); J. J. Lindner, 'Alle aandacht voor beleid nodig, vindt Drees Jr', *De Volkskrant* 13 February (1971); 'Indammen overheidsbesteding uiterst moeilijke zaak', *De Volkskrant* 18 May (1971).

48 Drees jr. was the son of Willem Drees sr., leader of the Dutch social democrat party (PvdA) and Dutch prime minister from 1948 till 1958.

49 'Thesaurie werkt op drie fronten'.

vers, Drees jr. founded an influential think tank focused on reducing public spending: the Institute for Research on Government Spending.[50] It became a prominent centre of Dutch public choice theory.[51] His political engagement took on a more explicit political form in the beginning of the 1970s. He became the leader of DS '70, a right-wing split from the social democrat party (PvdA) that opposed structural increase of state expenditure.[52] He developed into a prominent critic of the Den Uyl cabinet, whom he accused of 'capitulating to the demands of the trade unions'.[53] In this same period, Drees jr. introduced the 'benefit principle' (*profijtbeginsel*) into the Dutch public debate, which formed the basis for later privatization and new public management policies.[54]

Another key figure emerging in this time was Frans Rutten, who worked as a policymaker at the Ministry of Economic Affairs in the 1960s. In 1967, he became economics professor in Rotterdam. In his inaugural lecture, he argued that the increase in public spending (then at 35%) would lead to a decrease in corporate profitability and private investment.[55] In a classic supply-side argument, he posited that the curtailment of the public sector was a precondition for the creation of an attractive investment climate. Rutten was appointed head (secretary general) of the Ministry of Economic Affairs in 1973, and would remain in that position for seventeen years. He became one of the most influential economic policymakers in the Netherlands, and the country's leading critic of Keynesian economics. Rutten was positioned at the very heart of Dutch economic policymaking. He headed the powerful interministerial council overseeing macro-economic policy, the Central Economic Committee (CEC), whose reports were central to the budgeting process. He also directed the Economic Affairs policy institute AEP (*Directoraat Algemene Economische Politiek*). Rutten was a powerful public advocate of the wave of free market ideas coming from the Unit-

50 'Instituut gaat uitgaven overheid doorlichten', *De Volkskrant* 12 March (1969).

51 For key publications of Dutch public choice theory in the 1970s see: C. Goedhart, *Hoe collectief is de collectieve sector?* (Inaugural address; Amsterdam 1977); Th. Stevers, *Openbare financiën en ekonomie. De openbare financiën als instrument van ekonomische politiek* (Inaugural address; Leiden 1971); L. Koopmans, *Beheersing van de overheidsuitgaven* (Inaugural address; Deventer 1973).

52 J. J. Lindner, 'Een steile, rechtlijnige bestuurder', *De Volkskrant* 13 October (2000).

53 E. Brandt and K. van der Wild, 'Den Uyl had pressiegroepen kunnen intomen', *De Telegraaf* 20 October (1973).

54 The benefit principle implies that the cost of public services should as much as possible be borne by its users. See: W. Drees, *Gespiegeld in de tijd* (Amsterdam 2000).

55 F. Rutten, 'Over het macro-economische beleid voor de middellange termijn', *De Economist* 116:3 (1968) 287-308.

ed States. He later identified the reforms he presided over with the ideas of Milton Friedman.[56]

Striking is that the Dutch critique of Keynesianism predates the 1973 oil crisis and the leftist Den Uyl cabinet (1973-1977) – generally depicted as the peak of Keynesian thinking in the Netherlands (and the beginning of Dutch economic concerns). Also noteworthy is the senior positions such critics were able to occupy, in a period in which Keynesianism was effectively the reigning policy paradigm. As a short exploration shows, Willem Drees jr. and Frans Rutten were far from exceptional in their opposition to Keynesianism.

Conrad Oort, the successor of Drees jr. as Accountant General at the Ministry of Finance (1971-1977), was a student of Milton Friedman at the Chicago School of Economics, and was described by colleagues in his *Festschrift* as an economist who never denied 'his Chicago background'.[57] Lense Koopmans held his 1973 inaugural lecture at the Rotterdam economics faculty on the public choice theory of Willem Drees jr. and James Buchanan, while exploring the practical application of these ideas to cut back on spending and privatize public tasks.[58] Two years later, Lense Koopmans was appointed Deputy Director General at the Ministry of Finance, where he came to preside over the preparation of the Budget Memorandum (*Miljoenennota*).[59] Pieter Korteweg, an outspoken monetarist and advocate of the ideas of Milton Friedman, held his inaugural lecture on Anglo-American monetarism in 1973. He then worked with the influential monetarists (and later Ronald Reagan-advisers) Brunner and Meltzer in the US, and presented an economic model based on monetarism and rational expectations at the yearly congress of the Dutch Economics Association in 1978.[60] Described in the press as 'the Dutch Friedman', he was appointed Accountant General at the Ministry of Finance from 1981 till 1986, and became one of the principle architects of the reforms under Lubbers.[61]

56 F. Rutten, *Verval, herstel en groei. Lessen voor het economisch beleid gelet op het leergeld van twintig jaar* (Utrecht 1995) 37.

57 C. Kool, J. Muysken and T. van Veen, *Essays on money, banking and regulations. Essays in honour of C.J. Oort* (Deventer 1996) x.

58 Koopmans, *Beheersing van de overheidsuitgaven.*

59 B. de Haas and C. van Lotringen, *Wim Duisenberg. Van Friese volksjongen tot mister Euro* (Amsterdam 2003) 44.

60 Published in P. Korteweg, 'Herstel van economische groei', *Rotterdamse Monetaire Studies* 1 (1982) 3-26.

61 G. Driehuis and D. Kuin, 'Prof. Pieter Korteweg en de verrechtsing', *De Tijd* 6 March (1981); P. Korteweg, interview by Merijn Oudenampsen (Bosch en Duin, 7 January 2020); P. Korteweg, *Over de beheers-*

Similar views could be found at the Ministry of Economic Affairs. In the course of the 1970s and 1980s, Rutten assembled a team of talented young economists around the AEP, the so-called 'Rutten-boys'. These were all 'supply-side' economists who introduced monetarist, new classical and supply-side thinking to the Dutch policy field. Among the staff was Anton Knoester, who had written his PhD under Korteweg and Rutten on monetarist macro-economic modelling, Jarig van Sinderen, an advocate of Reaganomics and supply-side economics, and the later CPB director and Finance Minister Gerrit Zalm, who published papers with telling titles such as the 'myth of government investments'.[62] In so doing, Rutten and the AEP effectively took up the role of brokering new ideas in the Dutch policy field that free market think tanks played in the Anglophone world.[63]

## The shift from Keynesianism to a neoliberal supply-side approach

Internationally, Dutch civil servants were ahead of the game with their anti-Keynesian stance. For the larger part of the 1970s, economists at the OECD and the IMF still offered policy advice with a Keynesian slant. After the oil crisis of 1973 and the economic slump that followed, the OECD, the IMF and the EU called on the Netherlands and Germany to expand in order to stimulate international demand, and to compensate for countries that could not afford to do so.[64] This became known as the so-called 'locomotive theory', as promoted by the US president Carter. The expansionary policies of the leftist Den Uyl government (1973-

*baarheid van de geldhoeveelheid in Nederland* (Haarlem 1973). See also the PhD of Eduard Bomhoff, who was supervised by Korteweg. E. Bomhoff, *Inflation, the quantity theory and rational expectations* (Nijmegen 1980).

62 A. Knoester, *Over geld en economische politiek* (Leiden 1980) J. van Sinderen and A. Ravenstein, *New classicals en supply-siders. Een overzicht van hun ideeën en beleidsaanbevelingen* (The Hague 1986); G. Zalm, *De mythe van de overheidsinvesteringen* (The Hague 1985).

63 On the role of the AEP in brokering new ideas, see: A. Geelhoed, 'Making a difference. De beleidsagenda en AEP', *Tijdschrift voor Politieke Economie* 24:1 (2002) 60-72. For the Dutch reception of rational expectations theory; J. van Sinderen and A. van Ravenstein, 'Meer markt en minder overheid. De visies van nieuw-klassieken en aanbodeconomen', *ESB* 72:3590 (1987) 68-72.

64 L. Warlouzet, *Governing Europe in a globalizing world. Neoliberalism and its alternatives following the 1973 oil crisis* (London 2017) 144-145. See also M. Leimgruber and M. Schmelzer, *The OECD and the international political economy since 1948* (Cham 2017); J. Clifton and D. Díaz-Fuentes, 'The OECD and phases in the international political economy, 1961–2011', *Review of International Political Economy* 18:5 (2011) 552-569;

1977) however, soon became the object of serious internal opposition from senior civil servants at the Ministry of Finance and Economic Affairs.

Nevertheless, significant parts of the Dutch policy making fields were still decidedly Keynesian in orientation. This included economists in the major political parties, at the trade unions, and at the universities. As a result, economic policy making devolved into a constant skirmish between the supply-side and Keynesian camps in the 1970s. The intensity of their continuing disagreement, Frans Rutten argued, was due to the clear political implications of the debate: 'the opposition between new classicals and neo-Keynesians can run parallel to that of liberal champions of the free market and socialist advocates of detailed government regulation.'[65] This internal strife came to a point where the traditional meetings to coordinate economic policy between the different ministries (such as the aforementioned CEC) stopped functioning, due to bitter disputes and fundamental disagreements. According to Hans Weitenberg, then assistant director of the Bureau for Economic Policy Analysis (CPB), Den Uyl stopped these meetings in order to try 'to keep the senior officials of the Ministry of Finance and Economic Affairs out of it'.[66] As the monetarist Anton Knoester would later write in an overview of Dutch economic policy, the Den Uyl cabinet formed the beginning of the turn to supply-side thinking in the Netherlands.[67] Surprisingly, this was despite Den Uyl's own opinions on the matter.

An important element in the turn towards supply-side policies was a new model of economic forecasting, developed in 1974 by economists Den Hartog and Tjan at the CPB, called VINTAF.[68] It was presented in 1975 at the annual meeting of the Dutch Economics Association, in an intervention that was understood as a public critique of the employment plans of the Den Uyl cabinet.[69] VINTAF was in essence a neoclassi-

65 F. W. Rutten, *Verval, herstel en groei. Lessen voor het economisch beleid gelet op het leergeld van twintig jaar* (Utrecht 1995) 26.

66 Van Tijn and Van Weezel, *Inzake het kabinet Lubbers*, 77.

67 A. Knoester, *Economische politiek in Nederland* (Leiden 1989).

68 U. Becker and C. Hendriks, 'As the Central Planning Bureau says: The Dutch wage restraint paradigm, its sustaining epistemic community and its relevance for comparative research', *Review of International Political Economy*, 15:5 (2008) 826–850; T. Kayzel, 'A night train in broad daylight. Changing economic expertise at the Dutch Central Planning Bureau 1945-1977', *Œconomia. History, Methodology, Philosophy*, 9:2 (2019) 337–70, https://doi.org/10.4000/oeconomia.5613; M. Varisli, *Grenzen aan de groei? Sociaal-economische debatten in Nederland in de jaren 1971-1983* (Master thesis in History; University of Amsterdam 2018).

69 Kayzel, 'A night train in broad daylight', 351.

cal growth model, and it provided the basis for a series of reports of the CPB and the CEC in the years that followed. The VINTAF model differed from previous forecasting models, in that it claimed a causal link between high wages and the high tax burden on one side, and growing unemployment on the other. Consequentially, the policy advice based on this model leaned more in the direction of wage moderation and austerity, while Keynesian expansionary policies had less of an effect than in previous, more Keynesian models.[70] When first used, VINTAF was highly controversial, and Den Uyl refused to accept the data and policy implications from the new model.[71] The CPB soon found itself under fire from both sides.

In response to a 1977 CEC report based on VINTAF, a group of neo-Keynesian economists initiated a prominent debate at the leading Dutch economics journal ESB, later called 'the Economics Debate'.[72] The neo-Keynesian critics agreed that there was a correlation between high wages and unemployment. But that high wages caused unemployment was assumed in the model a-priori rather than proven empirically.[73] The new model was based on a political preference for a supply-side approach, rather than on empirical reality, they contended. For the neo-Keynesians, the real problem was the low-added value of certain sectors of Dutch business, such as textiles and shipbuilding. They favoured a public investment strategy to create more high-value added work, in addition to job-sharing schemes. The neo-Keynesian camp published a public letter ahead of the 1977 elections, in which they defended the expansionary policies of Den Uyl and warned to not 'one-sidedly blame the tax burden or wages for unemployment'. The signatories were 24 economics professors including leading names such as Tinbergen, De Galan, Halberstadt, Van der Zwan, Driehuis, Heertje and Pen.[74] The Keynesian camp was marginalized however, when Den Uyl failed to form government in 1977 and 1981. Den Uyl ruefully conceded that 'monetarists, new classicals and supply-siders have conquered the battlefield'.[75]

70 F. den Butter, 'De onderbouwing van het loonmatigingsbeleid in Nederland', *ESB* 74 (1989) 688-692; Kayzel, 'A night train in broad daylight'.

71 De Haas and Van Lotringen, *Wim Duisenberg*, 85.

72 P. Lansbergen, *Het economiedebat. Economen contra Den Uyl en Van Agt* (Amsterdam 1980); W. Driehuis and A. van der Zwan (eds.), *De voorbereiding van het economisch beleid kritisch bezien* (Leiden 1978).

73 A van der Zwan, interview by Merijn Oudenampsen (Amsterdam, 20 November 2019).

74 'Oproep hoogleraren economie', *Trouw* 21 May (1977).

75 See A. van der Zwan, *Nederland in zaken. investeren, winst en werkgelegenheid* (Utrecht 1985) 311.

*Illustration 1 "The band 'No Nonsense', performing their latest hit", cartoon by Peter van Straaten. Despite the pragmatic words politicians used to set out the austerity policy of the eighties, it generated a lot of controversy. (source: collection Peter van Straaten – Presscollection NIBG).*

At the same time, the CPB was under attack from the supply-side camp, who found their economic models still far too Keynesian. The monetarists Korteweg and Bomhoff accused the CPB in a series of widely read interviews and opinion pieces to deliberately underestimate inflation.[76] They also claimed the models of the CPB served a political agenda, this time to downplay the seriousness of the crisis.[77] In their opinion, the models of the CPB hindered the real solution to Dutch troubles: a monetarist policy aimed at controlling the growth of the money supply. Another influential line of criticism came from the Ministry of Economic Affairs. In his new year articles in the leading Dutch economics journal ESB, Frans Rutten criticized the models of the CPB for not considering the full range of negative (micro-economic) impacts of the high level of public spending on the economy.[78] A painful problem for Rutten was that the cutbacks under Lubbers performed quite badly in the economic models of the CPB, due to the depression

76 'Inflatiecijfer CPB voor '77 2 procent te laag', *NRC Handelsblad* 10 November (1976); 'Economen tegen planbureau', *De Volkskrant* 21 May (1977).
77 Bomhoff 2019, personal communication.
78 F. Rutten, 'Naar een hogere economische groei', *ESB* 71:3537 (1986) 4-9.

of effective demand.[79] In the 1980s, the Ministry of Economic Affairs actively tried to convince the CPB to change its models, by publishing its own new classical models and by taking CPB economists on organized visits to new classical economists in the US.[80]

With the advent of the second oil crisis of 1979, the Dutch economic crisis deepened. Older labour-intensive industries could not cope with domestic high wages and international competition. Unemployment, which had been under 6% from 1974 to 1979, went up 3% every year, until it reached 15% in 1983. As a result, public spending surged, reaching 61% of GDP in 1983. In response to this economic emergency, proposals for supply-side reform coming from the ministries gained in political urgency.

The first attempt at a fundamental policy shift was the austerity agenda *Bestek '81*, taken up by the centre-right government Van Agt I (1977-1981). At that time however, Dutch political parties were still very much divided on economic policy. The Van Agt cabinet failed to muster enough political support to implement the reform agenda, in part due to the internal opposition within the Christian Democratic Party, led by Minister of Social Affairs (and Keynesian economist) Wil Albeda. A next important step was the influential 1980 report of the Scientific Council for Government Policy (WRR) on industrial policy, which argued for a break with Keynesian policies and a fundamental shift towards a supply-side approach. The report provoked an extensive public debate on the future of economic policy.

In response to the report, The Van Agt government appointed the Wagner Committee, a high profile advisory group operating outside the official corporatist and parliamentary institutions. It was comprised of senior civil servants from the Ministry of Economic Affairs and leading figures from Dutch industry, with more minor trade union representation.[81] The committee met in the house of its chairman Gerrit Wagner,

79 Van Sinderen 2019, personal communication; Zalm 2019, personal communication.

80 G. Zalm, De romantische boekhouder (Amsterdam 2009) 52-53; Van Sinderen 2019, personal communication; Zalm, 2019, personal communication.

81 Among the members of the committee were Dreesman (CEO Vroom en Dreesman Nederland B.V.), Pannenborg (vice-president Philips) Beek (president Unilever Research Laboratorium) and Langman (board of directors of the bank ABN). Trade union representation in the committee proved to be controversial. The Wagner committee invited the trade union economist Piet Vos. But Wim Kok was not happy with that choice, since Vos was on the liberal side of the trade union spectrum. At the second session of the Wagner committee, the FNV delegated economist Cor Inja instead, but he was refused by the Wagner committee. See 'Adviesorgaan wil Albeda en Kloos'. *De Volkskrant* 13 January (1982); F. Nypels and K. Tamboer, 'Moet de metaaldraaier soms bejaardenhelper worden?', *Het Parool* 12 September (1985); See also Varisli, *Grenzen aan de groei?*, 60.

the former CEO of Shell, and produced its first report *A New Industrial Elan* in 1981. Its impact was likened to a bombshell in the Dutch press.[82] As economic historian Jeroen Touwen argues, the 'turning point was the Wagner Report rather than the Wassenaar Agreement'. It was the Wagner Report that 'supplied the ideological basis for replacing government intervention with the market mechanism'.[83]

Officially, the committee restricted itself to industrial policy. But in reality, the report had a much broader scope: it contained proposals for public sector retrenchment, wage moderation, deregulation, the increase of wage differences, and labour market and social security reform. Also included was a proposal to increase the power and scope of the CEC, to subject a larger range of policy terrains (education, labour market, environment) to economic analysis.[84] While the report was welcomed enthousiastically by the right and by the employers, social democrats and trade unions were critical.[85] Wim Kok described the Wagner report as a first step towards the 'Americanization' of Dutch society: 'Give entrepreneurs full freedom, cut back the state, and everything will be alright.'[86]

The opposition to Wagner rallied behind the Schouten-plan, named after the Christian democrat economist D.B.J. Schouten, a leading corporatist policymaker at the Social and Economic Council (SER). His plan was a moderate Keynesian proposal that combined wage moderation with measures to stabilize effective demand.[87] A majority of Dutch economists supported the Schouten plan, but the government was wary to further increase the deficit.[88] Den Uyl wrote about the choice between Wagner and Schouten on the eve of the 1982 elections, in the pamphlet *Small Margins, Big Consequences.* Even though the crisis had

82 'Waardering Shell-topman kwam later', *Trouw* 10 October (2003).

83 L.J. Touwen, 'How does a coordinated market economy evolve? Effects of policy learning in the Netherlands in the 1980s', *Labor History* 49:4 (2008) 439-464, https://doi.org/10.1080/00236560802376904; Idem, *Coordination in transition. The Netherlands and the world economy, 1950-2010* (Leiden 2014) 271. Also Wolinetz sees the Wagner Committee rather than Wassenaar, as the crucial breakthrough. Wolinetz, 'Socio-economic bargaining in the Netherlands'.

84 J.M. Den Uyl, *Smalle marges, grote gevolgen* (Amsterdam 1982) 7.

85 'Nog altijd grote kansen Nederlandse industrie. Advies commissie industriebeleid hoopvol', *Nederlands Dagblad* 6 June (1981), https://resolver.kb.nl/resolve?urn=ddd:010627479.

86 Nypels and Tamboer, 'Moet de metaaldraaier soms bejaardenhelper worden ?'

87 The plan was seriously considered within the Christian Democrat Party. See the debate between Zijlstra, Albeda, Schouten en De Vries in: H. Borstlap, 'De economische crisis en het 'Plan-Schouten,'' *Christen Democratische Verkenningen* September (1982) 400-415.

88 K. Caljé, 'Nederland moet het goedkoopte-eiland van de wereld worden', *NRC Handelsblad* 13 July (1983).

seriously constrained policy options, Den Uyl stressed the fundamental ideological nature of the upcoming choice: 'the two scenarios on which the political debate focuses, that of the Wagner committee and the so-called Schouten plan, are de facto based on completely opposed visions on the desired economic order.'[89]

When the Christian Democrats won the elections in 1982, they chose the Wagner proposals and set out a new market-oriented course, together with the right-wing liberals (VVD). The first Lubbers cabinet, installed in 1982, adopted most the reform measures proposed by the Wagner Committee as official policy.[90] As the head of Economic Affairs, Frans Rutten had played a crucial role in the policy shift. He wrote the 1977 CEC report, advised on the WRR report, co-drafted *Bestek '81*, handpicked the members of the Wagner committee and served as its secretary writing the minutes of the meetings. Understandably, Rutten later argued that senior civil servants rather than trade unionists or politicians were at the forefront of the 1980s policy shift:

> In the beginning of the 1980s, the Dutch economy was in a deep recession. The Social Economic Council (SER) stopped functioning, the labour movement was obstructing and politicians would not come to their senses. On the initiative of two senior officials of the Finance Ministry and Economic Affairs, an informal club was created with business leaders and civil servants. That group set out a new economic course. When at the end of 1982, the first Lubbers cabinet entered power, the case had already been thought out.[91]

Both supporters and adversaries shared this perspective on Dutch bureaucratic elites as initiators of the paradigm shift of the 1980s, while politicians followed suit. Cees Oudshoorn, the current general director of the Dutch Employers Organisation, VNO-NCW, praised the Ministry of Economic Affairs for having 'made the case for Reaganomics in the Netherlands'.[92] He noted that 'the policy of economic recovery that was initiated in the 1980s by the Lubbers cabinets, had largely been suggested by the head of Economic Affairs.' Jan Pen, a leading Keynesian economist and a senior policymaker at Economic Affairs in the 1950s, told a

89 Den Uyl, *Smalle marges, grote gevolgen*, 7.

90 Wolinetz, 'Socio-economic bargaining in the Netherlands', 91; Touwen, 'How does a coordinated market economy evolve?', 454. Varisli, *Grenzen aan de groei?*, 62.

91 C. Rutenfrans, 'Simonis is net zo oppervlakkig als ik vroeger was' *Trouw* 3 July (1999).

92 E. Jorritsma and M. de Waard, 'De SG is weer staatsdienaar, geen mooie zangvogel', *NRC Handelsblad* 5 January (2009).

similar story of bureaucratic initiative with somewhat opposite appreciation:

> This bureaucratic power ('fourth branch of government') flexed its muscles between 1973 and 1990, the time of Rutten. There was a certain struggle going on between Social Affairs, where they wanted a slightly more leftist policy, and the Ministry of Finance, that decided on the budget. As much as possible, they ignored the Ministers that happened to be there. The battle became more and more ideological, because Rutten wanted more market and less government.[93]

The above analysis serves to show that senior civil servants played a key role in the policy-shift of the 1980s. The ideas for the policy shift under Lubbers were promoted by civil servants in the ministries and the policy making process was neither consensual nor corporatist in character. This raises an important question. In the US and the UK, the economic policymaking establishment was dominated by Keynesian economists and the advocates of supply-side ideas emerged from outside of the institutions.[94] What explains the Dutch divergence, with influential anti-Keynesian policy-makers in key positions already under the leftist government of Prime Minister Den Uyl, the country's most prominent advocate of Keynesianism?

Weir and Skocpol have argued that politicians and policymakers usually do not develop policy solutions out of nowhere. Instead, they tend to work with existent policy recipes that have been successfully applied previously, adjusting them to suit contemporary needs.[95] While international inspirations were important to the Dutch shift in economic thinking, they also relied on existing Dutch policy legacies. Statements by Dutch policymakers in the early 1980s show that the industrialization policies of the 1950s served as an important source of inspiration.[96] The Scientific Council for Government Policy (WRR), one of the most influential policy think tanks in the Netherlands, hailed the industrialization memoranda of the 1950s as a source of inspiration for the revitalization of the Dutch industrial sector, claiming that these

93 J. Pen, 'Economische Zaken moet blijven', *Het Parool* 15 May (1999).

94 Hall, 'Policy paradigms'; Blyth, *Great transformations.*

95 Weir and Skocpol, 'State structures', 118.

96 See H. Wijers, *Een nieuwe aanpak. Het industriebeleid en de betekenis van de MIP* (Scheveningen 1982); K. Tamboer, 'Hans Wijers komt als geroepen', *Het Parool* 14 September (1994), https://resolver.kb.nl/resolve?urn=ABCDDD:010842280; A. van der Zwan, 'Wederopbouw en mobilisatiepolitiek', *Socialisme & Democratie* 38:11 (1981) 518-531.

documents (with wage restraint at its core) had established a sound '"climate" for investment activity'.[97]

The elderly Jan van den Brink, minister of Economic Affairs in the early 1950s, now found himself publicly discussing the strengths, weaknesses and influence of thirty years-old policies with economic historians.[98] Social scientists also showed renewed interest in the policy legacy of the 1950s and started to study the industrialization policies of the 1950s, while political scientists observed that 'the government and entrepreneurs fall back on the successful industrialization-formula of the 1950s'.[99]

The renewed interest of policymakers and academics in the economic reconstruction policies of the 1950s may seem surprising. The Dutch industrialization program of the 1950s, as set out by Van den Brink's industrialization memoranda, seems a typical example of post-war Keynesian planning. However, economic historians have concluded that Van den Brink largely followed a supply-side approach to boost competitiveness and create employment.[100] To understand how Van den Brink's policies served as a source of inspiration for the policymakers of the 1980s, we need to examine how they were first established in the 1950s.

## The post-war reconstruction of the Netherlands: industrialization and the origins of neoliberal policy

The state-fostered industrialization program of the Netherlands took off during the 1950s in a political landscape characterized by deep disagreement over socio-economic policies. Before the Second World War, Dutch socio-economic policies had been dominated by a classical liberal *laissez faire* approach, defended by liberal parties, but also

97 Wetenschappelijke Raad voor het Regeringsbeleid (WRR), *Plaats en toekomst van de Nederlandse industrie* (The Hague 1980) 163-164; 161.

98 R.T. Griffiths, 'Enkele kanttekeningen bij de eerste industrialisatienota's van J.R.M. van den Brink', *Bijdragen en Mededelingen betreffende de Geschiedenis der Nederlanden* 101:1 (1986) 110-117; J.R.M. van den Brink, 'Indicatieve planning als beleidsinstrument van de industrialisatiepolitiek in de jaren vijftig', *Bijdragen en Mededelingen betreffende de Geschiedenis der Nederlanden* 101:1 (1986) 118-127.

99 F.J. ter Heide, *Ordening en verdeling. Besluitvorming over sociaal-economisch beleid in Nederland 1949-1958* (Kampen 1986) 12; H. de Liagre Böhl, J. Nekkers and L. Slot, *Nederland industrialiseert. Politieke en ideologiese strijd rondom het naoorlogse industrialisatiebeleid* (Nijmegen 1981) 11.

100 J. Peet and E. Nijhof, *Een voortdurend experiment. Overheidsbeleid en het Nederlandse bedrijfsleven* (Amsterdam 2016) 148.

by the three main Christian democratic parties, who consistently held a parliamentary majority since 1917. Various indicators bear witness to the dominance of classical economic thought in the Netherlands: the Dutch had been among the last Western European countries to abolish the gold standard, participation of social democrats in government coalitions was effectively blocked until 1939, while welfare state arrangements at the national level developed at a slow pace.[101] Much of this changed during the Second World War, when the Dutch cabinet fled to London and found itself in the heart of the Allied debate on social security. Inspired by the British Beveridge Report on social insurance (1942), the Dutch cabinet installed a committee to examine the opportunities for the establishment of social security in the post-war Netherlands.[102]

The report of this so-called *Van Rhijn Committee* initially seemed to provide a major challenge to the Dutch pre-war socio-economic order. Pre-war social democrats, social liberals and a small group of progressive Christian democrats teamed up and established the Dutch Labour Party in 1946, which imitated its British counterpart to such extent, that they literally copied their election posters.[103] By aiming for the establishment of 'social security' in alignment with and complementary to the market economy, the supporters of the Labour Party challenged the existing socio-economic order. They also hoped to enforce a 'breakthrough' in Dutch politics, by luring Christian democratic workers away from the Christian democratic parties and ending the Christian democratic majority in parliament.[104] However, the social democrats encountered fierce opposition of self-proclaimed 'neoliberals'. Operating not by means of a parliamentary party but in more loosely organized networks, these pro-market advocates aimed for influence *within* the Christian democratic parties, hoping to gain their support for their anti-socialist, market-oriented program.[105] According to the neoliberals, the state should not delimit the market by means of social security, nor should it allow the market to run its course. Instead, the state should

101 H. Langeveld, *Schipper naast God. Hendrikus Colijn 1869-1944* (Amsterdam 2004) 216-217.

102 Commissie-Van Rhijn, *Sociale zekerheid. Rapport van de commissie, ingesteld bij beschikking van den minister van sociale zaken van 26 maart 1943, met de opdracht algemeene richtlijnen vast te stellen voor de toekomstige ontwikkeling der sociale verzekering in Nederland*, vol. 1 (The Hague 1945).

103 D.J. Elzinga and G. Voerman, *Om de stembus. Verkiezingsaffiches 1918-1998* (Amsterdam/Antwerp 2002) 85.

104 P. van Praag jr., *Strategie illusie. Elf jaar intern debat in de PvdA (1966-1977)* (Amsterdam 1990) 16-17.

105 B. Mellink, 'Towards the centre. Early neoliberals in the Netherlands and the rise of the welfare state, 1945-1958', *Contemporary European History* 29:1 (2020) 30-43, 35.

foster competition by combatting monopolies and cartels, while actively setting the conditions for an overarching socio-economic framework characterized by permanent competition.

Social democrats and the neoliberals both aimed to extend their influence at the expense of the Christian democratic parties. This made the Christian democratic parties vulnerable at the socio-economic level, as they united employers and employees on religious grounds and were therefore easily exposed to conflict between these parties with (possible) opposing socio-economic interests. This was especially the case for the Catholics, who had joined a coalition with the social democrats after the Second World War, much to the dismay of anti-socialist conservatives within the party, led by (among others) former minister of Colonial Affairs Charles Welter. When the Catholics obtained the ministership of Economic Affairs during the coalition negotiations of 1946, party leader Carl Romme appointed Gerardus Huysmans, a candidate with a strong right-wing profile, and confessed in private correspondence that he envisaged Huysmans as 'the conscience of Mr. Welter when he asserts that we adopt a socialist political course.'[106]

Had Huysmans been allowed to proceed as minister of Economic Affairs, his proposed industrialization policies would likely have failed, as the new minister sowed discord in an already highly politicized debate. On his first day in office, Huysmans asked his secretary for a list of policy officials appointed by his social-democratic predecessor and removed them within one and a half years.[107] He continued by openly embracing the free market and developing an industrialization program intended to restore market forces, a stance not well-received by the social democratic coalition partner. However, Huysmans had to quit his job in 1948 due to an illness that led to his untimely death. He was succeeded by the young economist Jan van den Brink, a far more tentative politician, who faced the difficult job of accommodating the KVP's right wing, while securing the support of the labour unions and the social democrats.

As political scientists have rightly concluded, Van den Brink's industrialization program was mostly a continuation of Huysmans's policy agenda, aimed at the restoration of market forces.[108] Its main tenets can be illustrated by focusing on the role of Albert Winsemius, the fu-

106 Nationaal Archief (hereafter NA), Archive of mr. dr. C.P.M. Romme [2.21.144], inv. 33, letter from C.P.M. Romme to F.J.F.M. Duynstee, 1 January 1947, 1.

107 De Liagre Böhl, Nekkers and Slot, *Nederland industrialiseert,* 146.

108 Ibid., 218 and 224.

ture economic advisor of Singapore, at the time appointed as Director-General of Industrialization and chairman of the Main Committee for Industrialization. At the inaugural meeting of the Main Committee, which consisted of policymakers and the social partners, Winsemius introduced his policy tenets. He did

> not conceive the issue of industrialization primarily as an issue of employment [...] We have to take our export figures into account. In this regard, our cost level is vital. [...] We are therefore obliged to take responsible measures by attempting to increase labour productivity, while using every opportunity to lower the costs of labour. On the global market, the only question is which party delivers at the lowest price. We have to ensure that we offer the lowest price.[109]

Winsemius's economic views were competition-oriented and aligned with neoliberal and neomercantilist assumptions. In line with neoliberal norms, Winsemius believed that the state should actively establish market conditions, as opposed to delimiting the market or allowing it to run its course. He expected these measures to enhance the opportunities for Dutch entrepreneurs on the global market, resulting in an increase of export. At the same time, however, Winsemius's conception of the global economy as a zero-sum game in which the Netherlands could only increase its share at the expense of others, bore resemblances to neomercantilist thought. The logical outcome of both was a race to the bottom, in which the Netherlands had to increase its competitiveness by an increase of labour productivity and by lowering its wage level. This policy solution attributed the lacking competitiveness of the Dutch industrial sector exclusively to the factor labour, which had allegedly become too costly.

Winsemius's views were shared by minister of Economic Affairs Jan van den Brink. Van den Brink likely developed these views before he appointed Winsemius. Before he took office as minister, he had been full professor of Economics in Tilburg, where he had taken an interest in the intellectual achievements of early neoliberal economists and their supply-side solutions for the recovery of post-war Western-European economies. Among these early neoliberals was the West German economist Ludwig Erhard who, like Van den Brink, would assume the posi-

109 Historisch Centrum Overijssel (hereafter HCO), Archieve of the Hengelosche Elektrische en Mechanische Apparaten Fabriek (hereafter HEEMAF), inv. 1328, Minutes of the inaugural meeting of the Main Comittee for Industrialization, 3 October 1949, 12.

tion of minister of Economic Affairs on behalf of the Christian democrats in 1948. In the same year, just months before both men acquired their new jobs, they met to discuss Erhard's views on the state-fostered market economy.[110] In his memoirs, published in 1984, Van den Brink emphasized that he did not aspire to copy Erhard's pro-market plans, which he deemed overly individualist. However, he emphatically preferred Erhard's approach over the socialist alternative and aimed to reconcile his Christian democratic values with the economic agenda of the German minister.[111]

This reconciliation of Christian democratic and neoliberal thought was crucial for the industrialization agenda of Van den Brink, not just because of the minister's own political aspirations, but also because he had to ensure sufficient support. As Van den Brink recalled in later life, it had been crucial 'to gain support of business elites in these economic policies and its tenets, without losing trust among employees, the trade unions and the social democratic coalition partner'.[112] Two steps had to be taken to meet these needs. First, the social partners had to subscribe to the new industrialization agenda, and the most constructive way to obtain this goal was to show employers and employees what they would gain from industrialization. Second, the resulting compromise had to hold appeal for Christian democrats and social democrats to keep the coalition intact and to secure a parliamentary majority.

Securing the support of the social partners initially seemed a tedious affair. Winsemius's rather bluntly formulated pro-market approach in the Main Committee for Industrialization, alongside his plea for low wages, appealed to employers but estranged the trade unions. The self-proclaimed neoliberal entrepreneur Henri Keus was among the first employers within the Main Committee to signal this problem. In private correspondence with his fellow-employer T.J. Twijnstra, he showed himself pleasantly surprised by Winsemius views, but he also feared commotion among the representatives of the trade unions if they did not understand why this deal should appeal to them.[113] Keus therefore organized a special meeting of employers and employees in addition to the meetings of the Main Committee. The aim of this meeting was to secure trade union support for a 'sound' investment climate, characterized by low taxes and cheap labour.

110 Van den Brink. *Zoeken naar een 'heilstaat',* 367.

111 Ibid., 369.

112 Idem, 'Indicatieve planning als beleidsinstrument', 119.

113 HCO, HEEMAF, inv. 1329, Letter from H.I. Keus to T.J. Twijnstra, 25 January 1950, 2.

When the meeting finally took place, Keus and his fellow employers secured the support of the trade unions with surprising ease. Both parties agreed on the necessity of 'capital formation within the enterprise as a precondition for the increase of employment', leading to mutual support for tax cuts within the business sector.[114] The outcomes of the meeting were undoubtedly influenced by the absence of the most left-wing representative of the trade unions, H. Oosterhuis and the presence of trade union representative D.W. Ormel, who also specialized in the academic work of the prominent neoliberal economist Wilhelm Röpke on behalf of the Protestant Anti-Revolutionary Party.[115] 'I was surprised', Keus wrote a few weeks later in private correspondence, 'that Mr. Ormel clearly expressed his support for the views held by [fellow-entrepreneur] Mr. Spoorenberg and me, and agreed that a revision of our fiscal system could wait no longer.'[116] After January 1950, fundamental debates regarding tax cuts were off the table.

The resulting consensus among the social partners, secured at the initiative of Keus, cleared the way for minister Van den Brink to push his policy agenda in parliament. This was a delicate job, as the minister required the support of the social democrats. The initial commotion among members of the Main Committee for Industrialization, although short-lived, demonstrated that he could not take the support of the social democrats for granted. However, Van den Brink managed to present his policy as an economic necessity. He argued that industrialization fostered Dutch export, which was required for the import of raw materials. In other words: Dutch industrialization should be oriented at the international rather than the domestic market to obtain the raw materials it required – a typical catch-22 situation. More importantly, the minister argued that industrialization contributed to job growth at a time when declining trade and an increasingly efficient agricultural sector were unable to do so.[117] Van den Brink estimated an increase of the Dutch workforce of at least 40,000 jobs annually, which tuned in with the social democratic emphasis on full employment.[118] The brochure *The Netherlands Industrializes*, issued in 1950 to communicate

114 HCO, HEEMAF, inv. 1328, Minutes of the meeting of the Main Committee for Industrialization, 7 November 1949, 1.

115 D.W. Ormel, 'Röpke', in: S.U. Zuidema (ed.), *Denkers van deze tijd III. Marx, Schumpeter, Keynes, Röpke* (Franeker 1957) 203-261.

116 HCO, HEEMAF, inv. 1329, letter from Keus to Twijnstra, 30 January 1950, 1.

117 HCO, HEEMAF, inv. 1328, 'Installatie hoofdcommissie voor de industrialisatie', 19 September 1949, 1.

118 Ibid., 2.

the government's plans to the general public, even mentioned the ambition to create 215,000 jobs within three years.[119]

It may be tempting to interpret Van den Brink's policy agenda as an example of state planning, or even as Keynesian, due to the minister's emphasis on job growth in defence of his policy agenda. However, although Van den Brink explicitly mentioned employment among the key policy objectives of his industrialization policies, he was careful to avoid plan socialism or Keynesian interventions to attain his policy tenets. Keynes's *General Theory* derived from the insight that, contrary to Say's Law, supply and demand tend to intersect *below* the level of full employment under free market conditions.[120] According to Keynes's analysis, free markets therefore produced a suboptimal employment of production factors such as labour, in other words: unemployment. According to this theory, the state should substitute for declining demand during economic slumps by fostering consumption and investment (demand management). Van den Brink defended the opposite solution and proposed to combat unemployment by adopting a 'facilitative policy' (*voorwaardenscheppend beleid*): the state should stimulate the economy through deregulation, tax cuts and fixing wages below the market price, to secure the competitiveness of the Dutch export sector on the global market. This supply-side logic, simultaneously defended by Director-General Albert Winsemius in the Main Committee for Industrialization, moved in the direction of what Cornel Ban calls 'embedded neoliberalism': an ideological hybrid that raises support for macroeconomic orthodoxy, deregulation and privatization.[121] As Peet and Nijhof rightly remarked, 'the socio-economic policies of the 1950s were to a large extent supply-side policies'.[122]

One of Van den Brink's key talents as a politician – which explains to a large extent the renewed appeal of his policy agenda in the 1980s – was his ability to sell his pro-market policy agenda as an optimal synthesis of liberal, Christian democratic and social democratic thought. He somewhat vaguely proposed 'indicative planning' underpinned by interventions with a 'global character', based on estimates rather than set targets.[123] The minister declared that 'given the [...] existing, and by

119 HCO, HEEMAF, inv. 1330, brochure 'Nederland industrialiseert', 8.

120 J. M. Keynes, *The general theory of employment, interest and money* (London 1936) 15-17 and 26.

121 C. Ban, *Ruling ideas. How global neoliberalism goes local* (Oxford 2016) 5.

122 Peet and Nijhof, *Een voortdurend experiment,* 148.

123 Rijksbegroting voor het dienstjaar 1950, stuk 1400 X 6, bijlage IV, memorie van toelichting, 'Nota inzake de industrialisatie van Nederland', 23.

the vast majority of the Dutch population desired socio-economic organization – (industrialization – BM & MO) should stem from private economic decisions'.[124] In line with the Catholic doctrine of subsidiarity, Van den Brink emphasized the complementary role of the state in society: state interventions were only feasible if private initiative failed.[125] However, the state should foster the private initiative by setting the conditions for a 'industrial climate'. Tax cuts for entrepreneurs, deregulations and fixed wages below the market rate were the main instruments to attain this goal.[126] As long as the industrial sector flourished, the subsequent economic growth would create 215,000 jobs in less than four years.

Van den Brink's policy agenda was a refined mixture of ideas. It complied with the social democratic tenet of full employment but achieved this tenet by employing supply-side policy instruments that contributed to the restoration of free market forces, while securing an active role of the state in fostering the economy. A tripartite consultation structure in corporatist fashion contributed to the support of the social partners. The Protestant trade union delegate Ormel eventually described capital accumulation and employment as 'Siamese twins' and his Catholic colleague J.A. Middelhuis also underlined the necessity of capital accumulation in the business sector to warrant employment.[127]

This specific combination of job creation, supply-side economics and consensus-oriented corporatism resurfaced when policymakers in the 1980s, confronted with a declining industrial sector, initiated a second wave of wage moderation. When the political scientist F.J. ter Heide studied the socio-economic policies of the 1950s in the 1980s, he observed that 'the 1950s serve in many respects as a source of inspiration for the 1950s. A first source of inspiration are the industrialization policies, designed in 1949 designed and applied in subsequent years'.[128] In its influential report *Position and Future of Dutch Industry*, published in 1980 by the influential Scientific Council for Government Policy, the council explained why Van den Brink's policies held such appeal. The so-called Main Committee for Industrialization, the council argued, had brought employers, employees and policy officials round the

124 Ibid.

125 Ibid., 28.

126 Ibid., 29.

127 HCO, HEEMAF, inv. 1328, minutes of the meeting between employers and employees initiated by H.I. Keus, 7 November 1949, 1.

128 Ter Heide, *Ordening en verdeling*, 12.

table.[129] It had offered employers and employees the opportunity to offer policy advise to officials, while tying the involved parties to the common tenet of industrialization. Citing the analysis of W. van Brakel, the former secretary of the main committee who analysed Dutch industrialization policies in the 1950s, the Scientific Council stated:

> The fact remains that these factors [the installation of the Main Committee and the appointment of a Director-General for Industrialization] all contributed in their own way to the establishment of the right "climate" for investment activities. On the one hand, they emphatically drew the attention to the vital opportunities for individual entrepreneurs and the national economy in a well-documented way. On the other hand, they underlined the strong willingness of the government to create favourable conditions for private investment activities.[130]

The Scientific Council thus subscribed to Van Brakel's analysis that a key feature of the Main Committee for Industrialization was its ability to generate support. By bringing employees, employers and policy officials together, the committee fostered consensus. As in the 1950s, the three parties would once again conclude in the 1980s that a facilitative investment climate strengthened the Dutch economy and that, therefore, entrepreneur-centred policies served the public interest.

## Conclusion

In the existing literature, the Dutch paradigm shift of the 1980s has long been ascribed to the power of social learning and corporatist compromise. This explanation however, rests on surprisingly shaky foundations, since there is little evidence for social learning and corporatist compromise. We have argued that not the trade unions, but rather senior civil servants were the primary drivers of supply-side reform. The Dutch case then conforms to state-centered explanations of policy change, as developed by Skocpol, Weir and Heclo. This does not imply that corporatism plays no role in Dutch developments, but merely that corporatism was not the driving factor in the Dutch paradigm shift of the 1980s. Instead, the analysis put forward in this article points to the

129 WRR, *Plaats en toekomst*, 163.
130 Ibid.

central role of the Dutch state in disciplining labour and restructuring Dutch corporatism on a new footing, within a supply-side framework.

If we look beyond their primary focus on consensus, there are arguments to be found in the work of Visser and Hemerijck that would support such a reading. Most notably, they emphasise the relevance of Fritz Scharpf's concept of the 'shadow of hierarchy', which refers to the ability of the state to cast its shadow over the bargaining table and 'shift the balance of bargaining power from one side to the other'.[131] Following this line of reasoning, it is the reassertion of the power of the Dutch state that is the crucial precondition for a market-oriented restructuring of Dutch corporatism (which is only fully achieved in the mid-1990s). Crucial here is that the initiative lies with the state, and the importance of the 1982 Wassenaar agreement is then demoted to being one of the products of the state-led paradigm shift, rather than the primary driver of that transformation.

While we believe that the role of administrative elites is key to the policy shift of the 1980s, we do not wish to overstate the autonomy of policymakers from societal pressures and interests, in particular that of Dutch business. The Ministry of Economic Affairs traditionally conceives of its role as that of a mediator between Dutch business, Dutch economic policy making and Dutch politics. The ties between business and senior economic policymakers at the Ministries of Finance and Economic Affairs have historically been remarkably close. Senior civil servants move on to sit in the boards of the largest Dutch companies and prominent business leaders get appointed to head the ministries. The Wagner commission that prepared the policy shift for the Lubbers cabinet can hardly be described as proof of the autonomy of civil servants.

Finally, we argue that a state-centred approach can provide important insights into the Dutch paradigm shift of the 1980s. In their work, Skocpol, Weir and Heclo argue that the ability of civil servants to act as the drivers of new policy ideas is dependent on the local policymaking infrastructure, and existing policy legacies. Both are important factors in the Netherlands that have received relatively little attention in comparative research. On the one hand, the exceptionally centralized, ostensibly depoliticized and universally respected nature of Dutch economic policymaking could help explain the outsized role of policymakers. The Netherlands lacks the powerful private think tanks with clear ideological profiles, such as in the UK and the US. Instead, bureau-

131 F. Scharpf, *Games real actors play* (Boulder 1997) 207.

cratic think tanks such as the CPB, the AEP and the WRR dominate the policymaking field. On the other hand, existing policy legacies can help explain the relatively early adaption of supply-side ideas in the Netherlands. In particular, the earlier experiences with supply-side and wage moderation policies during the industrialisation strategy of the 1950s became a recurring reference point in the 1980s. The Dutch academic field can be considered an important factor in the reproduction of such legacies, as many of the policymakers of the 1970s and 1980s received their training in the 1950s.

## About the authors

**Merijn Oudenampsen** (1979) is a sociologist and political scientist. He is postdoctoral researcher at the University of Amsterdam, working on a political history of neoliberalism in the Netherlands. He participates in the research project Market Makers, funded by the Netherlands Organization for Scientific Research (NWO). For his PhD, he wrote an intellectual history of the swing to the right in Dutch politics around the turn of the century. His PhD-thesis has been published by Routledge as *The Rise of the Dutch New Right* (2020) while it appeared in Dutch as *De conservatieve revolte* (Nijmegen: Vantilt, 2018).
Email: m.oudenampsen@uva.nl

**Bram Mellink** (1985) is assistant professor at the University of Amsterdam and postdoctoral researcher at Utrecht University. He investigates the role of ideas in politics and their translation into policy. His current research focuses on the influence of the early neoliberal movement in Western Europe on Dutch policy debates on welfare politics between 1945 and 1975. This research is part of the research project Market Makers, funded by the Netherlands Organization for Scientific Research (NWO).
Email: A.G.M.Mellink@uva.nl

# Towards a Politics of Restraint

*Public Choice Theory in the Dutch Labour Party of the 1970s*[1]

Thomas Kayzel

TSEG 18 (1): 53–78
DOI: 10.18352/tseg.1198

**Abstract**

Public choice theory, an analysis of politics based on economic principles, is often considered to be one of the major innovations in economics and political sciences in the second half of the twentieth century. In its formulation by James Buchanan and Gordon Tullock, public choice is commonly understood as one of the major theoretical building blocks in the development of neoliberal thought. It was also remarkably popular with economists and political scientists within the Dutch Labour Party (*Partij van de Arbeid*) in the mid-1970s. This latter fact is surprising since public choice was seemingly at odds with the Keynesian ideas around which the Labour Party had built its economic policy. This article investigates why and how public choice became popular in the Labour Party. In understanding the popularity of this theory, I will argue, it is important to see the popularity of neoliberal ideas not only in reaction to the economic tribulation of the period but also as a discussion on social planning and an expression of discontent with the democratization movement. Since the rise of neoliberalism in Dutch policymaking is often understood as coming from liberal and conservative channels, studying public choice within the Labour party will shed new light on the development of neoliberalism in the Netherlands.

1 The author wants to thank the editors of this special issue, Bram Mellink, Matthias van Rossum and Merijn Oudenampsen for their elaborate comments on multiple versions of this article and encouragement.

## Introduction

In 1975, the poet and novelist Gerrit Krol confused his readership by publishing an essay with the provocative title *The Common Man and Happiness or Why It's Not Right to Be a Union Member*. The author's intent was tricky to discern as the essay was filled with idiosyncratic abstract formulas expressing the freedom of which individual happiness would consist. As both a man of letters and a trained engineer, Krol was famous for taking the poetic power of mathematic formulas very seriously. At the same time, the tone of the essay could be highly ironic, and there was a strong possibility that Krol was satirising economists and political scientists attempting to formalise the most inner drives of human beings, giving meaning to the world by using axiomatic sets of formal language. Even the prize of the essay (12,50 guilders), together with the amount of time Krol had spent writing it and the satisfaction the reader could get out of it, were formalised into a simple cost-benefit model. Yet, Krol ended his essay with the sentence 'the sum of members united in interest groups is proportional to the degree of decline of that society.'[2] An invocation, with its reference to interest groups, eerily similar to the public choice theory discourse that enjoyed much popularity in the Labour Party (*Partij van de Arbeid*) at the time.

Public choice theory applies the techniques developed by economics to describe the behaviour of market actors to political actors. Politics in this theory is imagined as a field of competition by individual actors, each acting in accordance with their own preferences, making use of rational strategies to maximise the satisfaction of these preferences at the lowest costs. The rationality that the political agent applies is described via a so-called rational choice theory, an axiomatic set of formal prescribing rules that form the explanation of the behaviour of the actor. In short, political actors make decisions like economic actors make choices: based on optimal utility and rational strategies.

In the 1970s, Floor Hartog, Lenze Koopmans, Theo Stevers, Dick Wolfson, Arnold Heertje, Hans Daudt, Roel in 't Veld and Hans van den Doel, all members of the Labour party, applied public choice in one variant or another in both their academic work as well as their public writings. That the Labour party would become a hub of public choice theory is remarkable considering the prevalence of Keynesian ideas within the same party. The Dutch Labour party, following its British counter-

2 G. Krol, *De gewone man en het geluk of Waarom het niet goed is lid van een vakbond te zijn* (Amsterdam 1975).

part, had made Keynesian inspired policies into the spearhead of its economic program since the 1950s. The literature on the application of public choice in other countries suggests that the theory was often used to debunk Keynesian policies.

For example, Colin Hay has argued that public choice was deployed in the UK to explain why Keynesian demand management was nice in theory but would fail in practice. Because politicians were likely to bow to interest groups for electoral reasons, they would always artificially increase demand even when this was damaging for the economy. As such, public choice provided a very suited narrative to discredit Keynesian ideas in wake of the economic shocks of inflation and rising unemployment of the 1970s (often called the stagflation crisis).[3] Consequently, public choice has often been associated with the neoliberal-turn in politics and policymaking that many nations underwent in the 1980s. This article investigates why public choice could have gained a foothold in what on the surface seems a hostile environment as a stronghold of Keynesian thought and policy, the Dutch Labour Party.

The association between public choice and neoliberalism is no coincidence. The origins and development of public choice are diverse,[4] but critics of the theory have pointed out that a crucial part of its development is associated with military think tanks, most prominently the RAND-corporation, and that public choice research served as an ideological justification of capitalist liberal democracy and the denunciation of more socialist-oriented politics.[5] In its formulation by James Buchanan and Gordon Tullock, also known as the Virginia school, public choice became an instrumental building block in the development of neoliberal theory. Not only were Buchanan and Tullock involved in a network of neoliberal think tanks,[6] they also reformulated longstanding issues from neoliberal thought, such as the rent-seeking problem

3 C. Hay, *Why we hate politics* (Cambridge 2007) 106-107. See also: N. Thompson, 'Hollowing out the state. Public choice theory and the critique of Keynesian social democracy', *Contemporary British History* 22:3 (2008) 355-382, https://doi.org/10.1080/13619460701731913.

4 For an overview of sources, see: B. Cherrier and J.B. Fleury, 'Economists' interest in collective decision after World War II. A history', *Public Choice* 172:1-2 (2017) 23-44, https://doi.org/10.1007/s11127-017-0410-7; C. Herfeld, 'The diversity of rational choice theory. A review note', *Topoi* 39 (2020) 329-347, https://doi.org/10.1007/s11245-018-9588-7.

5 P. Mirowski, *Machine dreams. Economics becomes a cyborg science* (Cambridge 2002); S.M. Amadae, *Rationalizing capitalist democracy. The cold war origins of rational choice liberalism* (Chicago 2003); D.T. Rodgers, *Age of fracture* (Cambridge Mass. 2011) 63-64,85-94.

6 P. Mirowski and D. Plehwe (eds.), *The road from Mont Pelerin. The making of the neoliberal thought collective*, 1st edition (Cambridge Mass. 2009) 18.

and constitutionalism, in a public choice framework.[7] Moreover, their version of public choice has been applied in policymaking circles for the design of neoliberal policies.

The impact of public choice on post-war politics, especially in the neoliberal-turn made by many Western European and North-American countries throughout the 1980s, has been a fruitful research subject in recent years.[8] For example, in a recent controversial book, the historian Nancy MacLean has argued that public choice was picked up by a radical right-wing network funded by the industrialist Charles and David Koch as a central piece of argumentation of why securing minority interest in the democratic system through voter suppression, gerrymandering and appointment of partisan judges was necessary and justified.[9] Similarly, Hay argues in *Why We Hate Politics* (2007) that public choice has destroyed the idea of the public official as working for the common good. Consequently, trust in politicians, and more importantly the self-perception of the politicians, became low; resulting in ills of present-day politics: depoliticization, indifference towards politics, and technocracy.[10] In his analysis of the foundations of the EU, public choice gave shape to a framework in which important decisions such as inflation rates and budget rules were placed outside the democratic realm and instead left to technocrats. In general, this literature has set out a couple of structural points concerning public choice and the neoliberal-turn: (1) it was Buchanan and Tullock's version in particular that gained traction in policymaking circles, (2) public choice ideas were disseminated through a network of right-wing think tanks, and (3) public choice was a central element to relegate important political decisions to un-elected public offices, such as central banks and regulatory agencies.

7 T. Biebricher, 'Neoliberalism and democracy', *Constellations* 22:2 (2015) 257-260, https://doi.org/10.1111/1467-8675.12157.

8 Apart from the below named example's, see also: Thompson, 'Hollowing out the state'; T. Biebricher, *The political theory of neoliberalism* (Stanford 2018); M. Olssen, 'Neoliberalism and democracy: A Foucauldian perspective on public choice theory, ordoliberalism, and the concept of the public good', in: D. Cahill et al. (eds.), *The SAGE handbook of neoliberalism* (London 2018) 384-396.

9 N. MacLean, *Democracy in chains. The deep history of the radical right's stealth plan for America* (New York 2017) xvi-xvii. Unsurprisingly, the economics community was not amused by the associations with central piece of theory with racism. For an overview of the ensuing discussion, see: P. Mirowski, 'The eighteenth brumaire of James Buchanan. Review of Nancy MacLean, Democracy in chains', *Boundary 2* 46:1 (2019) 197-219, https://doi.org/DOI 10.1215/01903659-7271411.

10 Hay, *Why we hate politics*, 110-113. Cf. P. Mair, *Ruling the void. The hollowing of Western democracy* (New York 2013).

Although the rise of neoliberal thought has been an international phenomenon, in recent years scholars have argued – also in reaction to the US and UK dominated narratives – that the precise reception and implementation of neoliberal ideas were shaped by local circumstances and therefore many national varieties in neoliberalism can be discerned.[11] Therefore, answering the main question of this article, it is important to go beyond the international literature on public choice and neoliberalism and investigate the particularities of Dutch political debate at the time. With what issues did public choice resonate at the time and why were those issues prominent in the Labour party? I will argue that it were not only economic problems that propelled the attractiveness of public choice but also discontent with the discussion on democratization. In the 1970s, the latter discussion had taken a very particular form in the Netherlands. Under the auspices of social planning, democratization became strongly associated with the growing public sector. Hence public choice functioned mainly as an attack against the growing welfare state.

The Dutch history of public choice, as I will argue in this article, shows some remarkable deviations from the main points of the international literature (as formulated above), even if the main structure remains intact. Most striking was that the public choice did not only enter the public debate through right-wing think tanks or political parties but through economists and political scientists associated with the Dutch Labour Party. Most literature on the rise of neoliberalism, both international and national, suggests that adoption of neoliberal ideas by social democratic parties in the so-called Third Way of the 1990s, was due to external pressure. Hay, for example, suggests that the UK Labour Party based its monetary policies on the established neoliberal policy-paradigm of the Conservatives; hoping to gain credibility by adhering to the 'there is no alternative' slogan that was made famous by Margaret Thatcher.[12] In a recent book on the Dutch context, Duco Hellema and Margriet van Lith argue that neoliberalism entered Dutch politics through the liberal and Christian democratic parties, and the Labour Party adopted these ideas in order to enter government once again, after twelve years of opposition. They suggest that the neoliberal turn of the Labour Party was a

11 For an example of an plea of localized histories of neoliberalism, see: B. Jackson, 'Currents of neo-liberalism. British political ideologies and the new right, c.1955-1979', *English Historical Review* cxxxi:551 (2016) 823-850, https://doi.org/doi:10.1093/ehr/cew237.

12 C. Hay, 'The normalizing role of rationalist assumptions in the institutional embedding of neoliberalism', *Economy and Society* 33:4 (2004) 500-527, https://doi.org/10.1080/0308514042000285260.

relatively swift affair, pushed through by a group of young reformers.[13] In contrast to these narratives, I will argue that already in the 1970s neoliberal ideas entered the Labour party and that the party had internal motivations for adopting these ideas. This suggests that the neoliberal turn of the party at the end of the 1980s was not solely due to external pressure and that this turn was a long time in the making.

The starting point of my analysis of public choice within the labour party is their think tank the *Wiardi Beckman Stichting*, which was at the time an important platform for the introduction of new ideas and discussions of both ideological issues of social democracy and political strategies. The main source of research are the articles published in the think tanks periodical, *Socialism and Democracy* (*Socialisme en democratie*) for which both prominent Labour party members were writing at the time, such as Labour leader Joop Den Uyl, as well as scientist and scholars associated with the party. In my analysis, I have identified a set of social scientists who used public choice (inspired) arguments, or reacted against it. These include the above-mentioned set of Heertje, Daudt, Stevers, Van den Doel, In 't Veld, Wolfson, as well as Lucas Reijnders, Arnoud Weeda, Bart Tromp and Wim Duisenberg. In the second step of my analysis, I surveyed the academic writings of these scientists on the topics discussed within the Labour party at the time. I have chosen to focus on two contributors to these debates in particular, one economist and one political scientist: Theo Stevers and Hans Daudt. Stevers and Daudt were both prominent and controversial voices in these debates and in their writings the issues of public choice received their most recognisable formulations. Furthermore, the writings of Stevers provide a perfect bridge with earlier debates on public choice in the economics subdiscipline of public finance from the 1950s, showing a longer history of public choice in Dutch politics. Similarly, Daudt works on democratization within the Labour party in the 1960s provide a clear link between earlier writings on democratization and public choice theory.

The article starts by exploring the origins of public choice in the Netherlands. Public choice first became popular as part of public finance in the 1950s and 1960s but remained confined to academic circles and policymakers in the ministry of finance. The second section of the article discusses the so-called Economists' Debate within the Labour party which concerned the many economic issues that plagued the 1970s. It was within this discussion that public choice came to wider prominence.

13 D. Hellema and M. Van Lith, *Dat hadden we nooit moeten doen. De PvdA en de neoliberale revolutie van de jaren negentig* (Amsterdam 2020).

The third section will turn to the discussions on democracy and show that public choice had a similar impact there, while the last section will address how the public choice discourse was connected to a larger discussion on social planning. These three issues prominently discussed within the Labour party – public spending, democratization and social planning – form the reasons why public choice could become so popular.

## Public finance and public choice

In the Netherlands, public choice theory first gained traction in relation to public spending in the 1950s. Already in the early period, the growth of public spending was mainly a concern of neoliberal economists. Subsequently, public choice was strongly associated with neoliberal thought, even before Buchanan or Tullock became household names.

In the 1950s, the rising popularity of Keynesian ideas in policymaking circles had provoked a counter-reaction amongst economists and ministers with a strongly neoliberal character.[14] Economists, such as Amsterdam professor Pieter Hennipman, feared that a large growth of the government expenditure needed to manage aggregated demand in the economy and counter unemployment, as Keynesian ideas promoted, would set the state on an inevitable course to socialism.[15] Saving Dutch democracy from this fate, restricting the state budget was of crucial importance. Such sentiments were also shared by the ministers of economic affairs Jan van den Brink (1948-1952) and Jelle Zijlstra (1952-1958), who opposed the more statist course of the Labour party, resulting in much bickering and unclear contours of economic policy.[16]

What made matters more alarming for neoliberals, was the idea that the growth of public spending was not the consequence of a simple political choice inspired by Keynesianism but a structural feature of the

14 For spread of Keynesian ideas in policymaking circles, see: M.L. Bemelmans-Videc, 'Economen in overheidsdienst. Bijdragen van Nederlandse economen aan de vorming van het sociaal-economische beleid, 1945-1975' (Rotterdam 1984) Chapter 2; T. Kayzel, 'A night train in broad daylight. Changing economic expertise at the Dutch Central Planning Bureau 1945-1977', *Œconomia* 9:2 (2019) 351-352, https://doi.org/10.4000/oeconomia.5613.

15 B. Mellink, 'Towards the centre. Early neoliberals in the Netherlands and the rise of the welfare state, 1945-1958', *Contemporary European History* 29:1 (2019) 30-43, https://doi.org/10.1017/S0960777318000887.

16 J. Harmsma, '"Voorbij de oude ballast". Neoliberalisme en het nieuwe marktdenken van Nederlandse economen (1945-1952)', *Sociologie* 15:3 (2019) 253-270, https://doi.org/10.5117/soc2019.3.002.harm.

modern state as such. If it were not for strict rules and robust institutions, the modern state would always undermine itself or would become socialist. How this structural feature of increased spending exactly worked was elaborated by Willem Drees Jr. (the son of the prime minister of the time) in his dissertation *On the Level of Government Expenditure in the Netherlands after the War* (1955). Drees's thesis very likely marks the first application of a form of public choice analysis in a Dutch context; even a couple years before Anthony Downs, Buchanan and Tullock came with their famous formulations. Through a study of policymaking process at the ministry of finance, Drees argued that the rise of public spending was caused not so much by democratic decision-making but rather the result of the micro-actions of the public officials that favoured policies from which they would benefit. Moreover, ministers and policymakers responsible for spending in the public or semi-public sectors, such as education, defence and health care had little to gain from more frugality in their departments. Hence, these ministries formed natural fronts against the minister of finance, forcing an increase in spending. Policymakers and ministers of social services lacked the overview to understand that an increase in spending might be beneficial to their departments but could threaten the common good.[17]

Drees's analysis spurred the conviction among conservative economics circles that restricting the budget beyond democratic decision-making was necessary to protect the capitalist order. Putting his money where his mouth was, Drees became director-general of the national budget (*Directeur-Generaal Rijksbegroting*), a public office overseeing the budgeting process, in 1956; and chief treasurer in 1969, further propagating ideas of budget norms within policymaking circles.[18] Drees shared this conviction with other newly appointed public officials, such as Frans Rutten and Lenze Koopmans.[19] The wish for public finance rules became a reality in 1961 when Zijlstra, who became minister of finance in 1958, introduced a budgeting norm which made the public spending dependent on the projected tax-incomes for the coming years, thus restricting the government's budget outside of decisions made in parliament.[20]

17 W. Drees Jr., *On the level of government expenditure in the Netherlands after the war*, Aspecten der economische politiek, III (Leiden 1955) 62-67.

18 M. Oudenampsen and B. Mellink, 'The roots of Dutch frugality. The role of public choice theory in Dutch budgetary policy', Forthcoming.

19 See for example: F. Rutten, 'Over het macro-economische beleid voor de middellange termijn', *De Economist* 116:3 (1968) 287-308.

20 See: J. Zijlstra, 'Het belang van vaste beleidsbakens', in: *Het sociaal-economisch beleid in de tweede helft van de twintigste eeuw. Opstellen aangeboden aan Prof. dr. F.W. Rutten* (Groningen 1990).

Although ideas on the use of public choice had gained a strong foothold in policymaking circles and were further disseminated in the subdiscipline of public finance – a very popular topic in the Dutch universities – they could not turn the tide with regards to public spending. With continuing economic growth, the end of wage-moderation and the further expansion of the social security system, restricting budgets was not attractive to most ministers. Zijlstra's norm did too little to change that. In 1966, the cabinet of prime minister Jo Calls fell in a dramatic fashion over a conflict with members of parliament of the Catholic People's Party concerning the national budget.[21] But even this event did little to reverse the overall political attitude that higher budgets were no really a problem. Furthermore, in the consensus-driven corporatist politics of the mid-1950s and early 1960s, the opposition between neoliberalism and Keynesianism started to matter less and less. Keynesian ideas were adopted by centre right-wing government more out of pragmatism than out of ideology. As such, ideas on public choice never gained a wider audience and seemed to have lost relevance at the end of the 1960s.

## The economists' debate

After falling into obscurity, public choice theory made a strong comeback in the mid-1970s. Although still strongly associated with public finances, the theory gained a new audience and new applications in the wake of the stagflation crisis. The dominant narrative is that the combination of inflation and rising unemployment was an anomaly in Keynesian theory and therefore sent the whole paradigm into a crisis. But, as thorough readers of Thomas Kuhn know, one anomaly does not cause a paradigm to sway. More issues were plaguing the economic order and the dominant knowledge about it; moreover, public choice helped to formulate a challenger paradigm. This confusion surrounding Keynesianism and stagflation is best illustrated by the fierce debates within Labour party circles between economists, later dubbed the economists' debate (*het economendebat*).[22]

21 H. Notenboom, *De val van het kabinet-Cals. De financiële politiek van de Katholieke Volkspartij in de parlementaire periode 1963-1967* (The Hague 1991) 63-76.

22 For an overview of the debate by some of its participants, see: H. Van den Doel, *Het biefstuksocialisme en de economie*, 2nd ed. (Utrecht 1979) Chapter 4; A. Weeda, 'Van economendebat tot economiediscussie', *Socialisme en Democratie* 36:1 (1979) 3-15; P. Lansbergen, *Het economiedebat. Economen contra Den Uyl en Van Agt* (Amsterdam 1980).

Already in the late 1960s, inflation was rising but seldom conceived of as a problem before the early 1970s. Even without unemployment, neoliberal economists, such as Rutten and Heertje, saw rising inflation as a sign of an overburdened economy. Through index linking, raising wages kept inflation stuck in a rising spiral. They argued that the resulting high costs of labour would affect the private consumption and investments, leaving industries in a bad shape. Many pessimistic economists interpreted the sudden rise in unemployment after the oil-crisis of 1973 as confirmation of their beliefs.[23] But the link between inflation and unemployment was not easily established. The two were negatively linked in the infamous Phillips-curve – often taken as a central piece of post-war monetary policy and although not strictly Keynesian still strongly associated with it – but detractors of Keynesian theory had similarly no idea how the two phenomena correlated positively.[24]

An answer to this problem was formulated by the Dutch Central Planning Bureau (CPB) in 1974 with the publication of the so-called Hartog-Tjan model. The economic planners argued that the strong rise in wages had led Dutch industries to relatively invest more in capital goods rather than labour to boost productivity. Labour was simply too expensive. Such a discrepancy between investments in labour and capital had not been noticed when the economy was booming but with the downturn, this problem became painfully visible through a spike in unemployment. In a follow-up, the CPB used the newly developed VINTAF-model to further link the high wage-costs to the growing fiscal burden: by expanding social insurances, businesses and employees had to pay higher taxes, resulting in higher wage-costs and less spendable private income.[25] Soon after, the government was accused by economists of passing on the costs of social insurances to the employers.[26]

23 A. Heertje, 'De miljoenennota en de economische orde', *Economische en Statistische Berichten* 59:2972 (1974) 880-882; Lansbergen, *Het economiedebat*, 19-22.

24 For the tarnished reputation of the Phillip-curve, see: J. Forder, 'Friedman's Nobel lecture and the Phillips curve myth', *Journal of the History of Economic Thought* 32:3 (2010) 329-348, https://doi.org/10.1017/S1053837210000301.

25 H. Den Hartog and Hok Soei Tjan, 'Investeringen, lonen, prijzen en arbeidsplaatsen. Een jaargangenmodel met vaste coëfficienten voor Nederland', *CPB Occasional Paper* 8 (1974); H. Den Hartog, Hok Soei Tjan, and T. Van de Klundert, 'Structurele ontwikkeling van de werkgelegenheid in macro economisch perspectief', Paper for the Annual Meeting of the Dutch Society of Economics in The Hague, September 1975.

26 The Dutch term used was 'afwenteling' which became something of a buzz word in economic literature in the Netherlands. See for example: Van den Doel, *Het biefstuksocialisme en de economie*, 44.

The CPB's analysis was grist on the mill of neoliberal thinkers: in their eyes, the growth of government expenditure had led to the large fiscal burden which was was overburdening the economy.[27] However, the CPB's figures were also highly contested. Economists from the University of Amsterdam (sometimes called the Amsterdam School) – and close advisors to Labour leader and prime minister Joop Den Uyl – Wim Driehuis and Arie van der Zwan, opened a fierce attack on the models of the CPB.[28] To them, the problem of unemployment was not primarily the fiscal burden but rather a demand-excess and dwindling investments of the government in the private sector.[29] These debates did not only rage within the economic profession and policymaker circles but also in national newspapers and political parties. Within the Labour party, these discussions took a surprising turn: the question whether a growing public sector would mean the end of capitalism – the same question that occupied economists just after the Second World War – returned with a twist.

One of the most controversial voices in this debate was the Tilburg professor and Labour member, Theo Stevers. Denoting himself a prophet of doom, he straightforwardly warned against the end of capitalism and liberal democracy if the public sector would grow any further. With this warning, Stevers continued the tradition of public finances and its neoliberal interpretation from the 1950s. In the mid-1970s, such alarming words were usually taken as an exaggeration,[30] however, Stevers had some credibility since he had already provided an explanation for the co-occurrence of inflation and unemployment in 1971, a couple of years before stagflation would hit the Dutch economy.[31] In his book *Public Finance and Economics*, Stevers had argued that as a result of the high social insurances' costs the spendable income of employees had relatively decreased. This not only hampered the private consumptions but also led to a constant demand from labour unions for higher wages. These demands then, in turn, led to strong inflation, while declining investments and consumption caused the economy to

27 The CPB-models themselves had been partly inspired by neoliberal concerns, see: Kayzel, 'A night train in broad daylight', 355-356.

28 W. Driehuis and A. Van der Zwan, 'De voorbereidingen van het economisch beleid kritisch bezien (part I & II)', *Economische en Statistische Berichten* 31 August (1977).

29 W. Driehuis, 'An analysis of the impact of demand and cost factors on employment', *De Economist* 127:2 (1979) 255-286.

30 See for example: J. Pen in *De Tijd* 13 October (1978).

31 Works by Lansbergen and Weeda (op. cit. n. 22.) praise Stevers for his insight.

stagnate.[32] Stevers thought of these problems not as accidental, or the effect of wrong political choices. Rather these problems were inherent to Keynesianism. State intervention in the economy always had negative side-effects that the government could not foresee. In the Keynesianism framework, these effects had to be remedied by more interventions, this time in a more ad-hoc manner and less planned. Yet mopping up of the dirt of previous policy would only give way to more negative side-effects, thus setting a negative spiral of even more interventions into motion.[33]

In an article written five years later, when rising unemployment was a fact, Stevers repeated this analysis in a more explicit public choice framework. Although the solution to the whole crisis was, according to his view, the decrease in government spending, he had little hope that the government would actually do so. Similar to Drees's analysis, Stevers asserted that Government spending was not completely autonomous – that is, free to change by the government's political will – but could be described as endogenous to an economic system. State finance was stuck in a spiral in which more spending led to higher wage demands by trade unions, unemployment, and higher taxes, which led in turn to more spending. Using public choice theory, Stevers argued that the complicity of politicians and unions in this spiral was caused by the influence of interest groups. In contrast with the general labouring population, interest groups only represented partial interest and had, in good public choice fashion, little eye for the overall negative consequences of their actions. Stevers applied marginal-utility theory to elucidate why unions and political parties were willing to listen to minorities even if those would only make up a small part of their support. Interest groups were, namely, the most volatile members of their voter base; keeping them aboard was vital for electoral success. Unions and parties were thus eager to facilitate their wishes even if it went against the interests of the majority of their loyal voters. With this influence of minorities over political organizations, pressure for higher wages and rising government expenditure was kept high, even when the consequences of those measures were negative to the general working population.[34]

Stevers's most dramatic statement on the matter came in an op-ed for *De Volkskrant*, one of the major newspapers of the Netherlands, in

32 T. Stevers, *Openbare financiën en ekonomie* (Leiden 1971) 266-279.

33 Ibid., 282-285.

34 Idem, 'Is het overheidsbeleid endogeen?', *Economische en Statistische Berichten* (1976) 1037-1040.

1976. The growth of public spending amounted to an unlimited growth of the public sector, which would soon 'trample' the private sector, ending capitalism. Here it became clear that Stevers's real concern was not so much unemployment or inflation itself but rather the crisis it caused. With the worsening of the crisis – a likely scenario given the above-described spiral of inflation – the unemployment issue could no longer be solved in indirect manners such as a demand-push. With mounting political tensions, Stevers predicted that the government would take more extreme measures to counter unemployment: directly intervening in the management of businesses and forcing the unemployed into work. This was not only the end of free enterprise but also of democracy since 'bureaucracy apparatus [would] grow and become more powerful' giving bureaucrats all the decision-power (see illustration 1).[35]

One of Stevers's fiercest critics was the Amsterdam economist Hans van den Doel, who, picking up Stevers's gauntlet, departed from much of the same presumption Stevers had used. Most strikingly, Van den Doel also made use of a public choice framework in order to make his analysis, even if he arrived at opposite conclusions. Van den Doel agreed with the CPB that the rising costs of social insurances were passed on to employers and that returning to measures of wage moderation was the most effective way of countering unemployment. Accordingly, he scolded the trade unions for sticking to their demands for higher wages.[36] However, contrary to Stevers, Van den Doel did not blame minority interest groups within unions and political parties for this predicament. He argued that the union reaction was understandable, employers first tried to pass the cost of social insurance on to employees by restraining wages. As a reaction, the unions tried in turn to pass the cost back on to the employers. To Van den Doel, the unwieldy corporatist system was ultimately the cause of the unproductive blame game: lacking a clear decision-making structure and easily manipulated to the benefit of CEOs, the costs of social insurance were endlessly tossed around.[37]

Moreover, Van den Doel and Stevers clashed completely in their evaluation of the growth of the public sector. Van den Doel argued that employees in general had a higher preference for social security than for higher spendable income. If there was a trade-off between social security and wages, the choice was easily made. That this meant a growth

35 T. Stevers, 'Daling werkloosheid vrome wens', *De Volkskrant* 22 September (1976).

36 Van den Doel, *Het biefstuksocialisme en de economie*, 75.

37 Ibid., 44.

*Illustration 1 A train disaster [...] Political cartoon on Stevers' dire vision of the economy. Stevers attemps to slow down the train representing the Den Uyl-Cabinet, while the economy (the train tracks) is crumbeling, plunging the train in a sea of choas and coercion (source: Caricature by Opland, NIBG Presscollection BG D88/481, IISH).*

of the fiscal burden and a growth of the public sector did not bother Van den Doel: they were in the common interest, and a diminishing private sector in relation to a public sector only seemed natural.[38]

Public choice in the Labour party rose to prominence in the context of debates over stagflation. This was partly a return of the discourse on public spending from the 1950s, now adjusted for new concerns. But public choice also became popular because the problem of unemployment and inflation was conceived by both neoliberal thinkers as well as their detractors as a problem of collective decision-making: the corporatist system was the issue, either because unions and political parties were taken hostage by short-sighted interest groups, or because the system allowed for the cost of social insurance to be endlessly tossed around. In other words, economists feared that the economic crisis was in essence caused by muddled decision-making. Public choice came to be the ultimate tool to analyse the decision-making structures and to turn opaque choices transparent again.

38 Ibid., 60.

## Democratization and its discontents

Why did discussions within the Labour party form such a fertile ground for the re-emergence of public choice in the 1970s, even when the party had rejected neoliberalism in an earlier stage?[39] The economic issues only go so far to explain the attractiveness of those ideas. Indeed, public choice pointed to the costs of social security that were tossed around but, as the writings of Stevers attest to, the problem that public choice tried to address was ultimately political in nature, not economic. In this section, I will argue that further propelling the popularity of public choice were discussions on democratization. Since the identity of the Labour party was strongly tied up with the idea of democratization under the notion of a 'participatory party', the issue cut right to the core of social democratic politics of the time.

In the mid-1960s, a strong call for democratization emerged in Dutch society.[40] The mass-democracy of the post-war order had been unable to fully deliver on its promise for emancipation; structural inequality in power and income remained an inherent part of society. Consequently, further demands for democratization were formulated, entailing both a better system for parliamentary representation, as well as introducing democratic decision-making in parts of society where this was previously absent: corporations, public and semi-public organization, from factories and psychiatric wards to universities and public housing.

The New Left movement within the Labour party had given a clear expression of this sentiment in their first manifesto *Ten Past Red* (1966), when they wrote: 'a political democracy in a socialist state can only become a reality if [...] everyone is given the opportunity to take part in the decision-making process' and 'the type of participation the average citizen has in parliamentary politics should roughly be extended to the lower levels of government.'[41] These concerns were quickly picked up by the party establishment, publishing a report on democratization

39 Why so many neoliberal economists preoccupied with public finances were members of the Labour party in the first place is subject of another article. See also: M. Oudenampsen, 'A dialectic of freedom. The Dutch post-war clash between socialism and neoliberalism', *Socialism and Democracy* 30:1 (2016) 128-148, https://doi.org/10.1080/08854300.2015.1132648.

40 I. De Haan, *Zelfbestuur en staatsbeheer. Het politieke debat over burgerschap en rechtsstaat in de twintigste eeuw* (Amsterdam 1993) 100-116; D. Hellema, *Nederland en de jaren zeventig* (Amsterdam 2012) Chapter 1.

41 H. Van den Doel et al., *Tien over rood. Uitdagingen van nieuw links aan de PvdA* (Amsterdam 1966) 21-22. The title of this manifesto is a reference to a type of carom billiards game, making it somewhat impossible to translate properly.

the next year, *A Vote That Counts* (1967). Although the report focussed mainly on parliamentary reforms and was more motivated by strengthening the electoral position of the party, the chairmen of the party, Sjeng Tans, stressed in his introduction that 'a well-functioning parliament does not stand on its own. Equality of all citizens should also be expressed in reorganizing the structure of our society.'[42] Accordingly, the report argued that besides political parties 'also other political organizations, action committees, ad-hoc groups and clubs, should indirectly participate in [a political] coalition,'[43] thus arguing for the participation of extra-parliamentary political movements in the Labour party.

By the mid-1970s, however, much of this enthusiasm for democratization had disappeared, or even reversed into a strong discontent. One of the best expressions of these dissatisfactions are the writings of the professor of political sciences at the University of Amsterdam and Labour party member, Hans Daudt. Although Daudt always remained committed to democratization in name, he made a strong U-turn somewhere in the early 1970s about what 'good' democratization actually entailed. In 1967 he had contributed to *A Vote That Counts* report but by 1976 he decried the democratization ideal that the report had embraced as 'a confused democratic ideology, prescribing that democracy would not only imply that everyone has the right to bring all their preferences into the process of political considerations but in addition, that everyone would have the right for their preferences to be satisfied.'[44]

As in Stevers's diagnosis of the national budget, Daudt laid the blame for this 'confused democratic ideology' with interest groups. The notion of interest group had been central to the pluralist school in American political science, associated with the names Robert Dahl and Seymour Martin Lipset, whose works Daudt had helped to introduce in Dutch political science. The focus on interest groups was also evident in *A Vote That Counts* report. The report spoke of action committees, pressure groups and interest groups. Action committees were generally evaluated positively, while pressure groups were more of a mixed bag. Pressure groups could undermine the primacy of the parliament and the representative character of the political system but also play a vital role in involving citizens in the policymaking process.[45] Such an assessment

42 J. Den Uyl et al., *Een stem die telt. Vernieuwing van de parlementaire democratie* (Amsterdam 1967) 3.

43 Ibid., 52.

44 H. Daudt, 'De politieke toekomst van de verzorgingsstaat', in: J. Van Doorn and K. Schuyt (eds.), *De stagnerende verzorgingsstaat* (Amsterdam 1978) 202.

45 Den Uyl et al., *Een stem die telt*, 27-28.

corresponded to Daudt's own academic research on pressure groups within the EEG: they could be an addition to democracy if regulated properly.[46] Moreover, pressure groups were seen as an essential counterweight to the power of bureaucratic elites. Interest groups, in contrast, were seen as a negative force. These groups represented the interest of the establishment, trying to prevent the growing influence of the people on the political process, and consequently had to be opposed and excluded from political coalitions.[47]

This differentiation disappeared from Daudt's later work. When Daudt analyzed the process of democratization, he reframed the ideal that underlying the effort of involving action committees and pressure groups in parliamentary politics as follows: 'more and more demands enter as points of conflict in the sphere of political decision-making [... of] groups whose preferences were previously not expressed, or less explicitly expressed.'[48] In short, Daudt understood newly emancipated of social groups like women, students, eco-activists and workers as interest groups whose demands had entered the political sphere in a process of democratization. The problem was, Daudt argued, that all these demands were overburdening the state. And the state did not (yet) have the capacity to comply with all those demands. In such a case, the state had two options: either expanding social service to meet all the demand and thereby growing significantly or only serve the interests of a select few of the interest groups.

Making use of two British neoliberal authors Samuel Brittan and Robert Moss, Daudt argued that neither option was particularly attractive: a growing welfare state would burden the private sector too much, resulting in an economic crisis – here Daudt called the US neoliberal Milton Friedman's variant of the argument too simplistic, although he agreed with the conclusion.[49] For the second option, Daudt used public choice theory to argue that a government in power serving only minority interest was actually possible in a representative democracy. Minorities would, namely, form an alliance with bureaucrats as both shared interest in a growing welfare state: minorities to meet their demands, bureaucrats since a large state meant stability and employment securi-

46 H. Daudt, *Pressiegroepen in de EEG*, Europese monografieën vol. 3 (Deventer 1965).

47 Den Uyl et al., *Een stem die telt*, 81-82.

48 Daudt, 'De politieke toekomst van de verzorgingsstaat', 201.

49 H. Daudt, 'Verzorgingsstaat, democratie en socialisme', *Het Eerste Jaarboek voor het Democratisch Socialisme* (1979) 23.

ty.[50] The second option thus also amounted to a growing public sector. Moreover, serving only some interest groups would result in the disillusionment of the majority of citizens with the democratic system, resulting in an anti-democratic attitude.[51] From these dire analyses, Daudt drew the implicit conclusion that a growing welfare state would eventually end capitalism and democracy.[52]

Although Daudt was particularly pessimistic in his analysis, his concern for the influence of interest groups on politics was more widely shared within the Labour party. For example, party ideologue and stern opponent of the New Left movement, Bart Tromp feared that the party had been taken over by interest groups. Pushing for their own specific agenda, he argued, there was a danger that interest groups would exclude the concerns of the majority or the common good.[53] Labour's democratization strategy in the late 1960s had been to become an intermediary between the concerns of the street and the state apparatus, identifying itself as a participatory party. By the mid-1970s this was seen by those sceptical of New Left as precisely the problem.

Daudt's solution to this quandary was to restrict democracy, by working out a manner in which the presumed grip of interest groups on the state apparatus could be broken. One of the ways in which this was possible, he argued, was to only allow parliamentary voting on outlines of policy while leaving the details for policymakers to figure out.[54] In this manner, interest groups had less opportunity to manipulate the details of policy to their benefit. Moreover, Daudt proposed to use plebiscites in order to correct policymakers when they threatened to stray too far from the majority interests. In other words, plebiscites were a good mechanism to protect majority interest against minority interests.[55] Such proposals were in the same spirit as the budgeting norms

50 Daudt, 'De politieke toekomst van de verzorgingsstaat', 207; See also: H. Daudt and D. Rae, 'The Ostrogorski Paradox. A peculiarity of compound majority decision', *European Journal of Political Research* 4:4 (1976) 391-398.

51 Daudt, 'De politieke toekomst van de verzorgingsstaat', 202.

52 Daudt does not put it with so much words, but references cases in which it had already happened, see: Daudt, 198.

53 B. Tromp, 'Socialisme, organisatie en democratie', *Socialisme en Democratie* 33:4 (1976) 155-172.

54 Daudt, 'De politieke toekomst van de verzorgingsstaat', 199.

55 In the literature on neoliberalism and democracy, it is commonly understood that the aims of neoliberalism with regards to democracy are precisely the opposite: that restricting majority interest is the neoliberal goal. See, for example: P. Mirowski, *Never let a serious crisis go to waste. How neoliberalism survived the financial meltdown* (New York 2013); MacLean, *Democracy in chains*; W. Brown, *In the ruins of neoliberalism. The rise of antidemocratic politics in the West* (New York 2019). Only a few authors have pointed out that plebiscites are the exception to this rule. See: Biebricher, 'Neoliberalism and democ-

proposed by Drees and later Stevers: shielding off a part of the policy-making process from democratic influences in order to protect the political and economic order.

When the Minister of Finance, Wim Duisenberg, wrote his alternative party manifesto for the Labour party in 1976, he appealed to the same principles. An alternative program was necessary, according to Duisenberg, because the existing one reflected too much the partial interests of minorities and was therefore way too long. 'Is it not the natural inclination of an administrator to seek freedom to manoeuvre and not to be hindered by a 'participatory party'?'[56] he asked rhetorically. Interest groups, in other words, bounded politicians too much, making it impossible to properly execute their task. To counter this, he proposed to fix the baseline of policies over multiple years, not making them the subject of democratic voting, while leaving the details to parliament. Although this was the opposite of Daudt's proposal, it was based on the same intent and rationale.

Already in the discussion on stagflation, the use of public choice indicated a strong discomfort about the muddiness of the decision-making process. The institutions that should be making the decisions – governments, captains of industry, trade unions and political parties, in short, the political establishment – were wavering; becoming a plaything for sinister interest groups acting in the background. In the discussion on democratization within the Labour party, the power of these shady groups within the Labour party itself were made the subject of discussion. Public choice allowed to formulate a discontent with the party's embrace of action groups in the 1960s and its rebranding as a participatory party. It also made a link between issues of democratization and economic issues. The structural spending problem of the modern state, already identified by Drees, was now given a democratic explanation mechanism: emancipation of minorities caused an increase of the public sector and threatened through their alliance with the bureaucrats to trample the private sector. In order to protect democracy from itself, democracy had to be restrained.

racy', Q. Slobodian, 'Demos veto and demos exit. The neoliberals who embraced referenda and secession', *Journal of Australian Political Economy* forthcoming (2020).Further research on this connection is needed.

56 W. Duisenberg, 'Een alternatief verkiezingsprogram', *Socialisme en Democratie* 33:5 (1976) 211.

## Social planning and the market

One lingering fear addressed by public choice in the debates within the Labour party was, as I have argued, that democratization had given way to indecisive politics, or shadowy undemocratic decision-making. Another fear that popped up again and again in these discussions was the growing public sector of the welfare state that would 'trample' the private sector. Evidently, the perceived problem of the public sector was tied in with the issue of government spending, as it was believed that most of the rising government budget went into social security provided by the public sector. However, the fear for the public sector went further than budgets or democratization alone; it was also tied up with a discussion on social planning. Fearing that under the auspice of social planning, the state would justify intrusion in each part of society, neoliberal authors started to push the market as an alternative.

Near the end of the 1960s, the OECD started to shift its focus to set of non-economic issues that seemed to plague the industrialised societies of its member countries. The mass protest of May '68 had shocked the OECD – and not only because the riot began in close proximity of the organization's headquarters – as they conceived the protest as part of larger friction within society caused by social change: due to newfound wealth, social habits had started to shift, with individualization, secularization, generational conflicts, youth culture and alienation as a consequence. In short, May '68 was unintentionally caused by the growth policies of the OECD. Together with issues of environmental pollution and the depletion of natural recourses, these problems were thematised as 'the unforeseen side-effects of long-term economic growth.' In internal reports, the OECD suggested that such problems could be tackled by more social planning.[57]

The issues coined as 'the unforeseen side-effects of long-term economic growth' were also an impetus on the social planning debate in the Netherlands. For a longer time, social scientists wanted to prove their social relevance by developing closer ties to the policymaking process and the 'side-effects of growth' formed the perfect vehicle for this

57 M. Schmelzer, 'The crisis before the crisis. The "problems of modern society" and the OECD, 1968–74', *European Review of History. Revue Européenne d'histoire* 19:6 (2012) 999-1020, https://doi.org/10.1080/13507486.2012.739148; E. Seefried, 'Rethinking progress. On the origin of the modern sustainability discourse, 1970-2000', *Journal of Modern European History* 13:3 (2015) 377-400; J. Andersson, *The future of the world. Futurology, futurists, and the struggle for the post-cold war imagination* (Oxford 2018) Chapter 5.

ambition. The CPB was taken to be a successful example of scientific advice to the government and other social sciences sought to emulate their example.[58] In 1969 a research committee, led by former CPB-director Pieter de Wolff, recommended that the government establish social and cultural, and environmental planning bureaus, next to the already existing economic-focussed CPB. The focus of this new planning should be long-term to counter the negative effects of growth.[59] Such a message was further driven home by the influential report *The Limits to Growth* (1972) by The Club of Rome, which also made a strong impact on the political discussion in the Netherlands. Within the Labour party, such planning ambitions were for example carried by Sicco Mansholt, the former President of the European Commission and earlier Minister of Agriculture, became an outspoken advocate for new environmental policies and de-growth measures and sought the cooperation of all the left parties on these matters.[60]

This enthusiasm for a planned society became inextricably bound up with the discourse on democratization. Many social scientists believed that involving the targeted social groups in the policymaking process in a more direct manner would ultimately benefit the efficiency of a policy. It was also a way to seek democratic legitimization for political power that could otherwise be understood as technocracy.[61] For instance, when urban planning Theo Quené reorganized the National Planning Service (*Rijksplanologische Dienst*) in 1966, he described his ideal as 'a kind of Social and Economic Council for spatial planning' involving '[n]ature and environment lobby [...] Housing Council, Roadbuilders lobby, but also the Construction Union and Federation of Labour Unions.'[62] Consequently, new ideals of social planning became tied up with the demand of democratization in the Dutch political discourse. The sociologist Jan-Willem Duyvendak has described this pecu-

58 P. Den Hoed, 'Een keur van raadgevers. Honderd jaar vaste adviescolleges', in: P. Den Hoed and A.-G. Keizer (eds.),*Op steenworp afstand. Op de brug tussen wetenschap en politiek WRR 35 jaar* (Amsterdam 2007) Chapter 4.

59 P. De Wolff, *Rapport van de Commissie Voorbereiding Onderzoek Toekomstige Maatschappij-Structuur* (The Hague 1970).

60 L. Jansen et al., (eds.), *Barsten in de groei. Productie en konsumptie tegen de achtergrond van welzijn, derde wereld, milieu en macht* (Baarn 1974).

61 J. Andersson and A.-G. Keizer, 'Governing the future. Science, policy and public participation in the construction of the long term in the Netherlands and Sweden', *History and Technology* 30:1-2 (2014) 104-122, https://doi.org/10.1080/07341512.2014.932563.

62 Quené in an interview with Jan Buevink en Paul Den Hoed for the 35th anniversary of the Scientific Council for Government Policy in 2007, in: Den Hoed and Keizer (eds.), *Op steenworp afstand*, 428.

liar meeting of top-down governance and bottom-up democracy as the *planning of emancipation.*[63]

When in the 1970s a backlash against democratization started, social planning soon met a similar fate. Under new ideas of planning social and cultural wellbeing became an increasingly important issue for the government, resulting in a growth of the social service sector but also in an increase in bureaucracy. This latter part formed an anathema for many political commentators. For example, when Daudt spoke about 'the expanding army of civil servants and semi-civil servants' and 'the many vacancies for social workers in newspapers requiting for the new priestly caste,'[64] he unambiguously had the social planning discourse in mind.

Similarly, on the left, a discomfort with the increased state and its bureaucracy was clearly discernible. Daudt's invocation of a 'priestly caste' echoes Hans Achterhuis's *The Market of Wellbeing and Happiness* (1979), which attacked the public services and social workers for excessive bureaucratization and professionalization.[65] Achterhuis was not so much concerned with the public sector *vis a vis* the private sector but feared that increased social planning turned social work into a cold detached practised governed by a disproportionate number of rules. Such fears tapped into the image of the untrustworthy bureaucrat and social worker propagated by public choice as someone who would serve the ideology of the state rather than of the people.[66]

As became clear in the previous section, the neoliberal solution to the problem of a large public sector was restraining democracy. At the same time, authors such as Daudt and Heertje acknowledged that abstaining from satisfying the demand of dominant interest groups could result in anti-democratic stances. Moreover, after radical social change had unleashed the spirit of emancipation, it was unlikely to be contained again. Neither were environmental and recourse problems likely to disappear after the influence of interest group was curbed. So, what was the alternative to social planning?

63 J.W. Duyvendak, *De planning van ontplooiing, Wetenschap, politiek en de maakbare samenleving*, Nederlandse cultuur in Europese context, monografieën en studies 15 (The Hague 1999).

64 Daudt, 'Verzorgingsstaat, democratie en socialisme'.

65 H. Achterhuis, *De markt van welzijn en geluk* (Amsterdam 1979).

66 Similar critiques on bureaucratization and social workers within the Labour party were formulated by Bram Peper and Trudy van Asperen, see: B. Peper, *Vorming van welzijnsbeleid. evolutie en evaluatie van het opbouwwerk* (Amsterdam 1972); T. Van Asperen, 'Met de beste bedoelingen... Over de ideologie van de verzorgingsstaat', in Idem, *Het bedachte leven. Beschouwingen over maatschappij, zingeving en ethiek* (Amsterdam 1993) 11-30.

Heertje and Daudt framed the problem as follows: the state's supply of social services did not correspond to society's demand of those services. In contrast to Van den Doel, who believed that the people simply wanted more social services, Heertje and Daudt argued that the demand for social security was artificial, driven-up through the devilish alliance of interest groups and bureaucrats. The solution was to let the public sector grow in accordance with the 'real' social demands.[67] The problem for the government was that it had no reliable techniques to measure these demands. The state over-relied on crude macroeconomic indicators that valued measurable material welfare over true welfare. And it had been a narrow reliance on crude indicators that had caused 'the unforeseen side-effects of long-term growth' in the first place. Heertje argued that only subjective valuations of individual citizens could determine the real demand for social services. Such subjective valuations were by definition unmeasurable by a government but could only be understood or acted upon through market-mechanisms.[68] In other words, Heertje was suggesting that only a real market of social services could determine how much people valued social services. He proposed similar solutions to environmental problems, which according to him could only be solved through technological innovation, which was best left to the market.[69] Such sentiment was sometimes also shared on the left-wing of the party. For example, eco-activist Lucas Reijnders, writing for *Socialism and Democracy* argued against government planning in general and the management of technological innovation in particular, as the state would only propagate 'system-based rationality, [a] very particular logic of the state' that did not correspond to the rationality of the citizen. Unsurprisingly, he referenced public choice literature to make this point.[70]

Heertje's conceptualization of the market can be understood as the proper channel through which the unleashed social forces of emancipation, environmentalism and de-growth concerns could be canalised in a manner that would not threaten the political-economic order. In essence, this was an older neoliberal argument that gained traction again

67 Daudt, 'Verzorgingsstaat, democratie en socialisme', 22; A. Heertje, 'De toekomst van het stelsel', in: J. Van Doorn and K. Schuyt (eds.), *De stagnerende verzorgingsstaat* (Amsterdam 1978) 165-188.

68 Heertje, 'De toekomst van het stelsel', 171. Heertje's argument of subjective valuation has a longer history and goes back to his mentor, the earlier mentioned Pieter Hennipman, see: A. Wilts, *Economie als maatschappijwetenschap. Een sociologische geschiedenis van de economische wetenschap in Nederland (c. 1930-1960)* (Amsterdam 1997) 127-128.

69 A. Heertje, *Beheersing van de technische ontwikkeling*, Economische Notities 2 (Amsterdam 1978).

70 L. Reijnders, 'Dan maar Albanië', *Socialisme en Democratie* 37:2 (1980) 78-80.

in the mid-seventies in the wake of democratization, environmental and economic problems: the demands of mass-democracy should be diverted away from the state through the market. Or, to put it in other terms, the market should act as a mediator between the democratic demands and the state.[71] Although not primarily a public choice argument, the point was driven home by this theory: choices concerning the environment and emancipation were not taken on the right level, no central government could provide the choice architecture in which individual valuation could be aggregated. And if choices were made on the central level they were distorted by the interests of minorities and bureaucracy.

## Conclusion

Public choice in the 1970s in the Labour party helped to advance the core neoliberal message in a new guise while addressing new issues. In essence, public choice relayed an argument in favour of a strong but small state and a market sector framed by, but clearly distinguished from, the state. A state strong enough to make decisive choices independently of shadowy corporatist powers, but small enough that it would not pose a threat to the private sector; and an independent economy that could successfully satisfy the demand of society without making that demand artificially higher for social services.

Why did this message, that was seemingly rejected in an earlier stage, re-enter the Dutch Labour party? By attacking Keynesianism and democratization, public choice addressed the issues around which the Labour party had built its identity in the 1960s. These matters were already broadly under discussion before public choice re-entered the scene. Public choice facilitated a longer latent discontent with the course the party had taken in the early seventies. New Left had been relatively successful in putting their concerns on the agenda. Moreover, faced with new issues of long-term growth, such as environmental pollution, depleting natural recourses and the fate of development countries, the Labour party was moving to the left, seeking coalitions with parties on the left rather than entering again a coalition with a right-wing party.[72]

Public choice was very much a reaction against New Left ideas, but strikingly also resonated with some of the issues that the more radical

71 For the neoliberalism idea of the market as mediator of mass democracy, see: O. Innset, *Reinventing liberalism. Early neoliberalism in context, 1920-1947* (Florence 2017).

72 Hellema, *Nederland en de jaren zeventig*, 139-150.

wing of the party was pushing. Fear for bureaucratization was shared by both sides, as well the disdain for the narrow macroeconomic indicators that had driven economic policy in the 1950s and 1960s, including Keynesian programs. In that sense, there was a strong scepticism also among the left-wing whether Keynesianism provided any solution to the multiple crises of the mid-1970s. However, as I have argued, the concerns which public choice addressed went further back, to discussions on social planning, to which both New Left thinkers and neoliberals were reacting. Social planning was an attempt to manage the side-effects of state planning through more state planning: precisely the spiralling motion neoliberals feared the most.

How does the case of the Dutch Labour party compare to the international literature on public choice and the neoliberal turn? Much of the beats of the popularity of public choice in the US and UK were very similar. Public choice became attractive for arguing against Keynesianism in the stagflation crisis. And on a political level, public choice pointed the finger to interest groups, often understood as trade unions and labour-power, as the culprit for the economic crisis. The answer that public choice formulated was to restrain democracy, relegating important decisions to presumed neutral and technocratic institutions. But there are also significant differences. The push for neoliberal ideas did not only come from right-wing channels; internal discussion specific to the Labour Party created fertile ground for public choice arguments. Consequently, neoliberalism took a different form than was the case in the UK or US. Neoliberalism was not formulated in opposition to social democratic ideas of the welfare state, rather Daudt, Heertje and Stevers presented their proposals for restraining the welfare state as saving the state from itself. They considered the US discourse led by Friedman as too simplistic and aggressive, not completely applicable to the Dutch case. But they drew the same conclusions: they feared for the instability of the political and economic order.

Although, as other articles in this special issue argue, resistance against neoliberalism within the Labour party continued until the late 1980s, the party became susceptible to parts of neoliberalism already in an early stage. Especially the idea that interest groups posed a threat to the common good and therefore democracy should be more restrained became an accepted idea. The Labour party was not simply building on the foundation of right-wing parties when it started to adopt neoliberal-policies in 1989, as the UK case, studied by Hay, suggested. Neither was the Labour party pushed into neoliberal policies through solely outside forces, as Hellema and Van Lith recently argued. It had a long internal discussion in which neoliberal ideas were already disseminated.

A good example of this early entry of neoliberal ideas was Den Uyl's famous election speech in the Amsterdam concert hall Paradiso in 1982. Although he strongly warned of the rise of New Right forces of neoliberalism and neoconservatism, he admitted at the same time that 'democratization for the sake of democratization runs the risk of making democracy indecisive. [... And] democratization creates a bureaucracy in which only a small elite can find its way.'[73] Democratization had not distributed political power equally but concentrated it in the hand of 'a new class of social workers (*nieuwverzorgende klasse*).'[74] It was a sentiment that democratization had led to obscuring clear political choices, which was shared by both the neoliberals and the radical left. It was also a sentiment that public choice helped to formulate and was quickly accepted, as Den Uyl's speech attest to, within the Labour party.

## About the author

**Tom Kayzel** (1990) is a PhD Candidate at the Amsterdam School for Cultural Analysis at the University of Amsterdam and associated with the Vossius Center for the History of Humanities and Sciences at the same university. He is currently working on a history of twentieth century social and economic planning in the Netherlands, with a focus on the Dutch Central Planning Bureau, and the conceptualization of the future in Dutch politics.
Email: t.n.kayzel@uva.nl.

73 J. Den Uyl, *Tegen de stroom in* (Amsterdam 1982) 12-13.

74 Ibid., 22.

# De Europese Commissie als motor van verandering

*Staatssteun, neoliberalisme en de sluiting van de Amsterdamse scheepswerven, 1976-1986*

Sjoerd Keulen en Ronald Kroeze

TSEG 18 (1): 79–108
DOI: 10.18352/tseg.1199

**Abstract**

By analyzing the case of the closure of the Amsterdam shipyards in the 1980s, this article shows how the European Commission actively promoted a neoliberal turn in policies towards state support for economic sectors in Western-Europe. Besides the EC, the article also makes clear that quite early on leading civil servants within the Dutch ministries of Economic Affairs and of Finance embraced neoliberal ideas as an answer to tackle the economic crisis of the 1970s. A third, often neglected actor in explanations on the rise of neoliberalism were management consultants – in this case from management consultancy firm McKinsey – who wrote alarming reports about the shipbuilding industry and promoted ideas that emphasized the importance of business principles and individual managers as key for improvement, thereby offering an alternative to macroeconomic Keynesian models of growth.

## Inleiding

Tot de parlementaire enquête naar het faillissement van het scheepsbouwconglomeraat Rijn-Schelde-Verolme (RSV) in 1983-1984 was staatssteun in de Nederlandse industriepolitiek onomstreden en een geëigend middel om de werkgelegenheid te beschermen.[1] Deze rede-

1 J.L. van Zanden, 'The Netherlands: The history of an empty box', in: J. Foreman-Peck en G. Federico (red.), *European industrial policy. The twentieth-century experience* (Oxford 2006) 177-193; B. Strath, *The politics of de-industrialisation. The contraction of the West European shipbuilding industry* (Londen 1987).

natie werd begin jaren tachtig verdrongen door het nieuwe neoliberale anti-staatssteundiscours van marktwerking, vrije concurrentie en vrijhandel.[2] Aan de hand van de casus van de sluiting van de ADM en NSM-scheepswerven in Amsterdam onderzoeken we hoe de snelle omslag van het Keynesiaanse macro-economische beleid naar het neoliberale discours van vrijhandel en concurrentie plaatsvond in zowel de ambtenarij als de politiek. We laten daarbij zien hoe een relatief nieuwe speler – de Europese Commissie – dit neoliberale discours via het staatssteunrecht vrij plotseling dominant maakte en vervolgens de vormgeving van het scheepsbouwbeleid in Nederland kon meebepalen. Juist de verandering van een ogenschijnlijk rationele set staatsrechtsregels, in de vorm van het mededingingsrecht, moet worden gezien als '*deeply political and needs to be understood in a broader context*', zoals de rechtssociologen Buch-Hansen en Wigger eerder al betoogden.[3] Dit sluit aan bij conclusies van de historicus Warzoulet die de veranderingen in staatssteunregels van de EEG ziet als het voorbeeld van de relatief vroege acceptatie van neoliberalisme door de Europese Commissie.[4] De scheepsbouw en de RSV-casus in het bijzonder zijn goede casestudies om deze transitie nader te onderzoeken, omdat de scheepsbouw de meeste staatssteun ontving en deze in een kort tijdsbestek verloor.[5]

Daarnaast brengt deze casus een belangrijke tweede actor in beeld die invloed had op de snelle omslag: topambtenaren die al vroeg het neoliberale denken omarmden. Intern zagen Nederlandse topambtenaren RSV als het voorbeeld van falende Keynesiaanse subsidiepolitiek.[6] Dit sluit aan bij Van Grinsven, die wees op het belang van de rol van topambtenaren achter de schermen, en Mellink en Oudenampsen die wezen op de langere traditie van neoliberaal ideologisch denken buiten de politiek. Een derde actor was managementconsultancybureau McKinsey die rapporten schreef over de crisis in de scheepsbouw en als oplossing een omslag adviseerde waarbij concurrentie en op het bedrijfsleven geïnspireerde managementconcepten werden gepro-

2 L. Warlouzet, 'The collapse of the French shipyard of Dunkirk and EEC state-aid control (1977-86)', *Business History* 62:5 (2020) 858-878.

3 H. Buch-Hansen en A. Wigger, 'Revisiting 50 years of market-making. The neoliberal transformation of European competition policy', *Review of International Political Economy* 17:1 (2010) 20-44.

4 L.Warlouzet, *Governing Europe in a globalizing world. Neoliberalism and its alternatives following the 1973 oil crisis* (Londen 2017); Idem, 'Competition', in: É. Bussière e. a. (red.), *The history of the European Commission 1973-1986* (Luxemburg 2014), 291-301

5 Van Zanden, 'The history of an empty box'.

6 Zoals geciteerd in: P. van Grinsven, 'De zure appel in tijden van economische crisis', in: C. van Baalen e.a. (red.), *Parlementair Jaarboek* (2009) 59-71, 63.

moot.[7] We willen met deze *in-depth* studie van een Nederlandse casus onderzoeken hoe de neoliberale omslag zich voltrok, wie de belangrijkste actoren waren, waardoor ze geïnspireerd werden en hoe ze de crisis begrepen en vervolgens handelden.

We illustreren dit alles door een *multi-level governance*-perspectief te gebruiken.[8] Dit perspectief uit het veld van de Europese Studies, wordt gezien als het incorporeren van historisch institutionalisme en heeft als belangrijkste toegevoegde waarde dat het niet staat-centrische verklaringen biedt voor de manier waarop macht en beleid worden gemaakt.[9] Dit perspectief wijst ons erop dat een verandering in het verleden vaak niet door één actor (bijvoorbeeld de nationale overheid) wordt bewerkstelligd, maar door meerdere actoren die op verschillende bestuursniveaus actief zijn en elkaar wederzijds beïnvloeden.[10] Een dergelijke governancebenadering wordt nog weinig gebruikt in historisch onderzoek.[11] Wel is in eerdere studies naar politiek-economisch beleid en de rol van de Nederlandse overheid in de economie in de periode na 1945 door onder andere Jan Luiten van Zanden opgemerkt dat er verschillende perioden kunnen worden onderscheiden van meer en minder inmenging van de overheid in de economie. Ook is daarbij opgemerkt dat de scheepsbouw een belangrijke ontvanger van subsidies was maar die in de jaren 1980 verloor. Opvallend genoeg wordt de rol van de Europese Commissie daarbij niet genoemd en krijgen ook topambtenaren en managementconsultants nauwelijks aandacht.[12]

De benadering in dit artikel is ook geïnspireerd door de *cultural turn*, zoals voorgestaan door met name de Cambridge School met historici als John Pocock en Quentin Skinner.[13] Zij lieten zien hoe nieuwe vormen van tijdgebonden politieke taal niet slechts de politiek beschrijven maar ook aanzetten tot inhoudelijke veranderingen zijn.[14] Dus wanneer

7 R. Kroeze en S. Keulen, 'Managerpolitiek. Waarom historici oog voor management moeten hebben', *BMGN – Low Countries Historical Review* 127:2 (2012) 97-112.

8 L. Hooghe en G. Marks, *Multi-level governance and European integration* (Lanham 2001).

9 S. Piattoni, 'Multi-level governance. A historical and conceptual analysis', *European Integration* 31:2 (2009) 163-180.

10 Voor een uitgebreide toepassing: S. Keulen en R. Kroeze, 'The rise of neoliberalism and the termination of Keynesian policies. A multi-level governance analysis of the closure of the Amsterdam Shipyards (1968-1986)', *Enterprise & Society* 22:1 (2020) 212-246. In dit artikel wordt de neoliberale omslag ook verbonden met veranderingen in de scheepsbouw in Frankrijk, Engeland en West-Duitsland.

11 W. van Meurs, *Never mind the gap. Comparison in political history* (Nijmegen 2018).

12 Van Zanden, 'The history of an empty box'.

13 E.A. Clark, *History, theory, text. Historians and the linguistic turn* (Cambridge 2004) 138-140.

14 J.G.A. Pocock, 'Verbalizing a political act. Towards a politics of speech', in: idem, *Political thought*

een nieuw politiek discours dominant wordt, zal dit leiden tot inhoudelijke veranderingen en de manier waarop politiek wordt bedreven.[15] Eerder heeft Hall al een baanbrekend artikel geschreven over de *paradigm shift* van Keynesiaans naar neoliberaal beleid die zich in Engeland voltrok en daarbij gewezen op hoe een discourswijziging en de acties van (nieuwe) actoren, inclusief hun wisselwerking, leidt tot een grootschalige verandering.[16]

Concreet laat ons artikel zien hoe acties op verschillende bestuursniveaus (de gemeente Amsterdam, departementen en regering in Den Haag, de Tweede Kamer en de Europese Commissie, in het bijzonder de DG Mededinging) leidden tot vergaande neoliberale veranderingen in het staatssteunbeleid. Door te kijken naar de argumentatie van ambtenaren, ministers, parlementariërs en door de politiek aangezochte adviseurs en de reacties die dit uitlokte, ook van vakbonden en zakelijke leiders, zien we hoe deze neoliberale omslag zich in het Nederlandse politiek-bestuurlijke domein voltrok en kunnen we wijzigingen op beleidsniveau volgen. Om de verschillende bestuursniveaus te kunnen onderzoeken is gebruik gemaakt van diverse bronnen: archiefstukken en correspondentie tussen het ministerie van Economische Zaken en de Europese Commissie, adviesrapporten en Kamerstukken. Om een beter beeld te krijgen van de beleidsopvattingen van met name de Europese spelers is gebruik gemaakt van het *oral history* archief van de Europese Commissie, een type bron dat belangrijk is voor onderzoek naar contemporaine geschiedenis.[17] Voor met name de Amsterdamse inbreng is vanwege een gebrek aan een gestructureerd archief gebruik gemaakt van gedigitaliseerde kranten en daarin werd geschreven over de rol van Amsterdam.

Het artikel is als volgt opgebouwd. Allereerst wordt de historiografie van het neoliberalisme en de neoliberale wortels van het Europese staatssteunbeleid besproken. De tweede paragraaf gaat over de conglomeratiebeweging in de Nederlandse scheepsbouw die een reactie was op de instortende scheepsbouwmarkt van de jaren zeventig. Daarna wordt de toenemende invloed van de DG Mededinging van de Europese Commissie besproken die een neoliberaal concurrentiebeleid

*and history. Essays on theory and method* (Cambridge 2009) 33-50; K. Palonen, *Quentin Skinner. History, politics, rhetoric* (Cambridge 2003).

15 F. Ankersmit, *Aesthetic politics. Political philosophy beyond fact and value* (Stanford 1996) 159.

16 P.A. Hall, 'Policy paradigms, social learning, and the state. The case of economic policymaking in Britain', *Comparative Politics* 25:3 (1993) 275-296.

17 S. Keulen en R. Kroeze, 'Back to business: a next step in the field of oral history. The usefulness of oral history for leadership and organizational research', *Oral History Review* 39:1 (2012) 15-36.

ontwikkelde. In de volgende paragraaf worden de eerste voorzichtige neoliberale wijzigingen in het Nederlandse scheepsbouwbeleid besproken. De laatste paragraaf gaat in op de definitieve wijziging van het staatssteunbeleid onder het kabinet-Lubbers I (1982-1986) en de katalyserende rol die de RSV-enquête hierin speelde.

## Historiografie van het neoliberalisme

Het neoliberalisme is een lastig concept, omdat het als containerbegrip en als een afkeurend bijvoeglijk naamwoord wordt gebruikt voor doorgeschoten marktwerking bij publieke instellingen en doordat verschillende wetenschapsgebieden het totaal anders gebruiken. Binnen de wetenschap, zo lieten Oudenampsen en Mellink zien, wordt neoliberalisme op ten minste drie manieren begrepen: als marxistische structuralistische benadering met veel aandacht voor de invloed van het kapitalisme en bedrijfsleven in de moderne samenleving, een sociaalwetenschappelijk foucaultiaanse benadering van bestuur(sveranderingen) en ten derde een fase in de geschiedenis van politieke ideeën.[18]

In de historiografie bestaat er brede consensus over dat neoliberalisme zijn wortels heeft in het crisisdenken van de jaren dertig toen een groep economische intellectuelen ageerde tegen de zich uitbreidende overheidsinterventies in de economie, zoals het *New Deal*-programma in de Verenigde Staten. Deze neoliberalen pleitten voor het herstel van *laisser-faire*, maar met een duidelijke rol voor de overheid die als marktmeester moest toezien op eerlijke concurrentie. Zij kwamen voor de Tweede Wereldoorlog bijvoorbeeld samen in een van de Lippmann colloquia in Parijs en vanaf 1947 in de door Friedrich von Hayek opgerichte *Mont Pèlerin Society*.[19] Deze neoliberalen vormden niet slechts een praatclub maar waren gericht op het bewerkstelligen van politieke verandering.[20] Binnen het neoliberalisme waren nadrukkelijk verschil-

18 M. Oudenampsen en B. Mellink, 'Voorbij de controverse. Het Nederlandse neoliberalisme als onderwerp van onderzoek', *Beleid en Maatschappij* 46:2 (2019) 235-254, 244; W. Davies, 'Neoliberalism: A bibliographic review', *Theory, Culture & Society* 48:1 (2014) 1-9.

19 P. Mirowski en D. Plehwe (red.), *The road from Mont Pèlerin. The making of the Neoliberal thought collective* (Londen 2009); A. Burgin, *The great persuasion. Reinventing free markets since the depression* (Londen 2012); Q. Slobobidian, *Globalists. The end of empire and the birth of neoliberalism* (Londen 2018).

20 B. Mellink, 'Politici zonder partij. Sociale zekerheid en de geboorte van het neoliberalisme in Nederland (1945-1958)', *BMGN-Low Countries Historical Review* 132:4 (2017) 25-52.

lende scholen te onderscheiden als de Duitse ordoliberalen, de Chicago school en de Oostenrijkse school. Deze neoliberale scholen hadden een verschillende epistemologie en mensbeeld en opereerden binnen verschillende nationale contexten, waardoor de aangedragen economische visies en oplossingen verschilden.[21] Een deel van de spraakverwarring over het begrip neoliberalisme komt hier uit voort. Wel hadden ze een gemeenschappelijke afkeer van enerzijds ongebreideld *laisser-faire* denken dat het negentiende-eeuwse economisch liberalisme kenmerkte en anderzijds van het keynesianisme dat vooral na 1945 aan aanhang won.

Neoliberalisme claimde, zo bezien, een middenpositie te zijn waarin de overheid als een krachtige marktmeester ervoor moest zorgen dat belangrijke marktmechanismes goed functioneerden, zonder dat teveel overheidsinterventie de kracht van de markt verstoorde. In de politieke ideologie van de neoliberalen vormden in een stevig juridisch systeem verankerde vrije mededinging en concurrentie de cruciale uitgangspunten. Deze combinatie van principes raakte na de jaren zeventig enigszins uit beeld doordat de Chicago school met de beeldbepalende mediagenieke Amerikaanse econoom Milton Friedman de dominante neoliberale stroming werd en de staat als hindermacht voor een vrije markt voorstelde.[22] Zo ontstond het populaire beeld van het neoliberalisme dat met het recept *stabilize, privatize and liberalize* (de zogenaamde *Washington Consensus*) tal van overheden dwong om zich terug te trekken uit beleidsterreinen.[23] Overigens betekende dit vaak niet dat de staat of politiek geen rol meer in de economie speelde, want overal moesten keuzes gemaakt worden over of en waar men zich uit terug trok en op welke wijze dat gebeurde.

Na deze eerste intellectuele golf van het neoliberalisme, volgde de 'neoliberale doorbraak' vanaf het uitbreken van de oliecrises van de jaren zeventig.[24] Door de ongekende schokken in de economie waarmee dit gepaard ging, vonden de neoliberale ideeën die waren gepromoot door aanhangers van de eerste golf, een welwillend oor onder bestuurders en politici die zochten naar een oplossing voor de crisis, ook omdat als Keynesiaans bekendstaande oplossingen, zoals de economie stimuleren door de vraag van de overheid te vergroten (*demand management*), weinig positief effect sorteerde en leidde tot stagflatie (een

21 Plehwe, 'Introduction', in: Mirowski and Plehwe (red.), *The road from Mont Pèlerin.*

22 Burgin, *The great persuasion.*

23 P. Ther, *Europe since 1989. A History* (Princeton 2016).

24 D. Stedman Jones, *Masters of the universe. Hayek, Friedman, and the birth of neoliberal politics* (Princeton 2012) 215.

stagnerende economie en oplopende inflatie). De toenemende kritiek op het Keynesianisme viel samen met meer waardering voor het monetarisme dat stelde dat de overheid niet de vraag maar het aanbod (van geld) moest bespelen (*supply side economics*), en in dit geval beperken, om de economie vlot te trekken. De theorie van het monetarisme werd al snel beschouwd als een aanvulling op of zelfs een inherent onderdeel van het neoliberalisme. De promotie van deze combinatie van factoren en beschikbare ideeën door bepaalde economen, denktanks en ambtenaren leidde ertoe dat zowel in het Verenigd Koninkrijk als in de Verenigde Staten betrekkelijk snel de ambtelijke toppen van de ministeries van Financiën Keynesiaanse opvattingen inruilden voor neoliberale, een verandering die ook in andere departementen snel navolging kreeg.[25] De politiek met als meest bekende exponenten Thatcher en Reagan volgde pas hierna. Oudenampsen en Mellink demonstreerden een zelfde verandering en periodisering voor Nederland, waar de ministeries van Financiën en Economische Zaken 'vroege bolwerken van principiële oppositie tegen keynesiaans beleid' waren.[26] Voor deze ambtelijke en politieke verandering geldt dat dit niet zwart-wit was, de historicus Stedman geeft tal van voorbeelden van neoliberale veranderingen die al begin jaren zeventig onder de Amerikaanse democratische president Jimmy Carter plaatsvonden, dus al voor het aantreden van de republikeinse president Ronald Reagan. Tevens laat hij zien dat al in de jaren zeventig in zowel de Verenigde Staten als binnen de Britse labourregering, er brede consensus bestond dat voortaan de beteugeling van de inflatie en niet langer volledige werkloosheid (een ander bekend Keynesiaans beleidsdoel) het belangrijkste was.[27]

De oliecrises en stagflatie van de jaren zeventig zijn niet alleen voor nationale overheden een keerpunt maar ook voor het Europese integratiebeleid. Binnen de Europese organen had het neoliberale denken diepere wortels, ook omdat neoliberale denkers de casus van de Europese integratie actief volgden en becommentarieerden. De verschillende neoliberale scholen voerden sinds de oprichting van de Europese Economische Gemeenschappen (EEG) in Rome in 1957 een debat of Europese integratie binnen de neoliberale kaders paste of niet. Alhoe-

25 Stedman Jones, *Masters of the universe*, 215 e.v.; J. Tomlinson, *Managing the economy, managing the people. Narratives of economic life in Britain from Beveridge to Brexit* (Oxford 2017) 63-87.

26 M. Oudenampsen en B. Mellink, 'Bureaucrats first: The leading role of policymakers in the Dutch economic paradigm-shift of the 1980s', *TSEG – The Low Countries Journal of Social and Economic History* 18:1 (2021); Oudenampsen en Mellink, 'Voorbij de controverse', 247.

27 Stedman Jones, *Masters of the universe*, 215-254.

wel het landbouwbeleid of de economische banden met de oude koloniën vanwege de opzichtige rol van overheidsinterventies lastig als neoliberaal beschouwd konden worden, gold één Europees beleidsterrein vanaf het begin als duidelijk neoliberaal: mededinging, ofwel de set van regels die vrije marktwerking en concurrentie moesten bevorderen en staatssteun begrenzen. In de eerste Europese Commissie zag de Duitse Eurocommissaris voor mededinging Hans von der Groeben zijn beleidsterrein als duidelijk 'neoliberaal' en als het epicentrum van het Europese beleid. Geholpen door met name de Duitse neoliberalen van de tweede generatie werkte hij begin jaren zestig het nog ongedefinieerde en brede oprichtingsverdrag zo uit dat de Commissie de centrale rol in het toezicht op en het afdwingen van naleving van staatssteunregels kreeg toebedeeld en het Europees hof volledige jurisdictie en een boete-instrument om dit te handhaven.[28] De historicus Warzoulet die onderzocht in hoeverre de Europese Commissie met neoliberaal beleid reageerde op de crises van de jaren zeventig, stelde vast dat op de verschillende beleidsterreinen waarop de EEG actief was grote verschillen bestonden tussen de aangehangen politiek-economische opvattingen, maar hij stelde ook dat mededinging 'the main vehicle for a neoliberal transformation of Europe' zou worden.[29]

## De Amsterdamse scheepsbouw en de samenvoegingen in de jaren zeventig

Om te begrijpen waarom de scheepsbouwsector en de Amsterdamse in het bijzonder een interessante casus is om de opmars van het neoliberalisme te onderzoeken, is het goed te beseffen dat de Amsterdamse haven en scheepsbouw een prominente rol speelden in het Nederlandse wederopbouwbeleid na de Tweede Wereldoorlog. Met bijna 50.000 werknemers produceerden de scheepsbouw en reparatiewerven zo'n 12% van het totale industriële volume van Nederland. De twee belangrijkste Amsterdamse werven waren de in Amsterdam-Noord gesitueerde Nederlandsche Dok en Scheepsbouw Maatschappij (NDSM) en Amsterdamsche Droogdok Maatschappij (ADM).[30] De NDSM behoorde tot de 'zeven zusters', de grootste scheepsbouwers van Nederland, en had

28 Slobiodian, *Globalists,* 206-212.

29 Warlouzet, *Governing Europe,* 13, 156-181.

30 D. Bosscher, 'De oude en de nieuwe stad', in: P. de Rooy (red.), *De geschiedenis van Amsterdam. Volume IV 1900-2000* (Amsterdam 2007) 357-399, 351.

eind jaren zestig ongeveer 3.500 werknemers. Voor ADM werkten circa 1.500 werknemers en tezamen waren ze verantwoordelijk voor 9% van de totale werkgelegenheid in de Nederlandse scheepsbouw en reparatiesector die in 1967 in totaal uit 252, veelal kleine, bedrijven bestond.[31]

Tijdens de wederopbouw legde de Nederlandse regering veel nadruk op een door de overheid gestimuleerde industrialisatie, waarbij een geleide loonpolitiek voor een comparatief kostenvoordeel moest zorgen. Na de economische groei in de jaren vijftig en zestig werd uiteindelijk in 1963 zowel de geleide loonpolitiek als dit industriebeleid losgelaten. De lonen stegen hierna snel waardoor Nederland het land met relatief de hoogste lonen werd. Dit maakte vooral de arbeidsintensieve industrie – zoals de scheepsbouw – duurder, met als gevolg dat de werkgelegenheid in deze sector vanaf 1967 snel afnam.[32] Tegelijkertijd was er nog steeds een sterk besef dat een crisis zoals in de jaren dertig, met hoge werkloosheid en grote publieke onvrede, moest worden voorkomen. De Tweede Kamer vroeg daarom aan de regering een onderzoek in te stellen naar de scheepsbouw, een sector die in de jaren dertig nog in de wereldwijde top-drie stond qua productie maar was afgezakt tot plek veertien. De commissie-Keyzer, bestaande uit bankiers, scheepsbouwers, vakbonden en regeringsvertegenwoordigers, adviseerde om subsidie te geven aan de scheepsbouw, zoals ook elders in Europa gebeurde. Het tweede advies was in te zetten op samenvoegingen van de Nederlandse scheepsbouwers, nieuwe productiemethoden en specialisatie.[33]

Als een gevolg van het Keyzer-advies werd de scheepsbouwer Verolme in 1968 door de Nederlandse overheid gedwongen het verlieslijdende NDSM over te nemen in ruil voor overheidssubsidie voor een nieuw droogdok voor de bouw van mammoettankers waar veel vraag naar was op dat moment. De directeur van NDSM (Goedkoop) zou later voor de RSV-enquête getuigen dat hij geen moment geloofde dat dit initiatief ertoe kon leiden dat de NDSM weer concurrerend zou worden ten opzichte van de snelgroeiende scheepsbouwsector in Japan.[34] Toch ging het door. Niet veel later volgden verdere samenvoegingen en concentraties en werd een nationale kampioen gecreëerd: Rijn-Schelde-Verolme

31 Aantallen uit: S. van der Velden, 'The Dutch shipbuilding industry', in: R. Varela, H. Murphy en M. van der Linden (red.), *Shipbuilding and ship repair workers around the world. Case studies 1950-2010* (Amsterdam 2017) 221-246; Strath, *The politics of de-industrialisation*, 157.

32 J.L. van Zanden, *The economic history of the Netherlands* (Londen 1997), 81; Van Zanden, 'The history of an empty box', 184.

33 Strath, *The politics of de-industrialization*, 158, 159.

34 Kamerstuk II 1984/5, 17718 (RSV-enquête), nr. 16, 30, 31 en nr. 21, 5.

(RSV). Alle zeven zusters werden hierin samengevoegd, ADM was hierbij in 1978 de hekkensluiter. Het belangrijkste argument voor de vorming van RSV was dat het bijdroeg aan een reductie van de overcapaciteit. Al snel werd echter capaciteitsreductie ondergeschikt gemaakt aan het behoud van werkgelegenheid.[35]

De Amsterdamse scheepsbouwers moesten de verliezen van NDSM op zich te nemen en werden gedwongen zich te specialiseren. Binnen het RSV verband moest NDSM zich gaan concentreren op de bouw van nieuwe schepen en ADM op scheepsreparatie.[36] RSV president-directeur Dirk Stikker getuigde later dat hij liever NDSM had gesloten, maar dat dat politiek onhaalbaar was: zowel het Amsterdamse stadsbestuur als de minister van Economische Zaken waren hier tegen.[37]

Deze trend van concentratie als antwoord op de goedkopere scheepsbouw in Zuidoost-Azië zien we in heel West-Europa. Door de oliecrises en het wegvallen van de vraag naar mammoettankers grepen de regeringen van bijvoorbeeld Frankrijk, het Verenigd Koninkrijk en West-Duitsland naar dezelfde middelen: verdere concentratie en overheidssubsidies om arbeidsplaatsen zoveel mogelijk te behouden.[38]

De Nederlandse industrie in de brede zin werd zwaar getroffen door de oliecrises. Zo verdween in de textiel- kleding- en schoeiselindustrie in de periode 1970-1984 70% van de werkgelegenheid. De scheepsbouw en machinebouwindustrie zaten ook in zwaar weer, maar kregen meer steun omdat ze tot de kern van de Nederlandse industrie(politiek) werden gerekend. Deze industriepolitiek was weliswaar officieel beëindigd in 1963 maar dat betekende allerminst dat overheidsingrijpen stopte, zonder dat hierbij een beleidsplan werd gevolgd. Daarom is deze periode ook wel als 'industrial policies without a plan' gekenschetst.[39] Met een reeks individuele acties werden vooral arbeidsintensieve bedrijven samengevoegd in de hoop dat er zo grotere, meer competitieve bedrijven zouden ontstaan.[40] De oprichting van RSV past daar in. Dit beleid was ook ingegeven doordat het in de publieke opinie 'onaanvaardbaar ge-

35 Ibid., 93.

36 Van der Velden, 'The Dutch shipbuilding industry'; Kamerstuk II 1984/5, 17718, nr. 16, 171, 172; C.P.P. van Romburgh en E.K Spits, *Nederlandsche Dok en Scheepsbouw Maatschappij* (Rotterdam 1996).

37 President-directeur Stikker in: Kamerstuk 1984/5, 17718, nr. 21, 1422.

38 Keulen en Kroeze, 'The rise of neoliberalism', 13-15.

39 Van Zanden, 'The history of an empty box', 185.

40 B. Dankbaar en E.-J. Velzing, 'Industriebeleid in Nederland', in: B. Dankbaar en T. van den Berg (red.) *Samen toekomst met techniek* (Hoofddorp 2013) 7; H.J. Hesselink, *Strategische besluitvorming in een neergaande bedrijfstak. Onderzoek naar de strategische maatregelen in de KRL textiel-industrie in de periode 1950-2000* (Enschede 2010) 180-182, 263-266.

acht' werd om mensen te ontslaan zolang delen van een bedrijf nog winst maakten.[41] Zo raakte de overheid steeds meer betrokken en gaf het steeds meer subsidie om bedrijven aan te zetten tot herstructurering.[42] Tussen 1975 en 1985 ging ongeveer 6 miljard euro staatssteun (prijsniveau van 2012) naar bedrijven als DAF, Volvo, Fokker, RSV, Stork en Hoogovens.[43]

De Nederlandse scheepsbouw was de sector die het sterkst werd gesubsidieerd.[44] In de jaren zeventig raakte RSV verder in de problemen vanwege een sterke afname van de vraag door de oliecrises en de toenemende concurrentie vanuit Zuidoost-Azië. Uiteindelijk gaf de overheid door de jaren heen fl. 2,7 miljard staatsteun (de waarde in huidige koopkracht is ongeveer € 2,3 miljard), zonder het parlement hierover in te lichten. Toen de subsidies voor herstructurering niet het gewenste resultaat hadden, begon de directie van RSV de problemen steeds meer als verantwoordelijkheid van de overheid te beschouwen. Het was immers de overheid die de herstructurering had geëist en betaald, voornamelijk om de werkgelegenheid te behouden. De directie verwachtte daarom ook dat meer subsidie gegeven zou worden. De president-commissaris van RSV, Jan de Vries, stelde onomwonden tijdens de enquête dat RSV een 'sociale werkplaats' was in die tijd:

> 'Wij waren niet bezig een goed lopende commerciële onderneming op haar zwakke punten te ondersteunen. Wij waren bezig een grote schare werknemers op een acceptabele wijze bezig te houden. Ook in die tijd zaten al plukken in de kantines. Dat kan voor niemand een verborgen zaak zijn geweest.'[45]

In december 1977 was de situatie nog verder verslechterd. Iedere hoop dat de economische crisis tijdelijk zou zijn verdween na de tweede oliecrisis eind jaren zeventig. Daarnaast bleek RSV nog steeds niet succesvol in het terugdringen van de kosten en het verhogen van de inkomsten door productiviteitsgroei en efficiëntie. Het bouwen van mammoettankers was geen goede keuze gebleken, de verliezen van deze divisie drukten zwaar op de resultaten van RSV als geheel.

Een nieuwe beleidscommissie, bestaande uit ambtenaren, scheepsbouwers en vakbonden, werd ingesteld om nieuwe plannen te ontwik-

41 K. Sluyterman, *Kerende kansen. Het Nederlandse bedrijfsleven in de 20e eeuw* (Amsterdam 2005) 249.

42 Ibid.

43 Van Zanden, *Economic history*; Dankbaar en Velzing, 'Industriebeleid in Nederland', 9.

44 Van Zanden, 'The history of an empty box', 187.

45 Kamerstuk II 1984/5, 17718, nr. 21, 1185.

kelen voor reductie van de overcapaciteit. Unaniem adviseerde deze commissie in 1978 om de zwakste werven te sluiten, maar dat leidde al snel tot de Noord-Zuid tegenstelling. De keuze om de Amsterdamse NDSM (noord) te sluiten en de Rotterdamse werven (zuid) open te houden stuitte op groot verzet in Amsterdam en deed de vakbonden uit elkaar vallen. De Amsterdamse vertegenwoordiging verliet de beleidscommissie uit protest.[46] De positie van de vakbond werd hierdoor ernstig verzwakt.

Wat wel volgde was een beroemde staking in Amsterdam in 1978 waarbij de lokale afdeling van de NKV-NVV (vanaf 1981 FNV) werd gesteund door een brede coalitie bestaande uit het stadsbestuur en alle raadsfracties en ondersteund door een keur aan solidariteitsacties van bijvoorbeeld ambtenaren van naburige gemeenten en de vrouwenbeweging. De staking viel samen met de Provinciale Statenverkiezingen en werd daarom veelvuldig bezocht door landelijke politieke kopstukken die zich uitspraken tegen sluiting van de Amsterdamse werf en zo de stakers een extra steun in de rug gaven. De kritiek richtte zich toen al ten dele op de rol van de EEG, die werd gezien als een aanstichter van het sluiten van de scheepswerven.[47] Tijdens de protesten toonde het Amsterdamse stadsbestuur zich bereid om te investeren in NDSM. Wethouder Enneüs Heerma (Christen-Democratisch Appèl, CDA) en de vakbonden stelden een plan op waarbij werd voorgesteld dat de ADM, die werd gezien als meest rendabel, delen van NDSM zou overnemen.[48]

Het gevolg was dat NDSM gedeeltelijk werd gered door 400 van de in totaal 3000 NDSM-werknemers onder te brengen in een nieuw bedrijf NSM (Nederlandse Scheepsbouw Maatschappij). Nog eens 950 werknemers gingen over naar ADM als onderdeel van een sociaal plan en de rest werd ontslagen of ging met vervroegd pensioen.[49] De Nederlandse staat en Amsterdam werden aandeelhouders in de NSM; Amsterdam kocht evenveel aandelen als de Nederlandse staat en stond medegarant voor leningen.[50] NSM werd orders toegezegd afkomstig van RSV, 'een toezegging waarvan het departement en RSV in oktober 1978 reeds wisten dat zij vermoedelijk niet gerealiseerd kon worden', zo concludeerde de RSV-enquêtecommissie achteraf.[51]

46 Strath, *The politics of de-industrialization*, 163, 164, 173-175.

47 Van Romburgh en Spits, *Nederlandsche Dok en Scheepsbouw Maatschappij*, 62.

48 'Amsterdam wil in nieuwe werf delen. Nieuwe hoop voor NDSM', *NRC Handelsblad* 11 september (1978); 'Amsterdam bereid tot steun werfcombinatie', *De Telegraaf* 11 september (1978) 1.

49 Strath, *The politics of de-industrialization*, 178.

50 Kamerstuk II 1980/1, 14969, nr. 65.

51 Kamerstuk II 1984/5, 17718, nr. 16, 487.

*Illustratie 1 Op de publieke tribune van de Tweede Kamer volgen de Amsterdamse wethouders Schaefer (l, PvdA) en Heerma (r, CDA) de beraadslagingen tussen de Kamer en minister Van Aardenne (VVD) van Economische Zaken over extra steun voor ADM, 19 januari 1983 (bron: foto Rob C. Croes, fotocollectie Anefo, Nationaal Archief).*

## Het herwonnen vertrouwen van het Europese directoraat Mededinging

Ondertussen had men op de burelen in Brussel ook niet stilgezeten, want in alle landen van de toenmalige Europese Economische Gemeenschap verkeerde de scheepsbouw in grote economische problemen in de jaren zeventig.[52] Al jarenlang steunden nationale en lokale overheden in West-Europa de scheepsbouw in hun landen. Net als in Nederland werden subsidies gegeven onder de voorwaarden dat scheepsbouwers samengingen, herstructureerden en competitiever werden om zo de werkgelegenheid op peil te houden. Naarmate de teleurstelling over de resultaten van deze interventies toenam, werd de belangrijkste reden voor staatssubsidies behoud van werkgelegenheid.[53] Mede hierom werd de Europese Commissie kritischer.

Hoewel er al in het verdrag van Rome van 1957 was afgesproken dat staatssteun aan de scheepsbouw moesten worden teruggebracht, was de Europese Commissie lange tijd niet erg actief in het bestrijden van staatssteun. Het stond ook betrekkelijk machteloos tegen de lidstaten,

52 Strath, *The politics of de-industrialization.*

53 Keulen en Kroeze, 'The rise of neoliberalism'.

omdat deze (soms bewust) staatssteun niet of te laat aanmelden bij de Europese Commissie. Dit gold temeer voor industrieën die onder druk stonden zoals staal, textiel en scheepsbouw.[54] Nederland was hier geen uitzondering op.[55]

Begin 1980 veranderde dit, niet in de laatste plaats door de komst van een nieuwe eurocommissaris voor Mededinging, de voormalig Nederlandse minister van Financiën Frans Andriessen (CDA), die een wijziging op het gebied van staatssteun en mededinging inzette, die bijdroeg aan een 'herwonnen vertrouwen' in en binnen het Directoraat-Generaal IV Mededinging. Andriessen herinnerde zich: 'De DG Mededinging was volledig gesloten. Mijn voorganger was een man die blijkbaar vrij gesloten was. Daarom gooide ik de ramen open.'[56] Andriessen stelde een nieuwe directeur-generaal aan, de Duitser Manfred Caspari, omdat ook hij 'meer open was, hij was meer een entrepreneur die veel wist van wat er werkelijk gebeurde in de economische praktijk, niet in de theorie, maar in het werkelijke economische leven'.[57] Caspari kwam met een duidelijke agenda voor de hervorming van staatssteun omdat naar zijn idee 'deze sector totaal verwaarloosd was en men nu weer krachtig moest ingrijpen'. Daarmee ontstond een 'economische en intellectuele context' waarin krachtig concurrentie- en staatssteunbeleid ontstond.[58] En onder leiding van Andriessen en Gaspari werd in vier jaar veertienmaal tegen staatssteun besloten, terwijl in de kwart eeuw daarvoor slechts 21 zaken waren verboden.[59]

Hierbij kregen ze een fikse steun in de rug van het Europees Hof die in een serie arresten de Europese Commissie een exclusieve rol als beoordelaar van staatssteun gaf. Nederland werd in 1980 nadrukkelijk op de vingers getikt door het Europees Hof in het beroemde Philip Morris-arrest. Het Hof oordeelde dat staatssteun alleen geoorloofd was om de doelen van de Gemeenschap mee te behalen. Volgens het verdrag gold dit alleen voor gebieden met een abnormaal lage levensstandaard en hoge werkeloosheid. Omdat Nederland op dit vlak ver boven het Europees gemiddelde bleef, was daarmee staatssteun voor de Nederlandse

54 K. Middlemas, *Orchestrating Europe. The informal politics of the European Union 1973-95* (Londen 1995) 503.

55 Kamerstuk II 1984/5, 17718, nr. 16, 247.

56 Historical Archives of the European Union (hierna HAEU), Oral History, Interview Frans Andriessen, 6: via https://archives.eui.eu/en/oral_history.

57 HAEU Interview Andriessen, 9.

58 Middlemas, *Orchestrating Europe*, 503-504; Warlouzet, 'Competition', 295-296.

59 Middlemas, *Orchestrating Europe*, 504.

scheepsbouw al snel ontoelaatbaar. Maar bovenal wordt het arrest gezien als een *'political landmark ... a public statement about DG IV's right to restrict the freedom of national and subnational aid-donors in choosing where and when to grant subsidies'*, zoals Thomas stelt.[60] Vanaf 1983 begon Andriessen bovendien illegale staatssteun terug te vorderen. In het beroemde Boussac-vonnis bekrachtigde de rechter dat Frankrijk 300 miljoen francs moest terugbetalen, dat was tot een paar jaar daarvoor ondenkbaar geweest.[61]

Het nieuwe neoliberaal geïnspireerde denken over staatssteun werd voor het eerst getest op sectoren waarin de Commissie van oudsher via het Verdrag van Rome een rol had: de staal- en scheepsbouwsector. Beide sectoren waren in de woorden van Caspari 'niet-essentiële' sectoren met 'waanzinnige overcapaciteit' die via nationale steunmaatregelen tegen werkloosheid werden beschermd. De scheepsbouw was hierbij het grootste dossier.

In 1981 waarschuwde Andriessen het Europees Parlement in een toespraak over scheepsbouw al: 'het mag niet zo zijn dat als het ware een soort van "subsidiementaliteit" zou ontstaan waardoor deze sector permanent alleen maar met grote steun van overheidswege op de been zou kunnen worden gehouden. Dat zou een degradatie van deze sector zijn en op den duur zou dat ook niet vol te houden zijn.'[62] Om de scheepsbouwsector te saneren besloot DG IV om een 'rationalisatiekartel goed te keuren voor het ontmantelen van capaciteit' maar wel op voorwaarde, want 'zolang de marktherstelmaatregelen van kracht zijn zal er geen cent [aan staatssteun] worden goedgekeurd'.[63] De perceptie op de markt was binnen de Commissie bovendien veranderd, de problemen in de scheepsbouw werden nu gezien als 'structureel in plaats van conjunctureel'. In twee richtlijnen voor steunverlening aan de scheepsbouw uit 1981 en 1987 werden toegestane staatsteunmaatregelen snel teruggebracht. De Europese Commissie berekende dat hierdoor tot 1990 zo'n 30.000 banen zouden verdwijnen.[64]

60 K.P. Thomas, *Competing for capital. Europe and North America in a global era* (Washington 2000) 113, 114.

61 J.J. Piernas López, *The concept of state aid under EU Law. From internal market to competition and beyond* (Oxford 2015) 195.

62 Andriessen als geciteerd in: Kamerstuk II 1984/5, 17718, nr. 16, 247.

63 HAEU Interview Gaspari, 19.

64 López, *The concept of state aid*, 55, 56.

## De zure appel: de heroverweging van scheepsbouwsteun (1981-1982)

Vanaf 1980 zet een verandering van het Nederlandse scheepsbouwbeleid snel in. Allereerst begint het ministerie van Economische Zaken tegen de achtergrond van het Philip Morris-arrest steunverzoeken af te houden en af te bouwen. Dit had als gevolg dat er spanningen ontstonden tussen overheid, werfeigenaren die om steun bleven vragen en de vakbeweging die het geloof in herstructurering verloor. De grootste vakbond FNV stapte daarom in 1981 uit het georganiseerde tripartiete overleg tussen nationale overheid, werfeigenaren en vakbonden. Hierdoor verloor het ook invloed op het sociaal beleid dat werd afgesproken bij sluitingen. De vakbonden speelden ondanks protestacties geen werkelijke rol meer in het beleid.[65]

Deze door het ministerie van Economische Zaken ingezette koerswijzing was niet enkel een juridisch ingegeven keuze, maar ook een ideologische. Deze ideologische tint zien we voor het eerst terug in de Studiegroep Begrotingsruimte van 1978 en vervolgens in de serie Heroverwegingen uit 1981, een reeks ambtelijke rapporten geschreven onder auspiciën van het ministerie van Financiën met voorstellen om niet langer met de kaasschaaf te bezuinigen, maar het beleid drastisch te veranderen. Hierbij werden dertig beleidsterreinen onder de loep genomen, en voor elk terrein in ieder geval een plan gemaakt om 20% te bezuinigen. Eén van de Heroverwegingsrapporten ging ook over de scheepsbouw. De ambtelijke commissie concludeerde 'dat de politieke keuze is gemaakt voor een geleidelijke afbouw ten einde ernstige verstoring van het sociale klimaat te vermijden. Het is een politieke zaak om te bepalen welke prijs men hiervoor wil betalen. (...) Gezien de economische toekomstverwachtingen kan men zich afvragen of de prijs die afgelopen jaren in dit kader betaald is in de toekomst nog wel is op te brengen c.q. in relatie tot de economische orde zou moeten worden opgebracht.'[66] De Heroverwegingen worden wel de 'moeder aller operaties' genoemd en kwamen tijdens het kabinet-Lubbers I (1982-1986) tot volle wasdom in de serie Grote Operaties, waarvan de operatie privatisering en de -2% operatie de bekendste werden.[67]

65 Strath, *The politics of de-industrialization*, 180.

66 Kamerstuk II 1980/81,16625, nr. 31, 22.

67 F.K.M. van Nispen, *Het dossier heroverweging* (Delft 1992) 9.

Deze rapporten hebben ook als onderlegger gediend voor een ander uniek rapport, *De zure appel*, dat in 1982 als ongevraagd ambtelijk advies door de secretarissen-generaal van Financiën en Economische Zaken aan premier Van Agt werd gestuurd met voorstellen voor vergaande hervormingen, uit te voeren door het nieuwe kabinet dat zou aantreden na de verkiezingen van 1982. Met name Frans Rutten, als secretaris-generaal van Economische Zaken één van de auteurs van *De zure appel*, was één van de belangrijkste en meest vocale ambtelijke wegbereiders van het neoliberalisme in Nederland. In zijn nieuwjaarartikelen in het blad *Economisch Statistische Berichten* (ESB) verketterde hij de 'economische professie' die met 'simplistische keynesiaanse modellen bijgedragen [heeft] tot de euforie, dat volledige werkgelegenheid en "volledige" bezetting van de productiecapaciteit door macro-economische maatregelen van de overheid veilig zijn te stellen. Deze vergissing is van meer dan theoretische betekenis; zij heeft het centralisme in de hand gewerkt en daarmee aan de eigen verantwoordelijkheid van ondernemingen en werknemers afbreuk gedaan.'[68] Zijn recept was een beperkte staat die zich richtte op monetaristisch monetair beleid en het herstel van concurrentie en een vrije markt. Dat laatste moest tevens het centrale streven van de EEG worden.[69] Deze boodschap had Rutten ook al uitgedragen als secretaris van de commissie-Wagner I, een door minister van Economische Zaken Gijs van Aardenne (1977-1981, 1982-1986, VVD) ingestelde adviescommissies van werkgevers en werknemers onder leiding van oud-Shell bestuursvoorzitter Gerrit Wagner, die over de heroriëntatie van het industriebeleid het breed gedragen rapport *Nieuw industrieel elan* (1980) publiceerde. Hoe fundamenteel anders dit was dan het tot dan toe gevoerde beleid blijkt uit de benadering van werkgelegenheid: 'Werkgelegenheid hebben we niet vooropgesteld. Wij geloven niet dat je industriepolitiek moet voeren als panacee voor werkgelegenheid', aldus het lid Harrie Langman, in plaats daarvan moest de collectieve lastendruk omlaag en konden (private) investeringen omhoog.[70] In *De zure appel* werd RSV als het voorbeeld van falende Keynesiaanse subsidiepolitiek opgevoerd. Het was, aldus de schrijvers, een van de meest 'evidente voorbeelden van verloedering'. Zij zagen een 'fundamentele aantasting van de markteconomie' die alleen kon worden opgelost door 'harde, op het

68 F.W. Rutten, 'Prioriteit voor werkgelegenheid en economische groei', *ESB* 5 januari (1983) 4-7, 5.

69 Vergelijk: F.W. Rutten, 'De nationale economie is in groot gevaar', *ESB* 7 januari (1981) 4-7, 7; Idem, 'De kern van de afbraak', *ESB* 6 januari (1982) 4-7, 5.

70 M. Varisli, *Grenzen aan de groei? Sociaal-economische debatten in Nederland in de jaren 1971-1983* (masterscriptie geschiedenis UvA 2018) 61.

eerste gezicht asociaal aandoende maatregelen', waaronder een bezuinigingspakket van fl. 10 miljard per jaar.[71] Deze konden worden ingevuld met de bezuinigingsmaatregelen uit de Heroverwegingsrapporten.[72]

Deze redenatie werd grotendeels overgenomen in het regeerakkoord van het kabinet-Lubbers I, waarin bevordering van concurrentie, het belangrijkste speerpunt uit de tweede neoliberale golf, een belangrijk doel van het regeringsbeleid werd. 'Bij steun aan individuele bedrijven zal vanwege de schaarse overheidsmiddelen en het gevaar van concurrentievervalsing grote terughoudendheid worden betracht.' Ook is de invloed van Philip Morris duidelijk zichtbaar in de tekst, steun is alleen nog mogelijk in 'gebieden met duidelijk meer dan gemiddelde werkloosheid.'[73]

Deze neoliberale wijziging was eerder al ingezet in het beleid van het ministerie van Economische Zaken. Minister Frans Andriessen (CDA, 1977-1980) poogde al onder het kabinet-Van Agt I nieuwe steunaanvragen in de scheepsbouw te voorkomen. Dit gebeurde in een periode die de Europese Commissie omschreef als een 'crisis in de crisis', waarin de overcapaciteit verder opliep terwijl de orders en de prijzen nog verder terugliepen.[74]

Terwijl ministeries en ministers steeds meer een neoliberale koers gingen varen, was de Tweede Kamer hiervan nog niet overtuigd. In februari 1981 vroeg de Kamer na een succesvolle lobby van de gemeente Amsterdam en de vakbonden unaniem om een nieuw steunpakket voor de Amsterdamse werf NSM. De gemeente had een reddingsplan gepresenteerd ter waarde van fl. 25 miljoen gulden, maar minister van Economische Zaken Van Aardenne weigerde hier aan mee te werken. Hij meende dat het voorstel 'op grond van zakelijke overwegingen onvoldoende toekomstperspectief heeft om verdere steun te rechtvaardigen'. Wanneer de gemeente het plan toch wilde doorzetten zou hij de staatsaandelen in NSM 'afstoten'. Veel kans gaf hij het plan ook niet omdat hij problemen voorzag bij de goedkeuring die de Europese Commissie zou moeten verlenen. 'Opmerkelijk is hierbij dat reeds op de dag dat het plan van Amsterdam in de publiciteit kwam de commissiediensten mondeling van hun verontrusting blijk hebben gegeven', aldus Van Aar-

71 Van Grinsven, 'De zure appel', 63.

72 Van Nispen, *Het dossier,* 119.

73 Kamerstuk II 1982/83, 17555, nr. 7, 30.

74 Report from the Commission to the Council on the state of the shipbuilding industry in the Community. Situation at the beginning of 1985. COM (85) 548 final, 22 October 1985. Beschikbaar via (online) Archive of European Integration of the University of Pittsburgh (AEI), http://aei.pitt.edu/id/eprint/8834.

denne.[75] De Kamer was furieus over deze Kamerbrief van Van Aardenne en de terechtwijzing werd veroordeeld door alle partijen.[76]

Dat had echter geen effect in Brussel, de invloed van DG IV bleef groeien. Dat bleek wel in december 1981 toen de Europese Commissie een vooronderzoek opende naar het vermoeden van onterecht verleende staatssteun aan NSM en ADM in het verleden. De regering 'betreurde' deze stap, naar haar idee had het de Commissie altijd geïnformeerd over de steunpakketten. Ambtenaren van Economische Zaken hadden deze ook besproken in het maandelijkse ambtelijke overleg over de scheepsbouw met de andere lidstaten en de Europese Commissie. Tijdens eerder overleg hadden andere lidstaten nooit bezwaar gemaakt tegen de steun.[77] Een persoonlijke ontmoeting tussen Van Aardenne en Andriessen op 27 januari 1982 veranderde de mening van de eurocommissaris niet. Andriessen meende dat er 'ontoelaatbare' steun was verstrekt aan zowel NSM als ADM.

In hetzelfde jaar klopte ADM nogmaals aan voor nieuwe steun bij de gemeente en het Rijk. ADM had fl. 36 miljoen nodig om te overleven. De stad Amsterdam was bereid de helft van dit geld te lenen, maar Van Aardenne weigerde de andere helft bij te leggen. Zelf was hij van mening dat de omvang van de Amsterdamse haven een reparatiewerf als ADM rechtvaardigde. De reden om de steun desondanks te weigeren was het onderzoek van DG IV. Het directoraat-generaal had Van Aardenne laten weten dat een lening om een onmiddellijk bankroet te voorkomen niet zou worden geaccepteerd en dat in het verleden gegeven steunmaatregelen nog steeds onderzocht werden.[78] Andriessen had hiertoe in oktober 1982 een formeel onderzoek naar mogelijk ongeoorloofde staatssteun geopend.[79] Terwijl de Europese Commissie zijn onderzoek begon waren de ambtenaren van Economische Zaken er al van overtuigd dat het beleid moest veranderen, zoals ook bleek uit de Heroverweging en het *Zure appel*-rapport. Dit begonnen zij ook Europees uit te dragen. Vanaf 1982 vertelden ze de Europese collega's in het maandelijks overleg over de scheepsbouw, dat per 1985 alle steun aan de scheepsbouw zou zijn uitgefaseerd. De Nederlandse ambtenaren steunden nu ook na-

75 Kamerstuk II 1980/1, 14969, nr. 60, 63.

76 Kamerstuk II 1980/81, 14969, nr. 66.

77 Nationaal Archief (NA) 2.06.107, Ministerie van Economische Zaken: Directoraat-Generaal voor de Buitenlandse Economische Betrekkingen. 5595, De Nederlandse Scheepsbouwindustrie 1980-1983. Telexen aan DG IV, ongedateerd [december 1981?]; 20 januari 1982.

78 Kamerstuk II 1982/83, 17600XIII, nr. 15.

79 NA 2.06.107, 5596. Formele notificatie van de EC, 13 oktober 1982; NA 2.08.107, 5595. Telex aan Commissaris Andriessen, 31 januari 1983.

*Illustratie 2 ADM-medewerkers protesteren op het Binnenhof en ontmoeten minister Van Aardenne (VVD) van Economische Zaken, 8 december 1982 (bron: foto Rob C. Croes, fotocollectie Anefo, Nationaal Archief).*

drukkelijk de Europese Commissie in het zo snel mogelijk afkondigen van de zesde richtlijn die een 'situatie van staatsteunanarchie' moest voorkomen.[80]

## De RSV-enquête als katalysator: staatssteun gaat in de ban, 1983-1986

Met het aantreden van het kabinet-Lubbers I in 1982 werd het nieuwe neoliberale staatssteunbeleid nu ook krachtig publiekelijk uitgedragen. Deze regeringsploeg van 'managers in de politiek' liet zich openlijk inspireren door bedrijfsmatige managementmethoden en door managementconsultants van met name McKinsey. Ria Beckers (Politieke Partij Radikalen, PPR) meende bij het debat over de regeringsverklaring niet geheel ten onrechte 'dat de Nederlandse overheid met de Regering-Lubbers één groot McKinsey-bureau is geworden.'[81] McKinsey is een veelgenoemde verspreider van neoliberale ideeën in de jaren tachtig.[82]

80 NA 2.06.107,5595. Verslag 10 juni 1982, 1.

81 Keulen en Kroeze, 'Managerpolitiek'; S. Keulen, '1982: Managers in de politiek', in: L. Heerma van Voss e.a. (red.) *Wereldgeschiedenis van Nederland* (Amsterdam 2018) 689-695, 689.

82 J. O'Mahoney en A. Sturdy, 'Power and the diffusion of management ideas. The case of McKinsey &

Het bureau had ook veel invloed op het Nederlands bestuur. Verschillende departementen in Den Haag werden in de jaren zeventig en tachtig door McKinsey gereorganiseerd en (on)gevraagde adviesrapporten werden in beleid omgezet.[83] Dit neoliberalisme kan teruggevoerd worden naar één van de grondleggers van het moderne managementdenken: de Oostenrijkse neoliberaal Peter Drucker.[84] Drucker groeide uit tot auteur die het vaakst (zevenmaal) de McKinsey-award voor het beste artikel van de *Harvard Business Review* won. De verspreiding van bedrijfsmatige managementideeën wordt gezien als een van de meest kenmerkende verschijnselen van het neoliberale tijdperk.[85]

Vlak voor de formatie tijdens de toonaangevende NIVE-voorjaarsdag van het Nederlands Instituut voor Efficiency legden Pieter Winsemius, minister in Lubbers I maar toen nog firmant van McKinsey, en Frans Rutten uit hoe management paste binnen de neoliberale hervormingsagenda.[86] Vanuit Ruttens afkeur voor de Keynesiaanse macro-economische planning pleitte hij voor herstel van efficiëntie in de economie via micromanagement. 'Een basispunt van de economische wetenschap en van de organisatieleer in het bijzonder is voorts dat in een organisatie niet elke detail aan de top van de organisatie moet worden beslist. (...) Veel te veel detailproblemen – bijvoorbeeld betreffende bedrijven in nood – worden in Den Haag op het Binnenhof behandeld. (...) Het meer overlaten van beslissingen aan ondernemers en werknemers, zou de doelmatigheid van onze economie ten goede komen. Het zou ook beter passen bij de idealen van de democratie'.[87] Hij vervolgde:

> 'Bij het omkeren van trends en het keren van de afbraak hoort ook een in bepaalde opzichten verzwaarde taak voor het management. Ondernemers hechten terecht aan hun eigen verantwoordelijkheid. Die moet echter ook worden waargemaakt onder moeilijke omstandigheden en op moeilijke terreinen, zoals bij saneringen en bij loonsvorming. Goede en moedige managers hebben een sleutelrol te vervullen bij het herstel van een goede werking van onze economie.'[88]

Co.', *Management Learning* 47:3 (2016) 247-265.

83 Voor voorbeelden: S. Keulen, *Monumenten van beleid. De wisselwerking tussen Nederlands rijksoverheidsbeleid, sociale wetenschappen en politieke cultuur, 1945-2002* (Hilversum 2014) 188, 191, 199, 217.

84 D. Stone, *Goodbye to all that? The story of Europe since 1945* (Oxford 2014) 181.

85 M. Eagleton-Pierce, *Neoliberalism. The key concepts* (Londen 2016) 114.

86 Zie ook: Keulen, *Monumenten van beleid*, 179-228.

87 F.W. Rutten, 'Bevordering van een efficiënte werking van onze nationale economie', in: *Management in perspectief* (Den Haag 1982) 7-17, 14, 15.

88 Ibid., 15.

Hier presenteerde Rutten management, inclusief de rol die individuele managers moesten spelen in plaats van de overheid, als micro-economische oplossing voor macro-economische vraagstukken.

Hoe groot het vertrouwen was in deze nieuwe vorm van managementdenken en managementconsultancy bleek wel tijdens het eindspel om RSV. Vanaf de formatie van Lubbers I voerde Van Aardenne de druk op het op omvallen staande RSV snel op. Van Aardenne maakte duidelijk dat van overheidskrediet alleen nog sprake kon zijn als het gehele bestuur ermee instemde 'dat McKinsey wordt ingehuurd en dat aanbevelingen van dit bureau, voorzover geaccordeerd door de overheid, zullen worden uitgevoerd'. De begeleidingsgroep van ambtenaren die namens de overheid het saneringsproces moest begeleiden zou eveneens onder voorzitterschap van McKinsey komen te staan.[89] Deze relatief nieuwe actor kreeg zo een belangrijke rol die overigens in deze tijd door sommigen al kritisch werd besproken.[90] Op 25 januari 1983 presenteerde de projectgroep onder leiding van McKinsey haar ontluisterende eindrapport aan de meest betrokken bewindslieden. Van de 28 bedrijven waaruit het RSV-conglomeraat bestond, waren er op dat moment slechts zeven rendabel. Of zoals één van de projectgroepleden het concern omschreef; het probleem was dat 'RSV niet uit een aantal goede en een aantal slechte appels bestaat. Er zijn vrijwel geen echt gave appels'. Alleen al voor 1983 was een half miljard gulden nodig om het bedrijf overeind te houden, een bedrag dat in de jaren daarna zou oplopen tot jaarlijkse bijdragen van fl. 650 miljoen. 'Zonder deze externe middelen was de totale ineenstorting van het concern onvermijdelijk.'[91] En zelfs met die steun liep een groot deel van de werkgelegenheid gevaar, 10.000 mensen zouden hun baan kunnen verliezen. De conclusies werden snel overgenomen: al een week later besloot de regering geen geld meer te steken in het RSV-concern. Het conglomeraat moest dezelfde week nog surseance van betaling aanvragen en stortte als een kaartenhuis in elkaar. Een maand later besloot de Tweede Kamer voor het eerst sinds de oorlogsenquête een parlementaire enquête te houden naar het RSV-drama.

89 Kamerstuk II 1984/5, 17718, nr. 16, 422, 423.

90 Zie bijvoorbeeld: 'CPN-fractie vraagt parlementaire enquête over RSV', *De Waarheid* 11 februari (1983) 1. De onvrede over de rol van McKinsey uitten sommigen ook bij beleidswijzingen in jaren daarvoor en daarna: 'McKinsey, *De Waarheid* 15 december (1976) 3; 'Werven: Minister breekt nu de geherstructureerde scheepsbouw af', *NRC Handelsblad* 3 mei (1985) 11.

91 Kamerstuk II 1984/5, 17718, nr. 18, bijlage 74.

Ondertussen bleef Andriessen in de Tweede Kamer de druk opvoeren door er telkens op te wijzen dat de Europese Commissie 'steunverleningsoperaties in de lidstaten zeer kritisch volgt'. Eerdere steunmaatregelen waren toen 'nog steeds niet goedgekeurd' waardoor de kans op terugbetaling bestond. En zo hield de minister de Kamer voor: 'Indien de Commissie weigert haar goedkeuring te verlenen, moet een goedkeuring van verdere steunoperaties welhaast uitgesloten worden geacht.'[92]

In deze context begon ook het parlement te schuiven over de wenselijkheid van Keynesiaans steunbeleid. Kwam de weigering van nieuwe steun Van Aardenne in 1981 nog op een kamerbrede veroordeling te staan, een jaar later waren de regeringspartijen al een stuk sceptischer. In een debat van 8 december 1982, met het Amsterdamse college van B&W op de publieke tribune, lieten het christendemocratische CDA en de liberale Volkspartij voor Vrijheid en Democratie (VVD) nu een heel ander geluid horen. 'De fractie van de VVD is een verklaard tegenstandster van financiële overheidssteun aan individuele bedrijven', heette het nu. 'Concurrentievervalsing is vrijwel steeds het onbedoelde nevenproduct van dit soort hulp, en concurrentievervalsing is waarachtig niet het enige bezwaar', zo meende VVD-woordvoerder H.H. Jacobse.[93] Toch was nog niet iedereen overtuigd. De grootste oppositiepartij, de sociaaldemocratische Partij van de Arbeid (PvdA), meende met de rest van de oppositie dat een reparatiewerf een 'publieke voorziening' was en of die nu publiek of privaat werd uitgebaat veranderde daar niets aan. De partij vond het 'slecht beleid en onbegrijpelijk dat de minister (...) bezwaren oproept (...) die er eventueel in de Europese Commissie zouden kunnen zijn. Zo iets doet men niet. Bezwaren roep je niet op als je iets wilt voortzetten. Bezwaren roep je niet op als je een beleid wilt voeren dat positief gericht is.'[94]

In januari 1983 werd een met algemene stemmen door de Kamer gevraagd rapport van een commissie van 'wijze mannen' gepresenteerd. Het rapport schetste een somber beeld van de vooruitzichten van het bedrijf. Het openhouden van de werf zou in ieder geval fl. 50 miljoen subsidie kosten, zonder dat er tekenen van marktherstel waren. Van Aardenne wees dit af, 'in haar nationale verantwoordelijkheid' kon de

92 Kamerstuk II 1982/83, 17600XIII, nr. 15.

93 Handelingen II 1982/83 1019, 1020.

94 Ibid., 1018.

minister geen nieuwe subsidie verstrekken.[95] In een hierop volgend debat in de Senaat lichtte Van Aardenne zijn besluit toe met de woorden:

> 'Brussel is kritisch op dit soort zaken. Dat is terecht, want men beoordeelt daar de overheidssteun en of dat dan steun van de rijksoverheid of van de gemeente is, doet er in dat geval niet zo veel toe. Het gaat om de beoordeling van de eventuele concurrentievervalsing.'[96]

In Amsterdam was het gemeentebestuur door stomheid geslagen door dit besluit. De wethouders Heerma (CDA) en Jan Schaefer (PvdA) hadden juist voor het oog van de tv-camera's vanuit de portiersloge van de ADM een 111 uur durende inzamelingsactie gehouden om ADM te redden. Arbeiders en het publiek waren naar het stadhuis gekomen om geld te doneren om de werf open te houden. De ontbrekende fl. 15 miljoen werd gevonden doordat de stad de twee drijvende dokken van de werf had opgekocht om weer terug te verhuren.[97]

De Europese Commissie werd over deze laatste steunoperatie niet geïnformeerd, maar hoorde er snel over en nam het mee in haar eindconclusie van 28 april 1983. Het was een opmerkelijk besluit waarin commissaris Andriessen de overheidssteun voor ADM goedgekeurde omdat het samenging met de ontmanteling van het RSV-concern als geheel. 'Het heeft in ieder geval wel moeite gekost om de commissie tot de beslissing over ADM te krijgen. Ik verwacht geen al te grote problemen met de goedkeuring van de RSV-operatie, juist vanwege het feit dat er zo'n afslanking plaatsvindt. Ik heb hierover echter nog geen contact gehad. Ik heb commissaris Andriessen wel ingelicht over de problemen, voor zover hij die nog niet uit de krant kende', aldus minister Van Aardenne in de Tweede Kamer.[98]

Dat Nederlandse ambtenaren zich niet als neutrale volgers van de politieke leiding opstelden, bleek wel uit het feit dat zij intern hun ongenoegen uitten: zij waren zeer verbaasd dat de steun aan ADM was goedgekeurd. En niet alleen zij. In het maandelijks overleg tussen de nationale ambtenaren en de Europese Commissie over scheepsbouw vroeg de Duitse delegatie hoe het kon dat de steun aan ADM was goedgekeurd. De Commissieambtenaren lichtten toe dat dit kwam doordat

95 Ibid., 1603; Kamerstuk II 1982/83, 17600XIII, nr. 25.

96 Handelingen I 1982/83, 531.

97 I. Bos, 'Enneüs Heerma', *Groene Amsterdammer* 40:5 (1994); Kamerstuk II 1982/83 17600XIII, nr. 135, 3, 4.

98 Handelingen II 1982/83, 3700.

ADM de enige reparatiewerf was en dat steun samenging met vermindering van arbeidskrachten en tot verrassing van Economische Zaken ook omdat '(merkwaardig genoeg) het feit dat de steun van de lagere overheid beperkt is'.[99] Waarschijnlijk mede hierom, ondanks dat er geen bezwaar was van de kant van de Europese Commissie, ging Van Aardenne er niet toe over om de ADM of andere scheepswerven nieuwe steun te bieden vanuit de rijksoverheid. Hieruit blijkt dat de kritische houding van ambtenaren effect sorteerde. In dezelfde werkgroepvergadering deelden de Nederlandse ambtenaren namelijk mee dat binnen het jaar Nederland de laatste staatsteun zal beëindigen. Omdat 'gezien de moeilijke situatie van de scheepsbouwsector in de wereld, waardoor eigenlijk elke nationale steun verloren gaat. Een nationale oplossing van de problemen is dan ook niet meer mogelijk'.[100] De tweede reden was dat de grootste ontvanger van steun, het RSV-concern nu failliet was. Immers, in februari 1983 was RSV falliet gegaan. Dit faillissement maakte het besluit eenvoudiger om verdere staatssteun per direct te blokkeren.

De parlementaire enquête naar het RSV-debacle die in maart 1983 was gestart, presenteerde ondertussen een ontluisterend beeld van de samenwerking tussen bedrijfsleven en overheid. De samenvattingen van de openbare verhoren trokken steeds grotere kijkersaantallen op de televisie. Betrokkenen hadden moeite overtuigend uit te leggen wat RSV met al het geld had gedaan en hoe het had gefunctioneerd, verschillende verhoren resulteerden in grote hilariteit en ontluisterende conclusies over de 'RSV-show'.[101] In december 1984 trok de parlementaire enquêtecommissie met leden van de uiterst linkse Communistische Partij Nederland (CPN) tot de uiterst rechtse reformatorisch-conservatieve Staatskundig Gereformeerde Partij (SGP) een gemeenschappelijke conclusie waaruit duidelijk werd dat het Keynesiaanse interventiebeleid had afgedaan. Want ondanks de Kamerbrede steun voor het beleid,

> 'valt het te betwijfelen of de strijd om het zo lang mogelijk openhouden van de reeds jarenlang onrendabele scheepsbouwcapaciteit juist uit sociale overwegingen kon worden beschouwd als een aanvaardbaar beleidsalternatief. (...) Want de problemen waren niet van tijdelijke aard maar

99 NA 2.06.107, 5596. Verslag 7 juni 1983.

100 NA 2.06.107, 5596. Verslagen 7 juni en 21 september 1983.

101 R. Kroeze en S. Keulen, '"More exciting than Watergate, more real than Dynasty". Transparency's rise: the Dutch RSV-enquiry and the context of the 1980s', in: J.I. Engels and F. Monier (red.), *History of transparency in politics and society* (Göttingen 2020) 137-152.

> structureel van karakter. Een conjuncturele opleving betekende nog geen levensvatbare Nederlandse scheepsbouw. (...) [D]e pogingen om die werven zoveel mogelijk en zo lang mogelijk open te houden waren een voortdurende bron van onzekerheid en een lange reeks van desillusies.'[102]

De parlementaire enquête werkte voor de Kamer als katalysator om een einde te maken aan het op werkgelegenheid gerichte Keynesiaanse beleid en om voortaan de markt zijn werk te laten doen. De enquête bezegelde een al door de minister en zijn ambtenaren ingezette verandering in het industriebeleid waarin, aldus de economisch historicus Van Zanden, non-interventie voortaan de norm werd.[103] Hierbij borduurde de politiek voort op de neoliberaal geïnspireerde rapporten van de hierboven aangehaalde commissie-Wagner en eerder genoemde ambtelijke adviezen, evenals op rapporten zoals *Plaats en Toekomst van de Nederlandse industrie* (1980) van de Wetenschappelijke Raad voor het Regeringsbeleid dat eveneens een meer marktgericht industriebeleid voorschreef.[104]

Tussen 1983 en 1986 werd het RSV-concern opgedeeld in zes bedrijven, deze bleken in de praktijk niet altijd even stabiel en winstgevend als gehoopt. Dit gold ook voor NSM en ADM. Het Amsterdamse gemeentebestuur bleef zijn best doen om de werkgelegenheid van beide bedrijven te behouden. Nieuwe pogingen om kredieten en steun los te weken bij de nationale overheid liepen op niets uit.[105] De NSM zou nooit herstellen en werd bankroet verklaard in mei 1984. Wethouder Heerma probeerde hierop nog éénmaal de werf door te starten, maar ook die poging liep op niets uit.[106] De ADM verging het niet veel beter. In januari 1985 was de kas leeg en konden de lonen niet langer betaald worden. Minister Van Aardenne liet weten dat 'in een situatie van dreiging van een faillissement de huidige financiers, te weten de banken, primair verantwoordelijk zijn (...)' en dat 'van de rijksoverheid geen bijdrage in het benodigde boedelkrediet viel te verwachten'.[107]

Van Aardenne presenteerde dit nadrukkelijk als één van de geleerde lessen van de RSV-enquête. Deze mening werd nu gedeeld door de meeste partijen in de Tweede Kamer. De PvdA sprak nu over 'het on-

102 Kamerstuk II 1984/5, 17718, nr. 16, 462.

103 Van Zanden, 'History of an empty box', 188.

104 Zie hiervoor: Varisli, *Grenzen aan de groei?*

105 Kamerstuk II, 1984/85, 18600XIII, nr. 87.

106 'Oud-Shell man bekijkt werf NSM', *NRC Handelsblad* 1 juni (1984) 13.

107 Kamerstuk II 1984/85 18600XIII, 87.

vermijdelijke faillissement'.[108] D66 benadrukte: 'Wij kennen de RSV-geschiedenis. Het lijkt erop dat enige lessen zijn getrokken uit het gebeurde. Het lijkt er echter ook op dat er fouten zijn gemaakt. Het faillissement van de ADM is onvermijdelijk. Iedereen erkent dat, tot en met de vakbeweging toe.'[109] Ook in de bijdrage van het CDA kwam het nieuwe neoliberale adagium duidelijk naar voren. De partij pleitte voor een oplossing die 'met twee voeten op de grond staat, gebaseerd is op marktconformiteit en gericht is op een rendement dat perspectief biedt.'[110] Alleen onder de leden van de kleine linkse oppositiepartijen waren er nog pleitbezorgers voor Keynesiaanse steunmaatregelen te vinden. Willems (PSP): 'Ik waarschuw nog eens dat dit niet betekent dat men tegen steunverlening in het algemeen zou moeten zijn. Dat is wel een beetje het sfeertje dat dreigt te ontstaan na het RSV-drama. Wij vinden dat steunverlening uiterst zinvol kan zijn.'[111] De ADM-reparatiewerf vond echter geen steun bij de rijksoverheid en sloot binnen een maand, in februari 1985, de deuren. Overgebleven restanten van het RSV-concern werden in de jaren erna gesloten of opgekocht door private partijen en gereorganiseerd.

## Conclusie

De sluiting van de Amsterdamse werven past in een Europees patroon van afbouw van staatssteun aan verlieslijdende werven. In alle lidstaten moest het beleid van fusies en centralisatie om werkgelegenheid te beschermen plaatsmaken voor een beleid gericht op concurrentie. In Groot-Brittannië verdwenen hierbij tussen 1977 en 1987 82.000 banen in de scheepsbouw die tot de komst van Thatcher vrijwel geheel in één genationaliseerde firma waren ondergebracht. In Frankrijk waren de werven ook tot conglomeraten gefuseerd die niet onderling mochten concurreren, maar in de jaren tachtig moest de regering mede op aandringen van de Europese Commissie ingrijpen op werven waar de bouw tot 90% gesubsidieerd werd, de Franse centrale Rekenkamer berekende dat het goedkoper was om orders te weigeren en uitkeringen te verstrekken dan schepen te bouwen. Ook in West-Duitsland opende de Commissie onderzoeken naar staatsteun in de gefuseerde werven waar-

108 Handelingen II 1984/85, 2803.
109 Ibid., 2802.
110 Ibid., 2805.
111 Ibid., 2801.

bij de federale overheid tegenover subsidiewillige bondslanden als Bremen kwam te staan.

Onze studie toont aan de hand van de Nederlandse casus aan dat dit veranderingsproces werd bevorderd en tegengewerkt op verschillende bestuursniveaus: lokaal, nationaal en Europees. De interactie en dynamiek die hierbij ontstond, bleek van belang voor het verloop van het proces. De komst van een nieuwe actor in de politiek veranderde daarbij vrij plotseling het speelveld. De Europese Commissie, vooral in de vorm van het DG IV Mededinging die zeer invloedrijk werd, speelde deze transformerende sleutelrol. Het ideologische denken dat DG IV in de jaren tachtig uitdroeg is terug te voeren op de eerste golf neoliberalen. De Nederlandse commissaris Andriessen promootte deze omslag.

Maar ook andere actoren en factoren moeten meegenomen worden om te begrijpen waarom Nederland een van de eerste Europese landen was waar zich de wisseling van Keynesiaans georiënteerde staatssteun naar neoliberalisme voltrok. Dit was deels omdat binnen de ministeries van Financiën en Economische Zaken het neoliberale vertoog al ingang had gevonden. Topambtenaren probeerden in lezingen en rapporten de politiek warm te maken voor op neoliberale gedachten gestoelde heroverwegingen. Een tweede factor voor de snelle acceptatie was de specifieke band tussen de Europese commissie en Nederland: de veranderingsgezinde commissaris Andriessen kwam uit Nederland en Nederland werd op de vingers getikt door het Europese Hof in de rechtszaak over Philip Morris. Onder deze omstandigheden werden Nederlandse ambtenaren die al openstonden voor een verandering erin gesterkt dat zo'n verandering in neoliberale richting – dus met afbouw van staatssteun – moest plaatsvinden, zoals privédiscussies met Europese collega's illustreren. En toen deze Europese ambtenaren zelf weer wat leken te verslappen – ze keurden de Amsterdamse steun aan ADM goed in 1983 – waren het de Nederlandse ambtenaren van Economische Zaken die hun ongenoegen daarover uitspraken en samen met hun minister met vermelding naar de Europese mededingingswetgeving geen steun van de rijksoverheid meer zouden verlenen. Veel meer dan vanuit de politiek, was er dus vroege en aanhoudende druk vanuit de ambtenarij en de Europese Commissie om tot verandering over te gaan.

Nederlandse ministers, zoals Van Aardenne die werd gevoed door zijn ambtenaren, stonden zeker na het aantreden van het kabinet-Lubbers I in 1982, open voor de Europese druk omdat het paste in de bredere bezuinigingsagenda van het kabinet om bedrijfsmatig denken en privatisering te stimuleren als middel om de economische recessie te beëindigen. Dat het kabinet-Lubbers een McKinsey-afdeling leek, zoals het wel werd gezien bij haar presentatie, bleek ook niet zonder effect. McKinsey was een consultancybureau van aanzien, één van de bekendste wegbereiders van neoliberaal denken en kon haar ideeën in haar rol van adviseur aan het ministerie van Economische Zaken uitdragen en presenteren als het enige juiste. Zij kreeg die ruimte ook uitdrukkelijk van de minister. Het managementdenken dat McKinsey uitdroeg was aanlokkelijk, omdat het de nadruk legde op de rol van individuele consultants, managers en ondernemers om de economie vlot te trekken en daarmee een micro-economisch alternatief bood voor de Keynesiaanse macromodellen van centrale plannen en overheidssteun die steeds minder overtuigden in een tijd van stagflatie.

Het niveau van de politiek was het laatste niveau dat veranderde en het neoliberale vertoog overnam. Toen topambtenaren en ministers al klaar waren om staatssteun af te zweren, bepleitte de voltallige Kamer nog hulp aan de Amsterdamse werven. Hoewel vanaf 1982 de voorkeuren veranderen, was het de RSV-enquête die een katalysatorfunctie speelde, omdat het op ontluisterende wijze de enorme schaal en ineffectiviteit van de staatssteun toonde. Het leidde tot de uiteindelijke conclusie dat de Keynesiaanse politiek – massale overheidssteun om banen te behouden – niet langer acceptabel werd geacht door de grote politieke partijen. Staatssteun werd niet meer gezien als sociaal – het oude Keynesiaanse argument – maar als marktverstoring, concurrentiebederf en onrendabel – het neoliberale argument. In het Nederlandse geval duurde de acceptatie van het nieuwe paradigma ongeveer vijf jaar – wat relatief snel is in vergelijking met de andere West-Europese landen. De verklaring hiervoor ligt in de interactie tussen de actoren die actief waren op verschillende *governance*-niveaus in combinatie met enkele specifiek voor Nederland belangrijke omstandigheden, zoals het Philip-Morris-arrest en de impact van het RSV-debacle.

## Over de auteurs

**Ronald Kroeze** (1983) is universitair hoofddocent politieke geschiedenis aan de Vrije Universiteit Amsterdam. Hij promoveerde op de geschiedenis van politieke corruptie en richt zich in zijn onderzoek op (anti)corruptie, koloniaal bestuur, oral history en de rol van management in bedrijfsleven en politiek in de moderne tijd. Hij was als visiting scholar verbonden aan University of Oxford en Humboldt-Universität zu Berlin. Een eerdere publicatie van hem is R. Kroeze, A. Vitória en G. Geltner (red.), *Anticorruption in History* (Oxford: Oxford University Press, 2018).
Email: d.b.r.kroeze@vu.nl

**Sjoerd Keulen** (1982) is specialistisch adviseur en coördinator van de Algemene Rekenkamer. Hij onderzoekt verantwoording en beleidsevaluaties en de geschiedenis van financieel management en begrotingsbeleid. In 2014 promoveerde hij aan de Universiteit van Amsterdam op het proefschrift *Monumenten van Beleid. De wisselwerking tussen Nederlands rijksoverheidsbeleid, sociale wetenschappen en politieke cultuur, 1945-2002* (Hilversum: Uitgeverij Verloren, 2014).
Email: s.keulen@rekenkamer.nl

Samen schreven Keulen en Kroeze eerder onder meer: 'Managerpolitiek. Waarom historici oog voor management moeten hebben', *BMGN* 127:2 (2012) 97-112; 'The rise of neoliberalism and the termination of Keynesian policies. A multilevel governance analysis of the closure of the Amsterdam shipyards, 1968-1986', *Enterprise & Society* (2020) 1-35 en '"More exciting than Watergate, more real than Dynasty". Transparency's rise: the Dutch RSV-enquiry and the context of the 1980s', in: J.I. Engels en F. Monier (red.), *History of transparency in politics and society* (Göttingen: Vandenhoeck & Ruprecht, 2020)137-152.

# Flexland in wording

*De reactie en strategie van de vakbeweging ten aanzien van flexibilisering in Nederland in de jaren tachtig*

Rosa Kösters, Loran van Diepen, Moira van Dijk en Matthias van Rossum

TSEG 18 (1): 109–146
DOI: 10.18352/tseg.1200

**Abstract**

Internationally, the 1980s marked a shift in economic policy. In the Netherlands, it was the decade of the supposedly moderate neoliberal turn and of the first round of flexibilization. Nowadays, the degree of flexibility of the Dutch labour market is exceptionally high compared to neighbouring countries. This article examines how the trade union movement in the 1980s responded to increasing flexibilization, which strategy was used, and how this contributed to early Dutch flexibilization. In contrast to the literature with an institutional perspective, this article analyzes the trade union movement from a social-historical perspective and as a social movement organization. As a result, it argues that the effects of rising flexibilization were signalled very early on within the trade unions. Be that as it may, both the priorities that followed from the agreements with employer organizations and the internal dynamics, were decisive for the trade union movement's relatively late and unassertive responses towards the flexibilization of labour in the 1980s.

## Inleiding

Sinds de financiële crisis van 2008 is het onderwerp flexibilisering niet meer weg te denken uit het Nederlandse publieke debat. 'Flex' wordt daarbij in één adem genoemd met het 'neoliberalisme'. Zo zei de invloedrijke socioloog en politicoloog Anton Hemerijck begin 2019 dat het Europese financieel-economische beleid: 'is geïnspireerd door het neoliberale dogma: flexibiliseren, liberaliseren, privatiseren, bezuinigen op sociale bescherming'.[1] Tegelijkertijd is het neoliberalisme volgens historicus Bram Mellink en socioloog Merijn Oudenampsen 'hét containerbegrip geworden voor alle kwalen van onze tijd'.[2] Daarmee blijft het veelal onduidelijk hoe flexibilisering van arbeid en neoliberale beleidsvorming zich tot elkaar verhouden, wat de historische relatie is tussen deze processen en hoe zich dit heeft ontwikkeld in Nederland.

Arbeidssocioloog Maarten Keune plaatst het begin van de geleidelijke ideologische verschuiving waarmee een sterke nadruk op arbeidsmarkt flexibiliteit kwam te liggen, rond het einde van de jaren zeventig.[3] Historici en politicologen dateren het begin van de opleving van het neoliberalisme in dezelfde periode.[4] De politiek-maatschappelijke stroming vond in de loop van de jaren tachtig op diverse beleidsterreinen een ingang, ook in de manier waarop de sociale partners tegen arbeidsrelaties aankeken. De toenemende werkloosheid stond hoog op de agenda en de kabinetten onder leiding van Lubbers (1982-1994) bestreden deze met aanbod gestuurd beleid. Die reactie kreeg in de loop van de jaren negentig in binnen- en buitenland veel lof: in Nederland zou zich een wonder hebben voltrokken. Anton Hemerijck en zijn collega socioloog Jelle Visser publiceerden hierover in 1997 het toonaangevend boek *A Dutch Miracle*. Ze concludeerden dat de belangrijkste beleids- en mentaliteitsveranderingen lagen in de brede erkenning van regering, werkgevers- en werknemersorganisaties dat voor een hoger investeringsniveau, welke essentieel zou zijn voor de creatie van meer banen, een hogere winstgevendheid nodig was. Om dit te bereiken stond loonmatiging centraal in het in 1982 tussen werkgevers- en werknemersorganisaties afgesloten Akkoord van Wassenaar. Het akkoord moest bijdragen aan het verlagen van de reële wisselkoers en het verbeteren van het prijsconcurrentievermogen van Nederlandse bedrij-

1 M. ten Hooven, 'De uitholling van Nederland. Dertig jaar neoliberalisme', *De Groene Amsterdammer* 13 maart (2019) https://www.groene.nl/artikel/de-uitholling-van-nederland/. Geraadpleegd op 5 februari 2020.

2 M. Oudenampsen en B. Mellink, 'Neoliberalisme is de schuld van alles. Toch?', *De Correspondent* 28 augustus (2019) https://decorrespondent.nl/10426/neoliberalisme-is-de-schuld-van-alles-toch/1114113591734-5021aded. Geraadpleegd op 5 februari 2020.

3 M. Keune, 'Is het flexizekerheidsconcept (in) de beperking meester?', in: E. Sol en C. Nysten (red.), *Wat is de zekerheid in flex en zeker?* (Amsterdam 2011) 53-72, 56-57.

4 D. Hellema, *Nederland en de jaren zeventig* (Amsterdam 2012) 261; P. de Rooy, *Ons stipje op de wereldkaart. De politieke cultuur van Nederland in de negentiende en twintigste eeuw* (Amsterdam 2014) 268; M. Oudenampsen, 'In de boksring van de vrijheid. Den Uyl versus Hayek', in: M. Hurenkamp en R. Cuperus (red.), *Omstreden vrijheid* (Amsterdam 2015) 112-135, 132; J. Kennedy, *Een beknopte geschiedenis van Nederland* (Amsterdam 2017) 365-369.

ven en producten.[5] In de literatuur over het neoliberalisme en het corporatisme in de jaren tachtig hebben auteurs als Visser en Hemerijck, maar ook de Duitse politicoloog Peter Katzenstein, de Duitse socioloog Wolfgang Streeck en Engelse socioloog Colin Crouch daarbij altijd gewezen op hoe zich in corporatistische landen als Nederland minder radicale marktgerichte tendensen voordeden.[6]

Dit vertoog wordt inmiddels echter geproblematiseerd door de mate van flexibilisering van de Nederlandse arbeidsmarkt, die vergeleken met omringende landen uitzonderlijk hoog is.[7] In een recent verschenen rapport van de Wetenschappelijke Raad voor het Regeringsbeleid (WRR), *Het betere werk,* stelt de raad vast dat Nederland momenteel koploper is in Europa: 36 procent van de werkenden heeft geen vast contract en de flexibilisering van werk is hier de afgelopen decennia meer dan verdubbeld.[8] Als het gaat over het verband tussen de opleving van het neoliberalisme en de toenemende flexibilisering is het dus de vraag hoe het komt dat juist dit 'gematigde' land zo'n sterke flexibilisering kent. Eén van de stappen die voorafgaat aan het beantwoorden van die vraag is het benoemen van factoren die daarbij een rol hebben gespeeld. De historische indicaties voor de omvang van flexibele arbeidsverhoudingen, die wij voor het recente verkennende onderzoek *Precaire Polder* hebben verzameld, wezen op de vroege praktische en tastbare gevolgen van de neoliberale omslag.[9] Uit de beschikbare gegevens blijkt dat het midden en het eind van de jaren tachtig zich kenmerkten door een sterke jaarlijkse stijging van het aantal werknemers op flexibele arbeidscontracten en – vooral – het aantal werknemers bij uitzendbureaus (in 1984-1986 zo'n 7-9 procent; in 1989 maar liefst 9-15 procent).

5 J. Visser en A. Hemerijck, *'A Dutch miracle'. Job growth, welfare reform and corporatism in the Netherlands* (Amsterdam 1997) 13 en 16.

6 Ibid.; P.J. Katzenstein, *Corporatism and change. Austria, Switzerland, and the politics of industry* (Ithaca/ Londen 1984); Idem, *Small states in world markets. Industrial policy in Europe* (Ithaca/ Londen 1985); C. Crouch en W. Streeck (red.), *The diversity of democracy. Corporatism, social order and political conflict* (Cheltenham 2006).

7 H. Borstlap e.a., *In wat voor land willen wij werken? Naar een nieuw ontwerp voor de regulering van werk* (z.p. 2020) 21; J. Leupen, 'Geen land heeft zo'n flexibele arbeidsmarkt als Nederland. Trend naar flex is een voorbode voor Europa, zegt Guy Ryder', *Financieel Dagblad* 9 december (2015).

8 G.B.M. Engbersen e.a. (WRR), *Het betere werk. De nieuwe maatschappelijke opdracht* (Den Haag 2020) 11. Zie ook: M. Kremer, R. Went en A. Knottnerus (WRR), *Voor de zekerheid. De toekomst van flexibel werkenden en de moderne organisatie van arbeid* (Den Haag 2017) 19; CBP, *Flexibiliteit op de arbeidsmarkt* (z.p. 2016) 3; 'Report from the commission to the European Parliament, the Council, the European Central Bank and the European Economic and Social Committee', *Alert Mechanism Report* (2016).

9 M. van Dijk e.a., *Precaire polder. Rapport in het kader van het onderzoeksproject Historische Verkenning Vakbeweging* (Amsterdam 2018) 28-32.

De relatieve stijging van de flexgraad van werknemers (het percentage flexibele werknemers ten opzichte van de totale beroepsbevolking) was in de jaren 1984 en 1989-1990 zelfs 6 procent of hoger (zie grafiek 1). Volgens het Centraal Bureau voor Statistiek (CBS) nam het aantal geregistreerde flexwerkers in de periode 1983-1990 met ruim 200.000 toe.

Dit artikel onderzoekt hoe de vakbeweging zich in de jaren tachtig verhield tot de toenemende flexibilisering, welke strategie werd gehanteerd, en hoe dit heeft bijgedragen aan de vroege Nederlandse flexibilisering. Door terug te gaan naar dit decennium onderzoeken we de eerste ronde van groei van flexibele arbeidsverhoudingen, die dus plaats vond al ver voor de tot nu toe vooral onderzochte fase van regulering van flexibele arbeidsverhoudingen in de jaren negentig. Met deze studie kiezen we bovendien een andere invalshoek dan de bestaande historiografie, die andere kernfactoren via andere perspectieven bestudeerd. We laten zien dat voor een beter begrip van veranderingen in de organisatie van werk en de arbeidsmarkt ten tijde van de opkomst van het neoliberalisme, het niet voldoende is alleen veranderingen in ideeën en in de beleidsmatige vormgeving van de welvaartsstaat te bestuderen. De reactie van de vakbeweging is ook een kernfactor om de flexibilisering in Nederland in deze periode te kunnen begrijpen. Vanuit een sociaalhistorisch perspectief analyseren we de vakbeweging daarbij als sociale bewegingsorganisatie. Het institutionele perspectief in het recent internationaal vergelijkend onderzoek – voortbouwend op de kaders uit de jaren tachtig en negentig van auteurs als Visser en Hemerijck – is niet blind voor deze worsteling van de vakbonden met de opkomst van flexibilisering, maar kent zijn beperkingen.[10] Het heeft de neiging om de vakbeweging te bestuderen als een actor met primair formele invloed op economische besluitvorming in de landelijke politiek, terwijl de vakbeweging juist ook gekenmerkt wordt door een veel complexere eigenstandige organisatorische en sociale dynamiek, en door de verschillende rollen die zij in het politiek-sociale landschap vervult. De vakbeweging neemt deel aan het sociaal overleg met regering en werkgeversorganisaties in bijvoorbeeld de Sociaal-Economische Raad (SER; adviesraad) en de Stichting van de Arbeid (StvdA; overlegorgaan) en sluit in die rol landelijke akkoorden die resulteren in wetgeving, zoals het Flexakkoord uit 1996. Maar de vakbeweging is tegelijkertijd een so-

10 Voor recente bijdragen op dit terrein zie onder andere: B. Palier (red.), *A long goodbye to Bismarck? The politics of welfare reform in continental Europe* (Amsterdam 2010); K. Thelen, *Varieties of liberalization and the new politics of social solidarity* (New York 2014); P. Emmenegger, *The power to dismiss. Trade unions and the regulation of job security in Western Europe* (Oxford 2014).

ciale beweging die op verschillende andere niveaus actief is. Vakbonden combineren daarbij het afsluiten van ondernemings- en bedrijfstakcao's (en het daarvoor actievoeren) met diverse andere strategieën die invloed uitoefenen op de arbeidsvoorwaarden van werkenden (zelforganisatie, opleiding, maar bijvoorbeeld ook controle en naleving). Het overgrote deel van de in Nederland afgesloten cao's wordt algemeen verbindend verklaard en geldt daarna voor alle bedrijven en werknemers in een bepaalde branche waardoor de meeste Nederlandse werknemers onder een cao vallen (tussen 2000 en 2009 gemiddeld meer dan 80 procent).[11] De cao- en arbeidsvoorwaardenstrategie en inzet is een cruciale factor in vorming van de arbeidsmarkt en was dus ook een relevante factor in de opkomst van flexibele arbeidsverhoudingen. En de vakbeweging is een sociale beweging die mensen, vooral werknemers, organiseert rond een breed scala aan economische belangen en maatschappelijke thema's.[12] Juist de combinatie van krachten gegenereerd aan en door de landelijke overlegtafels enerzijds, als de interne dynamiek van de vakbeweging als sociale beweging anderzijds, blijken bepalend te zijn geweest voor de houding van de Federatie Nederlandse Vakbeweging (FNV) tegenover flexibilisering in de jaren tachtig.

De positie van de vakbeweging is nog weinig systematisch onderzocht, en daarom bestudeerden wij de archieven van de FNV als de bond die het grootste deel van de Nederlandse vakbeweging vertegenwoordigt. De FNV is een vakbondsorganisatie met eigen individuele leden en een vakcentrale met dertien aangesloten bonden (in 1980 bijna 1,08 miljoen leden; in 2019 iets meer dan 1,01 miljoen leden). Daarop volgt het Christelijk Nationaal Vakverbond (CNV), een werknemersorganisatie op christelijke grondslag (in 1980 304.000 leden; in 2019 236.000 leden). Tot slot zijn er de Vakcentrale voor Professionals (VCP; tot 2014 de Vakcentrale MHP), die de belangen van hoger opgeleide en leidinggevende werknemers in het bedrijfsleven en bij de overheid wil behartigen (in 1980 118.000 leden; in 2019 164.000 leden), en de overige vakverenigingen (in 1980 in totaal 289.000 leden; in 2019 in totaal 188.000 leden).[13] Sinds de tweede helft van de negentiende eeuw kent

11 J. Visser, *The institutional characteristics of trade unions, wage setting, state intervention and social pacts*. ICTWSS Database, version 4.0, *Amsterdam Institute for Advanced Labour Studies*, 2013, http://www.aias-uvanet.nl

12 M. van Dijk en M. van Rossum, 'Terugblikken om meer te zien! Een historische reflectie op vakbeweging, strategie en onderzoek', in: S. Boumans en W. Eshuis (red.), *Positie en strategie vakbeweging. Beschouwingen, analyses en voorstellen* (Amsterdam 2018) 84-91.

13 'Historie leden vakverenigingen 1901-2019', *Centraal Bureau voor de Statistiek* 25 oktober (2019) https://www.cbs.nl/nl-nl/cijfers/detail/70061ned.

Nederland vooral vakbonden die volgens het principe van de 'moderne' vakbond zijn georganiseerd: betaalde bestuurders (bezoldigden) komen op basis van (democratisch) centraal vastgelegd beleid op voor de belangen van de leden (en niet-leden). De afgelopen veertig jaar zijn deze bonden daarbij, net als in de rest van de wereld, geconfronteerd met een afnemende organisatiegraad. Tussen 1995 en 2011 liep de organisatiegraad terug van 28 tot 20 procent.[14] Van alle werknemers in de leeftijd van 15 tot 75 jaar was in de periode 2012-2016 gemiddeld 19 procent lid van een vakbond.[15] Halverwege 2016 was de organisatiegraad ruim 17 procent.[16]

De FNV was in de jaren tachtig getuige van de opkomst van een veelheid aan vormen van flexibilisering en maakte daarbij een – ook nu nog analytisch relevant – onderscheid tussen *interne* flexibilisering, *externe* flexibilisering, *numerieke* en *functionele* flexibiliteit (zie tabel 2). Interne flexibilisering betekent de verruiming van de inzetbaarheid van werknemers binnen een bedrijf door flexibiliteit in werktijden en werkzaamheden, terwijl externe flexibilisering gaat over flexibele contractvormen (bv. oproep- en uitzendkrachten). In het geval van *numerieke* flexibiliteit varieert de kwantiteit van de arbeid ofwel extern door aanvullende krachten in te huren, ofwel intern door de werkroosters van degenen die al in dienst zijn te veranderen. *Functionele* flexibiliteit gaat gepaard met een verandering in de kwaliteit of de functie van arbeid. Daarbij is de primaire doelstelling van werkgevers bij al deze vormen van flexibilisering hetzelfde, maar de gevolgen voor werknemers (zoals de mate van onzekerheid die dit oplevert) verschillen.[17] In dit artikel kijken wij tevens naar deze verschillende vormen en de interrelaties. We signaleren voor de onderzochte periode een duidelijk verband tussen deeltijdverkorting enerzijds en diverse vormen van flexibilisering anderzijds.

Het artikel bouwt voort op een eerder verkennend historisch onderzoeksproject naar de FNV-archieven dat was gebaseerd op brede systematische steekproeven in de archieven van de FNV-vakbonden.

14 'Organisatiegraad van Werknemers 1995-2011', *Centraal Bureau voor de Statistiek* 31 mei (2015) https://www.cbs.nl/nl-nl/maatwerk/2012/22/organisatiegraad-van-werknemers-1995-2011.

15 W. Gielen en J. Floris, *Wie is er nog lid van een vakbond? Inzicht in lidmaatschap, belang en tevredenheid* (Den Haag 2018) 6.

16 M. Tamminga, *De vuist van de vakbond. Een recente geschiedenis* (Amsterdam 2017) 22.

17 L. Delsen, *Exit poldermodel? Sociaal-economische ontwikkelingen in Nederland* (Assen 2000) 76-77. Zie ook: C. Passchier en W. Sprenger, *Alledaagse flexibilisering. Uitkomsten van een onderzoek naar de praktijk van flexibele arbeidsrelaties onder vakbondsbestuurders, klachtenbehandelaars en ondernemingsraden* (Amsterdam 1998).

De steekproeven richtten zich op drie strategische vindplaatsen die inzicht geven in de uitdagingen die de vakbeweging tegenkwam en de strategieën die zij daarbij hanteerde: te weten de dossiers van bondsbesturen en bondsraden (van drie belangrijke bonden: Industriebond, Dienstenbond en de ambtenarenbond Abvakabo), dossiers van actiemateriaal (Bouwbond, Dienstenbond, Industriebond, Vervoersbond, Voedingsbond en de Abvakabo) en dossiers rond scholing (Dienstenbond, Industriebond, Abvakabo en Vakbondsschool). Dit leverde een goed voorlopig overzicht op, welke uitwees dat op basis van deze archieven een diepgaander onderzoek mogelijk was naar de omgang van de FNV met flexibele arbeid in deze periode.[18] Voor dit artikel is gericht verder onderzoek gedaan naar cao-coördinatiedossiers van de vakcentrale. In de cao-coördinatie zien we zowel de rol van vakbeweging als overlegpartner van bewindspersonen en Kamerleden, als de vakbeweging die vormgeeft aan arbeidsverhoudingen door afspraken via cao's en andere strategiën ten aanzien van arbeidsvoorwaarden. De dossiers vormen een cruciale schakel om te bestuderen hoe centraal beleid van de vakbeweging tot stand kwam en wat de invloed was van – en de wisselwerking met – het beleid en de praktijk bij de bij de FNV aangesloten bonden. Ze bestaan uit vastgestelde (meerjaren) arbeidsvoorwaardenbeleidsplannen, jaarlijkse nota's over het arbeidsvoorwaardenbeleid van de vakcentrale en op bondsniveau, voorbeeld-cao's, evaluaties van cao-onderhandelingen en reacties vanuit bonden (in correspondentie, discussiestukken en nota's ten behoeve van congressen en als gevolg daarvan de aanpassing van de concepteksten). Om de werking van de vakbeweging en de dynamiek tussen de verschillende lagen van de organisatie te analyseren, is een systematische analyse gemaakt van cao-dossiers uit de jaren 1983-1989. Het ging om honderden pagina's aan stukken, overgeleverd in zes volle archiefdozen.

Uit het cao-coördinatieoverleg volgen diverse nieuwe inzichten. Visser en Hemerijck legden de nadruk op hoe de economische crisis een nieuwe opstelling van de vakbeweging ten aanzien van het Nederlandse arbeidsmarktbeleid had geprovoceerd.[19] Uit *Precaire Polder* volgde de veronderstelling dat de (top van de) vakbeweging dacht het sociaal overleg op landelijk niveau te kunnen gebruiken in de strijd tegen de hoge werkeloosheid van de jaren tachtig, maar daardoor het zicht verloor op de toenemende flexibilisering.[20] Uit de cao-dossiers blijkt dat

18 Van Dijk e.a., *Precaire polder*, 16-19.

19 Visser en Hemerijck, *'A Dutch miracle'*, 17.

20 Van Dijk e.a., *Precaire polder*.

om de rol en houding van de vakbeweging te verklaren niet de crisis zelf, maar met name de dynamiek die ontstond door het akkoord van belang was. Daarbij was van blindheid bij de FNV geen sprake. Zowel bij de vakcentrale als in de aangesloten bonden werd flexibilisering vrijwel direct na het Akkoord van Wassenaar als een serieus probleem benoemd.

Dit artikel laat zien hoe de vakcentrale en de bonden in deze jaren een geïnformeerde en behoorlijk kritische houding aannamen tegenover het nieuwe postindustriële concept van werk dat breekt met de volledige werkgelegenheid op basis van voltijdse werkuren en arbeidsovereenkomsten voor onbepaalde tijd. Bovendien legde de top van de vakbeweging zelf direct een expliciete relatie tussen de toenemende flexibilisering en het Akkoord van Wassenaar. Tegelijkertijd wordt duidelijk dat zowel de vakcentrale als de vakbonden afzagen van hardere middelen. Weliswaar zijn in de loop van de jaren tachtig en negentig speciale werkgroepen, campagnes en zelfs wat acties rond flexibilisering opgezet, maar vooral met de hoop de uitwassen van flexibele arbeidsverhoudingen tegen te gaan en – opvallend – vrijwel altijd met relatief 'zachte' middelen, zoals het opzetten van informatievoorzieningen (middels bijvoorbeeld een Flexlijn), het organiseren van milde publieksacties en soms door naar de rechter te stappen. Niet iedereen was het daarmee eens. Intern was de FNV zeer verdeeld over de juiste strategie. Met name vrouwen streden voor een vakbond die een actievere houding aannam ten opzichte van flexibilisering. Dergelijke geluiden van onderaf kregen echter weinig (en steeds minder) gehoor. De top legde de prioriteit bij de afspraken gemaakt in het akkoord van Wassenaar en in de loop van de jaren tachtig trokken zij de interne organisatie van bovenaf strak. Na de bespreking van de historiografische context van het onderzoek zullen we deze bevindingen uiteenzetten door achtereenvolgens in te gaan op het Akkoord van Wassenaar, de relatie tussen dit akkoord en de flexibilisering, hoe ook de FNV dat verband opmerkte, de strategie die de vakcentrale vervolgens formuleerde en de reactie daarop vanuit de FNV-bonden.

**Grafiek 1 Relatieve ontwikkeling flexibele arbeidsverhoudingen, 1970-2012**

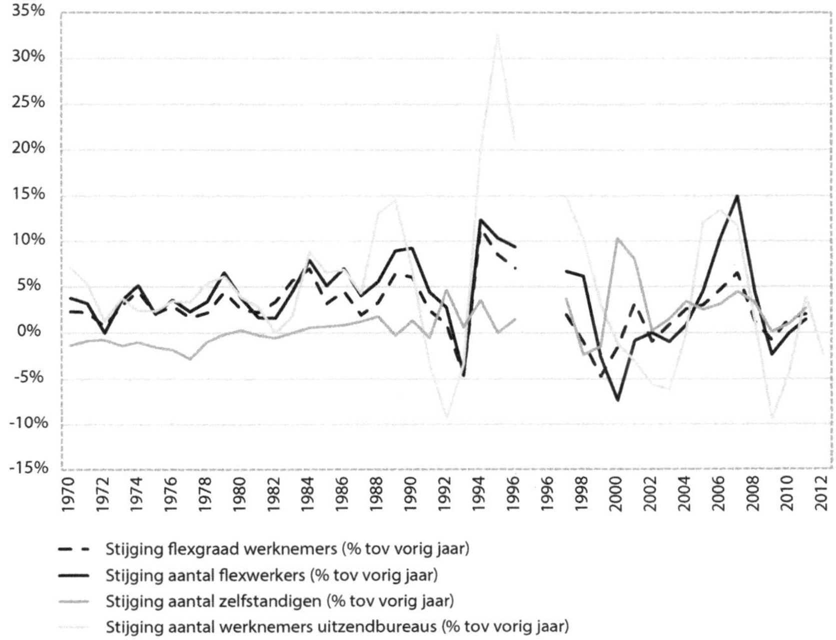


*Bron: CBS, Tijdreeksen Arbeidsrekeningen 1950-heden, werkgelegenheid; CBS, Beroepsbevolking; beroepsklassen 1996-2011.*

**Tabel 1 Vormen van flexibilisering[21]**

| | Extern | Intern |
|---|---|---|
| **Numeriek** | Uitzend- en oproepwerk<br>Tijdelijke dienstverbanden<br>Arbeidspools | Deeltijdwerk<br>Overwerk<br>Ploegenarbeid |
| **Functioneel** | Thuiswerk<br>Detachering<br>Freelance en onderaanneming | Functieroulatie<br>Overplaatsing<br>Taakverbreding en -verrijking |

21 L. Delsen en J. Visser, 'Flexibilisering van de arbeid via cao's', *Sociaal Maandblad Arbeid* 6 (1999) 296.

## Debatten over de politieke economie, corporatisme en flexibilisering

De Nederlandse economisch historicus Jeroen Touwen combineert twee verklaringsmodellen die we vaker terugzien in de wetenschappelijke literatuur over de opkomst van flexibilisering. Touwen legt in zijn boek uit 2015 de nadruk op het gecoördineerde karakter van de veranderingen in de Nederlandse economie en op de economische wenselijkheid van flexibele arbeid. Vanaf de jaren tachtig groeide volgens Touwen de consensus onder Nederlandse instituties – werkgevers-, werknemersorganisaties en de overheid – dat privatisering en deregulering van de economie en flexibilisering van de arbeidsmarkt onvermijdelijke en noodzakelijke hervormingen waren. De periode 1980-2010 kan volgens Touwen dan ook niet worden aangemerkt als een periode van meedogenloze neoliberale hervormingen. Hij acht het beter om te spreken van 'pragmatische aanpassingen aan globaliserende markten'.[22] In de recente internationale literatuur over de opkomst van *precarious work* circuleert het idee dat bedrijven hun arbeidsorganisatie in deze *era of fast capitalism* snel en tegen geringe kosten moesten kunnen aanpassen aan conjunctuurschommelingen en concurrentiedruk op vergelijkbare wijze een belangrijke rol.[23] In de jaren tachtig en negentig waren politicologen en sociologen als Visser, Hemerijck en Katzenstein net zo overtuigd dat veranderende internationale markten vroegen om flexibele bedrijven in een flexibele economie.[24]

Het is echter maar de vraag of onvermijdelijkheid als verklaring stand houdt. Arbeidseconoom Ronald Dekker stelt dat politieke partijen en gezaghebbende instellingen zijn 'bevangen door het defaitistische idee' dat Nederland 'slechts een scheepje [...] op de woelige baren van de wereldeconomie' is, waardoor zij nauwelijks tegenwicht bieden aan de 'marktretoriek van onvermijdelijke flexibilisering'.[25] Adviezen van internationale denktanks en organisaties als het Internationaal Monetair Fonds (IMF), de Wereldbank en de Organisatie voor Economische Samenwerking en Ontwikkeling (OESO) over de noodzaak van

22 J. Touwen, *Coordination in transition. The Netherlands and the world economy, 1950-2010* (Leiden/Boston 2015) 339.

23 A. Herod en R. Lambert, 'Neoliberalism, precarious work and remaking the geography of global capitalism', in: Idem (red.), *Neoliberal capitalism and precarious work. Ethnographies of accommodation and resistance* (Cheltenham 2016) 1-42, 20; L. Kösters, en W. Smits, 'Tijdelijk werk. Nederland in Europees perspectief', in: R. van Gaalen e.a. (red.), *Dynamiek op de Nederlandse arbeidsmarkt. De focus op flexibilisering* (Den Haag 2015) 128-150.

24 Visser en Hemerijck, *'A Dutch miracle'*; Katzenstein, *Small states*.

25 R. Dekker, 'Als alles flexibel wordt', *Socialisme & Democratie* 9 (2011) 110-118, 110.

flexibele Europese arbeidsmarkten hebben volgens Dekker bijgedragen aan de consensus dat flexibilisering onontkoombaar is. Bedrijfshistorica Keetie Sluyterman wijst tevens op het vertekende beeld dat is ontstaan. Zij stelt dat het institutionele landschap van regering, werkgevers- en werknemersorganisaties overtuigd raakte van het idee dat een internationaal concurrerend bedrijfsleven de basis vormt voor economische groei en werkgelegenheid. Daardoor is volgens Sluyterman de werkgeverslobby vervolgens het gedachtegoed en de beeldvorming over de noodzakelijkheid en onvermijdelijkheid van flexibilisering gaan domineren.[26] Van de twee verklaringsmodellen blijft er daarmee één over.

Het idee dat bij het gecoördineerde overheidsbeleid de sleutel ligt voor het begrijpen van allerlei veranderingen in de politieke economie van de afgelopen decennia, kent zijn oorsprong in de jaren tachtig. *Small States in World Markets* (1985) van Katzenstein zette de toon – het boek is volgens de politicoloog Mark Blyth één van de drie grondleggers van het hedendaagse onderzoek naar politieke economieën.[27] Katzenstein verschoof de aandacht naar de corporatistische politieke structuren in kleine West-Europese landen, zoals Nederland, die tot dan toe van wetenschappers weinig aandacht kregen. Met hun democratisch corporatisme zouden juist zij hebben bewezen effectief om te kunnen gaan met een snel veranderende wereld en een voorbeeld zijn voor grote industriële landen.[28] Het in de jaren negentig ontstane enthousiasme (nationaal en internationaal) voor het Nederlandse Poldermodel, zoals bij Visser en Hemerijck, past in deze gedachtenlijn. Zij betoogden in *A Dutch Miracle* dat Nederland dankzij het poldermirakel de rest van Europa had ingehaald. Overleg, beleidsleren en consensusvorming tussen vakbonden, werkgeversorganisaties en de overheid waren cruciale factoren geweest in het overkomen van werkloosheid begin jaren tachtig en de goede prestaties van de arbeidsmarkt in de jaren negentig.[29]

26 K. Sluyterman, 'Ruthless neoliberal reform or pragmatic adjustment to globalizing markets. That's the question', *TSEG – The Low Countries Journal of Social and Economic History* 12:3 (2015) 83-86, 84; K. Sluyterman en B. Wubs, 'Multinationals as agents of change', in: K. Sluyterman (red.), *Varieties of capitalism and business history. The Dutch case* (New York 2015) 156-182, 172-175. Vgl: Katzenstein, *Small states*, 11.

27 Naast P. Gourevitch, *Politics in hard times. The great recession in comparative perspective* (Ithaca 1986) en P.A. Hall, *Governing the economy. The politics of state intervention in Britain and France* (New York 1986), M. Blyth, 'An approach to comparative analysis or a subfield within a subfield? Political economy', in: M.I. Lichbach en A.S. Zuckerman (red.), *Comparative politics. Rationality culture and structure* (Cambridge 2009) 193-219, 194.

28 Katzenstein, *Corporatism*; Idem, *Small states*.

29 Visser en Hemerijck, *'A Dutch miracle'*.

Het politiek-economisch onderzoek uit deze stroming maakte met het *varieties of capitalism*-debat de stap naar de eenentwintigste eeuw. De politiekeconomen Peter Hall en David Soskice kwamen in 2001 met een nieuw raamwerk om de institutionele overeenkomsten en verschillen tussen ontwikkelde economieën te begrijpen en gaven bedrijven daarbij een prominentere rol.[30] Een kerninzicht uit de internationaal vergelijkende literatuur over *varieties of capitalism* (*VoC*) is dat structurele economische veranderingen, zoals globalisering, geen uniforme uitwerking hebben, omdat ondernemingen in verschillende typen economieën verschillend reageren op vergelijkbare economische uitdagingen.[31] Tegelijkertijd wijst de theorie op hoe de reactie van bedrijven sterk wordt ingegeven door wetgeving en machtsverhoudingen onder de sociale partners in het landelijk overleg. Het *VoC*-debat heeft met historicus Touwen en in het samenwerkingsproject Bedrijfsleven in Nederland in de Twintigste eeuw (BINT), ook een plek gekregen in het Nederlandse historische onderzoek.[32] De nadruk op het belang van de mediërende rol van economische instituties, heeft zich dus vanuit het politicologisch onderzoek verspreid naar andere vakgebieden en bij diverse disciplines inmiddels stevig voet aan de grond gekregen.

Het debat over de opkomst van flexibilisering in landen als Nederland is gevormd door deze onderzoekstradities. In lijn met het *varieties of capitalism*-verklaringsmodel benadrukken historici zoals Touwen dat de keuze van een bedrijf om de arbeidsorganisatie te flexibiliseren sterk wordt ingegeven door de arbeidswetgeving en de machtsverhoudingen tussen werkgevers- en werknemersorganisaties. Een regering die zijn arbeidsmarkt dereguleert, creëert een cruciale voorwaarde voor de totstandkoming en groei van flexibele arbeidsverhoudingen.[33] Ook in de

30 P.A. Hall en D. Soskice, 'An introduction to varieties of capitalism', in: Idem (red.), *Varieties of capitalism. The institutional foundations of comparative advantage* (Oxford 2001) 1-68.

31 Ibid.; G. Esping-Andersen, *The three worlds of welfare capitalism* (Princeton 1990); G. Esping-Andersen en M. Regini (red.), *Why deregulate labour markets?* (Oxford 2000). Vgl.: J. Touwen, 'Varieties of capitalism en de Nederlandse economie in de periode 1950-2000', *TSEG* 3:1 (2006) 73-104.

32 J. van Gerwen en F. de Goey, *Ondernemers in Nederland. Variaties in ondernemen* (Amsterdam 2008); K. Sluyterman en B. Wubs, *Over grenzen. Multinationals en het Nederlandse kapitalisme* (Amsterdam 2009); B. Bouwens en J. Dankers, *Tussen concurrentie en concentratie. Belangenorganisaties, kartels, fusies en overnames* (Amsterdam 2012); E. Nijhof en A. van den Berg, *Het menselijk kapitaal. Sociaal ondernemersbeleid in Nederland* (Amsterdam 2012); J. Peet en E. Nijhof, *Een voortdurend experiment. Overheidsbeleid en het Nederlandse bedrijfsleven* (Amsterdam 2015); G. Westerhuis en A. de Jong, *Over geld en macht. Financiering en corporate governance van het Nederlandse bedrijfsleven* (Amsterdam 2015).

33 Touwen, *Coordination*; J. Barbier, 'A conceptual approach of the destandardization of employment in Europe since the 1970s', in: M. Koch en M. Fritz (red.), *Non-standard employment in Europe. Paradigms, prevalence and policy responses* (Basingstoke 2013) 13-28, 15-16.

internationale literatuur over de opkomst van flexibilisering en de afname van baanzekerheid bouwen auteurs voort op en combineren zij *VoC* en corporatische theorieën. Zo pleit politicoloog Kathleen Thelen in *Variaties of Liberalization and the New Politics of Social Solidarity* (2014) voor het toevoegen van een nieuwe categorie aan het *VoC*-model.[34] En politicoloog Patrick Emmenegger test in een in datzelfde jaar gepubliceerd onderzoek naast de VoC-verklaringen, ook een theorie over de invloed van sociaal katholicisme en de *power resource theory*. Hij komt tot de conclusie dat de laatste als verklaringsmodel relevant is wanneer deze wordt aangevuld met inzichten uit het historisch institutionalisme en zo onder andere de rol van vakbonden in de beleidsvorming meeneemt.[35] Op arbeidssociologisch onderzoek hebben discussies over corporatisme en de populariteit van het poldermodel eveneens een duidelijke invloed. Arbeidssocioloog Maarten Keune kijkt bijvoorbeeld naar wat hij de discursieve en institutionele fundamenten van het Nederlandse poldermodel noemt. Volgens Keune houden deze de sociale partners bij elkaar en voorzien hen van een gezamenlijke visie en beleidskader: 'degenen die zich buiten dit discours plaatsen met afwijkende gezichtspunten of beleidsvoorstellen, worden makkelijk weggezet als onverantwoordelijk of irrationeel. Dit overkomt met name de FNV nog weleens als zij, in de optiek van werkgevers of overheid, 'onverantwoordelijke' eisen stelt in cao-onderhandelingen'.[36] Dat in de hedendaagse Nederlandse literatuur over flexibilisering veel aandacht is voor het Flexakkoord uit 1996, bevestigt de hang naar akkoorden en politiek beleid.[37] Het gevolg is dat de meeste sociaalwetenschappelijke en historische studies over Nederland tot nu toe de nadruk leggen op de sterke stijging van flexibilisering en de nieuwe regulering daarvan middels wetgeving in de jaren negentig van de twintigste eeuw.

Wat opvalt is dat wetenschappers vooral kijken naar beleidsvorming, zonder de interne dynamiek van de daarin opererende economische instituties te kennen. In de recente internationaal vergelijkende literatuur ligt de focus op veranderingen in sociaal beleid. Politicologen bestuderen belastingen, uitkeringen, stelsels van sociale verzekeringen en publieke voorzieningen (Palier); of de institutionele ontwikkeling

34 Thelen, *Varieties*.

35 Emmenegger, *The power*.

36 M. Keune, 'Inleiding. De legitimiteit van het poldermodel in de eenentwintigste eeuw', in: Idem (red.), *Nog steeds een mirakel? De legitimiteit van het poldermodel in de eenentwintigste eeuw* (Amsterdam 2016) 9-37, 13.

37 K. Boonstra, 'De invloed van het sociaal akkoord op de Nederlandse arbeidswetgeving', in: Keune (red.), *Nog steeds een mirakel?* 197-223.

van loononderhandelingen, van de arbeidsmarkt en het onderwijs- en opleidingsbeleid (Thelen); of wettelijke regelingen rondom baanzekerheid voor de private sector (Emmenegger).[38] Daarmee ontbreekt een kernfactor in het begrijpen van de opkomende flexibilisering, namelijk de houding en de strategie van de vakbeweging die vorm krijgt aan de overlegtafels op landelijk, sectoraal en bedrijfsniveau en als gevolg van de interne dynamiek van deze gelaagde sociale beweging. Arbeidsjurist Klara Boonstra wees eerder al op begripsverwarring over flexibilisering binnen de vakbeweging waarmee ze bedoelt dat flexibilisering binnen de vakbeweging met verloop van tijd een andere, negatievere, betekenis heeft gekregen.[39] Dit artikel laat zien dat de houding van de FNV in de jaren tachtig sterk werd bepaald door de afspraken van het Akkoord van Wassenaar. Het gevolg was dat met name externe flexibilisering geen prioriteit en zelfs veel ruimte kreeg, terwijl deze ontwikkeling binnen de organisatie wel degelijk gesignaleerd werd.

Dat flexibilisering bij de vakbeweging niet hoog op de agenda kwam had deels te maken met machtsverhoudingen binnen de bonden en de federatie. Hier blijkt een andere onderzoekslijn in het flexibiliseringsdebat gericht op 'dualisering' of segmenterings-theorieën van belang. Dit model benadrukt dat structurele economische veranderingen niet voor alle werknemers dezelfde gevolgen hadden, omdat arbeidswetgeving en collectieve belangenbehartiging een deel van de arbeidsmarkt beschermt (*insiders*), terwijl een ander deel belangenbehartiging en juridische bescherming wordt ontzegd (*outsiders*). Kenmerken als gender, etniciteit, leeftijd en opleidingsniveau bepaalden (zij het in wisselende mate) veelal het onderscheid tussen *insiders* en *outsiders*.[40] Vakbonden en regeringen zagen sommige werknemers en sectoren als de *core workforce*, wat overigens mede werd ingegeven door electorale en organisatorische overwegingen, en behartigden daardoor vooral de belangen van deze groepen. In de jaren tachtig was het niet de *core workforce* die in Nederland als eerste te maken kreeg met flexibilisering en het waren met name de vrouwen binnen de FNV die de strijd daartegen op de agenda probeerden te krijgen. Van begripsverwarring over

38 Palier, *A long goodbye*, 20; Thelen, *Varieties*, 1-2 en 32; Emmenegger, *The power*, 3.

39 Boonstra, 'De invloed', 210-219; Tamminga, *De vuist van de vakbond*, 143. Zie ook: Keune, 'Is het flexizekerheidsconcept (in) de beperking meester?', 53-72, 56-57.

40 S. Mosoetsa, J. Stillermann en C. Tilly, 'Precarious labor, south and north. An introduction', *International Labor and Working-Class History* 89 (2016) 5-19; L. Hipp, J. Bernhardt en J. Allmendinger, 'Institutions and the prevalence of nonstandard employment', *Socio-Economic Review* 13 (2015) 351-377, 355.

flexibilisering was daarbij geen sprake, want de FNV benoemde flex al in de vroege jaren tachtig als nieuw probleem.

## Flexibilisering als actueel vraagstuk

Uit het onderzoeksrapport *Precaire Polder* blijkt dat een groep vrouwen binnen de FNV vrij snel aan de bel trok nadat dat zij begin jaren tachtig met flexibelere arbeid te maken kregen.[41] In 1983 richtte het FNV-Secretariaat voor vrouwelijke werknemers de FNV-brede werkgroep Marflex op die begon aan een inventarisatie van flexibel werk. In 1985 bracht de werkgroep de brochure *Flexibele arbeid onder de maat! Een vakbondsvrouwenstrategie tegen wegwerpbanen* naar buiten. Flexibilisering was op dat moment een 'toverwoord' geworden om het personeelsbestand op vijf terreinen flexibel te maken: arbeidstijden, arbeidsovereenkomsten, functies en niveaus, inkomen en regelgeving. De Marflex-vrouwen constateerden bovendien dat flexibele contracten 'in eerste instantie buiten het gezichtsveld van de vakbeweging' bleven.[42] In *Precaire Polder* volgde hieruit de hypothese dat vooral de lagere organisatiedelen de opkomende flexibilisering signaleerden.[43]

Uit het onderzoek in de cao-dossiers blijkt nu dat het hoogste orgaan van de FNV de ontwikkelingen net zo goed direct op het netvlies had. Al in een beleidsnota uit maart 1983 schreef het Federatiebestuur van de vakcentrale over het nieuwe werkgeversdoel: flexibilisering. Het bestuur benoemde het als een voor de bond relevant en actueel vraagstuk en achtte het noodzakelijk afspraken te maken over de grenzen waarbinnen flexibilisering kon plaatsvinden.[44] In oktober 1983 vervolgde het Federatiebestuur dat het wenselijk was om tot een nadere standpuntbepaling te komen om greep te kunnen houden op de ontwikkelingen.[45] Tegen de tijd dat de vakcentrale in 1984 het gecoördineerde arbeidsvoorwaardenbeleid voor 1985 en 1986 uitstippelde, had de FNV dat standpunt geformuleerd.

41 Van Dijk e.a., *Precaire polder*, 103.

42 FNV Secretariaat van vrouwelijke werknemers, *Flexibele arbeid. Onder de maat! Een vakbondsvrouwenstrategie tegen wegwerpbanen* (Amsterdam 1986) 5-6 en 42.

43 Van Dijk e.a., *Precaire polder*, 103-107.

44 Internationaal Instituut voor Sociale Geschiedenis (hierna IISG), Archief FNV (hierna FNV), inv. 2584, Circulaire 479. Aan de leden van de Fedeatie Raad t.k.n. aan de bondsbesturen (hierna Circulaire 479), 27 maart 1984.

45 IISG, FNV, inv. 2583, Circulaire 1432. Aan leden Beleidsadviesraad Werkgelegenheid en Sociaal-Economische Aangelegenheden (hierna Circulaire 1432), 19 oktober 1983.

In het gecoördineerde arbeidsvoorwaardenbeleid voor 1985 en 1986 stond dat ten dele sprake was van een positieve ontwikkeling. De arbeidsorganisatie diende meer aangepast te worden aan individuele behoeften en flexibilisering bood daarvoor mogelijkheden. De vakcentrale ging bovendien in zekere mate mee in het idee van flexibilisering als noodzakelijke ontwikkeling. Het was, zoals de nota FNV-uitgangspunten voor het arbeidsvoorwaardenbeleid 1987 schreef, 'ook in het belang van de werknemers dat ondernemingen snel en slagvaardig reageren op wisselende (markt)omstandigheden'.[46] Maar over het geheel genomen werd de tendens vooral als zeer negatief beoordeeld. 'Steeds meer werkgevers', aldus de Nota Uitgangspunten Arbeidsvoorwaardenbeleid 1985/1986, 'zien flexibilisering als een mogelijkheid om het personeelsbestand eenzijdig aan te passen aan de behoefte van de onderneming'.[47] Het leidde tot de marginalisering van specifieke groepen werknemers. 'Bepaalde vergaande vormen van flexibilisering' moesten daarom 'vermeden worden' en voor werknemers moest duidelijkheid komen over hoe hun arbeidspatronen konden veranderen.[48] In de centrale coördinatienota's voor het arbeidsvoorwaardenbeleid van de vakcentrale keerden flexibilisering en de negatieve gevolgen daarvan jaar in jaar uit terug.[49] Klara Boonstra schreef over de positieve connotatie van flexibilisering binnen de vakbeweging in de jaren tachtig, maar in de cao-coördinatie en -onderhandelingen lijkt daar zelden sprake van te zijn geweest.[50]

In het ontwikkelen van een eigen kijk op het postindustriële werk en de grenzen daaraan, maakte de FNV een onderscheid tussen interne flexibilisering, externe flexibilisering, *numerieke* en *functionele* flexibiliteit. Uit de arbeidvoorwaardennota's van bijvoorbeeld 1986, 1987 en 1988 blijkt

46 IISG, FNV, inv. 2584, FNV-uitgangspunten voor het arbeidsvoorwaardenbeleid 1987 (hierna Uitgangspunten AVB 1987), 6 oktober 1986.

47 IISG, FNV, inv. 2584, Nota inzake uitgangspunten voor het arbeidsvoorwaardenbeleid 1985/1986 (hierna Nota AVB 1985/1986), oktober 1984.

48 IISG, FNV, inv. 2584, Nota AVB 1985/1986, oktober 1984; IISG, FNV, inv. 2584, Circulaire 479, 27 maart 1984.

49 IISG, FNV, inv, 2584, Circulaire 1181. Aan de leden van Beleidsadviesraad Werkgelegenheid en Sociaal-Economische Aangelegenheden, 24 september 1985; IISG, FNV, inv. 2584, Circulaire 119. Aan de leden van de Federatieraad, 21 januari 1986; IISG, FNV, inv. 2585, FNV-uitgangspunten voor het arbeidsvoorwaardenbeleid 1988 (hierna Uitgangspunten AVB 1988), 1987.

50 Met begripsverwarring bedoelt Boonstra dat flexibilisering geruisloos een andere betekenis heeft gekregen. 'Voor het flexakkoord van 1996 wil het begrip flexibel primair zeggen: werk dat in deeltijd wordt verricht. Flexibele arbeid heeft honderdduizenden vrouwen de arbeidsmarkt op getrokken.' Vanwege dit emancipatie-effect kreeg flexibilisering positieve connotaties, ook binnen de vakbond. Flexibilisering stond synoniem voor deeltijdwerk en werd gewaardeerd omdat het betere combinaties tussen werk en privé mogelijk maakte. Zie Boonstra, 'De invloed' en Tamminga, *De vuist van de vakbond*, 143.

dat ze externe flexibilisering als ongewenst zag. De FNV was 'van mening dat de flexibilisering, ingepast in het bredere sociale beleid, via een interne flexibilisering van de arbeidsorganisatie, dat wil zeggen door een flexibelere organisatie van produktie en dienstverlening, tot stand moest komen [sic]'.[51] Interne functionele flexibilisering moest worden bereikt door: 'minder hiërarchische niveaus, een minder rigide opsplitsing van het werk in functies en taken' en 'voortdurende aandacht voor om-, her-, bijscholing'. Een dergelijke modernisering van de werkorganisatie kon volgens FNV ruimschoots bijdragen aan een flexibeler manier van opereren.[52]

Toch slaagde de vakcentrale en de afzonderlijke bonden er niet in de ongewenste flexibele contracten aan banden te leggen. In 1988 *bleef* het in de ogen van de Voedingsbond nodig flexibilisering aan te pakken.[53] Het Federatiebestuur constateerde een jaar eerder al dat in deze zaak weinig schot zat. De conclusie was dat de vakbeweging nog veel denkkracht en initiatieven op dit terrein moest ontwikkelen.[54] Een belangrijke oorzaak hiervoor was dat de opkomst van flexibilisering in verband stond met een andere kwestie waarop de FNV in deze periode haar pijlen richtte.

## Flexibilisering en het Akkoord van Wassenaar

In november 1982 sloten de sociale partners het beroemde en achteraf internationaal geprezen Akkoord van Wassenaar – destijds beter bekend als het Stichtingsakkoord. De rendementen daalden en de werkloosheid was in de jaren daarvoor gestegen. Werkgevers wilden kosten reduceren door overtollige werknemers te ontslaan, liever geen arbeidsduurverkorting en zeker niet met behoud van loon. Vanwege de oplopende werkloosheid wenste de vakbeweging echter herverdeling van arbeid door middel van arbeidsduurverkorting met behoud van loon. Na onderhandelingen kwamen regering, werkgevers- en werknemersorganisaties tot een gezamenlijke lange termijndoelstelling van behoud van werkgelegenheid door op de korte termijn in te zetten op arbeidsduurverkorting en door af te zien van prijscompensatie van de lonen. Het akkoord kwam tegemoet aan de wensen van beide partij-

51 IISG, FNV, inv. 2585, Uitgangspunten AVB 1988, 1987.

52 Ibid.; IISG, FNV, inv. 2584, Uitgangspunten AVB 1987, 6 oktober 1986.

53 IISG, FNV, inv. 2585, Nota arbeidsvoorwaardenbeleid 1989 van de Voedingsbond (hierna Nota AVB Voedingsbond 1989), 24 november 1988.

54 IISG, FNV, inv. 2585, Notitie 'FNV-arbeidsvoorwaardenbeleid en flexibilisering. Overwegingen en mogelijke uitwerkingen behorend bij paragraaf 4 van de nota "FNV-Uitgangspunten voor het arbeidsvoorwaarden 1987"' (hierna Notitie FNV-AVB en flexibilisering), 19 januari 1987.

en en minister De Koning van Sociale Zaken zei te streven naar een arbeidsduurverkorting tot 36 uur per week.[55] De aanbevelingen van november 1982 werden door de Stichting van de Arbeid in juli 1984 voor de daaropvolgende jaren herbevestigd.[56] Het gevolg was dat de FNV de rest van het decennium prioriteit gaf aan de invulling en de concretisering van de beginselafspraken over arbeidsduurverkorting en arbeidstijdverkorting – in de praktijk gebruikte de organisatie beide termen door elkaar heen. Bij arbeidsduurverkorting (adv) vermindert het aantal uren dat een werknemer op verschillende dagen werkt. In de jaren tachtig ging dat door verkorting van de werkweek, roostervrije dagen en de bevordering van deeltijdarbeid (interne flexibilisering).[57] Met arbeidstijdverkorting (atv) daalt de gemiddelde werktijd per werknemer, waarmee de werkwijze verschilt van adv maar het resultaat hetzelfde is.

Met de arbeidsduur- en arbeidstijdverkorting hoopte de vakbeweging de beschikbare werkgelegenheid te kunnen herverdelen. In het akkoord hadden werkgeversorganisaties de toezegging gedaan gezamenlijk naar arbeidstijdverkorting te streven. In cao's zouden bonden en werkgevers dat concretiseren en afspraken maken over de vraag hoe de arbeidstijdverkorting daadwerkelijk tot het behoud en de creatie van arbeidsplaatsen ging leiden.[58] In de maanden na het afsluiten van het Akkoord wees de top van de FNV op de mogelijke gevaren die de vakbeweging hierbij kon tegenkomen. Het Federatiebestuur stelde in maart 1983 dat flexibele arbeid aan de orde moest komen in de onderhandelingen met werkgevers over de herbezetting van de door atv vrijgekomen arbeidsplaatsen. De verwachting was dat werkgevers de atv wel eens zouden kunnen gaan gebruiken om in te zetten op vergaande *externe* flexibilisering.[59] Of, zoals een beleidsmedewerker van de vakcentrale in september 1983 in een college zijn toehoorders liet weten: de werkgevers hoopten aan het akkoord te verdienen omdat het een aanzet tot grotere flexibiliteit van de arbeidsvoorwaarden kon gaan betekenen.[60] Bestuurders op bondsniveau deelden deze zorgen. De Voe-

55 K.G. Tijdens, 'Arbeidsduurverkorting en het Akkoord van Wassenaar. Via deeltijdarbeid en verlofsparen naar CAO à la carte', *Tijdschrift voor Arbeidsvraagstukken* 18 (2002) 309-318, 309.

56 IISG, FNV, inv. 2584, Notitie strategie arbeidsvoorwaardenbeleid van B Akkerboom, 11 december 1984.

57 Tijdens, 'Arbeidsduurverkorting', 310.

58 IISG, FNV, inv. 2583, Notitie inzake de voortgang van het arbeidsvoorwaardenbeleid in 1984 (hierna Notitie voortgang AVB 1984), 29 juni 1983.

59 IISG, FNV, inv. 2584, Circulaire 479, 27 maart 1984.

60 IISG, FNV, inv. 2583, College 'Arbeidsvoorwaarden in Nederland' door B. Akkerboom, 11 september 1983.

dingsbond was in 1984 bang dat werkgevers de vrijgekomen ruimte op zouden vullen met afroepkrachten (externe numerieke flexibiliteit) en zwart betaalde krachten. Ook bij de andere bonden zag de Voedingsbond de zorgen hierover.[61]

In de loop van de jaren tachtig bleek dat deze zorgen niet onterecht waren. Vakbondsbestuurders van de federatie en de bonden legden een direct verband tussen de vakbondsinzet op arbeidsduur- en arbeidstijdverkorting en het toenemend aantal tijdelijke krachten, thuiswerk(st) ers, oproepkrachten of uitzendkrachten (externe numerieke en functionele flexibiliteit). Op het themacongres 'Vakbeweging en arbeidsmarkt' in 1986 benoemde de FNV de flexibilisering als 'het toverwoord waarmee werkgevers de vakbewegingsstrategie voor een algemene stapsgewijze arbeidsduurverkorting te lijf zijn gegaan'.[62] Zowel bij de Voedingsbond, die actief was in sectoren waar relatief veel vrouwen werkten, als bij de Industriebond, die vooral was gericht op de *core workforce*, was men van mening dat weinig herbezetting had plaatsgevonden en vooral extra tijdelijk personeel was aangenomen.[63] Het is belangrijk daarbij op te merken dat de FNV in de loop van de jaren tachtig wel positief stond tegenover het bereiken van herverdeling met deeltijdarbeid. Deeltijd werd als vorm van interne flexibilisering gezien, en vanwege het emancipatie effect aanvaardbaar geacht.[64] Wel wilde de FNV de positie van deeltijdwerknemers verbeteren door in te zetten op volwaardige regelingen voor deeltijd in cao's en de organisatie pleitte voor een gelijke beloning bij overwerk. De vrijwilligheid kwam in hun ogen te vaak in het gedrang en werkgevers vingen pieken in de productie vaker op door het tijdelijk langer laten werken van deeltijdwerknemers.[65]

Doordat werkgevers verschillende vormen van flexibilisering wisten te bewerkstelligen, leverde de arbeidstijdverkorting niet de nieuwe banen op die de FNV voor ogen had. Tussen 1986 en 1990 is een uitbreiding van de werkgelegenheid in arbeidsjaren met ruim één procent per jaar

61 IISG, FNV, inv. 2584, Notitie Voedingsbond over afroepkrachten en cao-beleid (hierna Notitie VB afroep en cao), 5 april 1984.

62 Geciteerd in: Van Dijk e.a., *Precaire polder*, 93.

63 IISG, FNV, inv. 2585, Nota arbeidsvoorwaardenbeleid 1990 van de Voedingsbond FNV (hierna Nota AVB VB 1990), december 1989; IISG, FNV, inv. 2585, Conceptnota arbeidsvoorwaardenbeleid 1989, 1988; IISG, FNV, inv. 2584, Cao-voorstellen cao-en metaalindustrie, 2 januari 1986.

64 IISG, FNV, inv. 2585, Vraagpuntennotitie arbeidsvoorwaardenbeleid 1988 (hierna Vraagpuntennotitie 1988), 15 juni 1987.

65 IISG, FNV, inv. 2584, Inventarisatie cao-resultaten 1985 (hierna Inventarisatie 1985), 30 augustus 1985; IISG, FNV, inv. 2584, Gemeenschappelijke uitgangspunten voor het arbeidsvoorwaardenbeleid 1986, 18 juni 1985; IISG, FNV, inv. 2584, Nota AVB 1985/1986, oktober 1984.

*Illustratie 1 Poster FNV & CNV (ontwerper onbekend), Werk 36 uur. Kies voor arbeidstijdverkorting, 1982 (bron: IISG BG D44/512).*

mogelijk gemaakt, waarbij het met name ging om laagbetaalde en parttime banen (interne flexibilisering) in de dienstensectoren waar vooral vrouwen in terechtkwamen.[66] In de metaal zag de Industriebond dat de toename van 'vreemde werknemers' door de uitbesteding van werk (externe flexibilisering) de beoogde effecten van de arbeidsduurverkorting in belangrijke mate wegnam.[67] De Voedingsbond pleitte in 1988 sterk voor het aan banden leggen van flexibele contracten 'niet alleen omdat flexibele arbeidscontracten de rechtspositie van werknemers aantasten, maar ook omdat een succesvol werkgelegenheidsbeleid daardoor ondergraven wordt'. 'Immers', zo vervolgde de Nota arbeidsvoorwaardenbeleid 1989, 'des te flexibeler werkgevers de arbeid in het produktieproces kunnen inplannen, des te minder noodzaak om vrijkomende arbeidsplaatsen (bijvoorbeeld als gevolg van arbeidstijdverkorting) op te vullen [sic]'.[68] Maar ondanks de terugkerende aandacht voor de problemen van flexwerk en de conclusie dat de inzet op arbeidstijdverkorting het alleen maar verder in de hand werkte, kreeg de strijd tegen flexibilisering weinig prioriteit. Waarom was de aanpak van de FNV terughoudend?

66 IISG, FNV, inv. 2586, Meerjarig arbeidsvoorwaardenbeleid 1990-1993, juni 1989.
67 IISG, FNV, inv. 2584, Cao-voorstellen cao-en metaalindustrie, 2 januari 1986.
68 IISG, FNV, inv. 2585, Nota AVB Voedingsbond 1989, 24 november 1988.

## Strategieën van de vakbeweging

Uit de gekozen strategieën en de daarbij ingezette middelen, is af te lezen welk beleid de FNV in de jaren tachtig voerde. Welke keuzes maakte de FNV destijds ten aanzien van arbeidstijdverkorting en flexibilisering? Ten eerste zijn er de nationale akkoorden tussen de sociale partners, zoals het Akkoord van Wassenaar. De federatie zag een akkoord destijds als het meest invloedrijke en belangrijkste instrument voor verandering. De arbeidstijd- en arbeidsduurverkorting wilde de federatie aan de landelijke overlegtafels beslechten. Als vicevoorzitter was Johan Stekelenburg er in 1987 en 1988 glashelder over: de FNV moest maatschappelijke problemen – in dit geval de werkloosheid – vooral via de weg van het landelijk overleg tot een oplossing brengen. Een gedecentraliseerd arbeidsvoorwaardenbeleid zou een veel minder effectieve bijdrage leveren aan de bestrijding daarvan. De FNV zou betere resultaten behalen wanneer bonden na overleg en afspraken op centraal niveau aan het cao-overleg begonnen. 'Zo is de kans naar mijn mening', aldus Stekelenburg, 'heel reëel aanwezig dat de optelsom van de resultaten van louter decentrale onderhandelingen in maatschappelijk en sociaaleconomisch opzicht, negatiever uitwerkt'.[69]

Een tweede instrument om vakbondseisen af te dwingen zijn de cao's. In de jaren tachtig was herverdeling door arbeidsduur- en arbeidstijdverkorting het hoofddoel binnen het cao-beleid. Na het Akkoord van Wassenaar werden voor bijna 50 procent van alle werknemers die onder een cao vielen in meerjarige cao's (ze liepen meestal tot 1985) afspraken gemaakt over arbeidsduurverkorting.[70] Binnen het centraal gecoördineerde arbeidsvoorwaardenbeleid van de FNV-vakcentrale voor de periode 1986-1990 bleef het uitgangspunt dat de werkloosheid nog niet voldoende was afgenomen, en dat verdergaande herverdeling door middel van arbeidsduurverkorting dus noodzakelijk bleef.[71] Of, zoals in een conceptversie van de nota-arbeidsvoorwaardenbeleid voor 1989 te lezen valt: 'Zoals de tachtiger jaren zijn begonnen, lijken ze ook te wor-

69 IISG, FNV, inv. 2585, Toespraak J. Stekelenburg 'De FNV-visie op het decentralisatieproces in het arbeidsvoorwaardenbeleid', 18 maart 1987.

70 IISG, FNV, inv, 2583, Circulaire 1432. 19 oktober 1983; IISG, FNV, inv. 2583, Notitie voortgang AVB 1984, 29 juni 1983; IISG, FNV, inv. 2584, Circulaire 90. Aan de leden van de Federatieraad, 16 januari 1985; IISG, FNV, inv. 2585, Vraagpuntennotitie 1988, 15 juni 1987; IISG, FNV, inv. 2585, Nota Arbeidsvoorwaarden 1989, 11 juli 1988.

71 IISG, FNV, inv. 2584, Circulaire 1111. Notitie over de voortgang van het arbeidsvoorwaardenbeleid 1985/1986, 28 augustus 1984.

den afgesloten. Werkgelegenheid staat bovenaan de verlanglijst'.[72] En die lijn wilde de FNV ook doortrekken naar de jaren negentig. In de in 1989 opgesteld nota *Meerjarige Arbeidsvoorwaardenbeleid 1990-1993* stond de werkgelegenheid wederom bovenaan in het eisenpakket. De inzet voor de komende vier jaar was het realiseren van de gemiddelde 35-urige werkweek.[73]

Bovendien was het hoogste niveau van de FNV bereid het derde vakbondsmiddel in te zetten voor arbeidsduurverkorting: het actievoeren. Op verschillende momenten in het onderhandelingsproces konden cao-acties op sector-, bedrijfstak-, of bedrijfsniveau plaatsvinden. Daarnaast kon de FNV besluiten over te gaan tot landelijke acties. In de regel was de federatie alleen bereid gezamenlijk de strijd aan te gaan, wanneer de kwestie waarover geen overeenstemming kwam voor het bestuur prioriteit had. En om genoeg mensen te kunnen mobiliseren voor een landelijke manifestatie gold meestal dat de besprekingen moesten zijn vastgelopen, het liefst in meerdere of toonaangevende bedrijven. Bij de atv en adv was dat het geval. Wanneer de FNV-bonden in maart 1985 weinig vorderingen maken in de cao-onderhandelingen ziet het Federatiebestuur een reële kans op lichte acties in de eerste helft van april en zwaardere acties in de tweede helft van de maand. Bij lichte acties werd gedacht aan korte werkonderbrekingen, stiptheidsacties en waarschuwingsstaken en bij zwaardere acties aan meerdaagse stakingen.[74] Hoewel het besluit om tot actie over te gaan, de keuze voor actievormen, de duur van acties en het tijdstip van de beëindiging van acties tot de autonomie van de bonden behoorden, zag de vakcentrale een rol voor zichzelf weggelegd bij de invulling van wat zij noemde 'gecoördineerde akties'.[75] De Beleidsadviesraad Werkgelegenheid en Sociaal-Economische Aangelegenheden van de vakcentrale coördineerde al de actie-strategische kant van het arbeidsvoorwaardenbeleid en de Federatieraad wilde spoedig een besluit nemen over het instellen van een coördinatiegroep acties.[76] Ook het bondsbestuur van de Industriebond FNV wilde uiteindelijk voor de 36-urige werkweek in actie komen.[77] Bij

72 IISG, FNV, inv. 2585, Eerste concept Arbeidsvoorwaardenbeleid 1989 (hierna Concept AVB 1989), 25 mei 1988.

73 IISG, FNV, inv. 2586, Coördinatienota Arbeidsvoorwaarden 1990, 13 december 1989.

74 IISG, FNV, inv. 2584, Notitie aan J. Maat, F. Drabbe, J. Stekelenburg, B. Akkerboom, J. van Hoof, 1985.

75 IISG, FNV, inv. 2584, Circulaire 459. Aan de leden van de Federatieraad, 26 maart 1985.

76 Ibid.

77 IISG, FNV, inv. 2584, Notitie voor de regionale teambijeenkomsten op 5 en 9 juni 1986. Poging tot evaluatie Arbeidsvoorwaardenbeleid (hierna Notitie regionale teambijeenkomsten), 3 juni 1986.

Hoogovens zette de bond werknemers aan tot acties voor cao-afspraken over adv.[78]

Welke van de drie middelen zette de vakbeweging in bij het tegengaan van de als negatief bestempelde vormen en gevolgen van flexibilisering? In de flexbiliseringsstrategie was het uitgangspunt dat 'arbeidsvoorwaarden voor niet-reguliere (afwijkende) contracten beter geregeld' moesten worden 'via de cao' en dus niet via centrale akkoorden of de politiek.[79] De kwestie kreeg een terugkerende rol in het centraal gecoördineerde arbeidsvoorwaardenbeleid. Volgens de nota *Uitgangspunten voor het Arbeidsvoorwaardenbeleid 1985/1986* lag daarbij voor het vakbondswerk in de onderneming en de ondernemingsraden de taak de wildgroei aan afroepcontracten, thuiswerk en andere marginale arbeid tegen te gaan (externe flexibilisering). Met de *FNV-uitgangspunten voor het arbeidsvoorwaardenbeleid 1987* benadrukte de vakcentrale deze stellingname opnieuw: 'Uitgangspunt daarbij is echter voor de FNV-bonden dat vormen van flexibiliteit in de arbeidsvoorwaarden via de CAO gereguleerd (en begrensd) dienen te worden'.[80]

Via de cao's, zo blijkt uit de evaluaties, wisten de bonden daarbij soms een succes te behalen. De Dienstenbond wist af te spreken dat bedrijven voor continue werkzaamheden geen hulp- en afroepkrachten mochten inzetten. Na langdurige onderhandelingen over ziekenhuiscao's, waar afroepkrachten buiten de cao vielen, slaagde de ambtenarenbond Abvakabo erin het aantal afroepkrachten als percentage van het totale werknemersbestand te beperken. Ook bij de PTT, het staatsbedrijf dat verantwoordelijk was voor de post, was overeenstemming bereikt over het terugdringen van afroepcontracten. De werkgever ging één-uurs contracten omzetten in een vast dienstverband naar keuze. Bij Druk en Papier ging het meer om het tegenhouden van achteruitgang. Het was gelukt om in de grafische cao's af te spreken dat de rechtspositie van thuiswerkers verbeterde, maar de bond had het schrappen van het verbod op thuiswerken niet weten te voorkomen.[81] De Dienstenbond was in onderhandeling met het KBB-concern (het moederconcern van grote warenhuizen als de Bijenkorf) en wist daar een aantal maatregelen te nemen tegen flexibel werk. Oproepkrachten mochten alleen incidenteel worden ingezet en zodra het werk een meer struc-

78 R. Kösters, *Hand- en ellebogenwerk. De transformatie op de werkvloer bij Hoogovens en Philips* (masterscriptie Universiteit van Amsterdam 2019) 85-86.

79 IISG, FNV, inv. 2584, Nota AVB 1985/1986, oktober 1984

80 IISG, FNV, inv. 2584, Uitgangspunten AVB 1987, 6 oktober 1986.

81 IISG, FNV, inv. 2584, Inventarisatie 1985, 30 augustus 1985.

tureel karakter kreeg moesten de warenhuizen een ander arbeidscontract aanbieden. Nul-urencontracten werden verboden, evenals werkweken van zes dagen. Bovendien werd het één derde-criterium voor het minimumloon afgeschaft, wat werknemers die minder dan een derde van de normale arbeidsduur werkten geen recht gaf op het minimumloon.[82] De Voedingsbond constateerde in 1985 dat in de eigen sector de rechtspositie van deeltijdwerkers inmiddels in het merendeel van de contracten redelijk goed geregeld was.[83] Bovendien wist de bond een enkele keer afroepcontracten en uitzendarbeid aan banden te leggen.[84] In 1989 kenden sommige voedingsbedrijven geen nulurencontracten meer, andere hanteerden een ondergrens van acht en 26 uur werken en weer andere kenden beperkingen overwerk voor deeltijdwerkers.[85]

Toch bleven de successen beperkt, terwijl binnen de organisatie de wens klonk om tot gezamenlijke uitgangspunten te komen en een gezamenlijk plan te trekken. De vakcentrale besloot daarom in 1986 actief met de toenemende flexibilisering aan de slag te willen. Met het verschijnen van twee interne notities *Eerste notitie over een aantal aspecten van flexibilisering van de arbeid die in het arbeidsvoorwaardenbeleid van belang zijn* (1986) en *FNV-arbeidsvoorwaardenbeleid en flexibilisering* (1987) kwam in het arbeidsvoorwaardenbeleid meer aandacht voor het thema.[86] Met de eerste nota wilde de FNV 'de weg inslaan naar het uitzetten van een meer brede strategie ten opzichte van het vraagstuk van de flexibilisering'.[87] In het gecoördineerde arbeidsvoorwaardenbeleid voor 1987 en 1988 (vastgesteld in 1986 en 1987) volgde de 'goede arbeidsverhoudingen' als belangrijkste thema na de werkgelegenheid, want de flexibilisering mocht niet leiden tot het creëren van groepen werknemers met tweederangs arbeidsvoorwaarden en rechtspositie.[88]

Die brede strategie kwam er in de jaren tachtig niet. Na 1987 verdween de gecoördineerde cao-strijd tegen flexibilisering verder naar

82 I. Kuijpers, 'Vier kanttekeningen bij de discussie over flexibilisering', in: P. de Beer (red.), *Onzeker werk. Achtergronden, gevolgen en strategie ten aanzien van flexibel werk* (Amsterdam 2016) 35-41, 35.

83 IISG, FNV, inv. 2584, Inventarisatie 1985, 30 augustus 1985.

84 IISG, FNV, inv. 2584, Discussienota arbeidsvoorwaardenbeleid 1986/1987 Voedingsbond (hierna Discussienota AVB VB 1986/1987), 1985.

85 IISG, FNV, inv. 2585, Nota AVB VB 1990, december 1989.

86 IISG, FNV, inv. 2585, Notitie 'FNV-AVB en flexibilisering', 19 januari 1987; IISG, FNV, inv. 2584, Notitie 'Eerste notitie over een aantal aspecten van flexibilisering van de arbeid die in het arbeidsvoorwaardenbeleid van belang zijn' (hierna Notitie 'Eerste notitie flexibilisering'), 27 augustus 1986.

87 IISG, FNV, inv. 2584, Notitie 'Eerste notitie flexibilisering', 27 augustus 1986.

88 IISG, FNV, inv. 2584, Uitgangspunten AVB 1987, 6 oktober 1986; IISG, FNV, inv. 2585, Uitgangspunten AVB 1988, 1987.

de achtergrond. De besturen van de bij de FNV aangesloten bonden wilden voor 1989 primair afspraken maken over de werkgelegenheid en de bestrijding van werkloosheid, het arbeidsmarkt- en scholingsbeleid; en gelijke inkomensontwikkeling voor werkenden en uitkeringsgerechtigden. De coördinatie van de FNV richtte zich op deze drie punten. De inzet was dat bonden alleen cao's zouden afsluiten indien er sprake was van evenwichtige afspraken over een duidelijk herkenbaar positief werkgelegenheidseffect, goed zichtbaar arbeidsmarkt- en scholingsbeleid, en een inkomensontwikkeling.[89] De grenzen aan flexibilisering kwamen verderop in de nota slechts kort aan bod, namelijk in de vorm van een vluchtige verwijzing naar de flexibiliteitsnota's van 1986 die als 'nog steeds actueel' werden bestempeld. In het samenvattend eisenpakket ontbrak de inzet daarop volledig.[90] Ook in het Meerjarig arbeidsvoorwaardenbeleid 1990-1993 stond het terugdringen van flexibele arbeid en het onder een cao brengen van thuiswerk(st)ers beduidend lager op de agenda dan daarvoor.[91] Het vakbondsbeleid gericht op de bevordering van werkgelegenheid en de bestrijding van werkeloosheid had in 1988 landelijk een nieuwe impuls gekregen. In het najaarsoverleg waren de sociale partners aan de overlegtafel overeengekomen dat zowel behoefte was aan maatregelen die de positie van laaggekwalificeerden en langdurig werklozen op de arbeidsmarkt versterkten als dat het daarbij onverminderd van betekenis was voort te gaan op de weg van het Stichtingsverband van 1982.[92] Het Akkoord van Wassenaar kreeg wederom een vervolg in 1993 toen de bonden opnieuw afspraken maakten waarbij loonmatiging werd uitgeruild voor extra banen.[93]

En waar de vakcentrale wel een coördinerende rol bij adv-acties voor zich zag, spraken bestuurders binnen de Federatieraad en het Federatiebestuur niet over het voeren van acties voor cao-eisen over flexibilisering. Ook binnen de afzonderlijke bonden lijken geen acties te zijn gevoerd voor betere cao-afspraken over flexibilisering. Onder het supermarktpersoneel kwam het in 1988 bijna zover. De Dienstenbond wilde onderbetaling en 'ongewenste flexibilisering' via de cao van 1989 aanpakken. Ondanks de lage organisatiegraad en het ontbreken van een actietraditie wist de bond veel medewerkers uit supermarkten via in-

89 IISG, FNV, inv. 2585, Nota Arbeidsvoorwaarden 1989, 11 juli 1988.

90 IISG, FNV, inv. 2585, Concept AVB 1989, 25 mei 1988.

91 IISG, FNV, inv. 2586, Coördinatienota Arbeidsvoorwaarden 1990, 13 december 1989.

92 IISG, FNV, inv. 2585, Concepttekst naar aanleiding van het najaarsoverleg 'Samen voor werk', 25 november 1988.

93 Van Dijk e.a., *Precaire polder*, 48.

formatiecampagnes en ledenraadplegingen te betrekken bij de onderhandelingen. Toen werkgevers de cao-onderhandelingen afbraken kon de Dienstenbond een grote aanhang mobiliseren en acties lagen op de loer. Maar enkel de aankondiging van een nieuwe actievormen, zogenoemde 'picket-lines', was voor werkgevers voldoende reden om de caoeisen (zij het nog steeds maar een deel daarvan) te accepteren.[94]

In tegenstelling tot de adv en atv, ontwikkelde de FNV tussen 1983 en 1989 geen gecoördineerde strategie met een brede en systematische inzet van diverse middelen tegen flexibilisering. Ondertussen leverde de 'uitruil' die de kern van het Akkoord van Wassenaar was niet het gewenste resultaat op. Vakbondshistoricus Sjaak van der Velden concludeerde: 'De arbeidstijd gemeten naar het aantal te werken uren in een voltijdsbaan daalde van 1829 in 1982 naar 1770 drie jaar later. Het werkloosheidspercentage bleef echter ongewijzigd hoog. Rond de 15 procent van de onzelfstandige beroepsbevolking volgens de toenmalige berekening.'[95] Uit het onderzoek van socioloog Kea Tijdens blijkt daarbij dat de vakbeweging beperkte invloed had op de herverdeling van werk. In de jaren 1986-1993 vond geen arbeidsduurverkorting meer plaats en maakten de sociale partners nauwelijks nog cao-afspraken over arbeidsduurverkorting zoals in de periode direct na het akkoord. Volgens Tijdens was voor de vakbeweging de teleurstellende herbezetting aanleiding om van verdere arbeidsduurverkorting af te zien en in de onderhandelingen opnieuw looneisen te stellen. Voor de werkgevers had arbeidsduurverkorting volgens Tijdens evenmin nog prioriteit.[96] De cao-dossiers laten zien dat het steeds meer moeite kostte om met werkgevers afspraken te maken, maar de arbeidsduur- en arbeidstijdverkorting verdween niet van de FNV-agenda. Dat inzicht heeft ook implicaties voor de kijk op hoe Wassenaar in de rest van het decennium doorwerkte. Tijdens wees al op de herverdeling van werk die er kwam middels de deeltijdarbeid. Dit artikel laat zien hoe Wassenaar het arbeidsvoorwaardenbeleid van de FNV bepaalde. Mede daardoor lag het terrein open voor de toenemende flexibilisering in de jaren tachtig.

94 Ibid., 109.

95 S. van der Velden, *Loonstrijd en loonontwikkeling in Nederland* (Amsterdam 2016) 40.

96 Tijdens, 'Arbeidsduurverkorting', 311.

## Interne dynamiek van de vakbeweging

De keuzes die de FNV met dit beleid maakte, waren niet onomstreden. De strategie na Wassenaar en ten aanzien van flexibilisering leverde de nodige interne discussies op. In februari en maart 1987 deden de vakbondsbestuurders Johan Stekelenburg en Henk Leemreize een ronde langs de grotere FNV-bonden om in informele sfeer van gedachten te wisselen over het arbeidsvoorwaardenbeleid voor de komende jaren. Ze spraken met (hoofd)bestuurders en medewerkers die verantwoordelijk waren voor het beleid en de coördinatie daarvan binnen de bonden. Stekelenburg en Leemreize kwamen tot de conclusie dat in veel van de bonden sprake was van een tweeslachtige stemming ten aanzien van een verdergaande adv tot een gemiddelde werkweek van 36 uur. 'Men beseft', zo kwam in de evaluatienotitie te staan, 'dat verdergaande adv moet in de strijd tegen de werkloosheid. Maar de twijfel groeit.'[97] Oorzaak daarvoor waren de slechte ervaringen met eerdere adv-rondes waarbij onvoldoende herbezetting had plaatsgevonden, de werkdruk was toegenomen en problemen ontstonden met het opnemen van roostervrije dagen. In de notitie stond ook beschreven dat de motivatie om door te gaan met het adv-beleid bij kaderleden groter leek dan bij gewone leden. Veel bonden zouden daarbij hebben benadrukt dat de inzet van de hele FNV nodig was om met de adv verder te komen; als mensen uit de verschillende bonden het gevoel kregen dat ze er alleen voor stonden, zouden ze afhaken.[98] Op wie doelden de federatiebestuurders? Hoe keken de (grote) afzonderlijke bonden in de jaren tachtig naar de FNV-strategieën voor adv en tegen flexibilisering, de prioriteiten die daarbij gesteld werden en de gevolgen daarvan? En hoe helpt de interne dynamiek van de vakbeweging te verklaren dat atv en adv, en niet de flexibilisering, de boventoon voerden?

De Industriebond FNV was een groot voorstander van de strijd voor arbeidsduur-, arbeidstijdverkorting en herverdeling van arbeid. De bond uitte daarbij kritiek op zowel de toewijding en inspanningen van de andere bonden als op de interne FNV-coördinatie. In 1985 was volgens de vakbondsbestuurders uit de industrie sprake van verdeeldheid over de prioriteiten in het beleid en de strategievraag. Terwijl de Industriebond zich naar eigen zeggen hard maakte voor de 36 uur, deed de rest dat (te) weinig. De Voedingsbond zou atv niet onbelangrijk vinden, maar

97 IISG, FNV, inv. 2585, Evaluatie van gesprekken met bonden over het arbeidsvoorwaardenbeleid in de komende jaren, 14 april 1987.

98 Ibid.

of ze het echt als belangrijkste thema zagen? De ambtenarenbond Abvakabo had zich in eerste instantie terughoudend opgesteld en ook dat leidde tot frustratie. De Industriebond zag zichzelf in 1986 alleen staan met de 'atv-verlangens'.[99] Na de evaluatie van het arbeidsvoorwaardenbeleid van 1987 bleek dat weinig veranderd. De Industriebond pleitte opnieuw voor atv, maar zag grote verschillen in de houding van collega bonden. Op de Abvakabo was wederom kritiek, die 'wisten zeker dat op háár leden bezuinigd zou worden, zónder herbezetting!' De Vervoersbond werd compleet in beslag genomen door een ontslagkwestie in het stukgoed in de Rotterdamse haven. De interne FNV-coördinatie bestempelde de Industriebond dat jaar als 'weinig doeltreffend' en de bond zag 'opnieuw tanend geloof in het instrument arbeidstijdverkorting'.[100] De conclusie was dat voor de atv meer aandacht moest komen. Ondertussen kreeg de flexibilisering in het arbeidsvoorwaardenbeleid van deze bond beduidend minder prioriteit dan bij sommige andere bonden.

Wat betreft de inzet op adv en atv week de Bouw- en Houtbond FNV niet veel af van de Industriebond. Volgens deze laatste had Bouw- en Hout in 1987 aan de atv-eis 'zeer lang willen vasthouden'.[101] Uit de Algemene uitgangspunten voor het arbeidsvoorwaardenbeleid 1989 blijkt dat de bond voor de bouw de nadruk wilde leggen op drie hoofdpunten die sterk met elkaar samenhingen: verbetering van de werkgelegenheid en bestrijding van de werkloosheid; het ontwikkelen van een arbeidsmarkt- en scholingsbeleid, gericht op de verbetering van de positie van werkzoekenden; en een inkomensontwikkeling, die zowel koopkrachtbehoud als een gelijke inkomensontwikkeling voor werkenden en uitkeringsgerechtigden mogelijk moest maken. Adv was daar bij uitstek het juiste middel voor. Want 'ook al wekken velen de indruk dat algemene arbeidstijdverkorting een gepasseerd station zou zijn, de Bouw- en Houtbond FNV is van mening, dat op termijn de 36-urige werkweek binnen ieders handbereik gebracht moet worden'.[102] In de nota en de bijgaande concept-cao voor 1989 werd tegelijkertijd over flexibilisering geen woord gerept.

Bij de Voedingsbond was dat anders. In de arbeidsvoorwaardendiscussies voor deze sector kreeg flexibilisering naast de arbeidstijdverkorting ruim aandacht.[103] In de cao-voorstellen voor 1984 en 1985 bij Turmac had de bond verschillende maatregelen opgenomen in reactie op

99 IISG, FNV, inv. 2584, Notitie regionale teambijeenkomsten, 3 juni 1986.
100 IISG, FNV, inv. 2585, Evaluatie Arbeidsvoorwaardenbeleid 1987, 1988.
101 Ibid.
102 IISG, FNV, inv. 2585, Concept cao-voorstellen Bouwbedrijf 1989, 25 augustus 1988.
103 IISG, FNV, inv. 2585, Conceptnota arbeidsvoorwaardenbeleid 1989, 1988.

de toenemende numerieke interne en externe flexibilisering. De bond wilde parttimers de eerste keus geven bij het ontstaan van fulltime vacatures en een spijtoptantenregeling in voeren voor mensen die vrijwillig van een fulltime naar een parttime dienstverband waren gegaan.[104] In 1985 had de bond het aan banden leggen van afroepcontracten in alle voorstellenbrieven opgenomen en daarvoor concrete maatregelen uitgewerkt.[105] Voor de twee daaropvolgende jaren bleef volgens de Voedingsbond 'verzet' geboden tegen het omzetten van vaste contracten voor onbepaalde duur in tijdelijke flexibele contracten en tegen het afroepcontract, dat hoog scoorde in de 'werkgeversfilosofie'.[106] Deze bond schroomde ook niet in de arbeidsvoorwaardenota voor 1990 erop te wijzen dat na Wassenaar weinig sprake was van herbezetting en dat de flexibilisering en het overwerk waren toegenomen. En ondertussen was het volgens de Voedingsbond hoog tijd om met een centraal akkoord wettelijke beperking van flexibele contracten te regelen. Tegenover de FNV-strategie voor een effectieve bestrijding van de werkloosheid door herverdeling middels atv en adv nam de Voedingsbond in de nota een aarzelende houding aan. Een goede oplossing voor de in het slob geraakte atv en de tegenvallende herverdelingsresultaten, zou alleen mogelijk zijn met een drie-partijenakkoord op centraal niveau, maar daar leek het klimaat niet rijp voor. Het was in de ogen van de bond weinig zinvol wanneer afzonderlijke bonden zouden pogen de kwestie op eigen kracht op te lossen voordat er een akkoord lag. De Voedingsbond voelde er weinig voor 'mensen de "barrikaden op te jagen" voor een uurtje per week of een paar dagen extra vrije tijd [sic]'. Bovendien zou 'de kater (...) des te groter zijn, als er geen waarborgen komen', zoals tot nu toe veelal het geval was geweest.[107]

Ook de Abvakabo had te maken met bezwaren tegen atv en adv vanuit de achterban – dat de leden voor de bond aanleiding gaven kritisch te zijn, had de Industriebond terecht opgemerkt. In een brief over het arbeidsvoorwaardenbeleid uit 1987 liet de Abvakabo aan de federatie weten dat hun achterban een discussie over verdergaande algemene arbeidstijdverkorting niet zou begrijpen. 'Wij willen onze ogen niet sluiten voor het werkgelegenheidsprobleem', schreef de bond, 'maar verdergaande arbeidstijdverkorting in een situatie waarin de overheid de door ons betaalde arbeidsplaatsen net zo snel weer afbreekt, is niet goed denk-

104 IISG, FNV, inv. 2584, Notitie VB afroep en cao, 5 april 1984.

105 IISG, FNV, inv. 2584, Inventarisatie 1985, 30 augustus 1985.

106 IISG, FNV, inv. 2584, Discussienota AVB VB 1986/1987, 1985.

107 IISG, FNV, inv. 2585, Nota AVB VB 1990, december 1989.

baar'.[108] Verdergaan met arbeidstijdverkorting moest alleen onder strenge voorwaarden ten aanzien van koopkrachtontwikkeling, de gelijke behandeling van man en vrouw, en volledige herbezetting zonder dat dit ten koste zou gaan van de Abvakabo-leden. Daarbij pleitte de ambtenarenbond voor afspraken op centraal niveau, maar wel onder twee duidelijke voorwaarden: dit mocht niet leiden tot eenzijdig opgedrongen arbeidstijdverkorting en met het kabinet konden alleen afspraken gemaakt worden als de gelijke behandeling van mannen en vrouwen op tafel kwam. Daarnaast was flexibilisering voor de Abvakabo een belangrijk thema. De bond schreef in de nota *Een nieuw begin: Discussienota inzake de te voeren strategie* uit 1986 dat ze wilde zorgen dat nieuwe ontwikkelingen waaronder flexibilisering een plaats zouden krijgen in het centraal overleg.[109]

Tot slot wilde de Vervoersbond tegen het einde van de jaren tachtig nadrukkelijk leren van de negatieve gevolgen van het FNV-beleid voor atv. De bond zag anno 1989 enerzijds alle reden om door te gaan met herverdeling van werk om zo nieuwe arbeidsplaatsen te scheppen. Anderzijds merkte deze op dat de ervaringen met arbeidstijdverkorting zeker niet altijd positief waren geweest. Door de verslechteringen die werkgevers en de overheid met de atv hadden doorgevoerd was de herbezetting voorkomen en het doel van de atv (meer banen) volgens de bond onvoldoende bereikt. 'Soms werden dus zelfs arbeidsomstandigheden verslechterd en bezuinigingen op het personeelsbestand doorgevoerd, waardoor met de ATV het tegendeel werd bereikt van wat bedoeld werd', aldus de arbeidsvoorwaardennota. In de toekomst wilde de bond niet meer dit risico lopen en de invulling van de herverdeling mocht alleen nog een verbetering van de arbeidsvoorwaarden of de kwaliteit van werk opleveren, dus 'minder onregelmatigheid' en door 'terugdringen van fleksibilisering [sic]'.[110]

De per bond sterk variërende aandacht voor flexibilisering had te maken met de verdeling en inzet van vrouwen binnen de FNV als geheel. Bij het aankaarten van (met name externe) flexibilisering als probleem hadden de Marflexvrouwen een voortrekkersrol gespeeld.[111] Op het niveau van de vakcentrale zagen bestuurders flexibilisering in 1986 als een probleem dat vooral specifieke werknemers trof. Het was daarom de taak van de FNV om zoveel mogelijk te voorkomen 'dat slechts bepaalde groepen werkne(e)m(st)ers de volle last van de flexibilisering in arbeidsvoor-

108 IISG, FNV, inv. 2584, Brief AbvaKabo aan FNV J. Stekelenburg, 9 maart 1987.

109 Ibid.; Van Dijk e.a. *Precaire polder*, 95.

110 IISG, FNV, inv. 2585, Conceptnota Voedingsbond arbeidsvoorwaardenbeleid 1989, 1988.

111 Van Dijk e.a., *Precaire polder*, 103-107.

waarden krijgen te dragen'.[112] Het waren bovendien de vrouwen van het vrouwensecretariaat (voor een deel dezelfde vrouwen als uit de Marflex-groep) die in de jaren tachtig draaiboeken voor cao-onderhandelingen opstelden met voorbeeldafspraken op het gebied van flexibilisering en vervolgens per jaar de behaalde resultaten op dat gebied inventariseerden.[113] Tegelijkertijd bestond een duidelijk verband tussen de bonden die flexibilisering als een van de prioriteiten zagen binnen het arbeidsvoorwaardenbeleid en het aantal vrouwelijke leden dat zij kenden, zoals tabel 2 toont. De Abvakabo kende een relatief hoog percentage vrouwelijke leden en vond flexibilisering een urgente kwestie. De Voedingsbond had misschien relatief weinig vrouwen ten opzichte van een Abvakabo, maar voor hen waren, zeker na het congres in 1988, vrouwen bij uitstek een doelgroep.[114] En in haar sectoren zag de Voedingsbond dat nu juist vrouwen in afroepcontracten werkten.[115] Binnen de FNV als geheel waren vrouwen sterk in de minderheid. Het aantal vrouwelijke vakbondsleden nam in jaren tachtig wel toe, net als het aantal werkzame vrouwen in Nederland. Voor de FNV waren en bleven vrouwen echter niet de *core workforce*, hun geluid werd minder vertaald in beleid en de belangenbehartiging was in mindere mate op hun prioriteiten gericht.

**Tabel 2 Vrouwen binnen de FNV en haar voorlopers**

| | Percentage vrouwelijke leden in verschillende NVV/FNV-bonden | | | Verdeling van totaal aantal vrouwelijke NVV/FNV-leden over de verschillende bonden, in procenten | | |
|---|---|---|---|---|---|---|
| | 1980 | 1986 | 1990 | 1980 | 1986 | 1990 |
| Industriebond | 5 % | 6% | 8% | 15% | 14% | 15% |
| Bouw en Hout | - | - | 1% | - | - | - |
| Voedingsbond | 11% | 14% | 17% | 4% | 5% | 5% |
| Abvakabo | 22 % | 26% | 34% | 43% | 43% | 45% |
| Vervoersbond | 3% | 3% | 5% | - | - | - |

*Bron: Corrie van Eijl, Maandag tolereren we niks meer, 334*

112 IISG, FNV, inv. 2584, Uitgangspunten AVB 1987, 6 oktober 1986.

113 IISG, FNV, inv. 2585, Draaiboek cao-onderhandelingen gericht op de verbetering van de positie van vrouwelijke werknemers, herziene versie 1988-1989, juli 1988; IISG, FNV, inv. 2585, Brief C. Inja, 20 januari 1987.

114 IISG, FNV, inv. 2585, Nota AVB VB 1990, december 1989.

115 IISG, FNV, inv. 2584, Notitie VB afroep en cao, 5 april 1984.

*Illustratie 2 Vrouwen demonstreren voor echte arbeidstijdverkorting in Utrecht, 26 maart 1983 (bron: foto Marcel Antonisse, fotocollectie Anefo, Nationaal Archief).*

Ideeën over wie de *core workforce* is, geven tegelijkertijd niet de volledige verklaring voor de houding van de FNV ten aanzien van flexibilisering en van arbeidsduur- en arbeidstijdverkorting. Net zo belangrijk was dat Wassenaar prioriteit kreeg, omdat er een akkoord lag en de organisatie in deze periode een draai maakte. De FNV en haar voorlopers hechtten al decennialang veel waarde aan centrale akkoorden. Na de oorlog kende Nederland het harmoniemodel op basis van de geleide loonpolitiek in ruil voor de opbouw van sociale zekerheid en voor werkgelegenheid. In de jaren zestig en zeventig leek het conflict even sterker de boventoon te gaan voeren. De jaren tachtig begonnen als een periode van interne discussie over professionalisering en centralisering, de rol van vakbondsdemocratie en over de vakbeweging als strijdbare organisatie van onderaf. De FNV reageerde op de economisch crisis met het voeren van acties én met het afsluiten van akkoorden.[116] In de loop van het decennium veranderde dit. In 1987 verschenen het rapport *FNV 2000*, dat het startpunt vormde voor een 'grootscheepse heroriëntatie van de vakcentrale en de aangesloten bonden. De vakbeweging moest herkenbaar worden, onder andere door veel werk te maken van persoonlijke dienstverlening aan de leden.'[117] Met de opkomst van het plan zette de FNV vooral in op professionalisering van de organisa-

116 Van Dijk e.a., *Precaire polder*, 47-48.

117 Ibid., 72.

tie en op een centralere rol voor de dienstverlening aan individuele leden. Ook binnen bonden vond een verschuiving plaats naar meer centralisatie, kanalisering en professionalisering. Er trad een verzakelijking op in de verhouding tussen leden en kaderleden en tussen kaderleden en vakbond. De werkorganisatie was in toenemende mate gericht op centraal overleg waardoor het contact met de basis verder onder druk kwam te staan.[118] In de jaren na Wassenaar, kreeg verdere inzet op en de uitwerking van het arbeidsduur en arbeidstijdverkortingsbeleid binnen de FNV de meeste prioriteit. Dat de Voedingsbond en de Abvakabo tegen het einde van het decennium vonden dat de beperking van flexibele contracten een plaats moest krijgen in het centraal overleg, of zelfs in een centraal akkoord, illustreert des te meer het belang dat de FNV en haar bonden aan akkoorden hechtten.

## Conclusie

Voor een beter begrip van flexibilisering, neoliberalisme en de relatie daartussen vormen de jaren tachtig een belangrijk decennium. Nederland kende als corporatistisch land destijds minder radicale markgerichte tendensen, zo betoogt de literatuur, maar in dezelfde periode vond een eerste ronde van sterke groei van flexibilisering plaats. Dit artikel gaat terug naar de eerste jaren na het Akkoord van Wassenaar en onderzoekt de houding en de strategie van de FNV-vakcentrale en -bonden ten aanzien van flexibilisering. Het laat zien dat de rol van de vakbeweging vraagt om een zelfstandige verklaring. En het geeft daarmee nieuw inzicht in een onderbelichte factor in het debat over de ontstaansgeschiedenis van de radicale flexibilisering van de Nederlandse arbeidsmarkt.

Vooralsnog is in wetenschappelijke studies over flexibilisering met name gekeken naar structurele veranderingen die flexibilisering onvermijdelijk en wenselijk zouden maken (o.a. Touwen) en naar de economische instituties die het op het hoogste (overleg)niveau mogelijk maakten (o.a. Sluyterman, Dekker, Keune, Boonstra, Thelen, Emmenegger). Uiteraard was de vakbeweging niet immuun voor het discours van de onvermijdelijkheid van flexibilisering als gevolg van mondiale economische ontwikkelingen, en had de vakbeweging, zoals Keetie Sluyterman en Maarten Keune laten zien, te maken met haar tanende machts-

118 Ibid., 81-82.

positie aan de onderhandelingstafels met werkgeversorganisaties en de regering. De jaren tachtig werden bovendien gekenmerkt door een economische crisis die hoge werkloosheid tot gevolg had en veranderingen in de economie versnelden die de macht van de vakbeweging onder druk zetten. Maar de vakbeweging was geen homogene beweging en de rol van de vakbeweging kan niet worden gereduceerd tot haar formele invloed op economische besluitvorming in de landelijke politiek. Om ook de veel complexere eigenstandige organisatorische en sociale dynamiek van de vakbeweging in ogenschouw te kunnen nemen, hanteert dit artikel een sociaalhistorisch perspectief. Door de verschillende vakbondsstrategieën ten aanzien van flexibilisering naast elkaar te leggen – van landelijke akkoorden tot de cao- en arbeidsvoorwaardenstrategie en het actievoeren – geven we een plaats aan de meerdere functies (of rollen) die de vakbeweging heeft in het Nederlandse politiek-sociale landschap. Zo komen we tot een diepgaander en meer historisch gecontextualiseerde verklaring voor de ruimte die al vroeg ontstond in Nederland voor de flexibilisering van arbeidsverhoudingen.

Het onderzoek op basis van de cao-dossiers laat zien dat de FNV de ontwikkelingen rond flexibilisering signaleerde én veel ruimte gaf. Vakbondsmensen van verschillende bonden, uit verschillende belangengroepen en uit verschillende niveaus binnen de vakbeweging waren zich destijds overduidelijk bewust van het feit dat snelle ontwikkelingen plaatsvonden op dit gebied. De FNV ontwikkelde daarom een eigen visie op werk in de postindustriële samenleving: de kansen en met name de problemen die specifieke vormen van flexibilisering creëerden. En men kwam tot de conclusie dat de opkomst van externe flexibilisering in verband stond met de beginselafspraken uit het Akkoord van Wassenaar. Al snel bleek dat de vakbondsinzet op arbeidsduur- en arbeidstijdverkorting invloed had op het toenemend aantal tijdelijke krachten, thuiswerk(st)ers, oproepkrachten of uitzendkrachten. Toch veranderde na deze constatering de strategie van de vakbeweging tegenover atv en flex niet. Geluiden van onderaf die vanaf midden jaren tachtig te horen waren, drongen weinig door. In de tweede helft van de jaren tachtig (vanaf 1986/1987) groeide de aandacht vanuit het vakbondskader (leden en professionals) en kreeg flexibilisering kort een belangrijkere plaats in het centraal gecoordineerde arbeidsvoorwaardenbeleid. Maar dat was van korte duur. Zelfs toen aan het eind van het decennium bleek dat de inzet op arbeidstijdverkorting nauwelijks vruchten afwierp, draaide de centrale strategie wederom om het vasthouden aan de afspraken van Wassenaar. Gedurende het gehele decennium zette de FNV de middelen die zij tot haar beschikking had (nationale akkoorden, arbeidsvoorwaardenbeleid en acties) vooral in om arbeidstijdverkorting te bewerkstelligen en veel minder om flexibilisering tegen te gaan. De werkorganisatie was daarbij met verloop van tijd in toenemende mate gericht op het centraal overleg. En terwijl de FNV de meeste tijd en energie stak in het verzilveren van de beginselafspraken over arbeidsduurverkorting en arbeidstijdverkorting, gaven werkgevers prioriteit aan flexibilisering en stuitten daarbij dus op weinig verzet van de FNV.

Niet alle bonden waren het eens met de gecoördineerde strategie tegenover atv en flex, waarbij bonden die kritisch waren over flex ook kritischer waren over de grote prioriteit die het doorvoeren van arbeidstijdverkorting kreeg. Mede door de interne verdeeldheid over de prioriteit van atv en de te volgen strategie ten aanzien van flexibilisering, en doordat vrouwen vaak nog niet tot de *core workforce* werden gerekend, kwam hier geen verandering in. De afspraken van Wassenaar en de inzet op het binnenhalen van die uitruil (het was immers een akkoord geweest van aanbevelingen en beloftes) kregen de prioriteit. Deze keuze betekende dat de FNV minder tijd en aandacht kon besteden aan het complexe flexilibiliseringsdossier. Doordat de werkorganisatie daarbij steeds meer belang hechtte aan het bereiken van doelstellingen via het centraal overleg, kwam het contact met de basis verder onder druk te staan. De negatieve effecten van de herordening en flexibilisering van de arbeidsmarkt werden om deze redenen niet bestreden. Dat beleid gaf werkgevers, die sterk inzetten op flexibilisering, de ruimte die ze nodig hadden: ze zagen hun kans schoon de vrijgekomen arbeidsplaatsen op te vullen met een flexibele schil. De vakbondstop deed in 1996 uiteindelijk een poging tot regulering door een landelijk akkoord. De wetenschappelijke literatuur besteedt tot op heden vrijwel alleen aandacht aan deze vertraagde reactie in het Flexakkoord van 1996.

Dit artikel keek naar de vakbeweging als sociale bewegingsorganisatie om beter te begrijpen wat de effecten van ideeën en beleid zijn en welke de rol instituties van het sociaal overleg in de totstandkoming daarvan spelen. Juist de combinatie van krachten gegenereerd *vanuit* en *door* een akkoord onder de sociale partners (op het hoogste niveau) enerzijds, alsmede de interne dynamiek anderzijds, waren bepalend voor de houding van de vakbeweging tegenover flexibilisering van arbeid in de jaren tachtig. Daarbij was niet de economische crisis zelf de belangrijkste ontwikkeling voor de FNV, maar vooral de veranderende dynamiek die ontstond door het Akkoord van Wassenaar. De les voor de huidige wetenschappelijke en maatschappelijke discussies over de ingrijpende veranderingen in de politieke economie in de afgelopen veertig jaar – en dan met name de doorbraak van het neoliberalisme – is dat het kijken naar veranderende ideeën en overheidsbeleid alleen niet voldoende is. Om de rol van de vakbeweging verder te ontleden zou vervolgonderzoek zich bijvoorbeeld kunnen richten op de congressen die de vakbeweging in deze periode organiseerde en de debatten die zich daar ontspinden, maar bijvoorbeeld ook op de effecten van organisatie- en actievormen ten aanzien van de veranderende sociaal-economische uitdagingen waarvoor de vakbeweging kwam te staan. Dit artikel keek onder andere naar concept- en discussienota's, die op de congressen zijn besproken en naar aanleiding daarvan zijn aangepast. Het bestuderen van congresverslagen, archiefmateriaal in bedrijfsdossiers en het afnemen van interviews zouden een volgende stap kunnen zijn. Het onderzoek naar de sterke veranderingen in de organisatie van werk en arbeidsmarkt in de afgelopen veertig jaar is in ieder geval gebaat bij meer aandacht voor de vakbeweging en haar interne dynamiek.

## Over de auteurs

**Rosa Kösters (1993)** is PhD Researcher at the International Institute of Social History (IISH). Her project looks at the consequences and reactions of Dutch workers and trade unions to changing labour relations from 1970-2020. She studied History at the University of Amsterdam (*cum laude*). For her research master thesis on the transformation in work and work floor solidarities at Philips and Hoogovens in the 1970s and 1980s, Rosa won the Dutch Thesis Award for Studies of the Labour Movement 2018. She participated in the IISH and FNV project *Exploring the recent History of Labour Union Practices* in 2017 and is co-author of *Precaire Polder*. In collaboration with The Scientific Bureau for the Dutch Trade Union Movement she published *De vakbond en de werkvloer, op zoek naar nieuwe relaties* (2020).
Email: rosa.kosters@iisg.nl

**Loran van Diepen (1990)** was a research assistant at the project *Exploring the recent History of Labour Union Practices* in 2017, which resulted in the report *Precaire Polder* (2018). In that year, he also completed his research master in History. In his thesis *Wie verdient welvaart?* he investigated how welfare policy in the Wieringermeerpolder (1910-1940) was profoundly influenced by ideas about the promotion of welfare in the Dutch East Indies. From 2018 to 2019 he was as an archivist at the International Institute of Social History (IISH) in-

volved in creating an inventory and descriptions for the FNV archive. In 2019 he returned to education. He now works as a teacher at primary school 't Koggeschip in Amsterdam.
Email: loran.vandiepen@hotmail.com

**Moira van Dijk (1980)** is a historian and currently works as a curator at the International Institute of Social History (IISH). She is responsible for collection development on Germany, the United Kingdom and international organizations. Before this, Moira was a researcher at the IISH involved in the (preliminary) study of the recent history of the Dutch trade union movement, for which she co-authored the report *Precaire Polder* and the article 'Terugblikken om meer te zien! Een historische reflectie op vakbeweging, strategie en onderzoek'.
Email: moira.van.dijk@iisg.nl

**Matthias van Rossum** is Senior Researcher at the International Institute of Social History (IISH). He currently holds the role of vice-chair at the European Labour History Network (ELHN). Matthias specializes in social and labour history and his publications cover in particular the history of slavery and the slave trade, social relations and strategies of resistance. As a (co-)applicant he is involved in projects in the field of diversity and racialisation (*Resilient Diversity*) and the history of slavery (*Exploring Slave Trade in Asia; Between local debts and global markets*). He was project leader of *Exploring the recent History of Labour Union Practices*, which resulted in the report *Precaire Polder*.
Email: mvr@iisg.nl

# Sound Toll Registers Online[1]

Jan Willem Veluwenkamp, Werner Scheltjens and Siem van der Woude

TSEG 18 (1): 147–160
DOI: 10.18352/tseg.1203

In 2020, the University of Groningen and Tresoar, the Frisian Historical and Literary Center in Leeuwarden, completed the online database providing instant and free access to the complete Sound Toll Registers. This database, Sound Toll Registers Online (STRO), is already available to everyone at www.soundtoll.nl. Huygens ING is now taking over STRO from Tresoar and the University of Groningen to ensure its quality, accessibility and continuity. The realization of STRO has been funded by the Dutch Research Council (NWO), several cultural foundations, the Samenwerkende Maritieme Fondsen (Cooperating Maritime Funds), ING Huygens, the University of Groningen and Tresoar. The keeper of the Sound Toll Registers, the Danish National Archives, has supported us with encouragement and scholarly advice while building the STRO database.

1 This article intends to give greater publicity to Sound Toll Registers Online and to promote its use for research. It is an independent and complete paper, although, in the course of the last several years, we published other articles with the same purpose and with largely the same content. Sometimes, in these articles, we also presented results of research using STRO. Accordingly, earlier versions of this article have been published as J.W. Veluwenkamp, 'Sonttolregisters Online', *Tijdschrift voor Zeegeschiedenis* 38:2 (2019) 75-78; W. Scheltjens, J. W. Veluwenkamp and S. van der Woude, 'A closer look. STRO as an instrument for the study of early modern maritime history', in: J.W. Veluwenkamp and W. Scheltjens (eds.), *Early modern shipping and trade. Novel approaches using Sound Toll Registers Online* (Leiden and Boston 2018) 1-18; J.W. Veluwenkamp, '"Die Sound Toll Registers Online" als Instrument für die Erforschung des frühneuzeitlichen Ostseehandels', in: P. Rauscher and A. Serles (eds.), *Wiegen – zählen – registrieren. Handelsgeschichtliche Massenquellen und die Erforschung mitteleuropäischer Märkte (13.-18. Jahrhundert)* (Innsbruck [etc.] 2015) 365-384; and as parts of W. Scheltjens and J.W. Veluwenkamp, 'Sound Toll Registers Online. Introduction and first research examples', *International Journal of Maritime History* XXIV:1 (2012) 301-330.

## The Sound Toll Registers and the Sound Toll Tables

The Sound Toll Registers (STR) are the records of the toll levied by the kings of Denmark on the ships passing through the Sound, the main strait connecting the North Sea and the Baltic Sea. For centuries, the kings' bureaucrats administered this Sound Toll – *Øresundstolden* in Danish – in the small town of Helsingør, north of Copenhagen, where the strait is at its narrowest. The accounts of the toll have been preserved for intermittent years between 1497 and 1573, and practically entirely for the period from 1574 to 1857, when the Sound Toll was abolished. They cover about 300 of the 360 years between 1497 and 1857. The Sound Toll Registers – or *Øresundstoldbøgerne* – contain information on about 1.8 million passages. They are stored by the Danish National Archives in Copenhagen, where more than 700 volumes occupy about 60 meters of shelf space.[2]

The information the kings' bureaucrats entered in the registers for each ship's passage was initially limited to the passage year, the name of the shipmaster, his place of residence, the toll amount paid and, when relevant, the toll amount paid for any cargo of wine. Information increased with the gradual introduction of additional tolls in the course of the centuries. It reached its more or less definitive form by the eighteenth century, when for each individual passage, both westward and eastward, the STR contain the declaration date, the name of the shipmaster, his place of residence,[3] his ports of departure and destination, the composition of the cargo and the toll paid.

The STR are well known as one of the great serial sources of early modern history and the only one with rich and detailed information on European shipping and trade that spans a period of four centuries. They are a central source for social, economic and maritime history on all levels: global, European, national, regional and local.[4] In the first half of the twentieth century, the Danish historians Nina Ellinger Bang and

2 E. Gøbel, 'The Sound Toll Registers Online project', *International Journal of Maritime History* XXII:2 (2010) 305-324, there 305-308.

3 There is a protracted historiographical discussion concerning the question if the STR actually list the shipmasters' places of residence. The – Danish – wording in the source is, for example: *Willem Blocker af Horn*. It is our interpretation that – generally – the shipmaster lived in the place mentioned – in this case Hoorn. Some, however, have argued that the toponym refers to the homeport of the ship. Boon discusses the matter briefly in P. Boon, 'Dutch connections to Scandinavia. The case of the West Frisian seaman abroad and at home', in: M. Guldberg, P. Holm and P.K. Madsen (eds.), *Facing the North Sea. West Jutland and the world* (Esbjerg 1993), 87-101, there 95-98.

4 Scheltjens, Veluwenkamp and Van der Woude, 'A closer look', 2.

*Illustration 1 Gerard van Keulen & son, The Sound in bird's eye view, seen to the south, Amsterdam 1727 (source: Nederlands Scheepvaart Museum).*

Knud Korst published a monumental seven-volume work providing an ample summary of the STR: *Tabeller over skibsfart og varetransport gennem Øresund*, internationally known as the Sound Toll Tables (STT).[5] Ever since the publication of the first volume of the STT in 1906, these tables, rather than the STR themselves, have been used in almost every major study of early modern European transport and trade; only a few researchers have dived into the original source.[6]

## Sound Toll Registers Online

Sound Toll Registers Online was initiated in 2006, by a project team from Tresoar and the University of Groningen, to improve access to the

5 N. Ellinger Bang and K. Korst, *Tabeller over skibsfart og vaeretransport gennem Oeresund 1497-1783*, 7 volumes (Copenhagen and Leipzig 1906-1953).

6 See also M. van Tielhof, *The 'mother of all trades'. The Baltic grain trade in Amsterdam from the late 16th to the early 19th century* (Leiden [etc.] 2002). Christensen has used both the STT and the STR in A.E. Christensen, *Dutch trade to the Baltic around 1600* (Copenhagen and The Hague 1941). The same is true for Boon in P. Boon, 'West Friesland and the Sound (1681-1720)', in: W.G. Heeres et al.(eds.), *From Dunkirk to Danzig. Shipping and trade in the North Sea and the Baltic, 1350-1850* (Hilversum 1988) 171-189. Scheltjens uses the STR in, for instance, W. Scheltjens, 'The changing geography of demand for Dutch maritime transport in the eighteenth century', *Histoire et Mesure* XXVII:2 (2012) 5-47. Ahonen uses the STR extensively in K. Ahonen, *From sugar triangle to cotton triangle. Trade and shipping between America and Baltic Russia, 1783-1860* (Jyväskylä 2005).

data included in the Sound Toll Registers.[7] After securing the necessary funding, we constructed the database in two phases. From 2009 to 2013, we outsourced the data entry to Breed, the sheltered workplace for Nijmegen and the surrounding area. We accepted or rejected the records Breed produced after a quality check by random sample.[8] Initially, we accepted an error rate of two percent, allowing two out of every hundred records Breed produced to contain serious faults. When it became evident that this quality level was set too high, we increased the accepted error rate to five percent. After accepting a batch of records, we corrected the data and added them to the online database.

In 2013, the cooperation with Breed was ended by mutual agreement. One of the reasons was of a financial nature, due to the unexpected workload required. In the years from 1633 to the nineteenth century, the information for each individual passage was recorded in one entry in the original Sound Toll Registers and, consequently, was entered in one record of the database. However, when Breed began to work on the registers from the years before 1634, it became clear that, in those years, it often occurred that the information for an individual passage was recorded in several entries in the STR and, consequently, had to be entered in several records in the database. This meant that to enter the data for the 300,000 passages that remained at that moment and to complete the database, an estimated 700,000 entries had to be completed. Since we had no budget for that, we had to organize the data entry in another way.

We turned to volunteers. To facilitate this, we contracted the Meertens Institute to create a data entry application, which allowed participants with a laptop and internet connection to work from home. In October 2013, a few volunteers began entering data and testing the system live.[9] When it was clear that the system worked properly, we began to recruit volunteers on a larger scale. By the spring of 2016, a stable group of about 50 participants had formed and was entering data. Many of them regularly attended the instruction and consultation meetings we held every week in Leeuwarden and Groningen, and every other week in Zwolle and Amsterdam. Here, we taught them how to

7 Jan Willem Veluwenkamp (University of Groningen) and Siem van der Woude (Tresoar) managed the project. George Welling (University of Groningen) designed the database in the application phase. Douwe de Vries (then Director of Tresoar) and the late Rienk Wegener Sleeswijk encouraged and supported us.

8 Mark de Lannoy, Johan Steendam and Ubo Kooijinga (Tresoar) carried out the checks.

9 Volunteers Siep Maat, Klaas Dantuma and Anneke Westerhuis did excellent work at that stage.

read the old Danish handwriting, discussed problems with reading and entering data, and gave feedback on the work they had delivered. Again, we added records to the database after checking them.

Sound Toll Registers Online includes for each passage[10] the following information:

- the passage date
- the shipmaster's name
- the shipmaster's place of residence
- the port of departure
- the port of destination (from the mid-1660s; before that, they were not recorded in the STR)
- the nature and quantity of the cargo
- the toll paid

The data was entered into the database in the Danish language as used in the original source, including all early modern spelling variants to avoid contamination by premature interpretation. The spelling variations of personal names, geographical names, commodity names, measures and weights are almost without limit. Obviously, standardized spelling facilitates data analysis, but so far we have only standardized the spelling of the geographical names, while preserving the original input in the database and keeping it accessible there.[11]

The database has four basic tables: passage, cargo, taxes and images. The *passage table* basically contains one record for each passage, including fields for the date and the shipmaster's name and place of residence. It does not contain fields for the cargo and the ports of departure and destination, as many ships carried several commodities and the ports of departure and destination could differ per commodity. Accordingly, the *cargo table* contains per passage records for each commodity mentioned there, including fields for the commodity's ports of departure and destination and for the tax paid per commodity. The separate *taxes table* contains records with fields for the tax or, in many cases, the several taxes levied per passage. The *images table* contains records with a field that connects the passage record with the scans of the relevant folio of the original source. The four tables are connectable by a common identity field.

10 More precisely: for each STR entry. As discussed in the main text, passages were often recorded in more than one entry in the STR before 1634.

11 George Welling (University of Groningen) and Frank Bosmans (Tresoar) standardized the geographical names.

*Illustration 2 Data entry for Sound Toll Registers Online at Tresoar, Leeuwarden, 2015. (© Bob de Boer Photography).*

STRO is essentially an instrument for historical research. It allows one to make all conceivable cross tabs and to carry out any statistical analysis.[12] It includes a user interface, facilitating the selection of passage records by applying search terms for time periods, shipmaster names and places of residence, ports of departure and destination, and cargoes.[13] Researchers may download the results and process them with applications like Microsoft Excel and Access.

## From the STR via the STT to STRO

The Sound Toll Registers are an extremely valuable source, but their sheer volume and detail make them virtually impossible to handle. It was in their effort to make the STR more suitable for researchers that Ellinger Bang and Kort produced the Sound Toll Tables (STT). As mentioned above, historians have indeed preferred using the STT to the STR. Accordingly, the STT have had enormous significance for historical research.

12 Welling and Bosmans also designed the database.

13 Bosmans produced the user interface in the execution phase.

The importance of the STT, however, should not conceal their shortcomings. These limitations have been extensively discussed in the historiography.[14] First of all, the STT only cover the years 1497-1783 while the STR also include the years 1784-1857. Second, they only present data on a high level of aggregation, so that individual passages have disappeared from sight. Third, the way they combine commodities in categories is sometimes quite haphazard and blurs details. As a result, the STT offer only limited possibilities for analyzing the original data.[15] These complications have even led many scholars to content themselves with consulting the articles Unger published when new volumes of the STT first were published, and which included condensed tables based on the STT.[16]

The unwieldiness of the STR and the limitations of the STT were among the reasons we built STRO. That does not mean that STRO is without intricacies or that it can be used thoughtlessly. It should be handled with care and with an understanding of its potential and its limitations. The individual researcher must be aware of these when using it. A few remarks explaining some of the complications of the STR and STRO offer clarification.

14 See, for example: Gøbel, 'The Sound Toll Registers Online project'; P. Jeannin, 'Les comptes du Sund comme source pour la construction d'indices généraux de l'activité économique en Europe (XVIe-XVIIe siècle)', in: P. Jeannin, *Marchands du Nord. Espaces et trafics à l'époque modern* (Paris 1996) 1-62; A.E. Christensen, 'Der handelsgeschichtliche Wert der Sundzollregister. Ein Beitrag zu seiner Beurteilung', *Hansische Geschichtsblätter* 59 (1934) 28-142; E.F. Heckscher, 'Öresundsräkenskaperna och deras behandlings', *Historisk Tidskrift* (1942) 170-186.

15 Gøbel, ,'The Sound Toll Registers Online project', 321-322; Jeannin, 'Les comptes du Sund'.

16 W.S. Unger, 'De Sonttabellen', *Tijdschrift voor Geschiedenis* 41 (1926) 137-155; W.S. Unger, 'De publikatie der Sonttabellen voltooid', *Tijdschrift voor Geschiedenis* 71 (1958) 147-205; W.S. Unger, 'Trade through the Sound in the seventeenth and eighteenth centuries', *The Economic History Review*, New Series 12:2 (1959) 206-221. A few examples of the use of the STT and Unger's articles in Dutch historiography are: C.J. van Bochove, *The economic consequences of the Dutch. Economic integration around the North Sea, 1500-1800* (Utrecht 2008) 264-265; Van Tielhof, *The 'mother of all trades'*, 43, 49, 51, 53, 55, 59, 70, 73; R.W. Unger, 'The Dutch trade in rye. Comparative capital requirements in the seventeenth and eighteenth centuries', in: C.A. Davids, W. Fritschy and L.A. van der Valk (eds.), *Kapitaal, ondernemerschap en beleid. Studies over economie en politiek in Nederland, Europa en Azië van 1500 tot heden. Afscheidsbundel voor prof.dr. P.W. Klein* (Amsterdam 1996) 121-140, there 127; J.I. Israel, *Dutch primacy in world trade, 1585-1740* (Oxford 1989) 57, 93, 118, 129, 139, 144, 202, 214, 216-217, 301, 366, 381; J.A. Faber, 'Friesland and the Baltic trade', in: Heeres et al. (eds.), *From Dunkirk to Danzig*, 13-21; E. Harder-Gersdorff, 'Avoiding Sound traffic and Sound toll. Russian leather and tallow going West via Archangel and Narva-Lübeck (1650-1710)' in: Heeres et al. (eds.), *From Dunkirk to Danzig*, 237-261, there 242-244; F. Snapper, 'Commerce, ships and war in the Baltic from the rise of the Hanseatic League till the French Revolution' in: Heeres et al. (eds.), *From Dunkirk to Danzig*, 405-428, there 420-422.

## The reliability of the Sound Toll Registers

The Sound Toll Registers are a fiscal source. The Danish bureaucrats kept them not to produce statistics for future researchers but to give an accounting of the toll they levied to the king. The STR have been the subject of extensive source criticism. The discussions amount to three main concerns about their reliability. First, there were other routes from Western Europe to the Baltic Sea area, including the ones through the Little Belt and the Great Belt, the overland route, the sea route to Russia via the North Cape and, from 1784 on, the Schleswig-Holstein Canal. Although each of these routes may not have offered a serious alternative to the Sound, taken together they should not be omitted from the analysis of trade flows.

Hardly anything is known about the traffic through the Little Belt except that this strait was hard to navigate because of its winding channels and strong currents, and using it implied a long detour for ships sailing to and from the Baltic Sea.[17] It was, probably, only significant for local transport.[18] Only a minority of the shipmasters sailed the Great Belt, as this channel was much harder to navigate than the Sound, while the same toll tariffs were applied in both straits.[19] The traffic here was mainly regional, predominantly connecting Lübeck and Rostock with Danish and Norwegian ports. The overland route to present-day eastern Germany, Poland and Russia was only relevant for the transport of low-weight, low-volume and expensive commodities.[20] The Schleswig-Holstein Canal between Tönning on the North Sea and Kiel on the Baltic Sea was opened in 1784, but only small ships could pass through it and it never attracted a lot of traffic.[21] Finally, the sea route to Russia via the White Sea port of Archangel was the main gateway to Russia during the long seventeenth century, when Russia did not have its own Baltic port. It was the main and preferred alternative for the routing of Russia's foreign trade via the Baltic Sea and the possessions of Sweden and other lands between the sea and Russia. Vital as it was to Russia, this route involved usually much less than ten percent of the Sound traffic.[22]

17 Gøbel, 'The Sound Toll Registers Online project', 319-320. Gøbel mentions that toll registers of the Little Belt have been preserved for the years 1816-1857; Jeannin, 'Les comptes du Sund', 12.

18 Jeannin, 'Les comptes du Sund', 12.

19 Gøbel, 'The Sound Toll Registers Online project', 319; Jeannin, 'Les comptes du Sund', 12.

20 Jeannin, 'Les comptes du Sund', 4, 6, 12.

21 Gøbel, 'The Sound Toll Registers Online project', 319-320.

22 Jeannin, 'Les comptes du Sund', 4-5.

The second concern about the STR's reliability involves fraud. This did not mean stealing through the Sound without paying the toll. The chance of success in this respect was very low, as officials observed and guarded the strait from Kronborg castle and with the royal guard ship cruising it. It is widely accepted that all ships that sailed through the Sound in the years covered by the STR were recorded. Shipmasters, nevertheless, certainly evaded payment of part of the toll due by making false declarations of the commodities. Clearance was based on the ships' documents, such as the bills of lading, though the customs officers were entitled to search the ships. Obviously, this did not stop all shipmasters from trying their luck. Comparison with other sources, especially customs accounts from individual ports – the dependability of which is incidentally problematic, too – has shown that the information on cargoes in the STR is generally correct but not complete.[23] The extent of the fraud differed per period and per commodities category. Expensive commodities of small volume were always more subject to fraud.[24] For bulky commodities like grain, flax and hemp, the picture is slightly different. Here, before 1618, especially in the period 1580-1618, fraud was enormous, fluctuating perhaps between 25 and 50 percent. This may be explained by the fact that the customs officers seem hardly to have checked the declarations. In 1618, this changed. From then on, the customs officers carried out more systematic checks, reducing fraud for conspicuous bulk goods.[25]

A third reason that the STR must be handled with care is the fact that sometimes parties were exempted from paying the toll. This applies to Danish ships and goods throughout the period and to Swedish vessels and commodities between 1650 and 1710.[26] Exempted passages were recorded, though often without mention of the relevant cargoes, and, in any case, usually without mention of their quantities. Nonetheless, alternative routes, fraud and exemptions cannot alter the fact that the STR are a great source and starting point for the study of trade and transport during the period covered. As always, the researcher must be aware of the limitations of the source, in this case especially with regard to cargoes.[27]

23 Gøbel, 'The Sound Toll Registers Online project', 319-321.

24 Jeannin, 'Les comptes du Sund', 33, 38; Van Tielhof, *The 'mother of all trades'*, 42.

25 Jeannin, 'Les comptes du Sund', 21, 37-39.

26 Jeannin, 'Les comptes du Sund', 39-40.

27 Gøbel, 'The Sound Toll Registers Online project', 319.

## The intricacies of Sound Toll Registers Online

STRO is an interpretation of the STR and not compiled as a source edition. It is constructed as an organic historical source fitted into a much more sterile database. With the source criticism of the STR in mind, the researcher also needs to understand the details of STRO. Only the most obvious of these can be briefly discussed here.

First and foremost, we have only entered the STR toll collection entries proper into the database and have omitted a large quantity of additional information. This mainly involves the recurrent introductory, accounting and justifying texts the toll officials noted. In addition, as the database has a strict format, we could not include the extra information the officials sometimes added in the passage entries. This information is diverse. It may involve the owner or addressee of part of the cargo, a ship having been stranded, or a rotted part of the cargo. In order not to completely lose sight of that information, we have, as a rule, put a reference in the field '*opmerking bron*'– 'remark on the source'. This reference is often worded only as '*stuk Deense tekst*' – 'piece of Danish text' – with no further details.

Not all entry problems were solved after extra information had been dealt with – or disposed of – in this way. The STR developed organically over more than three and a half centuries so that their form and precise content changed and varied from one period to the other. This means that we had to handle all kinds of peculiarities to fit the content of the STR entries proper into the database. The three most conspicuous examples are connected to the recording of the value of a commodity, the formulas '*giør*' and '*er*', and references in one STR entry to another. We briefly discuss them in the following paragraphs.

Usually, the STR record commodities – the components of the cargo – by stating the quantity, the unit of measure and the commodity, e.g., *60 læster rug* (60 lasts of rye).[28] Sometimes the unit of measure and the quantity involve an amount of money, e.g., *for 800 rd. kramerie* (for 800 rixdollars peddler's wares).[29] The value per unit of the commodity is also sometimes recorded, for example: *156 fad stads viin à 52 rd.* (156 casks of town wine at 52 rixdollars per cask).[30] In this case, we enter the value per cask into the database as part of the commodity: '*stads viin à 52 rd.*' Sometimes, the STR record commodities with a second meas-

28 www.soundtoll.nl, record 152363, 25 August 1783.

29 www.soundtoll.nl, record 81863, 11 November 1783.

30 www.soundtoll.nl, record 96205, 16 May 1783.

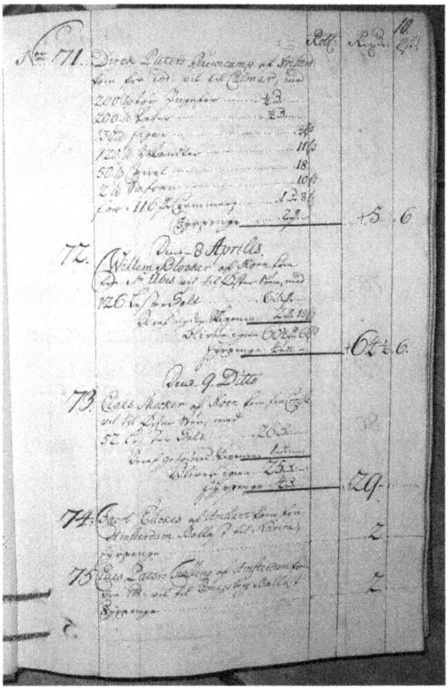

*Illustration 3 Entry from the Sound Toll Registers, 1734 (source: Danish National Archives, Copenhagen).*

ure, e.g., *42 læster rug etc. giør 50 2/5 læst* (42 lasts of rye etc., i.e., 50 2/5 lasts) or *36 læster hveede er 45 læst* (36 lasts of wheat, i.e., 45 lasts).[31] We have interpreted the formulas '*giør*' and '*er*' as 'that is to say' or 'i.e.'. In these cases, we have entered the second measure in a separate field as an alternative measure.

In approximately less than 0.6 percent of the STR entries, there is a reference to another entry, characterized by the term '*Vide Fol.*' and followed by the relevant folio number and passage number.[32] These references usually involve corrections of or additions to earlier entries. We have indicated these references concisely in the field '*opmerking bron*' – 'remark on the source' – as well as mentioning the folio and passage numbers and the relevant shipmaster name and place of residence. It is up to the researcher to further work through these references.

Finally, despite all efforts to maximize correct reproduction of the content of the STR entries, it is inevitable that the database contains many small errors and perhaps a few omissions. However, errors in the original spelling hardly affect the substance of the information. In other cases, the user will have to rely on their critical mind and knowledge to avoid mistakes and errant interpretations. We are confident that the

31 www.soundtoll.nl, record 75437, 23 March 1783; record 82520, 5 May 1783.

32 For example www.soundtoll.nl, record 119865, 21 August 1783.

quality of the information in the database allows all queries to produce accurate results. Moreover, the digitized originals in the database allow researchers to verify the information.

## Research and research prospects

Before STRO was available, historians used the STR and the STT mainly to produce statistics of rather generally categorized ship movements and commodity flows. Now, STRO allows the researcher to exploit easily the richness of the STR to a depth that used to be hardly attainable. Analyses that were previously almost inconceivable can now be carried out quickly and easily, and the STR's different dimensions – particularly place, time, cargoes and shipmasters – can be instantly combined in all the detail of the original source and on every conceivable level of aggregation.

Most evident is the utilization of STRO for the research of basic structures and developments of trade and transport of individual commodities or commodity categories on a local, regional, national or global level. An early publication exploring these possibilities discusses the flow of coffee to the Baltic region countries in the eighteenth century, including the breakdown into the countries from where the carrying ships left and where they were destined.[33] Another article analyzes Stockholm's foreign trade in the period from 1770 to 1790, including the breakdown into commodity categories per country of origin and destination.[34] Basic analyses like these also provide indications of the size, development and shifts of production and consumption of raw materials, textiles, luxuries, foodstuffs and many other things.[35] Consequently, they can help to study broader problem areas of social and economic history, like the industrial and industrious revolutions. An obvious point of departure in this respect is the development of the transport of industry-related commodities such as coal, machines and cotton through the Sound.[36]

33 M. Draper and J.W. Veluwenkamp, 'Sound Toll Registers Online and the eighteenth century Baltic coffee commerce', *Groniek* 200 (2014) 279-294.

34 S. Lilja, 'The Sound Toll Registers as a mirror of Stockholm's foreign trade c. 1770-1790', in: Veluwenkamp and Scheltjens (eds.), *Early modern shipping and trade*, 41-58.

35 See for example the analysis of the rhubarb and sarsaparilla traffic through the Sound in: J.W. Veluwenkamp and W. Scheltjens, 'Baltic drugs traffic, 1650-1850. Sound Toll Registers Online as a source for the import of exotic medicines in the Baltic Sea area', *Social History of Medicine* 31:1 (2018) 140-176.

36 Ahonen, *From sugar triangle to cotton triangle* could have been a fine example, but that study appeared years before the start of the STRO project and Ahonen uses the original STR.

STRO is a gold mine for detailed in-depth exploration and analysis. Micro-historical research employing STRO can focus on many things. A single port of departure or destination, one place of residence, however big or small, a route, a commodity, even the itineraries of any individual shipmaster may be the starting point for innovative research and contribute to the social and economic history of the early modern and modern periods. One example is an article presenting a methodology for estimating the volume of timber shipped from the Baltic Sea area to Spain in the period 1670-1806.[37] The history of the countless and clustered shipmaster communities all along the coasts of Europe and America lies largely fallow but can be fruitfully explored using STRO, as two studies on the shipmaster communities in the Dutch province of Friesland in the early modern period exemplify.[38] Apart from its significance for local and regional history, the study of these communities can contribute to understanding the structure and the development of the maritime labour market and national and international infrastructures and logistics and, consequently, to gaining insights into social and economic developments in general.[39]

Similarly, STRO can also help gauge the impact of political decisions and developments on international trade, revealing short-term crises and spikes in commodity flows and facilitating studies on the impact of trade blockades, port sieges, war and the threat of war on transport through the Sound. Indeed, practically any analysis of traffic using STRO will show the effects of war, with the French Revolutionary and Napoleonic Wars standing out.[40] Possibilities in this field are also shown in an analysis of the way the partitions of Poland and the connected mercantilist policies of Prussia and Russia rechannelled the trade flows between Western Europe and the Baltic Sea's southern ports.[41]

STRO is not a research agenda but a research instrument which is being used already. Examples are provided by two edited books, which

37 N. Gallagher, 'A methodology for estimating the volume of Baltic timber to Spain using the Sound Toll Registers: 1670-1806', *The International Journal of Maritime History* 28:4 (2016) 752-773.

38 J.J. Koopmans, *Vrachtvaarders van Europa. Een onderzoek naar schippers afkomstig uit Makkum in Friesland van 1600 tot 1820* (Hilversum 2020); S. Steenbeek, *Schipperen in Friesland. De ontwikkeling van maritieme schippersgemeenschappen in Friesland in de vroegmoderne tijd* (Groningen 2017).

39 An example is W. Scheltjens, *Dutch deltas. Emergence, functions and structure of the Low Countries' maritime transport system ca. 1300-1850* (Leiden and Boston 2015).

40 This is illustrated by J.W. Veluwenkamp, 'Pekelder schippers in de achttiende eeuw. Van turfvaart naar kustvaart' *Jaarboek Noordelijk Scheepvaartmuseum 2016* (Groningen 2017) 25-31.

41 M. Ressel, 'The impact of the Partitions of Poland on the structure of Baltic trade', in: Veluwenkamp and Scheltjens (eds.), *Early modern shipping and trade*, 21-40.

were published in 2018 and 2019.[42] We hope that researchers will continue to take advantage of STRO for a long time to come and trust that they will continue to find new topics and questions to study with the use of the database. It will stay in safe keeping with Huygens ING. Sound Toll Registers Online is now complete. It is available at any time for anyone to write history. If it were a ship, we would wish it a prosperous voyage!

## About the authors

**Werner Scheltjens** (1978) is professor of digital history at the University of Bamberg, Germany. His research interests are in preindustrial trade and transport history, maritime history, Eastern European history, digital research methods and historical metrology.
E-mail: werner.scheltjens@uni-bamberg.de

**Jan Willem Veluwenkamp** (1951) was associate professor of early modern history at the University of Groningen, The Netherlands, until he retired in 2017. He has published on the history of early modern entrepreneurship, trade and transport. Until his retirement, he was scholarly project manager of *Sound Toll Registers Online*, the electronic database for the complete Sound Toll Registers at www.soundtoll.nl.
E-mail: j.w.veluwenkamp@rug.nl

**Siem van der Woude** (1953) worked as a senior archivist at Tresoar, the regional archive of Friesland in Leeuwarden, until he retired in 2020. He has published on the history of Friesland. Beginning in 2000, he was project manager of Sound Toll Registers Online, the electronic database for the complete Sound Toll Registers at www.soundtoll.nl
E-mail: siemvdwoude@gmail.com

42 Veluwenkamp and Scheltjens (eds.), *Early modern shipping and trade*; M.-W. Serruys (ed.), *Proceedings of the sixth Sound Toll Registers Online conference, Antwerp, Belgium* (*22-23 October 2015*) (Antwerp 2019).

## Book Reviews

Rudolf A.A. Bosch, *Stedelijke macht tussen overvloed en stagnatie. Stadsfinanciën, sociaal-politieke structuren en economie in het hertogdom Gelre, ca. 1350-1550* (Hilversum: Uitgeverij Verloren, 2019). 581 p. ISBN 9789087047726.

DOI: 10.18352/tseg.1204

Middeleeuwse stadsfinanciën zijn notoir lastig te doorgronden. Hoewel het rekeningmateriaal de indruk wekt een afgeronde boekhouding te zijn, is dit vaak deels schijn. Het werkelijk doorgronden van de administratie is daarom een tijdrovende klus: vele tientallen lijvige rekeningboeken moeten op een rijtje worden gezet en met veel kunst- en vliegwerk moet er omgegaan worden met de onvermijdelijke hiaten. Daarbij is het bovendien zaak gebruik te maken van aanvullende documentatie – zoals kladrekeningen en persoonlijke administratie – die de historicus in staat stellen financiële feiten van boekhoudkundige fictie te onderscheiden. Rudolf Bosch onderneemt deze *tour de force* niet één, maar twee keer in deze studie naar de stadsfinanciën van Arnhem en Zutphen.

Het werd ook wel weer eens tijd voor een Gelderse bijdrage aan debatten over de laatmiddeleeuwse economie en samenleving, die in de afgelopen decennia inderdaad werden gekenmerkt door een sterke 'flandro- en hollandocentrische bias' (p. 16). Historici van deze regio's hebben onder meer betoogd dat financiële innovaties de basis legden voor de machtige en welvarende Bourgondisch-Habsburgse Nederlanden – en in het Noorden uiteindelijk ook voor De Republiek. Bosch presenteert het hertogdom Gelre als een soort controlegroep: hier was geen sprake van economische groei, maar juist van stagnatie. Lag dit dan aan een gebrekkig financieel systeem, zoals de historiografie lijkt te impliceren? Het bronnenmateriaal is alvast om van te watertanden: de Arnhemse stadsrekeningen zijn – vrijwel zonder onderbreking! – overgeleverd van het boekjaar 1353/1354 tot het begin van de moderne tijd, die van Zutphen zijn iets minder goed bewaard gebleven, maar gaan desondanks terug tot 1381.

De lezer wordt getrakteerd op twee eeuwen stadsfinanciën van twee steden. Wat levert dat op? Ten eerste een zeer gedegen overzicht van de middeleeuwse geschiedenis van de schatkist van respectievelijk Arnhem en Zutphen. Net als in naburige gewesten kwamen de stadsfinanciën van Arnhem en

Zutphen steeds meer onder druk te staan in de tweede helft van de vijftiende eeuw. Belastingen op levensmiddelen stegen en de publieke schuld groeide, door de aanhoudende verkoop van renten. Het droevige eindresultaat was een langdurige financiële crisis. Bosch ziet deze als een cruciale gebeurtenis, die vooral in Arnhem ruimte creëerde voor vernieuwing. De elite die zich van oudsher over de stadsfinanciën ontfermde, moest geleidelijk aan de boeken openen voor Arnhemse burgerij, die ook weleens wilde meelezen. Want: waarom werd zij eigenlijk jaar na jaar geconfronteerd met stijgende lasten? Vanaf 1483 kwam er daarom een burgercommissie die met stadsinkomsten onbetaalde renten diende uit te keren. En in 1487 vergrootte de burgerij haar invloed zelfs verder: de ambachtslieden verwierven het recht om zich in gilden te organiseren en zitting te nemen in het stadsbestuur.

De burgerij wendde haar politieke invloed aan om de publieke schuld te gaan saneren. Dat was onder meer nodig, omdat renteniers het recht hadden om stedelingen hoofdelijk aansprakelijk te stellen voor achterstallige rentebetalingen. Dit 'represaillerecht' kon leiden tot schuldgijzelingen en de confiscatie van handelswaar. In Arnhem stuurde de burgerij aan op het uitbetalen van renten aan vreemdelingen – die het handelsverkeer lam konden leggen – en het opschorten van rentebetalingen aan de Arnhemmers zelf. In ruil voor deze aanpak zou de burgerij akkoord gegaan zijn met hogere belastingen en slaagde Arnhem erin om renten te betalen en ook om de publieke schuld geleidelijk af te bouwen. In Zutphen kwam de burgerparticipatie in stedelijke financiën daarentegen niet echt van de grond, waardoor het stadsbestuur geen draagvlak had voor structurele belastingverhogingen. Daardoor stond de stad tot diep in de zestiende eeuw in het rood.

*No taxation without representation.* Door burgerinspraak te koppelen aan de sanering van de publieke schuld van Arnhem, levert Bosch een belangrijke bijdrage aan het debat over laatmiddeleeuwse stadsfinanciën – hoewel er nog wel wat werk verzet moet worden. Zo lijkt de auteur er impliciet van uit te gaan dat de Arnhemse burgers niet in eigen vlees sneden toen zij voorstelden rentebetalingen aan de Arnhemmers op te schorten (p. 202). Maar zonder een analyse van de sociaaleconomische achtergrond van Arnhemse rentekopers is dit moeilijk hard te maken en is het lastig om in te schatten welke belangen de burgerij had en hoe we de maatregelen die zij afdwongen moeten interpreteren. Hetzelfde geldt voor de suggestie dat vooral de 'handeldrijvende burgers van de stad' (p. 494) werden getroffen door represailles – en *niet* de elite: waren de laatsten werkelijk helemaal niet actief in de langeafstandshandel, of daarvan op zijn minst afhankelijk?

Buiten Gelre ontvingen steden die in zwaar weer verkeerden moratoria, waarmee het represaillerecht tijdelijk werd opgeschort en het weer mogelijk werd om op handelsreis te gaan. Op deze manier reikte vooral Filips de Schone vele steden de helpende hand – hij had daar ook alle belang bij, omdat hij voor zijn inkomsten en leningen grotendeels afhankelijk was van zijn steden en die mochten daarom absoluut niet in het slop raken. Volgens Bosch hoefden Arnhem en Zutphen niet op hulp van de hertog van Gelre te rekenen. Maar toch ontving Arnhem wel degelijk moratoria, in 1474 van Karel de Stoute en in 1505 van Filips de Schone (p. 490, 495) die destijds de scepter over Gelre zwaaiden. Weliswaar Bourgondisch-Habsburgse landsheren, maar toch… In hoeverre werd het herstel van de Arnhemse stadsfinanciën niet (ook) door deze moratoria mogelijk gemaakt?

*Stedelijke macht tussen overvloed en stagnatie* is een ambitieuze studie. De financiën van Arnhem en Zutphen worden onderling vergeleken. Ook wordt in kaart gebracht hoe de verhoudingen tussen de twee steden en de hertogen van Gelre zich ontwikkelden. Bovendien worden de stadsfinanciën en politieke economie van Arnhem en Zutphen gespiegeld aan die van steden elders in de Lage Landen. Ik was vooral getroffen door de overeenkomsten: ook steden in Gelre moesten blijkbaar mee in de financieringswedloop die de Bourgondiers en Habsburgers ontketenden in de Lage Landen. Overal waren er wel steden zich zolang in de schulden staken totdat grootschalige saneringen noodzakelijk werden. Of ze daarmee nu de Bourgondiërs en Habsburgers financieel ondersteunden, zoals in Vlaanderen, Brabant en Holland, of zich juist deze dynastieën van het lijf trachtten te houden, zoals in Gelre: linksom of rechtsom kwam de bodem van de stedelijke schatkist al snel in zicht.

Jaco Zuijderduijn, Universiteit Lund

Jessica Dijkman and Bas van Leeuwen (eds.), *An Economic History of Famine Resilience* (London/ New York: Routledge, 2019). 276 p. ISBN 9780367191283.

DOI: 10.18352/tseg.1205

Economic historians are increasingly turning their attention to disasters of all kinds. In many pre-industrial societies, famines were probably the most frequently occurring type of disaster. In industrial(izing) societies, famines were less frequent and probably more avoidable, but their impact could be all the more devastating. The impact of famines varied widely across time and space, depending not only on environmental factors but also on societal response mechanisms. How such responses shaped societies' 'famine resilience' is the topic of this edited volume, which is made up of thirteen chapters (including the introduction), contributed by sixteen authors. The volume has a long time span, with chapters covering antiquity (three), the early modern period (five) and the modern era (seven). The geographical scope is equally broad, with chapters covering societies across Africa, the Americas, Asia and Europe. Most chapters have a long-range vision or are explicitly comparative in nature.

Famine resilience is studied using a heuristic framework that distinguishes the state, the market and civil society which, the editors maintain, represent 'the three main coordination mechanisms that, in any society, allow people to allocate or share resources' (p. 2). The task the various authors set themselves in their chapters is to analyze the (shifting/uneven) role of these forces in facilitating or undermining famine resilience. Most chapters do so comparatively. The opening chapter (Van Leeuwen & Li) lays bare different famine drivers and responses in four core regions of antiquity. Subsequent chapters on the Romans (De Ligt), Ottomans (Çelik) and Incas (Covey) focus on comparisons within empires, stressing the spatially uneven role of governments and markets. Chapters on early modern northwestern Europe (Dijkman) and 1840s Belgium (Beeckaert & Vanhaute) uncover substantial variation among nearby countries and regions within one country, respectively.

Chapters on Indonesia (Bosma) and North India (Sharma) analyze shifting colonial discourses and policies towards food supply and famine relief. In a particularly compelling chapter, S.G. Wheatcroft compares Russia's and China's slide into prolonged food crisis during the early twentieth century and subsequent attempts at recovery. Pursuing a similar argument about collapsing resilience, Wang, Koryś and Tymiński make an unusual comparison between Chinese and Polish relief systems in the long run. Africa only enters the picture towards the end of the book, where Devereux explores how markets, states and civil society interacted, often unproductively, during four major twenty-first century famines. The closing chapter on famine and migration (L. Lucassen) stands out for its global approach.

This book will certainly attract those with an interest in historical famines and famine resilience, generally or in specific areas. Many of the chapters provide a relatively short, well-structured and lucid entry point into region-specific literatures, to which many of the authors themselves have contributed in greater length elsewhere. The tripartite framework – markets, states and civil society – proves a helpful overarching structuring device to which most authors adhere effectively. At times, it facilitates comparative arguments, as, for example, where colonial policies are confronted with indigenous civil society initiatives and markets, or where different famine resilience equilibria surface within and across ancient and early modern societies. The book is also full of compelling observations. Just to highlight some: food supply and poverty alleviation systems may function well under normal conditions but fail miserably when food supplies drop, and vice versa; elites may be intent upon avoiding starvation and providing relief during famines so as to legitimize systems of structural inequality and poverty; famines may trigger major historical events, contributing, for example, to the fall of dynasties from China to Ethiopia; if markets function efficiently, food may still not reach the poorest individuals and regions due to lack of effective demand and entitlement failure.

Most book titles that include *'An economic history of...'* then specify a country or region, providing a fairly clear (albeit broad) entry into what readers might expect. In this case, the title is somewhat enigmatic. Unfortunately, the significance of famine resilience for economic history remains underdefined throughout the book. Famine resilience may intersect with economic historians' broader research agendas in several ways. First, historical famines can be studied as economic events on their own terms, potentially yielding broader insights into individual and collective behavior, as well as the functioning of markets and institutions. Second, famine resilience can be compared across time and space as an entry point for understanding broader processes of economic change. The impact of famines, for example, may allow us to 'measure a society's temperature' concerning market integration, state capacity or socio-economic inequality. Third, famines can be analyzed as 'critical junctures', putting societies onto a different trajectory of (economic) change, sometimes even triggering wholesale revolutions. This volume yields insights relevant to each of these broader agendas, but the authors do not explicitly engage with them. It is unfortunate, indeed, that the introduction itself is brief (10 pages only). While ultimately, therefore, an overarching economic historical narrative on famine resilience is still needed, this volume takes substantial strides in that direction.

Michiel de Haas, Wageningen University

Jan Luiten van Zanden, Tine de Moor and Sarah Carmichael, *Capital Women. The European Marriage Pattern, Female Empowerment and Economic Development in Western Europe 1300-1800* (Oxford: Oxford University Press, 2019). 288 p. ISBN 9780190847883.

DOI: 10.18352/tseg.1207

This volume is a groundbreaking attempt to include women, their work, and their economic activities in the 'grand narrative' of the economic development of Northwest Europe and of the Low Countries, in particular. The book comes at the end of a series of articles and prognoses by the three authors and intends to be part of the debate on the very controversial and much discussed concept of the 'Little Divergence'.

The starting point is decidedly contemporary: the Gender Inequality Index (GII), i.e., the relationship between female schooling, girls' age at marriage and fertility rate, which reveals that where parents' investment in their daughters' education is low, the age at marriage is low and the fertility rate is high. Breaking this vicious circle requires external intervention, i.e., ad hoc state policies. All this is well known and can be demonstrated with quantitative data for the contemporary world, but is it possible to apply the same model to past centuries, in the absence of equally abundant and reliable statistical data? This is precisely the challenge, of fundamental importance, that Jan Luiten Van Zanden, Tine De Moor and Sarah Carmichael wanted to launch on the basis of the documentation available for the last centuries of the Middle Ages and for the early modern age, within a restricted territory, though with a very rich history.

The starting point is Hajnal's thesis on the European Marriage Pattern (EMP), which is said to have emerged west of the Trieste-St. Petersburg line, later clarified by Peter Laslett, who, within the EMP, distinguished Northwest from Mediterranean Europe. The hypothesis of the authors is that the EMP (in its Northwestern pattern) is characterized by power balances between husband and wife and between parents and children. Marriage is based on consent of both spouses (as prescribed by the Catholic, though not the Protestant religion), and women have a relatively large say in the marriage itself, especially when they contribute to the income of their households. The book analyzes the diffusion of female wage earners and the role of women in credit activities, and the idea that indicating the age of the subject it portrays is an index of the diffusion of 'numeracy' is particularly interesting, as is the use of the concept of 'numeracy' instead of 'literacy' to measure female education levels. Also very interesting is the chapter on 'beguinages', understood as places of female freedom, including economic freedom, since beguines did not have to renounce their earthly possessions, unlike nuns (at least in principle). The data and analyses on the chosen area are interesting and convincing, but the attempts at comparison with the Mediterranean region and Italy, in particular, are much less so, at least from the perspective of a historian of early modern Italy.

The reference text is the fundamental research of David Herlihy and Christiane Klapisch-Zuber on the Tuscan *Catasto* of 1427. The problem is that these data cannot be extended to the whole of Italy or to the whole historical period under consideration, nor can they be compared with much less numerous data on Holland in the eighteenth century. In the *Catasto*, for instance, the data on the age at marriage of girls are much more abundant for the wealthy groups (because the dowry paid to the daughters was deducted from the taxes), i.e., the groups in which, all over Europe, it was much more probable that marriage was decided by the families and that girls married earlier. The dowry system is one of the fundamental elements of the argument, as it is indicated as the cause of the lack of labour investment of young women and also of wives, since the dowry had to be provided by the families of origin and the wife would recover it in case of widowhood. Moreover, the fact that spouses' assets were not pooled would not have encouraged wives to take an active part in building up the common wealth. The fact is that, even in Italy, in the lower classes both men and women had to work, before and after marriage; indeed, the fact that the dowry, at least in theory, was indispensable to marriage encouraged girls without an inheritance to leave the family and to emigrate to the cities to find work in crafts or in service. In charitable institutions, poor or orphaned girls worked to earn a dowry while learning a trade that they could continue to practice later. The paradox of the dowry system, all aspects of which have yet to be fully explored, is that all the economic responsibility for the marriage fell on the woman, and it is no coincidence that the marriage contracts of sixteenth-century Venetian craftsmen included a 'counter-dowry', a contribution from the husband. The further down the social scale one goes, the more marriage is based on reciprocity and the pooling of resources. As early as the twelfth and thirteenth centuries, credit activities carried out by women were documented in Italy, and the diffusion of salaried work arrived just as early in Italy where, unlike much of northern Europe, even apprentices received a wage and rarely had to pay a 'skill premium' to the master, thus confirming the diffusion of wage relations though raising the question of the relationship between training and work. Finally, recent research has convincingly and conclusively demonstrated that Laslett's pattern of the Mediterranean family has no historical basis.

To affirm, in line with the most recent research of contemporary economists, that the 'Girl power index' and a higher rate of gender equality have been factors of economic development in the past is a very interesting approach, and there would be many other things to say about this book. We can only hope that in the future there will be a greater exchange of ideas and information among European historians, so that finally even the 'Little Divergence' will be reconsidered from a less schematic and rigid perspective.

Anna Bellavitis, Université de Rouen Normandie

Marianne Eekhout, *Memorabilia van de Tachtigjarige Oorlog* (Hilversum: Uitgeverij Verloren, 2020). 128 p. ISBN 9789087048372.

DOI: 10.18352/tseg.1211

Wat hebben een specerijenbus, lijsten met kanonskogels, en een waterspuitend Christusbeeld met elkaar te maken? Het zijn allen objecten waarmee in de Nederlandse Republiek en de Spaanse Nederlanden de herinnering aan de Tachtigjarige Oorlog in leven werd gehouden. In *Memorabilia van de Tachtigjarige Oorlog* zet Marianne Eekhout uiteen hoe veelzijdig en belangrijk de materiële herinneringen aan de oorlog waren – aan beide kanten van de noord-zuid grens. Dit compacte en vlot geschreven boek is een publieksversie van het proefschrift dat Eekhout in 2014 verdedigde. Het werk past, zoals Eekhout zelf aangeeft, duidelijk binnen de golf van hernieuwde interesse in de Tachtigjarige Oorlog. In de afgelopen jaren kreeg deze vorm in een tentoonstelling in het Rijksmuseum Amsterdam, een NTR-televisieserie, en de herdenking van verschillende historische ijkpunten. Volgens Eekhout is deze interesse in belangrijke mate opgewekt door onze eigentijdse omgang met de Tweede Wereldoorlog. Nu er steeds minder ooggetuigen overblijven is men gedwongen om de vraag te stellen hoe de herinneringen aan deze oorlog kunnen worden levend gehouden. Al in de zeventiende eeuw werd dezelfde vraag gesteld in relatie tot de Tachtigjarige Oorlog. Aan de hand van vijf hoofdstukken zet Eekhout uiteen hoe de inwoners van de Lage Landen van 1566 tot 1750 omgingen met de materiële herinneringen aan de gewapende conflicten die later historiografisch zouden worden geduid als de 'Tachtigjarige Oorlog'.

Het boek volgt een losjes chronologisch schema. De lezer volgt het verloop van de oorlog en de zeventiende- en achttiende-eeuwse nasleep, en komt bij elke fase nieuwe objecten en nieuwe opdrachtgevers tegen. Zo waren memorabilia uit de zestiende eeuw vaak 'in de strijd' ontstaan. Het waren kanonskogels, kapotte heiligenbeelden, of 'ontheemde' relieken. Al snel probeerden individuele burgers echter zelf invulling te geven aan de materiële herinneringscultuur door opdrachten uit te zetten voor schilderijen, zilverwerk en gevelstenen. Overheden kwamen pas later in zicht als opdrachtgevers. Hier waren het vooral de steden en stedelijke organisaties die het voortouw namen. Alhoewel grotere partijen zoals de Staten-Generaal of de gewestelijke autoriteiten minder actief waren dan steden, toont Eekhout aan dat zij zich zeker niet afzijdig hielden. Afsluitend wordt in het laatste hoofdstuk de herinnering na de Vrede van Münster besproken, en uiteengezet hoe er grotere en kleinere verzamelingen ontstonden die later vaak de basis vormden voor negentiende-eeuwse museale collecties.

In alle hoofdstukken is er een goede balans tussen detail en overzicht. Er komen tal van fascinerende objecten langs die allen met zorg zijn beschreven: van registers vol kanonschoten tot de beroemde Leidse kookpot. Tegelijkertijd laat Eekhout zien hoe de materiële herinneringscultuur is veranderd door de eeuwen heen, en hoe elke fase van conflict en herinnering zijn eigen materiële herinneringen voortbrengt. Hierbij is ook aandacht voor de wisselwerking tussen Noordelijke en Zuidelijke tradities, en tussen regionale en nationale herinneringskaders. Het boek laat hiermee bij uitstek zien dat de herinnering van de Tachtigjarige Oorlog als een meerstemmig verhaal kan worden benaderd. Soms leidt deze brede insteek tot wat kleine onevenwichtigheden: het zwaartepunt ligt impliciet vooral bij de Republiek, met kortere uitstapjes naar de gebruiken in de Zuidelijke Nederlanden.

Een grote meerwaarde van dit boek is dat de vele verschillende onderwerpen en voorwerpen zorgvuldig zijn ontsloten in drie verschillende indexen: personen, zaken en plaatsen. Samen met de uitgebreide literatuurlijst en illustratieverantwoording biedt het boek de lezer vele aanknopingspunten om de memorabilia zelf op te zoeken in musea en oude stadscentra. *Memorabilia van de Tachtigjarige Oorlog* is daarnaast rijkelijk en volledig in kleur geïllustreerd. Vanwege de beperkte afmetingen van het boek wordt sommige werken wat onrecht gedaan – een metersbreed schilderij of een complete gevel komen niet tot hun recht in een afbeelding van 6 bij 6 cm. Zonder enige twijfel zou dit mooie publieksboek niet misstaan in koffietafelvariant.

Michel van Duijnen, Vrije Universiteit Amsterdam

Hittjo Kruyswijk, *Gek, niet ziek? Lucas Lindeboom, Abraham Kuyper en de stichting van gereformeerde ziekenhuizen in Nederland (1880-1940)* [Donum Reeks.] (Amsterdam: HDC Centre for Religious History, 2020). 198 p. ISBN 9789072319401.

DOI: 10.18352/tseg.1214

Hoe komt het dat het gereformeerde volksdeel tien keer meer psychiatrische inrichtingen heeft voorgebracht dan algemene ziekenhuizen? Zouden gereformeerden zo veel vaker psychisch gestoord zijn geweest? Het omgekeerde blijkt het geval: gereformeerden waren, volgens gegevens uit 1909 en 1914, minder vaak opgenomen als psychiatrische patiënt dan hervormden of katholieken. Zou het lidmaatschap van de gereformeerde broederschap misschien een heilzame werking hebben op de geestelijke gezondheid?

In zijn boek *Gek, niet ziek?* doet de cardioloog en historicus Hittjo Kruyswijk onderzoek naar de grondlegger van het gereformeerde ziekenhuiswezen, Lucas Lindeboom, en naar de opvattingen van Abraham Kuyper over ziek zijn en beter worden. Ik beperk mij hier tot Abraham Kuyper, die uitgesproken ideeën had over de verzorging van krankzinnigen, die in zijn ogen in de eerste plaats een *sociaal* probleem waren. De verzorging van zieken en krankzinnigen was geen staatstaak, maar in eerste instantie een taak van de familie. Mochten bloedverwanten niet in de gelegenheid zijn hun krankzinnige familieleden te verzorgen, dan moeten ze 'elders' ondergebracht worden. Zij dienden verzorgd te worden door (1) De kerken van Jezus Christus, (2) Bij ontstentenis van de Kerk van Jezus trede de Christelijke Vereeniging op den voorgrond (3) Waar ook die macht terugbleef, de gewone particuliere nijverheid, die verpleegt tegen gereede betaling; niet om Godswil maar voor geld.' (p. 126). Pas als de krankzinnige niet 'in eigen kring' kan worden verpleegd, dan 'zou de Overheid tussen beide moeten komen.'

Die overheid moest vanaf 1841 al optreden omdat bij een opname in een inrichting niet alleen een arts, maar ook een rechter te pas kwam. Kuyper wilde de arts en de rechter vervangen door een curator, omdat hij volgens Kruyswijk krankzinnigheid meer als een maatschappelijk en juridisch probleem zag, dan een als medisch te behandelen ziekte. Overigens is Kuyper ook geen groot voorstander van ziekenhuizen, maar als het medisch noodzakelijk was moest een zieke in een hospitaal worden verpleegd. Dat gold nog in sterkere mate voor krankzinnigen. Hoewel Kuyper de eerste verantwoordelijkheid voor de verpleging van zieken bij de bloedverwanten legde, was hij in de praktijk een groot voorstander van het afzonderen van krankzinnigen. 'Wezenlijk krankzinnigen *stichten* gemeenlijk niet, maar *verwilderen* een gezin. (...) Zij moeten afgezonderd zijn.' De krankzinnige heeft dus een andere, en vooral ook lagere status dan de zieke. Treft de krankzinnige zelf enige blaam? Nee, dat nu ook weer niet. Weliswaar ziet Kuyper ziekte – en ook krankzinnigheid – als een straf van God, maar de gevolgen van de zondeval drukken op de gehele mensheid; ziekte is dus niet het gevolg van zonde van de patiënt zelf. Wel is het volgens Kuyper zo, dat God alles bepaalt op dit ondermaanse; hij is dus direct verantwoordelijk voor ziektes.

In de loop van de negentiende eeuw werden in de geneeskunde verschillende methodes ontwikkeld om lichamelijke ziektes te voorkomen of te genezen. Vaccinatie was daar een belangrijk voorbeeld van. Maar waarom zou men, als alles Gods wil was en ook ziektes door Hem gezonden werden moeite mogen doen om ziektes te voorkomen of zieken te genezen? Kuyper was voorstander van vaccinatie, hij zag het als een vorm van natuurgeneeswijze, door God (aan)geboden in het kader van de algemene genade. Zo weet hij ook hier weer een passende draai aan te geven. De legitimatie van de bestrijding van bacteriën (antisepsis, asepsis) ontleent hij wonderlijk genoeg aan de macht over het dierenrijk die de mens in het paradijs werd gegeven (p. 144). We mogen, aldus Kuyper, God niet vragen een zieke te genezen, maar we mogen zelf wel alles op alles zetten om ziektes te genezen.

Hoe zit dat bij krankzinnigheid? Krankzinnigheid is geen ziekte in de medische zin van het woord, noch kan het antwoord op de vraag 'wel of niet behandelen?' door de patiënt zelf gegeven worden. In Kuypers tijd waren er, zo schrijft Kruyswijk, nog weinig geneesmiddelen die hielpen tegen krankzinnigheid, buiten de kalmeringsmiddelen als broom. Liefderijke verzorging was vrijwel het enige dat bestond en een verzorging op basis van rust, reinheid en regelmaat was vaak heel effectief. Die verzorging werden aangevuld met badtherapieën en arbeidstherapie. Dat dit gebeurde in de afzondering van een inrichting, had te maken met de eerder genoemde opvatting van Kuyper dat krankzinnigen een verwilderende invloed hadden op het gezinsleven en het dorpsleven.

Wie de verhandeling van Kruyswijk leest kan zich niet aan de indruk onttrekken dat Kuyper weliswaar de suggestie weet te wekken dat hij zijn sociologische observaties en zijn morele oordelen afleidt van de Schrift of van zijn interpretatie daarvan, maar dat hij eigenlijk het omgekeerde doet. Zijn maatschappelijke en morele oordelen vormen de basis van zijn theologische bespiegelingen, die op zichzelf al behoorlijk tegenstrijdig zijn. Zo luidt de kop van een paragraaf in hoofdstuk 4: Hoe kan ziekte tegelijkertijd naar Gods wil en tegen Gods wil zijn? Met een zo tegenstrijdige Godsbesef moet het niet moeilijk zijn om voor alle maatschappelijke problemen een theologisch sluitende oplossing te vinden. Dat komt misschien nog het sterkst naar voren in Kuypers beschouwingen over de rol van arts en rechter bij de bepaling of iemand krankzinnig is. Zijn voorstel om het besluit tot opname aan een door de Rechter-commissaris aangewezen 'curator' over te laten, getuigt van een groot vertrouwen in de sociale omgeving van de krankzinnige. En ook het feit dat het besluit van de Rechtbank gebaseerd moet zijn op een medisch attest voorzien van een schriftelijke verklaring van onderzoek naar de geestelijke toestand door een predikant, pastoor of rabbijn, getuigt daarvan.

De theologie lijkt voor Abraham Kuyper een middel om zijn persoonlijke inzichten over hoe de maatschappij dient te worden ingericht kracht bij te zetten met de donder en bliksem uit het Oude Testament. Dat verklaart misschien ook zijn geweldige populariteit bij zijn achterban. Abraham Kuyper verwoordt de opvattingen van zijn achterban inzake familie en moraal en doet dat in zeer verheven en dwingende taal: de tale Kanaäns. Het verklaart in ieder geval het oordeel van Kruyswijk over de persoon van Kuyper: 'Over ziekenverzorging, geneeskunde en artsen had Kuyper evenals op veel ander gebied een uitgesproken mening die hij met grote overtuigingskracht en meer dan zachte dwang placht over te brengen.'(p. 123).

Meindert Fennema, Universiteit van Amsterdam

Maarten Hell, *De Amsterdamse herberg 1450-1800. Geestrijk centrum van het openbare leven* (Nijmegen: Van Tilt, 2017). 487 p. ISBN 9789460043437.

DOI: 10.18352/tseg.1210

Maarten Hell is een echte Amsterdamkenner en een geboren verteller. Met zijn boek (en proefschrift) over Amsterdamse herbergen, tappers, koffiehuizen en andere drinkgelegenheden levert hij een waardevolle bijdrage aan de sociale en culturele geschiedenis van de Republiek. De studie zit vol met leuke verhalen over vrouwen en mannen die eet- en drinkhuizen uitbaatten of die daar regelmatig als klant binnenkwamen. De auteur stelt zich tot doel het brede scala aan functies van drinkhuizen, en de verschuivingen die daarin tussen 1450 en 1800 hebben plaatsgevonden, te analyseren. De waard en de waardin staan centraal: hij onderzoekt vooral hoe zij hebben ingespeeld op de veranderende behoeften van hun gasten.

Het begrip 'herberg' wordt breed gedefinieerd en dekt alle openbaar toegankelijke etablissementen waar men (onder meer) alcoholische dranken voor kleinverbruik verkocht. In zijn inleiding geeft Hell een typologie van de voornaamste maatschappelijke functies die drinklokalen gewoonlijk vervulden. Zij voorzagen Amsterdammers en vreemdelingen van drank, voeding en onderdak. Zij brachten mensen met elkaar in contact en zorgden voor vermaak. Bovendien boden zij ruimte voor politieke activiteiten en discussies. Tenslotte speelden zij ook op diverse manieren een rol in de stedelijke economie. De politieke en economische functies hingen uiteraard in hoge mate samen met de concentratie van nieuws en informatie in herbergen. In de ondertitel van het boek legt de auteur de nadruk op de rol van de herberg in het openbare leven. Het conceptuele kader van het openbare leven, de openbare ruimte en de openbare orde had meer aandacht verdiend. Hell situeert zijn benadering in de lijn van Beat Kümin en Ann Tlusty, die in hun onderzoeken over drinkhuizen in Bern en in Beieren de herberg als fatsoenlijke multifunctionele maatschappelijke instelling hebben gerehabiliteerd.

Het lijvige boek is gebaseerd op een verbluffende hoeveelheid primaire bronnen. Het bestaat uit twintig hoofdstukken, onderverdeeld in twee delen van ongelijke afmeting. De eerste vier hoofdstukken zijn in grote lijnen chronologisch opgezet en betreffen de jaren 1450-1578. De overige zestien hoofdstukken gaan over de 'bloeiperiode' van het herbergwezen, die de auteur situeert tussen het jaar van de Amsterdamse Alteratie (1578) en 1800. In een aantal hoofdstukken schetst hij de ontwikkeling van bepaalde typen drinkgelegenheden, zoals herenherbergen, gildeherbergen, veilingherbergen, logementen voor vreemdelingen, slaaphuizen voor zeelieden en koffiehuizen. Andere delen gaan in op de sociale functies (spel en vermaak, prostitutie, criminaliteit), politieke activiteiten (partijstrijd en politisering aan het einde van de achttiende eeuw) en economische aspecten zoals de exploitatie van de herberg en reclame. Het boek eindigt met een korte epiloog die vooruitblikt op de ontwikkeling van de herberg in de negentiende eeuw. Het bijwerk bevat onder meer twee registers, één op persoonsnamen en één op de namen van de drinkhuizen. Dit is geen overbodige luxe, aangezien de informatie over één en dezelfde herberg dikwijls over meerdere hoofdstukken verspreid is.

De stedelijke overheid onderhield een complexe relatie met de uitbaters. In de vroegste periode was de herberg in diverse opzichten een verlengstuk van de autoriteiten. Herbergiers moesten hun gasten informeren over plaatselijke regelgeving en zij dienden strafbaar gedrag aan de overheid te melden. Net als in andere landen hadden zij bovendien een registratieplicht van vreemde logés. In de vijftiende en zestiende eeuw maakten herbergiers ook wel deel uit van het stadsbestuur. Zo was Jan Beth Jansz aan het einde van de vijftiende eeuw, behalve waard van De Witte Hond en zaakgelastigde van kooplieden uit het Oostzeegebied, ook lange tijd burgemeester. Later organiseerde de vroedschap ontvangsten van hoge gasten en regentenmaaltijden in geprivilegieerde herenherbergen zoals de Prinsenhof en de Herenlogementen. De regering had veel belang bij het welvaren van de drinkhuizen, want de accijnzen op de diverse dranken droegen in hoge mate bij tot de inkomsten van de stad.

De rol van herbergen in de ontwikkeling van het handelskapitalisme is ook een terugkerend thema (al benoemt de auteur dit niet als zodanig). Herbergiers hielden zich net als in omringende landen al vroeg bezig met kredietverlening, opslag van goederen, tussenhandel en de vertegenwoordiging van buitenlandse kooplieden. Sommige uitbaters specialiseerden zich in de dienstverlening aan zeelieden. Slaapbazen verschaften hen niet alleen onderdak en maaltijden, maar bemiddelden ook op de arbeidsmarkt en in het betalingsverkeer. In de achttiende eeuw functioneerde een aantal grote herbergen als veilinglokaal en zij vormden in die hoedanigheid een belangrijke schakel in de goederendistributie.

De verscheidenheid van de etablissementen blijkt duidelijk uit de herberginterieurs. Terwijl veel drinklokalen uit één ruimte bestonden en schamel waren ingericht, hingen in het Heidelbergse Wijnvat op het Rokin in 1663 maar liefst 28 schilderijen aan de muur, verspreid over dertien vertrekken. Herbergiers bezaten dikwijls spellen zoals 'verkeersborden' waarop werd gedobbeld. Ondernemende uitbaters probeerden publiek te trekken door de organisatie van opzienbarende attracties zoals hondengevechten, of lieten kaats- en kolfbanen aanleggen. Muziekoptredens lijken in de achttiende eeuw bijzonder populair te zijn geweest, wat wellicht verband houdt met veranderingen in feesttradities en met de opkomst van meer ingetogen vormen van vermaak. De meeste drinkhuizen werden uitgebaat door een herbergier en zijn vrouw. Alleenstaande vrouwen waren echter ook, vooral in de zeventiende eeuw, sterk vertegenwoordigd in het tappersbedrijf. De huur was voor uitbaters dikwijls de belangrijkste kostenpost. Veel herbergen waren in de zeventiende eeuw eigendom van bierbeschooiers, die tevens als leverancier optraden. Veranderingen in de drinkcultuur leidden in de achttiende eeuw echter tot verschuivingen in de eigendomsstructuur.

Het boek is rijk geïllustreerd met 80 pagina's kleurenreproducties van schilderijen van herberginterieurs, foto's van drinkgerei, portretten van tappers en plattegronden. Laten we hopen dat de auteur nog eens de gelegenheid krijgt om in het kader van een mooie tentoonstelling meer met dit materiaal te doen!

Anne Wegener Sleeswijk, Université Paris-1

Sharika D. Crawford, *The Last Turtlemen of the Caribbean. Waterscapes of Labor, Conservation, and Boundary Making* (Chapell Hill: University of North Carolina Press, 2020). 204 p. ISBN 9781469660202.

DOI: 10.18352/tseg.1213

Sometimes you pick up a book because it is sent to you for a review, and sometimes you end up wanting to write a review because you picked up a book that you really enjoyed reading from cover to cover. *The Last Turtlemen of the Caribbean* by Sharika D. Crawford falls into the latter category. *The Last Turtlemen* sketches the demise of the turtle industry in the Caribbean, looking specifically at the lives of the turtlemen of the Caymans from the late nineteenth century to the twentieth century. In five beautifully written chapters, *The Last Turtlemen* foregrounds the maritime space of the Caribbean and the people who worked there to argue the importance of the turtlemen and their lives at sea in shaping, contesting and claiming the circum-Caribbean. The book illuminates the working realities of turtlemen and the way their labour was affected by and affected in itself wider local, imperial and global socio-economic changes. The history of the turtlemen appeals to historians of all sorts; whether one is interested in transnational governance, labour and empire, or environmental change and conservation, there is a chapter for you in this book. The wide scope may for some be also considered a potential risk of the book: for someone interested in one of these specific themes, you are left wanting more only to find the next chapter does not delve into it deeper.

In five chapters we are taken through the ebb and flow of turtlemen's working lives and labouring landscapes. Chapter one sets out the basic biology and behaviour of sea turtles and gives a brief overview of the early modern history of the maritime space in which turtling took place, relating turtling as a form of labour, food and income to other imperial socio-economic endeavors and existing indigenous turtle-hunting practices. In chapter two Crawford argues that new technologies and capital investment changed the character of turtle hunting and the working lives of turtlemen as they were incorporated into a wider industry with global reach. The labouring landscape of the turtles comes to the fore in chapter three, where the connections between the Cayman Islands and the wider Caribbean are explored and it is argued that the increasingly long-distance migrations of turtlemen led to a transnational family and community of sorts as well as a shared maritime culture and exchange of knowledge. A chapter that will be of great interest to those interested in transnational governance and the use of imperial power dynamics by labourers is chapter four. In this chapter, disputes over turtling grounds are highlighted in relation to the development of sovereign states and tensions over maritime territorial sovereignty. Finally, chapter five caters to those interested in the rise of environmental activism. It draws from Archie Carr's archives and highlights how turtlemen's knowledge ended up contributing to the rise of an environmental movement calling for the end of turtling as turtle populations faced extinction.

As is apparent, the book touches upon many themes and histories, and this is both the strength and on occasion the weakness of the book. It is written with great care and does justice to the dynamic lives of the turtlemen, their lives at sea and their knowledge of turtles. Crawford highlights that their knowledge of turtles was immense and circulated throughout the Caribbean, but that it also contributed to the effectiveness of a trade that was in the end unsustainable.

It pains me to critique a book that I wish everyone would read. Even so, the book left me scratching my head as someone interested in the gendered dynamics of labour history. That is to say, the sources referenced many interviews with women, yet the importance of their stories was left implicit and the question 'but why turtle*men*' was not explicitly addressed. For example, the book does draw on interviews with women and references anecdotes where the social networks of these women is implicitly demonstrated to be important to the wage labour opportunities of men (e.g., p.76, p. 129-130). However, these stories are not explicitly referred to nor explained as such, with women instead often being referred to under the headings of 'wives, mothers, and sisters'. Similar issues might be found for those interested in transnational governance (why is there no comparison to the legal developments in maritime sovereignty and the later development of environmental personhood, for example?) or for anyone interested in one of the many themes the book addresses, such as the rise of an environmental conservation movement (i.e., how does this relate to the history of global activist movements?). It is therefore important to emphasize not to lose sight of the beauty of the book in its entirety and the way it relates the specific history of the turtlemen to many wider historic developments. *The Last Turtlemen* is therefore a great resource for teaching, as it raises a plethora of questions and refers to a great variety of archival sources, from colonial sources, to oral history and personal archives. For someone who really enjoyed the book, I can only state that the book is worthy of many sequels.

Stephanie van Dam, Cambridge University

Lodewijk Petram en Samuël Kruizinga, *De oorlog tegemoet. Nederlanders en de strijd om Spanje, 1936-1939* (Amsterdam: Atlas Contact, 2020). 352 p. ISBN 9789045032559.

DOI: 10.18352/tseg.1206

'Al die jongens hier willen godverdomme weg', verzuchtte de revolutionair-socialist Henk Sneevliet in 1937: 'ze willen allemaal naar Spanje'.[1] Daar was een jaar eerder een burgeroorlog uitgebroken tussen de democratisch gekozen volksfrontregering van socialisten, communisten en radicalen enerzijds en fascistische putschisten anderzijds. Terwijl die laatsten ruime militaire steun kregen van Hitler en Mussolini, kwam alleen de Sovjet-Unie de volksfrontregering mondjesmaat te hulp. Als reactie daarop trokken duizenden sympathisanten van over de hele wereld naar Spanje om de regeringstroepen te steunen. Zo ook bijna zevenhonderd socialisten, communisten en radicalen uit Nederland. Hoewel deze Spanjestrijders zichzelf zagen als antifascistische vrijheidsstrijders, zag het overgrote deel van de Nederlandse bevolking hen als extremistische *foreign fighters*.

1 K. ten Haaf, *In de geest van oktober. Het verhaal van Peter Drenth* (Groningen 1999).

In een nieuwe studie onderzoeken Petram en Kruizinga enerzijds wat de Nederlandse Spanjestrijders dreef, maar ook hoe de Nederlandse bevolking reageerde op de Spaanse Burgeroorlog en de pogingen van een kleine groep socialisten en communisten om mensen te werven om te gaan vechten in Spanje. Zij doen dat door de levens van een aantal Spanjegangers te reconstrueren en hun ervaringen te spiegelen aan de manier waarop de pers schreef over de burgeroorlog en de werving (het 'ronselen') van Spanjestrijders in Nederland.

Oudere literatuur over dit thema is vaak gebaseerd op interviews met communistische Spanjeveteranen. Petram en Kruizinga houden meer afstand en benadrukken dat Spanjestrijders lang niet altijd communist waren of werden gedreven door ideologische overwegingen. Zo waren er ook kansarme jongeren die in Nederland zó klem kwamen te zitten dat zij geen andere uitweg zagen dan naar Spanje te 'vluchten'. Zo waren er Marinus Onderwater, wiens vriendin zwanger was geworden, en Paul de Laat, die beschuldigd was van belastingfraude: 'Samen besloten ze het noodlot te ontvluchten. Spanje was een logische bestemming' (p. 83).

Een van de sterke kanten van het boek is de uitgebreide aandacht voor de manier waarop de Nederlandse pers en het publiek reageerden op de inspanningen van communisten om Spanjestrijders te werven. Sensationele en overtrokken krantenberichten, in combinatie met grote onduidelijkheid over het werkelijke aantal Spanjegangers, leidde tot grote onrust. Bij meerdere vermissingszaken in 1936 werd gevreesd dat de vermiste 'naar Spanje was gelokt'. In de meeste gevallen bleek daar niets van waar, zoals in het geval van een jongeman die stiekem de nacht bij zijn vriendin door had gebracht zonder dit aan zijn ouders te vertellen (p. 96). Juist dit soort anekdotes laten zien hoezeer 'Spanje' de Nederlanders bezighield.

Op meerdere plaatsen benadrukken Petram en Kruizinga 'dat de Nederlandse Spanjestrijders nooit de uniforme groep zijn geweest die de overheid, sommige kranten en de CPN, elk op hun eigen manier, meenden te zien' (p. 265). Toch lukt het Petram en Kruizinga uiteindelijk niet goed om de diversiteit onder de Spanjegangers goed tot haar recht te laten komen. Op basis van verschillende bronnen concluderen zij dat waarschijnlijk minder dan de helft van de Nederlandse Spanjestrijders lid was van de CPN (p. 136). Maar wie vormden dan die andere helft? Volgens Petram en Kruizinga waren zij 'voor een belangrijk deel nauwelijks politiek gemotiveerd' (p. 253). Hoewel het van grote waarde is om mensen als Onderwater en De Laat een plek te geven in de geschiedenis van Nederlandse Spanjegangers, is het omstreden of zij daadwerkelijk 'een belangrijk deel' uitmaakten van deze groep.

In feite richten Petram en Kruizinga hun onderzoek op twee categorieën Spanjestrijders: overtuigde CPN'ers en onfortuinlijke avonturiers. Daarbuiten komen vrijwel geen andere Spanjegangers aan bod, afgezien van de sociaaldemocratische jongere Krijn Breur. Het biografisch woordenboek 'Nederlandse vrijwilligers in de Spaanse Burgeroorlog', dat de levens van zo'n 650 Spanjestrijders omvat, noemt echter een groot aantal ideologisch gedreven Spanjestrijders van niet-communistische snit, waaronder sociaaldemocraten, linkssocialisten, revolutionair-socialisten en anarchisten.[2] Juist zij tonen wat een bont geheel de ideologisch gedreven Spanjestrijders vormden.

Daarbij hadden niet-communistische Spanjestrijders de nodige invloed op de hoofdstroom van de socialistische arbeidersbeweging: de sociaaldemocratie. De burgeroorlog was jarenlang voorpaginanieuws in *Het Volk*, het dagblad van de SDAP, die verscheurd werd door de vraag hoe men zich tegen Franco kon verzetten zonder de stalinisten in de kaart te spelen. In die context was het extra pijnlijk dat leden van de Onafhankelijk Socialistische Partij, die zich in 1933 van de SDAP hadden afgescheiden, wél naar Spanje afreisden om aldaar het fascisme te bestrijden. Uiteindelijk accepteerde de SDAP dat sociaaldemocraten naar Spanje afreisden als medisch personeel en steun gaven aan het comité Hulp aan Spanje. Deze worsteling van de toch belangrijkste linkse partij in Nederland krijgt weinig aandacht.

Deze insteek leidt ertoe dat bepaalde incidenten niet volledig correct geduid worden. Zo is er de zaak van Gerrit Schuring en Theo Wiering, die zich in december 1936 meldden bij de honorair consul voor Nederland in Madrid, na korte tijd aan het Republikeinse front verbleven te hebben. Ze vertelden de consul dat zij alleen maar naar Spanje waren gegaan om medische en technische hulp te bieden aan de Republikeinen, maar in plaats daarvan naar het front waren gestuurd. Op basis van hun verklaring en het verslag van de consul komen Schuring en Wiering naar voren als wat naïeve en onvoorbereide Spanjegangers. In werkelijkheid waren zij overtuigde revolutionairen (trotskisten), die vanwege hun politieke instelling zozeer door stalinisten werden dwarsgezeten en bedreigd dat zij voor hun leven vreesden en besloten te vluchten. Hun besluit om naar Spanje te vertrekken was nota bene ingegeven door een advertentie van Hulp aan Spanje in *Het Volk*.[3]

De diversiteit onder de Spanjestrijders had dus beter in kaart gebracht kunnen worden, evenals de worsteling van veel sociaaldemocraten met Spanje. Andere thema's komen beter uit de verf, zoals de Nederlandse reacties op de Spaanse Burgeroorlog en de werving van Spanjestrijders, de beschreven levensloop van een select aantal Spanjestrijders en de reconstructie van de

2 Nederlandse vrijwilligers in de Spaanse Burgeroorlog, https://spanjestrijders.nl.

3 Zie voor biografische gegevens over Schuring en Wiering ook B. de Cort, 'Biografieën van de leden van de Onafhankelijke Socialistische Partij (OSP, 1932-1935)' (2006, laatste bijwerking 2016) in het Internationaal Instituut voor Sociale Geschiedenis.

lange weg naar eerherstel voor de Spanjestrijders. Tot diep in de jaren vijftig werden zij namelijk als extremisten gezien en bleven zij staatloos omdat zij in vreemde krijgsdienst hadden gevochten. Zelfs Nederlanders die in de Waffen-SS hadden gevochten konden eerder aanspraak maken op hernaturalisatie dan veel Spanjeveteranen.

Bart van der Steen, Universiteit Leiden

David Onnekink and Gijs Rommelse, *The Dutch in the Early Modern World. A History of a Global Power* (Cambridge [etc.]: Cambridge University Press, 2019). 314 p. ISBN 9781107572928

DOI: 10.18352/tseg.1209

This book by David Onnekink and Gijs Rommelse sets out to give an introduction to early modern Dutch foreign policy. It is an accessible narrative of the history of the Dutch Republic placed in a wider international context. As a textbook, it has the merit of combining the Dutch, European and global scopes in the analysis. These different levels of analysis remain divided into chapters, however, and few connections are made between them. The book is largely based on secondary literature, yet that is not an issue since its aim is to provide a general overview of the history of the Dutch Republic in the early modern world. To achieve this goal, the work is divided into six chronological chapters from 1579 until 1795, each examining similar themes, such as Dutch history or European international relations. While a chronological division has the advantage of highlighting the evolution of each of these themes, it can also generate repetitions and render the narrative a little descriptive.

The authors take up the challenge of studying in parallel a wide array of topics and geographical contexts. The effort of bridging different historiographies, usually studied in isolation, should be commended in this case. As is expected in such an endeavour, some themes are more thoroughly discussed than others. For instance, the sections on the international dynamics in Europe and European diplomacy are strong. The authors demonstrate the highly personalized character of diplomacy in early modern Europe and the importance of individual social networks. Additionally, careful attention is given to identity formation and self-perception of the Dutch Republic throughout the chapters. The authors also show the non-national aspects of events shaping the Dutch Republic, such as the Dutch Revolt. Drawing from a wide range of artworks, the authors propose an object-based introduction to each chapter, which provides an original and tangible entry point into the Dutch Republic's history.

However, less attention is paid to the sections devoted to Dutch presence outside of Europe in each chapter. While the focus at the global level is understandably on the main Dutch colonies of Surinam and Indonesia, the narrative could have been less descriptive and engaged more with recent historiography. There is for instance very little about overseas diplomacy and the cultural brokers involved. The use of New Diplomatic History for the European context is laudable but could have been applied to the non-European context as well, as new literature has been produced in the last years on the topic. Nevertheless, an interesting analysis on religion or culture does bring to the fore other contexts, such as Elmina on the West African coast. The parts of the chapters dedicated to Dutch foreign policy in a global context are at times disconnected from the rest. It is unfortunate that the illustration chosen for the front cover of the book (Hooghly, a Dutch trading post in Bengal), is not mentioned in the book, as it would have been an interesting case to develop in a narrative centered on foreign Dutch policy.

Overall, the book provides a comprehensible overview of the place of the Dutch Republic in the early modern world, although the links to the non-European contexts are somewhat superficial at times. It is a good and manageable first introduction to the political and diplomatic history of the Dutch Republic.

Elisabeth Heijmans, University of Antwerp.

Ewout Frankema and Anne Booth (eds.), *Fiscal Capacity and the Colonial State in Asia and Africa, c. 1850-1960* [Cambridge Studies in Economic History.] (Cambridge [etc.]: Cambridge University Press, 2020). 303 p. ISBN 9781108494267.

DOI: 10.18352/tseg.1208

Currently, many countries in the Global South are struggling to build their fiscal capacity. Without well-functioning taxation systems to raise government revenues in relation to GDP, they lack resources to provide public goods and services to enhance socio-economic development. Moreover, without economic growth and increasing incomes, revenues will remain modest. Consequently, building state capacity, including fiscal capacity, is considered a major development challenge. Because most developing countries have a history of being colonized, and capacity building is a slow and arduous process, scholars regularly question the links between colonial state formation and the role of colonial legacies after independence.

In this edited volume, Ewout Frankema and Anne Booth, together with eight additional authors, aim at examining the evolution of fiscal capacity in the context of the colonial state formation in Asia and Africa. In the earlier days of colonialism, the administrative ambitions of the colonial powers in terms of developing taxation and investing in socio-economic development were relatively modest. With the expansion of imperialism in the late nineteenth century, however, the costs for upkeep of the empires increased. As the European colonial powers did not want to burden their metropolitan economies and taxpayers with these costs, fiscal capacity had to be developed in the colonies themselves. This is the story of how the various colonial powers set up their colonial administrations, what concrete policies they implemented in relation to taxation and government spending, and how those policies interacted with local political structures and systems of production.

The book consists of nine chapters. Chapter one is an introduction by Frankema and Booth where they establish the motivation for the project, account for the existing literature, and argue for the lessons learned by comparing the various studies. The rest of the book is organized geographically. Starting with Asia, chapter two is written by Anne Booth, who examines the changing role of the state in terms of fiscal capacity in Southeast Asia from 1900 to 1960. In chapter three, Tirthankar Roy investigates the extent to which constraints on borrowing explain why British India stayed a limited state. Montserrat López Jerez explores the relationship between the colonial tax system and local production systems in French Indochina in chapter four. In chapter five, Anne Booth and Kent Deng provide a comparison between Taiwan, Korea and Manchuria and challenge the view that Japanese colonial legacies were relatively speaking more beneficial for post-independence development of fiscal capacity. Turning to Africa, in chapter six Ewout Frankema and Marlous van Waijenburg downplay the principal differences between British and French colonial rule and instead highlight the variations in opportunities to tax trade. In chapter seven, Leigh Gardner discusses the early dependence on direct taxes, the role of settler communities and the regional coordination of tax and trade policies in East and Central Africa. Kleoniki Alexopoulou offers a study of the often overlooked Portuguese colonies and the balancing between local conditions and metropolitan vision in chapter eight. Finally, in chapter nine Abel Gwaindepi and Krige Siebrits highlight the specific challenges and opportunities of fiscal systems in mineral-rich colonies. All chapters go beyond single-country case studies in that they address whole regions or provide comparisons between colonies. Also, the chapters share a basic structure where both taxation and spending are consistently discussed.

The scholars present in-depth knowledge about the different colonial territories and produce detailed descriptions of local production systems, colonial administrations, taxation systems, priorities guiding colonial investments and spending, and so on. In total, the book includes as many as 54 figures and 42 tables with historical quantitative data. I would, however, have liked to see more than the three maps to help orient readers with specific locations. Looking at the chapters as a whole, the book contributes a richness of empirical evidence for the growing literature on colonial fiscal capacity. Meanwhile, most of the chapters are rather unspecific regarding their theoretical contribution, and I would have appreciated a clearer theoretical message regarding lessons learned from these insightful empirical studies.

The uniformity of the chapters provides a higher level of consistency than what is often found in a collection of essays. This helps the reader to identify common traits as well as inconsistencies between the different administrations and colonies. However, the chapters differ significantly in terms of type of data and methods used as well as concepts applied. While more could possibly have been done in terms of enforcing a more unified approach in the chapters, there will always be variations in colonial sources making fully comparable studies difficult.

Throughout the book, one central issue remains unresolved. What is the added value of the comparison, within and between Asia and Africa? The intraregional comparisons come out clearly in the different chapters showing the various administrations' relationship with the metropolitans and how that impacted fiscal policies. Even so, administrations consistently adapted to local socio-economic conditions, such as existing production systems, type of exports, and local politics. It appears that pragmatism governed by local conditions trumped imperial principles, or perhaps pragmatism was the imperial principle. As a result, even intraregional comparisons become challenging when local contexts differ.

Meanwhile, the actual comparison between Asia and Africa is only conducted in the introduction. Because the rest of the book is geographically divided, the individual chapters offer limited insights into similarities and differences between the two regions. I envision two ways to draw more from the comparison as well as learn about *global* patterns of colonial fiscal capacity formation. One could either conduct the Asia-Africa comparisons consistently in chapters based on themes like individual fiscal policies, taxation of certain sectors or crops, or specific colonial institutions; or one could add a concluding chapter with a more in-depth theoretical discussion based on the empirical chapters. Overall, however, this is a very enjoyable and rewarding read.

Ellen Hillbom, Lund University

Thomas Max Safley, *Family Firms and Merchant Capitalism in Early Modern Europe. The Business, Bankruptcy and Resilience of the Höchstetters of Augsburg* (Abingdon: Routledge, 2020). 287 p. ISBN 9780367137106.

DOI: 10.18352/tseg.1212

Crises have the potential to lay bare the structures and fault lines of economies and societies as Covid-19 has done today, or as the bankruptcy of Lehman Brothers did in September 2008, triggering the US subprime mortgage crisis, a worldwide financial crisis and a sudden awareness of increasing social and economic inequalities. The filing for bankruptcy of 'Ambrosius and Hans the Brothers Höchstetter and Company' on 1 July 1529, in the German city of Augsburg, mirrors events of 2008, and Thomas Max Safley shows this particular firm's failure to be equally revelatory for the workings of premodern capitalist economy and society, the economic life of the past, as he puts it.

The Höchstetters' spectacular failure produced a large trove of documents – described by the author as discovering Ali Baba's cave – that Safley meticulously uses to question and nuance key issues in premodern economic history: Can we talk about capitalism in this era? What was the role of family in the economy? Do concepts such as trust, networks and institutions help us understand the economic life of the past?

The book's narrative is structured by the chronology of the rags-to-riches-to-rags story of the Höchstetter family, with each chapter tackling one of economic history's key questions. How important was family in the management and capitalization of family firms; how capitalist were the Höchstetters' business practices; how was information obtained, assessed, managed and put to use in their firm; what role did institutions (such as laws) and organizations (such as courts and city and state governments) play in the economy in general and more specifically in the liquidation negotiations between the creditors – a large and socially wide group – and the Höchstetter firm; which social groups participated in the money and capital markets used by the Höchstetters to leverage their firm in an attempt to stave off bankruptcy; why did some of these investors choose to invest in a sinking ship while others were well aware of the difficulties and were paid back in full before things went sour; did the bankruptcy of 'Ambrosius and Hans the Brothers Höchstetter and Company' signify the end of the family – were the Höchstetters a perfect example of the so-called Buddenbrooks Syndrome? – or was the family resilient?

The recent historiography on merchants has – to a certain extent – somewhat dehumanized its subjects of interest. Merchants and their actions are supposed to have been guided by the structures of their networks; by the trust mechanism that underpins such relationships; by institutions in the sense of Douglass North's 'rules of the game' that produce more predictable behaviour in economic actors as well as in the sense of organizations like courts and city and state governments; and by economic rationality. By drawing on the case of the Höchstetters – not as well-known as the Fuggers but still a name that resonates among premodern historians – Thomas Max Safley in fact re-humanizes this economic history. His rich archival research reveals the role of human agency and choices, the negotiation processes, the paths of opportunism, deceit and solidarity. Members of the Höchstetter entourage or their creditors did not always follow the rules, sometimes because the rules were not clear or yet developed, sometimes because those rules did not suit them. Indeed, the complexity of the Höchstetter bankruptcy itself prompted new legislation in Augsburg to avoid the same problems in the future.

In any case, institutions are not set in stone and very much formed and shaped bottom-up, by the economic actors themselves. Their social relations and networks obviously mattered to them yet did not define them entirely. For example, several close family members and partners of Ambrosius I Höchstetter, the senior partner, were profligate and gambled away company money. Could they do so because they were family or despite being related to Ambrosius I? Safley also demonstrates that, even though the Höchstetter firm can be described as a family firm, not every family member was automatically involved in it. In addition, although all merchant companies included family members, each had its unique mix of family members and outsiders for its capital and management.

It does help that the Höchstetter history provides a range of absolutely fascinating characters, including the cunning Anton Fugger or Maximilian of Austria, imprisoned in Bruges during the Flemish Revolt and aided by Ambrosius I Höchstetter, all of them described by Safley in salient detail. Safley succeeds in bringing to life the premodern capitalist, defined by Max Weber as one who 'would sail through hell for profit, even if his sails were singed' (pp. 14-15), a description that matches the Höchstetters' adventures perfectly.

Safley synthesizes the German literature on the sixteenth-century South German merchant bankers, a wonderful scholarly gift to those who do not read German. The book is infused with a serious dose of German social sciences: Safley embeds his narrative in the works of Hayek, Sombart and Weber among many others. The Höchstetters are put into comparative perspective where possible: Safley clearly demonstrates that the Höchstetters relied on foreign support (from non-family and often from outside Augsburg itself) far more than their Fugger counterparts. This may have been due to their status as parvenus and/or the result of Ambrosius I leveraging the firm in order to survive the avalanche of crises it had to face. Hence, this is a well-developed case study with historiographical reverberations going well beyond Augsburg. Through its focus on premodern European merchant capitalists, this monograph is a welcome addition to the current vogue known as the New History of Capitalism, which concentrates on modern US economic history and therefore presupposes the absence or immaturity of capitalism prior to the eighteenth century.

Many questions remain, as the author himself acknowledges, and may perhaps never be answered. In this monograph, though, the author does not shy away from them, putting those questions center-stage. For example, Safley repeatedly refers to the decision-making process: as historians we know (part of) the information economic actors had, but we have no clue how such information was put into a business strategy from which we see the results emerge in the historical documents. In what way did Ambrosius I Höchstetter assess the risks of his attempt to create a European monopoly in mercury, a bold but in hindsight miscalculated and fatal move? We witness the actions that should have led to such a monopoly but not the ruminations in Ambrosius' mind that produced this strategy.

*Family Firms and Merchant Capitalism in Early Modern Europe* is a must-read for all social and economic historians of premodern Europe and scholars interested in capitalism. The book addresses the big questions of economic history, warns us of any blind belief in fashionable conceptual categories, and provides a rich understanding of the economic life in the past with an emphasis on its human dimension in all its beauty and ugliness.

Jeroen Puttevils, University of Antwerp

# Colophon

***TSEG – Low Countries Journal of Social and Economic History***

*TSEG – The Low Countries Journal of Social and Economic History* is the Dutch-Flemish journal of social and economic history. It is an open access, peer-reviewed, scientific journal that is granted an INT-1 status (the highest status for academic journals) by the European Science Foundation.

The journal publishes articles and reviews in the fields of social and economic history in the broadest sense, with a particular but not exclusive focus on the Low Countries. The journal has a strong interest in past forms of human interaction and how these shaped social, economic, cultural, and political patterns. Key notions are economic growth, power and (in)equality, group cultures, networks, identity, gender, ethnicity, ecology, trade and technique, entrepreneurship, labour, and social movements. The editors consider insights and theories from the social sciences (including economics) as a source of inspiration.

Contributions in Dutch and English are accepted.

From January 2021 onwards, *TSEG – The Low Countries Journal of Social and Economic History* is published on behalf of the International Institute of Social History (IISH) and Nederlandsch Economisch-Historisch Archief (NEHA) by Leuven University Press.

*TSEG – The Low Countries Journal of Social and Economic History* is het Nederlands-Vlaamse vaktijdschrift voor sociale en economische geschiedenis. Het is een open access, peer-reviewed wetenschappelijk tijdschrift met een INT1-status toegekend door de European Science Foundation.

*TSEG* richt zich op de sociale en economische geschiedenis in brede zin, met een focus op de Lage Landen, en bestudeert vooral de menselijke interacties in het verleden en hoe die vormgaven aan sociale, economische, culturele en politieke patronen. Sleutelbegrippen hierbij zijn: economische groei, macht en (on)gelijkheid, groepsculturen, netwerken, identiteit, gender, etniciteit, ecologie, bedrijf en techniek, ondernemerschap, arbeid en sociale bewegingen. De redactie beschouwt inzichten en theorieën uit de sociale wetenschappen (inclusief de economie) als een bron van inspiratie.

Het tijdschrift verwelkomt bijdragen in het Nederlands en het Engels.

Vanaf januari 2021 wordt *TSEG – The Low Countries Journal of Social and Economic History* namens het Internationaal Instituut voor Sociale Geschiedenis (IISG) en het Nederlandsch Economisch-Historisch Archief (NEHA) uitgegeven door Universitaire Pers Leuven.

**Journal Board**
Executive Editor: Jessica Dijkman, Utrecht University
Co-executive Editors: Wouter Ryckbosch, Free University Brussels, and Marion Pluskota, Leiden University
Managing Editor: Astrid Verburg, International Institute of Social History

**Open Access journal with a print edition**
3 issues annually (May / September / December)
Online ISSN: 2468-9068
Print ISSN: 1572-1701
Online available via www.openjournals.nl
More information on the journal: www.lup.be/tseg
Proposals and submissions: info@tseg.nl
Submission of materials for review consideration: Astrid Verburg (IISG), Postbus 2169, 1000 CD Amsterdam, T +31 20 668 58 66

**Copyright**
This journal provides immediate open access to its content on the principle that making research freely available to the public supports a greater global exchange of knowledge. Authors of articles published remain the copyright holders and grant third parties the right to use, reproduce, and share the article according to the Creative Commons CC BY 4.0 license agreement.

**Orders**
Subscription fee print edition (3 issues annually)*

| | |
|---|---|
| Institutional | € 120,00 |
| Individual | € 60,00 |
| Student/aio | € 35,00 |

Subscription form available on: www.lup.be/tseg
* VAT and postage fees for subscribers within Benelux are included. For subscribers outside Benelux a postage fee is applicable.
Unit price per printed issue: € 15,00 (excl. postage)
Send your orders to: orders@lup.be

Universitaire Pers Leuven/ Leuven University Press
Minderbroedersstraat 4, B-3000 Leuven, Belgium
info@lup.be
www.lup.be/tseg

Cover Illustration: Op de publieke tribune van de Tweede Kamer volgen de Amsterdamse wethouders Schaefer (l, PvdA) en Heerma (r, CDA) de beraadslagingen tussen de Kamer en minister Van Aardenne (VVD) van Economische Zaken over extra steun voor ADM, 19 januari 1983 (bron: foto Rob C. Croes, fotocollectie Anefo, Nationaal Archief).
Cover Design: WAT ontwerpers, Utrecht
Typesetting: Crius Group
ISBN 978 94 6270 290 5